AN IRRESISTIBLE ALLIANCE

A CYNSTER NEXT GENERATION NOVEL

STEPHANIE LAURENS

ABOUT AN IRRESISTIBLE ALLIANCE

A duke's second son with no responsibilities and a lady starved of the excitement her soul craves join forces to unravel a deadly, potentially catastrophic threat to the realm - that only continues to grow.

With his older brother's betrothal announced, Lord Michael Cynster is freed from the pressure of familial expectations. However, the allure of his previous hedonistic pursuits has paled. Then he learns of the mission his brother, Sebastian, and Lady Antonia Rawlings have been assisting with and volunteers to assist by hunting down the hoard of gunpowder now secreted somewhere in London.

Michael sets out to trace the carters who transported the gunpowder from Kent to London. His quest leads him to the Hendon Shipping Company, where he discovers his sole source of information is the only daughter of Jack and Kit Hendon, Miss Cleome Hendon, who although a fetchingly attractive lady, firmly holds the reins of the office in her small hands.

Cleo has fought to achieve her position in the company. Initially, managing the office was a challenge, but she now conquers all in just a few hours a week. With her three brothers all adventuring in America, she's been driven to the realization that she craves adventure, too.

When Michael Cynster walks in and asks about carters, Cleo's instincts leap. She wrings from him the full tale of his mission—and offers him a bargain. She will lead him to the carters he seeks if he agrees to include her as an equal partner in the mission.

Horrified, Michael attempts to resist, but ultimately finds himself agreeing—a sequence of events he quickly learns is common around Cleo. Then she delivers on her part of the bargain, and he finds there are benefits to allowing her to continue to investigate beside him—not least being that if she's there, then he knows she's safe.

But the further they go in tracing the gunpowder, the more deaths they uncover. And when they finally locate the barrels, they find themselves tangled in a fight to the death—one that forces them to face what has grown between them, to seize and defend what they both see as their path to the greatest adventure of all. A shared life. A shared future. A shared love.

Second volume in a trilogy. A Cynster Next Generation Novel – a classic historical romance with gothic overtones layered over a continuing intrigue. A full-length novel of 101,000 words.

OTHER TITLES BY STEPHANIE LAURENS

Mastered by Love

Black Cobra Quartet
The Untamed Bride
The Elusive Bride
The Brazen Bride
The Reckless Bride

The Adventurers Quartet
The Lady's Command
A Buccaneer at Heart
The Daredevil Snared
Lord of the Privateers

The Cavanaughs
The Designs of Lord Randolph Cavanaugh
The Pursuits of Lord Kit Cavanaugh
The Beguilement of Lady Eustacia Cavanaugh
The Obsessions of Lord Godfrey Cavanaugh (July 16, 2020)

Other Novels
The Lady Risks All
The Legend of Nimway Hall – 1750: Jacqueline

Medieval (As M.S.Laurens)
Desire's Prize

Novellas
Melting Ice – from the anthologies *Rough Around the Edges* and *Scandalous Brides*
Rose in Bloom – from the anthology *Scottish Brides*
Scandalous Lord Dere – from the anthology *Secrets of a Perfect Night*
Lost and Found – from the anthology *Hero, Come Back*
The Fall of Rogue Gerrard – from the anthology *It Happened One Night*
The Seduction of Sebastian Trantor – from the anthology *It Happened One*

Season

Short Stories

The Wedding Planner – from the anthology *Royal Weddings*

A Return Engagement – from the anthology *Royal Bridesmaids*

UK-Style Regency Romances

Tangled Reins

Four in Hand

Impetuous Innocent

Fair Juno

The Reasons for Marriage

A Lady of Expectations An Unwilling Conquest

A Comfortable Wife

AN IRRESISTIBLE ALLIANCE

AN IRRESISTIBLE ALLIANCE

Copyright © 2017 by Savdek Management Proprietary Limited

ISBN: 978-1-925559-39-2

Cover design by Savdek Management Pty. Ltd.

Cover and inside front couple photography and photographic composition

by Period Images © 2017

Cover background image photographic credit to Michael Spring

First print publication: May, 2017

Reissued print publication: July, 2019

Savdek Management Proprietary Limited, Melbourne, Australia.

www.stephanielaurens.com

Email: admin@stephanielaurens.com

The names Stephanie Laurens and the Cynsters, and the SL Logo, are registered trademarks of Savdek Management Proprietary Ltd.

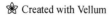 Created with Vellum

CAST OF CHARACTERS

Principal Characters:
Cynster, Lord Michael Magnus – *second son of Devil Cynster, Duke of St.*
Ives, and Honoria, née Anstruther-Wetherby
Hendon, Miss Cleome (Cleo) Annabelle – *only daughter of Jack, Lord*
Hendon and Katherine (Kit), née Cranmer

In London:

At Wolverstone House, Grosvenor Square:
Varisey, Lord Drake, Marquess of Winchelsea – *eldest son of Royce*
Varisey, Duke of Wolverstone, and Minerva, née Chesterton; heir to the
dukedom of Wolverstone
Hamilton – *the Wolverstones' London butler*
Finnegan – *the marquess's gentleman's gentleman*
Jeffreys – *a footman*
Various footmen and a maid

At St. Ives House, Grosvenor Square:
Crewe – *the Cynsters' butler*
Simpkins, Tom – *Lord Michael's gentleman's gentleman-cum-groom-*
cum-driver
Cynster, Lord Sebastian, Marquess of Earith – *eldest son of Devil Cynster,*

Duke of St. Ives, and Honoria, née Anstruther-Wetherby; heir to the dukedom of St. Ives, now engaged to Lady Antonia Rawlings

Rawlings, Lady Antonia – *eldest daughter of Gyles Rawlings, Earl of Chillingworth, and Francesca, née Rawlings; now engaged to Lord Sebastian Cynster, Marquess of Earith*

Cynster, Lord Sylvester (Devil), Duke of St. Ives – *Sebastian's, Michael's, and Louisa's father*

Cynster, Lady Honoria, Duchess of St. Ives – *Sebastian's, Michael's, and Louisa's mother; née Anstruther-Wetherby*

Cynster, Lady Louisa – *only daughter of Devil Cynster, Duke of St. Ives, and Honoria Anstruther-Wetherby; widely known as Lady Wild*

Tully – *a footman*

At the Hendon town house, Clarges Street:
Morris – *the Hendons' butler*
Jilly – *Cleo's maid*

At the Hendon Shipping Company Office, corner Fenchurch and Lime Streets:
Fitch – *head clerk*

At the Cranmers' town house, South Audley Street:
Cranmer, Geoffrey – *Kit Hendon's cousin, second cousin to Cleo*
Cranmer, Maude – *Geoffrey's wife*
Cranmer, Anthony – *Geoffrey's nephew, Cleo's third cousin*
Cranmer, Georgia – *Geoffrey's niece, Cleo's third cousin*
Herbert, Mrs. – *a Cranmer connection*
Winston, Mrs. – *a Cranmer connection*
Hepworth, Mr. – *a businessman visiting from Philadelphia*
Hepworth, Mrs. – *Mr. Hepworth's wife, also visiting from Philadelphia*
Hepworth, Miss Andrea – *Mr. Hepworth's daughter, also visiting from Philadelphia*
Hepworth, Mr. Robert – *Mr. Hepworth's son, also visiting from Philadelphia*

Elsewhere in Mayfair:
Rawlings, Lord Gyles, Earl of Chillingworth – *Antonia's father*
Rawlings, Lady Francesca, Countess of Chillingworth – *Gyles's wife and Antonia's mother*

The footman army – *comprised of footmen and grooms from all the Cynster households in London*

In the East End:
Carpenter, Joe – *a registered gunpowder carter*
Fields – *a registered gunpowder carter*
Landry, Mick – *a registered gunpowder carter*
Grimsby, Jack – *a registered gunpowder carter*
Carter, Martin – *a registered gunpowder carter*
Feeney, Walter – *a registered gunpowder carter*
Doolan, Terrance (Terry) – *a registered gunpowder carter; disappeared, believed murdered*
Dibney, Johnny – *registered apprentice to Doolan; disappeared, believed murdered*
Hendrick, Mrs. – *Johnny Dibney's landlady*
Oldham, Mrs. – *Oldham's wife*
Oldham, Mike – *a registered gunpowder carter*
Chilburn, the Honorable Mr. Lawton – *youngest son of Viscount Hawesley*
Three London Chartist militia leaders
Four London Chartist militiamen
Lovett – *London Chartist leader absent from town*
Hetherington – *London Chartist leader absent from town*

In Southwark:
Shepherd, Mr. – *owner of a warehouse in Morgan's Lane, Southwark*
Ellis – *head clerk at Shepherd's warehouse*
O'Toole – *foreman at Shepherd's warehouse; disappeared, believed murdered*
O'Toole, Mrs. – *O'Toole's wife*

In Whitehall:
Greville, Sir George – *the Home Secretary*
Waltham, Sir Harold – *the Home Secretary's principal private secretary*

In Kent:
Boyne, William, Lord Ennis – *of Pressingstoke Hall; deceased*
Boyne, Connell – *Lord Ennis's brother; also deceased*

In Northern England:
O'Connor, Mr. Feargus, MP – *head of the Chartist movement and owner of the Leeds-based* Northern Star *newspaper*

At a manor house in Berkshire:
An old gentleman – *pulling the strings of the plot*
Reed – *the old gentleman's manservant*

CHAPTER 1

OCTOBER 24, 1850. LONDON

*L*ord Michael Magnus Cynster sauntered down the grand staircase of St. Ives House as the long-case clock on the landing chimed the quarter hour. It was nearing two o'clock in the afternoon, a perfectly acceptable time for an unmarried gentleman of the ton to be descending to meet the day.

Would that his day held any appeal; it stretched before him, a vast emptiness he had no idea how to fill.

Out of habit, he maintained an amiable, easygoing expression, yet he was bored and restless. The only bright spot on his horizon was the news —hardly surprising, but at least a touch intriguing—that his older brother, Sebastian, had finally opened his eyes and seen what had been plain to all around him for the past decade.

Michael had had the news from his man, Tom Simpkins; apparently, Lady Antonia Rawlings had returned from Kent with Sebastian the previous evening—and had, it seemed, spent the night in his brother's bed.

If that didn't herald the sound of wedding bells chiming throughout the house—and, presumably, through Sebastian's thick skull—Michael would eat his hat.

As Michael stepped onto the black-and-white tiles of the front hall, Crewe, the family's London butler for the past decade, walked out of the library.

Michael smiled genially. "What-ho, Crewe! I hear my brother has finally seen the light regarding the position of his marchioness. Has he popped the question, do you know?"

Crewe's normally rigorously impassive mien eased into a small smile. "I believe Lord Sebastian is currently thus engaged, my lord. He and Lady Antonia left several hours ago for Green Street."

Antonia's father was the Earl of Chillingworth, and the family's town house was in Green Street. Michael imagined the scene and chuckled. "I would give a great deal to be a fly on the wall when Sebastian asks the earl for Antonia's hand."

"I'm sure the earl will be delighted."

"Indubitably, but for how long will Chillingworth drag out the interview before he admits that? That's the question."

"I'm sure Lord Sebastian will meet the challenge."

Michael had no doubt of that, either; once Sebastian set his mind on a course, very little could turn him from it.

"Will you be going out, my lord?"

Michael had halted several paces from the front door. He glanced at Crewe as realization struck; Sebastian and Antonia's upcoming union effectively released him from his careful existence of the past several years.

As he was not even a full year younger than Sebastian, until his older brother secured his wife—the future duchess—Michael had been almost equally in the matchmakers' sights. One of them had to marry and produce an heir, thus securing the dukedom for the principal line; the whole family and all of society had expected that.

But now Sebastian had finally taken the plunge…

Staring unseeing at Crewe, Michael murmured, "As soon as the news gets out, which it will almost immediately, I'll be able to slide out of the social spotlight. I won't need to pretend an interest in balls and soirees anymore."

The pressure to attend such events—to be visible and, supposedly, to cast his eye over the available young ladies as if possibly considering making a choice—hadn't come so much from his parents as from his great-aunts and myriad female connections. That he and Sebastian had both been circulating had, to some extent, lessened the pressure each had had to bear, yet waltzing through the ton while avoiding all the snares and pitfalls strewn in their paths by ambitious mamas had been…a challenge for the first few weeks, but thereafter, intensely wearying.

Being pursued primarily for one's social and financial status wasn't, all in all, a gratifying experience.

But now…now he was free. Free from all matrimonial pressure.

He could return to his carefree bachelor existence, at least for the foreseeable future.

Until *he* decided otherwise.

Michael smiled and refocused on Crewe. "Yes, I'm going out." Although he had no idea where.

Crewe duly retrieved Michael's greatcoat and cane from the coat rack.

After shrugging into the greatcoat, settling it across his shoulders, and tugging down his coat sleeves, Michael accepted the black cane with its silver stag's-head knob from Crewe. "I take it Their Graces have been informed?"

"Not yet, my lord. I understand Lord Sebastian intends to send a rider this afternoon. We anticipate the duke and duchess will arrive by tomorrow evening."

"And my sister?"

"Lady Louisa is not due back for several more days. It's possible she'll call in at Somersham Place first."

Michael nodded and turned to the door; as Crewe opened it, Michael said, "I'm not sure when I'll be back."

"Indeed, my lord." Crewe bowed.

Michael walked onto the front porch and paused. He heard the door shut quietly behind him.

He looked out at the park in the center of the square, taking in the children playing on the manicured lawns under the watchful eyes of nursemaids and governesses. Fashionable couples strolled the graveled walks, while carriages rolled sedately along the streets surrounding the park.

What now?

His earlier restless boredom swirled and surged anew; he felt rudderless—he had no direction. While he might now be free to resume his previously hedonistic life, the endless round of drinking, gaming, parties, dinners, and more gaming and even more drinking had, somewhat inexplicably, lost its allure.

The word "crossroads" hovered in his mind.

Impatient with such unproductive introspection, he shook his shoulders, descended the steps, turned left, and set out along the pavement—and found himself staring at Sebastian's back.

With Antonia Rawlings on his arm, his brother was walking east—but Green Street lay in the opposite direction. The pair must have already passed St. Ives House before Michael walked out of the door. But if they were coming from Green Street—and Michael had no reason to suspect they weren't—where were they going?

Curious, he lengthened his stride, closing the distance between them.

Sebastian and Antonia were discussing something; given their intensity and their brief gestures, Michael didn't think it was anything to do with a wedding.

Then the pair glanced up at the façades, slowed, and turned and climbed the steps to another house.

One glance, and Michael recognized the mansion. Wolverstone House.

Oh, ho! Something was up.

Intrigued, he followed the pair up the Wolverstone House steps.

Sebastian halted on the porch and rang the bell. At the sound of Michael's boots on the stone, he and Antonia turned; when they saw who it was, both smiled.

Michael grinned. Ignoring his brother, he grasped Antonia's hand and raised it to his lips. "I understand congratulations are in order, although you really would have done better with me."

Antonia laughed. Her fingers briefly gripped his. "I seriously doubt that would have worked." Using her hold on his hand, she drew him closer and stretched up to place a sisterly kiss on his cheek and received a similarly chaste buss in return. Sinking back to her heels, she studied his face. "But now you're my almost-brother-in-law, I can legitimately ask: What are you doing here?"

Michael glanced at Sebastian. "I was about to ask you two the same question." He grinned anew and thumped Sebastian on the shoulder. "What-ho, brother mine. I believe I should thank you for relieving me of the necessity of getting leg-shackled myself."

Sebastian met Antonia's gaze. "Don't mention it."

To Michael's eyes, his brother's expression appeared one step away from besotted.

Already?

The glossy black door of Wolverstone House swung open to reveal Hamilton, the Varisey family's London butler. When he saw Sebastian and Antonia, Hamilton's normally expressionless eyes twinkled, and his lips curved in a definite smile. "My lord, my lady." He bowed them in.

Michael trailed the pair into the front hall.

After closing the door, Hamilton relieved Antonia of her mantle, then accepted Sebastian's greatcoat, and finally, Michael's greatcoat and cane. After passing the garments to an underling summoned with just a look, Hamilton turned to Sebastian and Antonia and bowed. "We understand congratulations are in order. I speak for all the staff at Wolverstone House in saying we wish you both well."

"Thank you, Hamilton," Sebastian said.

"And our thanks to all the staff as well," Antonia added with one of her lovely smiles.

Sebastian's next words, "Is the marquess receiving?", answered Michael's principal question. He'd worked with Drake on covert missions before and had wondered if that was why—indeed, he had hoped that was why—Sebastian had come there. Antonia's presence, however, was a surprise. Even more than Sebastian, Michael, and the rest of their peers, Drake was rigidly opposed to the involvement of ladies in schemes such as his—in missions that had the potential to turn deadly at any time.

Hamilton informed Sebastian that the marquess was awaiting their arrival in the library. As Hamilton led the way, Sebastian caught Michael's eye and faintly raised one black brow.

With a nod, Michael accepted the unvoiced invitation and fell in behind Sebastian as he followed Antonia down the corridor and through the door Hamilton held open.

The library at Wolverstone House was a cozy, comfortable room that was predominantly the domain of the males of the family—the current duke, his heir, Drake, and Drake's three brothers. Glass-fronted bookcases lined the walls, the panes reflecting the flames leaping in the large fireplace directly opposite the door. The walls were covered in cream silk, and the areas between the bookcases played host to numerous paintings depicting hunting scenes and Northumberland landscapes. A large desk dominated one end of the room, but the primary focus was a setting of four well-stuffed, brown-leather armchairs and a long sofa arranged before the hearth.

As Hamilton shut the door, Drake rose from one of the armchairs. His gaze briefly scanned Antonia's face, then shifted to Sebastian's. Drake smiled. "Good afternoon. I take it the deed is done?"

Antonia swept forward. "If you mean are we officially engaged"—she glanced back at Sebastian—"then the answer is yes, as officially as we can be given Sebastian has yet to inform his parents."

Sebastian met her gaze. "I'll send a rider this afternoon—once we've finished here. It's not as if there's any doubt as to my parents giving us their blessing." He looked at Drake. "However, for reasons that ought to be obvious, I don't dare drag my heels over sending the news, which means that my mother, with my father in tow, will almost certainly arrive late tomorrow, and after that—"

"After that," Antonia cut in, "while Mama didn't mention an engagement ball, I'm sure she only refrained in deference to your mother, who is sure to have opinions on the subject."

Sebastian fleetingly closed his eyes and groaned. "I hoped we'd escaped that."

Antonia pityingly shook her head at him. "No chance. None whatsoever."

Drake humphed. "For such as us, my friend, there's no avoiding such things."

Sebastian sighed. "As I feared, once the news spreads, our ability to assist with the mission will almost certainly be severely curtailed."

Drake grimaced. "Indeed."

"But"—Sebastian turned to include Michael—"we have someone here who, courtesy of Antonia's and my engagement, is now free. Or at least, freer."

Michael met Drake's gaze and smiled winningly. "You might even say I'm at loose ends, so…" He looked from Drake to Sebastian, and finally at Antonia, and arched his brows. "What's going on?"

"That, in fact, is precisely our question." Drake waved them to the armchairs. Once they'd settled, Sebastian and Antonia on the sofa, Drake in a chair to their right, and Michael in an armchair facing Drake, he continued, "This is what we've uncovered so far.

"Foot soldiers of the Young Irelander movement—young hotheads in the lowest rank of the organization—believing they were acting at the behest of the Young Irelander hierarchy as a part of an officially sanctioned plot, obtained ten barrels of gunpowder. Exactly where from, we don't know, but that's largely irrelevant now. Connell Boyne, who was the manager for his brother, Lord Ennis's principal estate northwest of Limerick, organized for the barrels to be taken by ship from Limerick to the east coast of Kent, where they were delivered to a cave on his brother's English holding."

Michael glanced at Sebastian. "You and Antonia went to Kent."

Sebastian nodded. "We attended a house party at Ennis's estate, Pressingstoke Hall."

Michael blinked. "That must have been interesting."

"It was," Antonia dryly replied.

Imperturbably, Drake continued, "Ennis had sent me a letter saying he had word of some plot I needed to know about, but he would only tell me of it face-to-face. However, I'd had word of Young Irelander actions from my contacts in Dublin, and to follow that up, I had to go myself, so Sebastian stood in for me with Ennis. At that point, we didn't know the two matters were definitely connected—that we were investigating two stages of the same plot. Unfortunately, his lordship was fatally stabbed minutes before Sebastian was to meet with him. Ennis managed to utter the words 'gunpowder' and 'here' before he died. Subsequently, Sebastian and Antonia discovered the cave and evidence that the ten barrels had been stored there, but by then, Boyne had moved the barrels on, presumably to London." Drake paused, then, voice hardening, affirmed, "Almost certainly to London."

Michael frowned. "If London was the destination all along, why not just ship the barrels directly here?"

"Because," Drake said, "the movement of gunpowder within the capital is tightly controlled, but that control focuses on gunpowder produced by the local registered mills, both government and private, and any gunpowder brought in through the Port of London. By secretly landing the gunpowder in Kent and carting it in, Boyne—or rather, whoever was pulling his strings—avoided the net."

Michael looked at Sebastian. "Where's Boyne now?"

"Dead. He was killed by whoever he was reporting to."

"Presumably," Drake said, "to ensure he told no one who that person —the one he took his orders from—is." His tone grew grim. "After my trip to Ireland, the one thing I can state with absolute confidence is that whoever is behind this plot, it isn't anyone connected with the Young Irelander movement. They've been very cleverly used."

Silence fell while they contemplated that, then Drake continued, "So now we have ten barrels of gunpowder somewhere in London. Ten hundredweight—that's more than a thousand pounds, enough to blow up a very large building or several smaller ones—and we have no idea where it is, who is behind the plot, or what their target is." He paused, then went on, "One factor that might work in our favor is that whoever is behind this, they're being extraordinarily secretive. Extrapolating from that, it seems likely they're running this plot in stages and closing off each stage as it's completed—meaning killing off those involved to that point. As with Boyne, that effectively conceals not just the details of their past actions but also protects the identity of those giving the orders and their proposed next steps. If our plotters continue to adhere to such ruthless cautiousness, then while they may have meticulously planned each and every move all the way to lighting the fuse, they won't have yet activated—meaning organized and set in train—the people and the processes for the next stage."

He met the others' eyes. "What I'm saying is that we may have a small window of opportunity in which to find the gunpowder. Several days—possibly as long as a week. In my educated opinion, it's highly unlikely that the barrels were taken directly to the target. I think—I believe—that their true target is one fact those driving this plot will strive to keep secret from everyone, including all those they've used or think to use to achieve their purpose."

"So," Michael said, "the only people who know the true target are the instigators of the plot, and in fact, no one else will know until the very end?"

Drake nodded. "When even if those involved in that final stage wish to protest, it'll be too late."

Beside Sebastian, Antonia stirred. "That suggests the target is something...quite dreadful." She met Drake's golden eyes. "Something the Young Irelanders, or whatever disaffected ruffians the villains hire next, might object to—might balk at destroying."

"Indeed." Drake's tone was clipped and hard.

After a moment of silence, Michael asked, "Is there any way we can identify the target?"

Grimly, Drake shook his head. "Not without finding the gunpowder in place and set to explode or learning the identities of the villains." He grimaced. "And even knowing who they are, the specific target might not be instantly apparent. For example, if it had been a Young Irelander plot, their target or targets might have been any number of government buildings or places like the army barracks. But as this is not a Young Irelander plot"—he shrugged—"I don't think we can even hazard a guess."

Michael exchanged a glance with Sebastian, then they both looked at Drake, who appeared to have sunk into his thoughts—thoughts his expression stated were not pleasant.

"So that's where we are as of today." Sebastian caught Drake's eye. "What's next?"

Drake held Sebastian's gaze for a moment, then looked at Michael. "We need to do our damnedest to find the gunpowder. Only by locating it can we be certain of stopping this plot."

Michael nodded. "So where do we start?"

"That," Drake said, "will be up to you, at least over the next few days." He looked at Sebastian and grimaced. "I can barely believe it—and I'm starting to wonder if distracting me and getting me out of London is a part of this plot—but this morning, I received intelligence from two entirely separate sources that there's some sort of Chartist plot under way somewhere in London."

"The Chartists?" Sebastian looked incredulous. "When have they ever resorted to the sort of violence ten barrels of gunpowder implies?"

"Precisely. It was a stretch even for the Young Irelanders, although there have been smaller incidents of violence in their case. As for the Chartists, however, while they may protest and march en masse on Parliament, they're devoted to achieving voting reform through peaceful, legal means. They want—have always wanted—reform via an act of Parliament. Blowing up the place isn't in any way in keeping with their goals."

"So who has suggested they're involved?" Michael asked.

"No one—not in the sense of them being involved specifically with our ten barrels of gunpowder. But a contact I have in the London Working Men's Association sent word he'd heard whispers among the local leaders —not Lovett or Hetherington but the leaders of the local militia, as they style themselves—of some action about to start, some messenger expected from their headquarters in the north with news of something designed to make Parliament sit up and take notice again. Normally, I'd rely on Lovett and Hetherington to ensure the organization wasn't drawn into anything untoward, but—so my contact wrote—neither man is in London at this time. I'm not sure who is in charge, but it's not anyone I know—I can't just turn up and ask to be told what it's all about. But there was worse to come. An hour ago, I received a communiqué from Whitehall—it seems there've been whispers in the corridors about some renewed Chartist unrest." His expression one of disgust, Drake looked at Sebastian. "You know what they're like in Whitehall. Mention unrest, and they imagine the worst. More, I know that if I try to hunt down who started the rumors, I'll end chasing my tail."

Drake sighed. He leant back in his chair and looked at Michael. "As matters stand, the fastest way to resolve the question of Chartist involvement is for me to go north and speak with Feargus O'Connor."

O'Connor, Michael knew, was the de facto supreme leader of the Chartist movement and owner of the Leeds-based *Northern Star* newspaper.

"If anyone knows what those at the head of the Chartist movement have planned, it's O'Connor—and he'll tell me." Drake's smile was cold.

"Once I explain the situation to him—how I believe someone is plotting to drag the Chartist cause into the mud, ultimately to see it outlawed— I'm sure he'll tell me all I need to know about anything they have planned. And—as I doubt that they actually have anything planned—who to contact in London to set those in the London Working Men's Association right about what their leadership truly wants."

"How long do you think that will take?" Sebastian asked.

"Almost certainly longer than I would like." Drake calculated then offered, "Three days minimum, but more likely four. In this season, I'll be lucky to find O'Connor at his desk—I'll have to chase him into the country and hunt him down."

"Well," Michael said, "while you're hunting in the north, I'll hunt down here." He glanced at Sebastian, sitting on the sofa with one hand closed about one of Antonia's—Michael wasn't even sure his brother was aware of the contact; touching Antonia seemed to have already become an unconscious act—then met Drake's eyes. "As our two lovebirds here are going to be busy, I'll take on the search for the gunpowder."

Drake inclined his head. "Good. Where are you going to start?"

Michael had already thought about that. "You said there was ten hundredweight of gunpowder. They couldn't have moved that on one cart—not in one trip—so let's assume two carts were involved, and those carts wouldn't have been just any old farm cart with a rundown nag between the shafts. They would have had to be...well, carters' carts. The sort of carts that could manage the journey along the highway to London, loaded with heavy barrels, and no one would look twice. Right?"

Drake nodded. "So where did the carts come from?"

"Exactly." Michael glanced at Sebastian. "Might such carts have been hired locally from somewhere around Pressingstoke Hall?"

Sebastian pulled a face. "Dover's to the south, but I doubt carters from there would want to take a load to London, knowing they would be empty on the way back—unless they had organized a load for the return journey, but that would mean they'd have to have known of the trip far in advance…"

"No." Drake shook his head. "You're right about having to use professional carters with proper carts, but our plotters—whoever they are—wouldn't have risked using locals. Whoever drove those carts had to be prepared to move gunpowder illegally. There's no way the carters wouldn't have known what they were transporting, and they picked up the barrels from a cave off the beach—no chance of them not realizing no excise had been paid. So…" Drake tapped his steepled fingertips before his face.

Michael had seen Drake's father—the current Duke of Wolverstone—do the same thing when thinking some point through.

Eventually, Drake said, "If I was the villain behind this, I would have taken the time to find and recruit carters—or drivers with access to suitable carts—who were Young Irelander sympathizers." Drake looked at Sebastian. "Boyne had to be on the beach to lead them to the cave and the barrels—he would have got suspicious too early if the carters hadn't been a part of the movement. Or at least Irish." Drake tipped his head consideringly, then glanced at Michael. "Just being Irish would probably have been enough. They wouldn't have been discussing politics while moving the barrels."

His eyes on Drake's, Michael slowly nodded. "So I'm looking for two men, at least one of whom is Irish, if not both, with access to the right sort of carts to transport ten barrels of gunpowder into London." He paused, then added, "I seriously doubt I could fill that bill in any small town, and probably not even in Dover."

"London." Drake grimaced resignedly and sat up. "That fits with the care our villains are taking. You're looking for two drivers, most likely carters, most likely Irish and very possibly Young Irelander sympathizers, working out of London."

"As matters stand," Sebastian said, "other than the villains pulling the strings, the men who transported the barrels to London are our only route to the gunpowder."

"True." Michael surveyed the others, finally resting his gaze on Antonia. "So who do we know who would know about carters?"

Antonia opened her eyes wide. "I would have suggested asking Hamilton or Crewe, but I think you'll find that we—our households—use our own carts or carriages. We wouldn't hire carters, not on a routine basis—not enough to know the ins and outs of the trade."

Michael nodded. "So who do we know who has dealings with carters —the sort of carters we're after?"

After a moment, Sebastian offered, "You might see if any of Lord Hendon's sons are in town. They would probably have some idea—or at least be able to point you in the direction of someone who liaises with carters."

"And if you can't find them, try at the Hendon Shipping Company office," Drake said. "The company moves all sorts of goods from the docks to customers and warehouses all around London and the Home Counties, so someone in the office will surely know enough to steer you onto a worthwhile trail."

"Where is the office?" Michael reached for his notebook.

Drake looked nonplussed. He glanced at Sebastian, who shook his head.

When Michael looked at her, Antonia shrugged. "I've no idea."

Michael shoved the notebook back into his pocket. "Never mind. I'll find it." He looked at Drake. "My one remaining question—how much time do we have? If the gunpowder is already in London and has been since…" He broke off and looked at Sebastian. "When would the barrels have arrived here—in the capital?"

Sebastian looked at Antonia.

She frowned, then said, "The barrels left the Kent coast on the night of the day before yesterday or very early yesterday morning."

Sebastian nodded. "That's correct. So if they were brought straight up to town—and most likely they were—then they would have arrived in London yesterday, sometime in the morning."

"So the barrels have been here, in town, for twenty-four hours already." Michael looked at Drake. "How many days do you think we'll have to find the barrels before they're moved on, presumably to the intended target?"

"As I said earlier, we can probably count on a few more days, possibly up to a week." Drake pulled a face. "Successfully deploying that much gunpowder, in secret, into position to blow up some government building or monument will require extensive planning, and these villains have been so very careful, I can't imagine they'll rush at this point." Drake paused, then met Michael's eyes. "Let's just say that I'm not expecting to hear of any explosion in the next four or five days."

Michael grunted. "That's not quite as reassuring as you seem to think."

Drake shook his head. "Regardless, there's only one trail to follow, and you'll need to follow it step by logical step. That's all you—or we— can do. Incidentally"—he trapped Michael's gaze—"if you do happen to locate the barrels, watch them rather than seize them. I hope to be back before they're moved, and given that the Young Irelander connection has proved to be a deliberately misleading façade—and I'm fairly certain that this supposed Chartist involvement will turn out to be even less substantial—then our only avenue to identifying who is really behind this plot is via those barrels of gunpowder. If we find the barrels, we need to watch and wait, see who comes to fetch them, follow the barrels to their destination, then capture those involved before they have a chance to light any fuse. Up to this point, other than those directing the plot, everyone who has played a part in it, however minor, is dead. We need to seize someone still capable of speech."

With that acerbic comment, Drake came to his feet.

The others all rose.

Drake led them to the door. "I'll set out at first light for Leeds. If O'Connor reacts as I expect he will, I hope to return with the necessary contacts to halt any active support from the London Chartists—hopefully in time to stop the gunpowder being deployed, at least by them." He opened the door, waved the others through, then followed them into the front hall.

While Antonia donned her mantle and Sebastian and Michael shrugged into their greatcoats, Drake stood with his hands clasped behind his back, his feet apart, and studied the floor.

When the others were ready to leave, he looked up—at Michael. "You're right in thinking that, with the gunpowder now in London, some clock is ticking—it has to be—but unfortunately, we don't know on what timetable this plot is operating. However, there are already so many aspects about it that are simply not usual—not the way such games are normally played—that I'm in two minds over whether there's any need for urgency."

Drake paused, then went on, "I don't know how best to direct you. If —when—you find the gunpowder, if I'm not back, you should play it by ear. If you feel the location is safe enough—that it's not the target and you can mount a suitable watch over the place—then do so. If the barrels are already at the target, or what might be the target, then exercise your discretion." He glanced at Sebastian and smiled faintly. "In such a case, between the two of you, I'm sure you can arrange to seize the barrels."

Sebastian nodded, as did Michael.

"Don't worry," Michael said. "By the time you return, we'll have all in hand."

Drake looked skeptical. "I can only hope."

Hamilton took that as his cue to swing open the front door.

As the four walked toward the doorway, Michael glanced at Sebastian and Antonia, then looked across them at Drake. "One thing—we'll need to be careful about sending any messages to St. Ives House. Louisa's expected back in the next few days. Crewe seemed to think she would call in at Somersham first, presumably to see Grandmama, but given Louisa's propensity for turning up when you least expect her…"

His features hardening, Sebastian nodded curtly. "Indeed—and we all know what she's like. The very last thing any of us need is to have Lady Wild involving herself in this."

Sebastian, Michael, and Drake all shuddered, Drake most violently— most feelingly—of all.

"Lady Wild" was Louisa's nickname throughout the ton. Glancing at Drake, Antonia thought he had even paled a trifle. Intrigued, she caught his eye and arched a brow.

He correctly interpreted her unvoiced question; he waved her over the threshold and, as she stepped onto the porch, replied, "Her brothers have grown inured to her ways, but I have not. Her sheer recklessness makes my blood run cold." He halted in the doorway.

Antonia turned and fixed him with a disbelieving look. "*You?* Isn't that the pot calling the kettle black?"

Drake arched his brows in his usual arrogant fashion. "Not at all. I am the epitome of sane and considered compared to Lady Wild."

He sat in the shadows at a table tucked into a corner of the tavern in Weaver's Lane. Patience didn't come naturally to him, but tonight, confident and assured, with his wide-brimmed hat tipped forward to shade his face, he was prepared to sip his ale and wait for his contacts to arrive.

He might not be a guardsman, but he had his strengths; he could see why the old man had delegated this phase of the plan to him. There were, so the old man had informed him and the guardsman, three stages to the whole. And for each stage properly undertaken and successfully completed, he or the guardsman—whichever of them had been given that particular stage to run—would be awarded one third of the old man's estate.

As gentlemen with no prospects but an innate taste for living well, both he and the guardsman had accepted the old man's challenge. According to the old man, he would award the right to run the third and final stage to whichever of them completed their initial stage most cleanly —meaning who best ensured the old man's wishes were carried out smoothly and in complete secrecy.

The guardsman had performed to the old man's expectations in managing the first stage—in using the Young Irelander sympathizers to organize ten barrels of gunpowder, ship them to Kent, then transport the barrels by cart to London while leaving no trace that might lead back to either the guardsman or the old man.

Wrapped in the comforting shadows in the corner of the tavern, the man raised his mug of ale and took a slow, savoring draft. He'd been summoned by the old man that afternoon and given the location of the barrels, along with the keys to the warehouse in which the barrels were currently stored.

At an earlier audience, he'd been made privy to the names of those he needed to gull and all relevant information necessary to carry out the second stage. As far as he knew, the details of the second stage hadn't been shared with his competitor; the guardsman knew where the barrels were, but not where they were going.

As per the old man's instructions, the man had spent the first three days of that week rattling around the coffee houses and eateries around Whitehall, armed with names, positions, and many useful facts. He'd crossed paths with various, mostly distant acquaintances, had imbibed and eaten alongside them, and subtly raised hares; without actually stating anything as fact, he'd planted the seeds of the notion that the Chartists were stirring and action might be imminent. As he understood things, the rumors were designed to ensure that one Lord Drake Varisey, Marquess of Winchelsea—a nobleman the old man seemed to despise and hold in unqualified contempt, yet at the same time, be distinctly wary of—went off on a wild-goose chase, the better to pave the way for a straightforward and unfettered run through the old man's second stage.

That afternoon, he'd been happy to be able to report that all was in readiness to proceed, exactly as the old man had wished.

Yesterday, when he'd received a note from the guardsman informing him that the barrels had been delivered and describing their location, he'd progressed to contacting the local Chartist militia leaders via the London Working Men's Association headquarters. That hadn't been as difficult as he'd feared. As usual, the old man's information had been uncannily accurate; how the old boy managed it while remaining immured in the country, the man really didn't know, yet such an absolute grasp of every little detail and nuance of the situation commanded his admiration.

He'd only had to mention O'Connor's name to be assured that his message would be conveyed to the right quarters and the leaders would meet with him. He'd dropped only one hint of impending action; that was all the workers at the club had required to leap on his request.

He doubted the local leaders would be quite so easy to gull, but he'd nominated this tavern as a meeting place and tonight at ten o'clock as the time.

It was nearing the hour now. He sat in the shadows and, despite the impatience—a wish to push on—that rippled beneath his skin, reminded himself that all good things came to those who waited.

Even more specifically, he reminded himself of all the good things he would be able to buy with even one third of the old man's estate. Two thirds, and he'd live out his life in luxury. He felt confident of carrying out the old man's wishes to his satisfaction, if not his outright approbation —approval enough, at least, to convince the old man to entrust the third and final stage of the plan, whatever it might involve, to him.

In truth, this stage of the plan could not have been carried out by the guardsman; even in mufti, all guardsmen were instantly recognizable. Their stance, their rigid posture, gave them away; the Chartists would have taken one look at the guardsman and steered clear.

He, on the other hand, was a chameleon. He also had an abundance of charm; he fully expected to have the local Chartist leaders eating from the palm of his hand.

Or to be more accurate, swallowing his tall tale whole.

Barely audible above the raucous din, the clock on the wall above the bar weakly chimed the hour—and the main door was shoved open, and three men entered.

They were heavyset, middle-aged, and just a touch suspicious. They scanned the tavern. He made no move to attract their attention, just waited.

Eventually, they saw him, and hesitantly, sliding between other patrons' chairs, they approached.

When they reached the table where he sat, the oldest—the white-haired one in the center of the three—studied him, then asked, "Is it you we're supposed to see, then?"

The man smiled thinly and, with a wave, invited them to sit on the three empty stools arrayed around the table. "Please join me, gentlemen." He raised his hand and caught the serving girl's eye. As she walked over, he asked the three Chartists, "What's your pleasure? This round's on me...or rather"—he lowered his voice dramatically—"on Feargus O'Connor."

The three Chartists exchanged a glance, then the serving girl was there, and they ordered pints of ale.

When the girl retreated to the bar, the Chartists studied him anew with an interest that was easy to read. The oldest eventually asked, "What's this about, then?"

From under the brim of his hat, the man glanced past the Chartists, then murmured, "Let's wait until you have your drinks in front of you— no need to chance anyone overhearing."

His caution had the desired effect; the three were now convinced he brought highly sensitive information. He'd long ago learned that little touches like that carried more weight than protestations.

When the Chartists had foaming pints before them and the serving girl had departed, the three lifted their pints, took deep sips, then lowered the mugs. All three glanced guardedly around, then bent expectant looks on him, on his face shadowed by his hat brim.

He suppressed a self-satisfied smile; this was going to be even easier than he'd thought. He leant forward, fixed his gaze on the face of the oldest man, and quietly said, "O'Connor sent me down. He's...unhappy about the way things are going, but of course, he can't be seen to be inciting any action. Not now he's in Parliament himself. But he and the others up north feel the movement needs to ginger things up—to remind people we're here and that we've still got demands, demands the high and mighty haven't yet addressed."

The three murmured their agreement, keeping their voices down.

They leant in as the man let his voice sink even lower. "We need to make a bit of a statement, see? O'Connor and the others have agreed on that, and that the statement needs to be made here in London. They've worked out a plan, but their orders are that I keep all the details to the smallest number of people, so you'll excuse me if I don't explain."

The three exchanged glances, then the oldest looked directly into the man's shadowed eyes. "All right. But if you're not going to tell us what this plan's about, what are we meeting for, then?"

The man smiled and eased back; he knew he would get what he wanted. What he needed. "All I—well, O'Connor, really—wants from you is the loan of some muscle. I need four reliable men, but not just any men. Men who know how to do what's required—O'Connor and the others were sure you had the right men in your groups to help me carry out their plan."

The Chartists didn't even pause to exchange a glance. All three leant even farther forward. "What men?" the one on the right asked.

"Just four?" the man on the left queried.

The oldest man, the one in the center, asked, "What do you need them to do?"

He outlined his requirements.

And as the old man stuck away in the country had assured him, the Chartist militia leaders knew just the right helpers to steer his way. They promised him they would have all four meet him the following night.

"What name shall we tell them?" the oldest leader asked.

"Sharp." The man was sorely tempted to claim to be a captain, but that might be one contemptuous step too far. "John Sharp. And we won't meet here." He beckoned the serving girl. "The Dog and Duck tavern in Red Lion Street. Same time—ten o'clock."

The Chartists nodded readily, accepting his murmured comment that no one in Weaver's Lane needed to see the four of them together again, or even him with four of their fellows.

He tapped the side of his nose. "Best keep everything under wraps. O'Connor doesn't want any whispers getting around, not before the action."

He left the three at the table, sipping the second round he'd ordered for them. Only after he'd passed through the door into the welcoming darkness did he finally allow his triumph to show.

"Even easier than I'd thought." The old man would be proud if he knew. Lining up the men to carry out the next stage of his plot had cost seven pints of ale in a dingy tavern.

The man in the low-brimmed hat strode off down the cobbled street, and the night swallowed him whole.

CHAPTER 2

*M*uch to Michael's frustration, it was after ten o'clock the following morning when he finally found his way to the steps of the Hendon town house. He could barely credit that it had taken him so long to learn the address. "That's what comes of searching for ton addresses in London in October," he grumbled. "Most of the ton are somewhere else."

He'd assumed Crewe would know the address, but the butler hadn't. Subsequently, Michael had rifled the desk in the library, but his father had taken his address book with him. Reasoning that, if the Hendon sons—there were three of them—were in town, then they would appear at one or other of the customary haunts for fashionable gentlemen, he'd shrugged and gone out on the hunt. But trawling through the clubs had yielded only the information that the Hendons weren't about, and no one he'd been able to find knew of their London address.

In the small hours, annoyed over having wasted an entire evening, he'd returned to St. Ives House and his bedroom. There, he'd grumbled about the problem to his gentleman's gentleman, Tom.

Tom was two years older than Michael and had grown up on the Somersham Place estate. He'd originally been Michael's groom, then his sometime carriage driver. When the time had come for Michael to go on the town, and he'd been informed he needed a gentleman's gentleman to keep his clothes and effects in order, he'd asked for Tom to be trained by his father's man, and so now Tom effectively filled all three positions—

personal groom, sometime carriage driver, and gentleman's gentleman—to the satisfaction of all concerned.

Tom was also Michael's principal conduit for household information. In retrospect, Michael couldn't understand why he hadn't laid the problem of the Hendons' address before Tom immediately.

Once apprised of his need, Tom had advised that he would investigate and see what he could turn up by morning.

After consulting with his colleagues below stairs, Tom's morning suggestion had been to ask at the Half Moon Street house of Michael's father's cousin, Demon Cynster. Apparently, Lady Hendon was a superlative rider of exceptional horses, as was Demon's wife, Felicity. As the Hendon estate was on the north coast of Norfolk, not far from Demon's estate and stable complex outside Newmarket, it seemed likely the two ladies would be friends.

That prediction had proved accurate; although Demon and Felicity, better known as Flick, were in the country, the butler left in charge of the Half Moon Street house knew Michael well and promptly volunteered the Hendons' London address.

Michael paused on the pavement, looking at the houses, confirming that he'd finally reached Number 12, Clarges Street. Then he walked up the three steps, seized the knocker, and beat a tattoo on the glossy green door.

Several moments passed, then footsteps, slow but steady—a stately tread—approached. A second later, the door opened, revealing a butler somewhat older than the norm, of middling height and girth, correctly attired, with soft white hair neatly combed over his balding pate, a worn, lined face, and kindly blue eyes.

"Can I help you, sir?"

"Lord Michael Cynster." Michael handed the man one of his cards. "Are any of the family—the gentlemen—at home?"

The butler studied the card, then raised his gaze to Michael's face. "I'm afraid none of the family is currently here, my lord. Might I take a message?"

"I...no." Michael grimaced. "I need advice on a matter associated with business, and I need that rather urgently."

The butler regarded him steadily, then the man's features eased almost into a smile. "In that case, my lord, if I might suggest, you could ask at the Hendon Shipping Company office. If you ask to see the office manager, I suspect you'll be able to learn the answers to any questions you may have."

"The office manager?"

"Indeed, sir. I believe you'll discover the manager to be a font of information."

Michael brightened. At last, a possible source—no, a font. Just what he needed. "Thank you." He hefted his cane. "And where can I find this informative soul?"

"The Hendon Shipping Company office is located at the corner of Fenchurch Street and Lime Street in the City, my lord."

"Excellent." Michael raised the head of his cane in salute, then turned, clattered down the steps to the pavement, and hailed a passing hackney.

The hackney drew up.

"Corner of Fenchurch and Lime Streets," Michael called to the jarvey.

"Right you are, guv."

Michael settled on the seat as the hackney jerked into motion. Glancing out at the passing houses, he grinned. At last, he was off. At last, he'd found the opening to a trail, and his hunt for the gunpowder was —finally!—under way.

~

Miss Cleome Annabelle Hendon sat behind her desk in her private office. With her elbow on the desk and her chin propped in the palm of her hand, she stared at the three ledgers laid out before her.

Sales, Expenditures, and Profits, with all three ledgers reconciled to the last penny.

She surveyed the numbers—figures most businessmen would give their eyeteeth to boast of—and tried to discover inside herself some glimmer of the pride and self-satisfaction such a sight would once have brought her.

But it simply wasn't there.

When she'd first claimed her position in the company, every week, she'd taken the better part of three days to do the company's accounts. Now, she barely took two hours. She'd reduced what had once been a major battle to the most minor of engagements. Where once, every week, she'd savored a giddy rush of triumph, she now derived roughly as much satisfaction as she felt on correctly tying a bow.

In the early days of her occupying this office, there had been challenges galore. But now that she'd beaten every one of those challenges into submission, there was no longer any excitement left in her world.

Indeed, the office now ran so smoothly, so very much under her control even without her direct input, there was little reason for her to actually be there...

Her dissatisfaction—her disaffection with her present unchallenged and unchallenging state—welled. She set her jaw, picked up a pencil, and tapped its end on the desk.

Vigorously.

Unbidden, her thoughts veered to her brothers. Jarred, Robert, and Christopher were all out of the country. They'd sailed that summer for the Americas to investigate trading opportunities. Jarred was in New York, while Robert and Christopher had sailed to New Orleans. None of them was due back until mid-November; she had no doubt all three were enjoying their adventures to the giddy limit if not beyond.

That was what she needed—an adventure. A satisfying adventure of her own.

Something to test her, to engage her faculties and sharpen her wits. Considering her parents' colorful pasts, it was evident her family thrived on adventure; they might possibly even need it, at least in the sense of feeling fulfilled.

So her brothers were adventuring overseas, and in Norfolk, her parents were doubtless pursuing their own adventures of sorts. Meanwhile, she was the one left in London, holding the proverbial fort.

Admittedly, she'd fought to become the de facto lynchpin of the company, the one in control of all finances and more or less at the helm, deeming the position her sure route to independence and also a steady source of interest and excitement. She'd been correct about the former and even the latter; what she hadn't counted on was her own competence reducing the role to one she now found too easy.

With something close to disgust, she shut the ledgers one by one —*slap, slap, slap*—then stacked them and pushed them away.

She needed to find some adventure, some novel enterprise to lift her out of this rut.

But what?

She was staring unseeing across the room when a tap on the frame of her open door had her glancing that way.

Fitch, the head clerk, neatly attired, precise, and sharp-eyed, stepped over the threshold and halted. "There's a gentleman here, miss, asking for assistance with a matter of some importance. A Lord Michael Cynster—he called at your home, and Morris suggested he speak with our office manager."

Cleo blinked and sat up. Morris knew perfectly well that *she* was the office manager, and along with all the staff both at the house and the office, generally steered gentlemen away from her. But not this one. What made him so special? "Lord Michael Cynster?"

Even as the name left her lips, she saw him saunter into the doorway behind Fitch. Fitch wasn't that small, but Lord Michael filled the doorway, casting the slighter man into the shade.

Into near invisibility; Cleo's eyes and all her senses locked on the tall, broad-shouldered figure.

Very broad shoulders. Wide chest. Long legs and impressive height, with his dark hair—a dark brown close to sable—almost brushing the upper edge of the doorway. Features so chiseled, so perfectly cut and constructed, they would reliably capture and transfix the awareness of all females within sight.

Quite aside from the clue provided by his name, she instantly recognized his sort; blessed with a commanding presence and an easy, almost nonchalant assurance underpinned by the innate arrogance of the nobility, such men were inherently powerful personalities. More, they were men about whom women flocked, to her mind indiscriminately; in her experience, such men invariably held a high opinion of themselves and of their attractiveness to women. Sometimes, perhaps, that opinion was well founded, but often, it was not.

Normally, such men affected her not at all; their power bounced off the shield formed of her will, her intelligence, and her determination.

But this one...

With an easy, strangely gentle smile, one that reached and softened his dark-brown eyes, which, she noted, were fringed by ludicrously lush dark lashes, he stepped past Fitch and approached the desk.

That smile shouldn't have set butterflies flitting in her stomach, shouldn't have sent a teasing warmth sliding through her, yet it did. She hurriedly firmed her features into a stiffer, unrevealing mask.

When he paused before the desk, she arched a haughty brow. "And you are?"

His eyes met hers in a steady regard. Then his smile deepened a touch. "As your"—he glanced back at Fitch, then looked back at her—"head clerk said, I'm Lord Michael Cynster."

He drew a card from his pocket and offered it to her.

Cleo stared at the card, at the strong, slightly tanned fingers holding it. She didn't want to take it, but she forced herself to reach out and pluck the card from his hand.

Sure enough, the warmth of his fingers lingered on the ivory parchment. She dropped the card on her blotter; looking down, she noted that, yes, the name was as he'd said—not that she'd doubted who he was for an instant. His clothes—superbly tailored from expensive fabrics and fashionably cut with a hint of the austere—let alone the way he wore them and the manner in which he moved, like some overlarge, prowling, predatory cat, all screamed his station. The power of his presence, the intelligence in his features, and the strength conveyed by his squared chin simply underscored that.

Tamping down her leaping senses—she couldn't understand why they were so ridiculously exercised—she forced herself to look up at him, annoyed to find that it was, indeed, a very long way up. Keeping her expression studiously bland, in a distinctly chilly tone, she inquired, "I understand you're seeking assistance in some matter. How may we help you?"

Michael wasn't—definitely wasn't—used to being met by prickliness. In that respect, Miss Cleome Hendon was giving an excellent imitation of a hedgehog—one riled and ready to shoot quills his way. He didn't try a more beguiling smile; he had a strong suspicion that wouldn't go down well. Instead, he glanced around and spotted a nearby chair. He looked at her and gestured to the chair. "Do you mind if I sit?" If he didn't, she'd end with a crick in her neck and probably blame him.

She waved her permission. While he lifted the chair, set it before the desk, then leant his cane against the side and sat, she nodded to the clerk. "That will be all for the moment, Fitch. I'll ring if I need you."

The man bowed and departed, but left the door open. Michael glanced at it, but decided it didn't matter; the room was at the end of a long corridor, and the nearest clerks were at a sufficient distance—no one would be able to overhear their conversation.

"Well, Lord Michael?"

He returned his gaze to her face. "Please, just Michael. Our families are acquainted."

She dipped her head. A very pretty, well-shaped head with a wealth of strawberry-blond curls piled in a knot on top. The knot, a somewhat old-fashioned style for someone of her years, did not appear to be all that well anchored—wisps, even the stray lock, had already escaped and tumbled down to bob in lustrous curls about her heart-shaped face. Her complexion was soft ivory, with gently rounded cheeks delicately burnished with a rosy tint—a combination often referred to as peaches and cream. Quite delectable.

Eyes that were a combination of leafy green and golden brown regarded him steadily; for a gently bred miss, she had a gaze that was unusually open and direct. Almost challenging in its own right. Her features were delicate—finely arched brown brows over those large eyes, lashes a soft brown and long rather than thick. Her nose was straight, but with a slightly upturned tip. As for her mouth...

His lazy perusal halted with his gaze locked on her lips. Rosy pink, their curves distinctly lush, the upper straight, the lower full and ripe; he was suddenly conscious of a remarkably strong desire to taste them.

A strong enough compulsion to shake him into forcing his gaze to move on...to her figure. A swanlike neck, straight shoulders, and gently rounded, very feminine charms—that much was on show. With her perched behind the desk, he couldn't gauge her height, but what he could see suggested curves to match her lips. Lush, full, ripe.

His educated guess was that she was a pocket Venus with her curves hidden—or was that disguised?—by draperies. Her clothes were, he supposed, appropriate for the post of office manager of her family's company, being practical rather than fashionable—a rather severely cut jacket in honey-colored twill worn over a white lawn blouse with a ruffled jabot adorned with lace.

Her hands were delicate, fine boned, her long, slender fingers devoid of rings; as his gaze reached them, in a very deliberate fashion, she tapped the end of the pencil she was holding in her right hand on the blotter—a clear warning of mounting impatience.

He raised his gaze to her face and, more certain now, smiled easily. "I was hoping to speak with one or more of your brothers, but I understand they're not available to be consulted."

"They're in the Americas."

"Your parents?"

"In the country—at Castle Hendon on the north coast of Norfolk."

He made a small grimace and nodded. And said nothing more; instead of demanding, he would rather she asked.

She spent several moments regarding him with a mixture of distrust and curiosity; eventually, curiosity won. She sat straighter, reached up and poked the pencil she'd been holding beneath her topknot—favoring him with an excellent view of her distinctly feminine charms—then she lowered her arms, folded her hands on the blotter, and fixed her gaze on his face. "Lor—Michael, as I am the manager of this company, perhaps, if you tell me what you wish to know, I might be able to assist you. Unless your query concerns some subject peculiarly masculine in nature, I assure you that I'm significantly more likely than my brothers to have the answers you seek."

He was far too clever to grin. He hesitated for only a second before confiding, "I need to locate the drivers of two carts who delivered a particular cargo into London on Wednesday."

She studied him levelly for several seconds, then bluntly asked, "Why are you"—her gaze fleetingly swept over his figure—"interested in the drivers of carts?"

He blinked. He hadn't expected her to ask that. "I…need to find, to locate, the cargo they brought into the city."

Her gaze didn't waver. "Again, I ask: Why?" When he didn't immediately reply, her eyes narrowed on his. "What is this cargo?"

Michael realized he'd made a serious misstep; provoking the curiosity of a woman—a lady—of her ilk was never a good idea. He stuck to his guns, but strove to make his tone conciliatory. "I just need to find the cargo—some barrels. Ten, to be precise."

She opened her eyes wide. "Ten barrels of what?"

Cleo scented an intrigue; when she saw his jaw tighten and his lips—finely chiseled and distractingly mobile—firm into a straight line, she was sure of it. More confident, she leant forward, comfortably settling her forearms on the desk and holding his gaze with hers. "A gentleman of your ilk searching for barrels—barrels of anything? You have staff aplenty. And what possible interest could you have in barrels—again, barrels of anything—being brought into London?"

His face hardened. Absolute intransigence stared back at her. The line of his lips had turned to a rigid slash.

She studied his face, then smiled, letting her own confidence show. She lowered her voice and confided, "My brothers will tell you that there is no power in this world capable of overcoming my stubbornness. And trust me—they do know."

He stared at her as if she was a strange and unexpected puzzle. She waited, unperturbed by his scrutiny.

A scrutiny that steadily darkened until it was close to a glare.

When, with her lips still curved, she simply waited, he finally flung up a hand in a fencer's gesture of defeat. "Very well." His accents had turned exceedingly clipped, his tone hard—more real to her ears than his earlier softer, polished, and charming drawl. "If you must know, I'm working with Winchelsea—Drake Varisey." He pinned her with a penetrating glance. "Do you know about Drake? About what he does?"

She sifted through the accumulated information filed in her brain. "I've heard that he...*works*, for want of a more appropriate word, for the Home Secretary in pursuing those miscreants the usual authorities find it difficult to investigate."

Michael nodded. "A sound description as far as it goes. Drake is also tasked with pursuing plots that have the potential to threaten the realm."

She blinked and straightened. "And these barrels you're seeking have something to do with the latter?"

His curt nod sent a surge of expectant excitement through her. It had been so long since she'd felt such a thrill, she took an instant to savor it.

"The barrels I'm trying to find contain gunpowder."

The information acted like a bucket of cold water, effectively dousing her thrill. She stared at Michael Cynster's face—at the determination and strength so blatantly on display—and accepted that he wasn't in any way pulling her leg. "Gunpowder," she repeated. "Ten barrels. Somewhere in London." When he nodded again, she hesitated, then asked, "Are we talking about the usual barrels—a hundredweight each?"

Again, Michael nodded. "So now you understand why I'm searching for the drivers—I have to locate those barrels, and as soon as may be."

"Hmm." Her gaze now unfocused, Cleome Hendon stared past him at the open door. "Finding them will be a challenge."

He could almost see the wheels in her head turning. He forced himself to rein in his impatience and wait...

Then she blinked and refocused on his face. "I believe I know how to locate the men who drove those two carts. Trust me when I say that no one else in this office is likely to have the same knowledge, at least not to the extent of being able to lead you directly to it. And I am, needless to say, willing to assist you. However, I have one stipulation."

Her gaze locked on his face, she paused to draw breath, the lace of her jabot rising portentously; even before she spoke, he knew he wasn't going to like what he was about to hear.

"In return for my help, I want to be included in this action, through all of it from now until the end—and as an equal partner."

"What?" He gripped the wooden arms of the chair in an effort to remain seated and not leap to his feet.

With unshaken calm, she held up a staying hand. "Before you say anything, hear me out. My family thrives on adventure, but as the only girl, I have, thus far, been denied my...chance."

Panic trailed icy fingertips down his spine. He knew far too many ladies like her—ladies with a liking for intrigues and adventures, murder and violence notwithstanding, but...not on his watch. Although he could empathize, she would have to find some other adventure to slake her need. He cast about for an argument—any argument. "Managing this office—this company—isn't enough for you?" Even to his ears, his tone sounded faintly desperate.

"I thought it would be, but I was wrong." Her greeny-gold gaze captured his eyes, and her sincerity commanded his awareness. "When you walked through my door, I was sitting here racking my brains over how to uncover some intriguing, potentially exciting adventure in which to embroil myself. You, my dear Michael, walked in with my ticket to that adventure—and I've decided to take it."

He set his jaw. "No. I am not including you in this mission." When her chin only set more definitely—more stubbornly—he continued, "Two men and one woman—two gentlemen and a lady—have already been killed, and that was just getting the gunpowder onto the carts." He lowered his voice to a harsher register. "You cannot expect me to allow you to involve yourself in this."

She held his gaze steadily, levelly, then said, "Who said anything about being allowed? You are not my keeper."

Inflexible will met immovable object; he was determined to be immovable.

She seemed to read as much in his face, but to his disquiet, her confidence didn't falter. Then her lips lightly curved. "Now I know you're hunting these barrels, what's to stop me going out and finding the drivers involved—which, I assure you, I can do—and pursuing those barrels myself?" She tipped her head slightly; the pencil she'd stuck in her hair slipped, but didn't fall. "And of course, it's easy to understand why you—and through you, Winchelsea—want to lay your hands on more than a thousand pounds of gunpowder hidden somewhere in London as soon as you possibly can."

He wasn't going to be so easily manipulated. "Someone else must know how to find those drivers—you can't be the only one in London with that knowledge."

She inclined her head, but that irritatingly knowing smile of hers didn't wane. "That's certainly true." Her eyes locked with his. "But how many days are you willing to waste searching for that someone when you've already found me?"

He refused to give in. He held his ground.

Her expression hardened. "No, I am not going to change my mind and meekly tell you what you wish to know." Temper laced her tone. "You've heard my price—I'm afraid it's a case of take it or leave it, my lord."

Obviously, she was a lot more accustomed to driving hard bargains than he. He needed to find those drivers and, through them, the gunpowder. No matter how much it went against his grain, he was going to have to bend on this... He caught her gaze again. "You definitely know how to locate the drivers involved?"

She nodded decisively.

When he continued to fight his inner battle, as if she could see or sense it, her eyes on his, she again tipped her head—loosening that wretched pencil further, but it still didn't fall.

"Let me see if I can make this easier," she said. "*If* I locate the drivers involved, *then* you will accept me as an equal partner in this endeavor—this mission—and will share all relevant information with me, both relating to the history of the mission and, going forward, as matters unfurl."

That sounded like a contract—a binding agreement. Given her background, he probably shouldn't be surprised. However...she hadn't said anything about *participating* in any action, about being necessarily included in any action, but was only insisting on being kept informed of all developments.

If he had to agree to some degree of sharing in order to get her help, then that was an agreement he could accept.

"Done." He sat up and, over the desk, held out his hand to seal the deal.

She smiled in triumphant delight, reached out, and placed her fingers in his.

He gripped her hand—felt the silk-softness of her skin, the fragility of her fine bones—shook, and pretended not to notice the sharp catch in her breathing, the widening of her green-gold eyes, or the sudden tinge of color that rose to her cheeks. His own reaction to such signs was entirely familiar and, given his experience, easy enough to ignore.

The instant he eased his grip, she pulled her fingers free.

"Right, then." She looked down and bent to rummage in a drawer. Then she shut the drawer and straightened, a leather reticule and a pair of matching gloves in her hands. She plunked both items on the desk. "As time is of the essence, I suggest we go."

He came to his feet as she pushed back her chair and rose. "Go where?"

She glanced briefly at him, then away. "You'll see." With brisk movements, she pulled on her gloves.

He kept his expression studiously impassive, but inside, he was smiling like the hunter he truly was. Well, well—who would have thought that the feisty Miss Hendon was every bit as aware of him as he was of her?

If, later, he had any trouble keeping her out of situations in which she had no business being…in light of that unexpected susceptibility, he, better than most, knew just how to convince her to run home.

She picked up her reticule and came around the desk, clearly intending to lead the way.

She was taller than he'd expected—a touch over medium height— making her a pocket Venus as to curves, but with longer legs. Her height also brought her topknot level with his eyes.

As she swept past him, he held up a hand. "One moment."

She halted and regarded him through wide eyes. "What?"

The word was a touch breathless.

He smiled, strolled closer, and raised his hand. Slowly. He watched her eyes follow his fingers as he reached…for the pencil she'd anchored in her hair. He grasped it, drew it free, and presented it to her. "That seemed a rather strange ornament."

She uttered a sound between a laugh and a snort, took the pencil, swung back, and tossed it onto her desk. "Thank you." Briefly, she met his eyes, then she turned and swept to the door. "Come on."

He followed her out of the office and down the corridor to the clerks' domain just inside the reception area.

"Fitch, I'll be out for the rest of the day." She paused, then resumed her march toward the door. "Indeed, I may not look in for several days. If you have any questions, send a message to Clarges Street, and I'll come in."

"Of course, miss." The head clerk glanced at Michael with something akin to surprise. "Er...enjoy yourself, miss."

His office manager was already at the door.

Michael caught up with her and reached over her shoulder to hold the heavy panel open, so he heard her murmur, "As to that, Fitch, we'll see."

CHAPTER 3

*O*n the pavement outside the office, he asked, "Do we need a hackney?"

"Yes." As he turned away to summon one, she added, "Tell him to take us to Falcon Street, near where it runs into Aldersgate."

He had no idea what lay in that location.

A hackney pulled up. He opened the door, but before he could help her up, she grabbed her skirts in both hands and climbed in, in the process affording him a glimpse of nicely turned ankles encased in fine white stockings. Only once she'd let her skirts fall did he manage to haul his gaze up to the jarvey and relay the directions. Then he joined her in the carriage, settling alongside her as the hackney rattled off.

He opened his mouth to inquire as to their actual destination, but she beat him to speech.

"If this is one of Winchelsea's missions, and you're chasing these barrels, what's he doing?"

He glanced sidelong at her.

She turned her head, trapped his gaze, and arched one fine brow, pointedly if wordlessly reminding him of the agreement they'd so recently made. She hadn't yet located the drivers, but...

He swallowed a grunt and looked ahead. "Drake had to go north. There are political ramifications...in short, he—we—believe that someone is trying to paint the Chartists as being responsible, even though they know nothing about the plot—or so we think. Drake left for Leeds this morning to speak to the Chartist high command, as it were, to get a definite answer."

She frowned. "Why would someone want to implicate such a group? If someone, or some group, does something with gunpowder, isn't it more normal for them—the group responsible—to want the authorities, and the public, too, to know the disaster was their doing? What's the purpose of it, otherwise?"

"You have a point, but as Drake keeps saying, this plot isn't following any of the customary rules." After a moment of internal debate, he went on, "For instance, the first part of the plot—the procurement and transport of the gunpowder into London—was made to look like the actions of the Young Irelanders."

"Good heavens!" She shifted to face him.

He met her eyes. "Those three people who were killed—the two gentlemen were Young Irelander sympathizers, and the lady was the wife of one of them. However, while Young Irelander supporters were involved in acquiring and transporting the barrels, apparently believing this to be an officially sanctioned Young Irelander plot, by all the evidence Drake's gathered, it simply isn't. No one at any higher level in the organization knows anything about ten barrels of gunpowder being spirited into London."

Her frown had returned. She faced forward again. After a moment, she glanced at him. "Perhaps you'd better tell me about the earlier part of this plot—about how the ten barrels of gunpowder got to London."

He gave her a condensed version of events as the hackney rocked and rolled through the city traffic. They passed the Bank of England, and his short tale came to an end. Silence fell between them as the carriage continued north, eventually skirting the Guild-hall. At the sight of the building, he glanced at her, but the hackney rolled on several blocks farther before the driver drew his horse into the curb.

The jarvey raised the trap in the ceiling. "This where you wanted?"

Michael glanced at his companion to find her peering out of the carriage window.

She nodded. "Yes. This is the place."

What place? he wanted to demand, but held his tongue.

Impulsively, she reached for the door handle, but he beat her to it. He swung open the door, descended first, looked around, then turned and offered her his hand.

Lips tight, she met his eyes briefly, then gave him her gloved fingers and allowed him to help her to the pavement.

He sensed her reaction, yet as he'd supposed it would be, the effect of his touch was muted by her gloves. It was still there, however, which was oddly comforting.

He released her, paid off the jarvey, then turned to find her waiting with transparent impatience before an arched doorway. He looked up at the words engraved in the stone lintel. "Plaisterers Hall?"

"Indeed. Come on."

She led the way in, of course. He strolled at her heels as she traversed the tiled hallway. She paused briefly to glance at a board with various offices listed, then stated, "It's on the first floor."

He tried to determine which of the several offices listed as being on the first floor was their destination, but she was already sweeping toward the stairs, and he gave up the search in favor of keeping up with her.

At the top of the stairs, she released her skirts and smoothed them down, then she raised her head, settled her reticule on her wrist, and in a significantly more regal manner, swept down the corridor.

They passed various offices, their thick oak doors firmly closed. Halfway down the corridor lay an office with a divided door, the upper half of which stood open.

That was the office she made for. As she halted before the half door, Michael, halting behind her, read the words emblazoned in gold lettering on the wide timber sign mounted above the doorway. *The Worshipful Company of Carmen.*

Carmen? Were they carters? Was this the carters' guild? He should have thought...only he'd had no idea such an organization existed.

"Yes, miss?" A wizened man with a pair of pince-nez perched on the bridge of his nose came up to the counter-shelf protruding from the rear of the half door. "Can I help you?"

Stepping to the side, Michael saw his coconspirator smile rather distantly.

"I certainly hope so. I'm Miss Hendon of the Hendon Shipping Company. As you might be aware, we employ a great number of your members throughout the year on a wide variety of jobs. We are currently negotiating with several carters and would like to ensure that anyone we hire is on your list as a bona fide carter. As I understand it, this office registers all the carts and carters plying for trade in London. Is that correct?"

"Indeed, miss. Been keeping the register for centuries, we have."

"Excellent." Cleo allowed her somewhat chilly façade to thaw and leant closer to speak over the door. "We're particularly interested in carters who transport gunpowder. We need a reliable carter to fetch an order of several barrels once they're ready and take them to one of our ships for transport to Jamaica. We don't normally trade in gunpowder, you see—this is a favor for a very special client—so we don't have a regular carter lined up for the job. I don't suppose I could trouble you for the names of those carters known to transport gunpowder?"

"Oh, aye—that's a very specialized few, miss." The man turned and lumbered off to a cabinet containing numerous drawers in the far corner of the room. "As it happens, we keep copies of such a list—along with others of similar specialties—just for employers like you."

While the man opened a drawer and searched through various files, Cleo cast an eager—and quietly triumphant—look at her companion.

He met it with a steady gaze, but after a second, gave a tiny nod of encouragement. Perhaps even of admiration.

Smiling, she turned back to the counter as the old man returned, a single page in his hand.

"Here you go. Only fourteen on the list at present." He handed her the sheet and pointed as she turned it to peruse it. "The addresses are there, too—that's where you'll find them. All these men work for themselves. Most are older, it being a difficult area to move into."

"Why is that?" Cleo raised her gaze to the old man's face.

"Well, stands to reason, don't it?" The old man leant against the counter, crossing his arms, making himself comfortable—clearly very ready to chat. "They might get much higher fees, what with the danger money and all, but they have to have specially reinforced carts and much stronger horses, all of which costs money. They're not allowed to carry anything else, either, so sometimes business is slack. Other times, of course, they're rushing from one job to another, but they're only allowed to go so fast if they're loaded. Lots of regulations on trans-porting 'powder, and woe betide any of them who gets caught breaking our rules. Drummed out, they are, right smartly. All of which means that not so many carters want to go to the expense of buying a rig—cart, horses, and trappings—that can be registered for transporting 'powder."

Cleo nodded. After carefully folding the list of fourteen names and addresses, as she slipped it into her reticule, she asked, "Do other carters…well, moonlight, sometimes? Take gunpowder when they shouldn't?"

"Oh no." The old man shook his head. "Worth their registration to do that—and possibly more than that. The fraternity is very strict, you see—you stick to what you're registered for. We've nigh on a thousand members, but I guarantee only those fourteen would have any truck with moving 'powder. If anyone else tried it and was seen—and on the street, it's not easy to hide carts from other carters, you ken—then they'd be stripped of their registration and out on their ear in two shakes of a pig's tail."

Michael leant against the edge of the doorframe beside Cleo and spoke to the old man. "I would have thought that with all the mills in action, and so many with orders from the army and navy, that there would be work enough to keep many more than fourteen carters in business."

"Aye"—the old man nodded—"that there would be if the army didn't have its own band of carters. They have their own carts and soldiers to shift the stuff from the Royal Mills at Waltham and all the others that supply them—Faversham, Oare, Chilworth, and the like. Our fourteen members transport barrels from the private mills to the munitions works, the explosives factories, or the firework manufactories—or to be more accurate, mostly they deliver from the mills to the warehouses that supply those industries, and then later get hired again to move the stuff on to the factories when they order from the warehouses."

"I see." Michael had to admit to being impressed with the rich vein of information his would-be partner had uncovered. He glanced at her to see if she had any more questions.

She met his eyes briefly, then, fiddling with the strings of her reticule, said, "I understand that all gunpowder is packed in specially made hundredweight barrels, and if I recall aright, each barrel must be stamped with the emblem of the mill that produced it, and every barrel must be registered with the office of the Inspector General of Gunpowder, even the barrels produced by the private mills." She fixed her gaze on the old man's face and arched her brows. "Is that correct?"

He shrugged. "Far as I know, but I'm no expert on gunpowder." He grinned. "Only on carting it."

She smiled warmly at the man. "Thank you for your assistance. You've been most helpful." She patted her reticule. "This list will help enormously."

The old man waved them off. "Happy to be of service—well, that's partly why we're here. To help companies like yours find the right carter."

With another smile, Michael's would-be partner turned away. Michael nodded to the old man and followed her.

They went back along the corridor, then down the stairs. On regaining the pavement, she patted her reticule and met Michael's gaze, triumph in her eyes. "It sounds as if the name of the carter who fetched those ten barrels of gunpowder from Kent has to be on this list."

His expression impassive, he inclined his head. He hadn't missed the fact that the list now resided inside her tightly closed reticule.

He glanced around. She did the same.

"So." She returned her gaze to his face. "Shall we start visiting carters?"

Not if he could avoid it.

He reached for her arm and sensed the leap of her senses, which she valiantly strove to ignore. "First," he said, nodding down the street, "it's lunchtime. We should eat." He started her moving in that direction.

She gave a small humph, but fell in with his suggestion. He released her and matched his steps to hers.

~

"A very special customer in Jamaica?" Michael took a sip of ale and glanced across the scarred wooden table.

They were seated in a nook overlooking the small garden at the rear of the Bishop's Arms public house in Falcon Square. The clientele was quiet, mostly workers from nearby offices if the style of their attire spoke true. A serving girl had taken Miss Hendon's and Michael's orders and, in just a few minutes, had returned bearing plates of steak and kidney pie, with Miss Hendon's glass of cider and Michael's pint of ale.

"If one is going to lie," his would-be partner informed him, addressing her slice of pie with evident relish, "one should always include believable details. We do trade extensively with Jamaica."

Michael watched her convey a neat bite of pie to her mouth, watched her delectable lips close about the tines of the fork—and forced himself to look at his own plate. The pie was excellent, but was failing to hold his attention. He could read most females easily and was adept at managing them to his own ends. Miss Hendon, however, was made of sterner stuff;

she seemed determined to go her own road, to forge her own path no matter the distractions he placed before her.

He'd already tried to divert her—her senses if not directly her mind—on the short walk to Falcon Square. *Shall we start visiting carters? We?* He would very much rather she handed over the list of carters' names and addresses and left him to investigate; he was even prepared, subsequently, to fill her in on whatever he discovered. But the notion of investigating with her beside him—or to judge from events thus far, leading the way—filled him with a sense of foreboding.

In his view, ladies should remain safely at home, at least when it came to investigations—especially those involving gunpowder and unknown villains given to killing off anyone who learned of them.

So he'd played on her senses over the short walk—subtly, surreptitiously, doing nothing she could take exception to. A touch on her arm, directing her. His hand at the back of her waist, steering her across the street, then over the pub's threshold and to their table. All in an effort to divert her thoughts, to disconcert and even discompose her a trifle—even to discombobulate her if that was what it took to underline why insisting on continuing by his side was not a good idea.

She'd held her breath, held her nerve—and endeavored to let nothing of the susceptibility he was far too experienced not to know was affecting her show.

He could only reflect that she'd acknowledged from the first that she was diabolically stubborn.

So if he wasn't going to be able to deflect her in that way...what then?

He glanced at her again. He'd already seen enough of her to guess she belonged to that rare breed of lady who paid little attention to fashion. Locks of hair were progressively escaping the confines of her topknot, and there were wrinkles in the sleeves of her jacket from where she'd pushed them up while working in her office. Yet...the slightly rumpled look held definite appeal. Her trailing tresses were lustrous and silky, tempting any red-blooded male to touch. Her complexion was flawless, but also warm—inviting. And that rumpled, tumbled look...

She glanced up and caught him studying her. Faint color rose in her cheeks—which she ignored, and instead, haughtily arching her brows, she sent a faintly frosty, definitely challenging look his way.

Subtle measures weren't working. "Our agreement was that you would locate the drivers involved." He nodded toward where she'd set her reticule on the bench seat beside her—out of his sight, out of his reach. "We both agree that the names of the men I'm seeking must be on that list, so I accept that you've satisfied your side of our bargain. If you give me the list, I'll interview the men, find the pair I seek, then I'll dutifully come and report all."

She frowned at him. "I undertook to locate the drivers involved—that was the basis of our agreement. I haven't yet done that, so your capitulation is premature."

Capitulation? He felt his lips tighten and forced them to ease. "There's no need for you to stick by my side as I hunt down and interview fourteen different carters."

"On the contrary." Cleo had cleaned her plate; she pushed it aside, patted her lips with her napkin and set it down, then reached for her reticule. "There's every need. You forget—this is *my* adventure, not just yours. Not anymore."

With three brothers, she was well acquainted with the male propensity to push females out of anything exciting. She tugged at the neck of her reticule and muttered, "You men always want to keep all the fun for yourselves."

He grumbled something under his breath; she didn't think she needed to hear it.

Her reticule finally opened, and she drew out the list. She unfolded the page and spread it on the table, careful to keep it firmly anchored under her hand; she wouldn't put it past him to try to filch it from her. She ran her eyes down the list, scanning the addresses.

The tension emanating from the other side of the table was palpable, then she sensed rather than heard him sigh.

"All right. So who should *we* start with?"

That *we* was music to her ears. She curbed the impulse to smile brightly up at him; she didn't want him to think she could be so easily appeased.

Apparently relaxing, he continued, "Should we simply start at the top of the list and work our way down?" He paused, then asked, "Do you have any pertinent insights?"

Further mollified by the question, she glanced at the clock mounted on the wall above the fireplace, then looked down at the list and tapped one entry. "Given the time, the most sensible thing would be to start with the carter who lives farthest away."

She looked up and met a puzzled look. "It's just after two o'clock.

Carters start their day at dawn and normally head home about three in the afternoon. If we leave now, we should catch him"—she glanced down and tapped the list—"Mr. Joseph Carpenter, as he arrives home."

When her reluctant partner didn't reply, she looked at him in question; from his expression, he appeared to be deliberating.

Although his gaze remained on her face, Michael was, in fact, checking for other appointments. His parents were expected in Grosvenor Square that afternoon, but Sebastian and Antonia would be there to greet them, and, Michael judged, in the inevitable flap over their engagement, his parents were unlikely to notice his absence, at least not immediately. That said, he was perfectly content to stay away from Grosvenor Square until his mother got over her first transports, and pursuing the carters who ferried the gunpowder into London was a better than reasonable excuse to do so.

Refocusing on Miss Hendon's face, he inwardly admitted that he wasn't at all averse to spending more time in her company. And as he would be with her every step of the way, what danger could there be in simply talking to some carters? He nodded and straightened. "Very well." He paused, then caught her eye. "Incidentally, what is your name?"

He'd given her his when they were first introduced, and given her the freedom to use it, but he hadn't heard her addressed other than as Miss Hendon. "If we are to be *equal partners…*"

She studied him for a moment, as if debating whether to trust him even with that. But then she opened her luscious lips and said, "Cleome. But everyone calls me Cleo, and I suppose you may, too."

He arched a cool brow and thought about calling her Cleome, then decided to take the high ground and simply inclined his head. "Thank you."

She picked up her gloves and started to tug them on—taking her hand from the list. "One thing—when was the gunpowder collected in Kent?"

"It was taken from the cave either very late on Tuesday night or very early on Wednesday morning."

She paused in her tugging. "So it would have arrived in London at some time on Wednesday morning."

"Assuming the carters didn't dally on the way, yes." Eyes on the list, he considered, then said, "We should have asked at the carmen's office about whether the carters involved might have kept the barrels on their carts for temporary or even longer storage."

"I can answer that—they offload their cargoes immediately. All

London carters start every day with an empty cart. I suspect that's one of the guild's regulations—certainly they all adhere to that practice."

He nodded. "So if we work our way through the names on that list, we should—in theory, at least—find the carters we're after." Smoothly, he reached for the list.

Cleo snatched it up just before his fingers touched the paper. "Indeed." Across the table, she met his eyes—so very dark brown it was difficult to read any emotion in them—with an outright, entirely obvious, almost belligerent challenge in her own. She wasn't about to give up the list; she wasn't going to turn aside from her adventure. And nothing he could say or do—not even his flustering of her nonsensical senses— would make her retreat.

He studied her eyes, and she hoped he read all that and more in her gaze.

Finally satisfied that he had, she let her lips curve coolly, glanced at the list in her hand, then at him. "Now that we understand each other, shall we get started?"

The look he cast her could have ground rocks to dust, but then he reached into a pocket, tossed several coins on the table, and slid along the bench seat.

She rose and led the way to the door. She didn't need to glance behind to know he followed, but his expression—that of a feudal lord denied— was one she wished she could have savored for longer.

On the pavement in Falcon Square, he hailed a hackney, and Cleo read off the address she'd selected as lying farthest afield. She then made a point of stuffing the list back inside her reticule and tying the drawstrings tightly before steeling herself and allowing him to hand her into the carriage.

Somewhat to her relief, while her sensitivity to the contact lingered and her nerves still leapt, she didn't feel quite as discombobulated by the contact as she first had. The effect wasn't fading, but it seemed she was growing used to it.

She then had to endure a silent half hour of being jolted over the cobbles. Seated beside her, her reluctant partner didn't exactly pout, but a miasma of sulking male permeated the enclosed space. He wasn't getting what he wanted, and he didn't like it. He sat back, not exactly in a sprawl, but with his arms crossed over his chest.

Quite an impressive chest—not that she needed to notice that, much less dwell on it. They were partners in adventure, that was all. She knew far too much about the propensities of gentlemen like him; not only did she have three brothers who were very much cast from the same mold, she'd also had her two seasons of being paraded around the ton to observe and catalog the species. Gentlemen like Michael Cynster weren't, in her eyes, dangerous in the sense that she needed to fear he would seek to seduce her or damage her or her reputation in any way. Far from it. The very real threat he and those of his ilk posed was a predisposition to get in her way. To high-handedly interfere in her life, in the way she chose to live it.

Men like him had an ingrained but severely misguided notion that they had a right to interfere in ladies' lives.

Luckily, being aware of the danger meant she could block or deflect said interference.

The carriage slowed, then finally rocked to a halt. The jarvey opened the trap and called down, "This is Chicksand Street. Can't rightly take you farther, sir—lane's too narrow."

Michael sat up. He looked out at the houses, then glanced at his partner—at Cleo. She was peering out of the window on her side of the carriage.

She pointed along the street. "I think that's the lane we want."

Michael called upward, "This will do."

He opened the carriage door, stepped down, and handed Cleo out, then releasing her, called up to the jarvey, "Wait for us here. We won't be long."

The jarvey raised a finger in salute. "I'll wait right here, guv."

Michael turned—and realized Cleo hadn't waited. She'd already reached the intersection of a narrow lane and the slightly larger Chicksand Street. She stood peering up at the wall to one side, then her face cleared, and without so much as a glance in his direction, she set off down the lane.

He swore beneath his breath and strode after her.

The area wasn't the most salubrious part of town, and he really wasn't happy bringing her into such surroundings, but at least it wasn't the slums to the east or the teeming alleys closer to the docks. As she was determined to assist in speaking with the carters, this area was at least acceptable.

The lane was cobbled, and the pavements were narrow; the hackney might have been able to squeeze down had it not been for the handcarts, costermongers' carts, and drays drawn up on either side, many blocking the pavement in order to leave space enough for others to pass down the lane's center.

Cleo was just ahead of him, head bent as she consulted the list, then still sweeping along, she raised her head and scanned the numbers scrawled here and there on the doors.

The lower half of the lane was wider. As they reached that section, a little way ahead, Michael saw a carter on the box of a heavy cart pulled by two large shire horses draw the vehicle into the curb on the opposite side of the lane.

Cleo had seen the cart, too. She picked up her skirts and hurried forward. When the man heard her footsteps and glanced in her direction, she raised a hand and waved. "Hello—are you Mr. Joseph Carpenter?"

Michael lengthened his stride.

The carter saw him, but then looked across the street to where Cleo had come to a teetering halt. Her question hung in the air for a second, then the man—middle-aged and heavyset—nodded. "Aye. I'm Joe Carpenter. What can I do for you, miss?"

"Oh, wonderful!" Her face lighting with a transparently innocent smile, Cleo hurried across to stand beside the cart. "I'm Miss Hendon of the Hendon Shipping Company. I"—apparently remembering Michael, closing fast, she waved in his direction—"we are searching for an order of gunpowder that was picked up from Kent and brought into London on Wednesday."

As Michael reached her, she looked earnestly up at Joe Carpenter and stated, "Our company would like to make an offer for those barrels on behalf of a special client in Jamaica. You wouldn't happen to have ferried those barrels by any chance?"

Carpenter looked as though he wished he could say he had, but reluctantly, he shook his head. "No, miss. That weren't me."

Cleo fought to suppress her awareness of the large, hard body that was now far too close for her comfort, hovering protectively mere inches away and seriously impinging on her idiot senses. For Joe's benefit as well as her own, she grimaced, then thought to ask, "You don't happen to know which carter took the job?" She brandished the list. "The guild gave us the names and addresses of carters who transport gunpowder, but you're the first we've asked."

But again, Joe shook his head. "Sorry, miss. I haven't heard anything about any job in Kent. Could be any of the others, far as I know."

Cleo gave him another smile. "Thank you, anyway. At least we can strike your name off our list."

Joe tipped his cap to her. "Always happy to assist Hendon Shipping. Good luck to you, miss."

She started to turn away, but Michael gripped her arm and halted her.

Froze her, in fact, but he'd looked up at Joe, and she prayed he hadn't noticed the violence of her response, even as she battled to drag in a breath and overcome it.

His gaze on the carter, Michael ruthlessly blocked all awareness of Cleo's reaction from his mind and asked, "Has anyone borrowed your cart and team recently?"

"Nah." Carpenter looked fondly at his horses. "Some do ask, thinking to fetch something from here or there on the cheap, but our carts are registered for gunpowder only, see? Can't legally be used for aught else."

Michael thought rapidly. "But what if someone wanted to move gunpowder? Would any of the gunpowder carters—those on the guild list —loan their carts for that?"

Carpenter shook his head vehemently. "Oh no. We'd never do that. Has to be a registered driver, too. Anyone driving a registered cart has to be registered with the guild, and trust me, the guild would have conniptions if they got wind of a non-registered man driving a registered cart, and they always seem to find out anytime anyone bends the rules. It's worth our license—which means our business—to flout guild rules."

Michael glanced at Cleo; she seemed to have recovered from the jolt to her senses and was taking in Carpenter's words. He should, he supposed, release her, but his grip on her arm wasn't tight, and at least this way, she couldn't take off. He looked up at the carter again. "We're trying to figure out how the system works. If we understand correctly, then the carters who brought the gunpowder we're searching for into London have to be men on the list the guild gave us. In addition to that, the carts used to ferry the gunpowder must have belonged to men on the guild list—carts properly registered to carry gunpowder. Is that right?"

Carpenter's brows lowered as he worked through the statements, then his face cleared. He looked at Michael. "Aye. That's it. Both driver and cart have to be guild-registered, so all the possible men will be on your list."

"Thank you." Michael fished in his pocket and handed up half a crown. "First drink tonight is on us."

"Why, thank ye." Carpenter accepted the coin and doffed his cap to them both. "Hope you find what you're looking for, sir. Miss."

With a smiling nod, Michael turned away, easing his hold on Cleo's arm as he did. "Let's get back to the hackney."

Somewhat carefully, she lifted her arm free of his fingers and immediately became—or at least pretended to become— engrossed in the damned list. As they walked briskly up the lane, she seemed oblivious to all about her; Michael found himself steering her by dint of his size and physical presence around obstacles in their path.

When they reached the top of the lane and stepped into Chicksand Street, she finally consented to raise her head. The hackney was where they had left it; they picked up their pace and headed for it. When she still said nothing, he observed, "It seems that working our way through the guild list will, sooner or later, lead us to the carters who transported our ten barrels of gunpowder."

"Hmm." She glanced at the list again. "As that seems to be the case, I believe our next port of call should be Allen Street. It's just north of Cable Street."

He paused to relay the direction to the jarvey. When he turned to the carriage, it was to find the door open and Cleo already inside.

Grinning would not be wise. He took a moment to wipe any telltale expression from his face before climbing up, shutting the door, and settling beside her.

CHAPTER 4

*B*y the time they reached Cable Street and were once again
forced to leave the hackney to head into a warren of smaller
lanes, Michael had realized that Miss Cleome Hendon was a female who
possessed the power to get under his skin.

Despite the fact he could, if he wished, throw her into a sensual fluster
and at least make her pause, when it came to the world around her, she
was utterly fearless. As in, without fear. Fear—even caution—apparently
did not feature within the lexicon of her otherwise impressive
intelligence.

How or why that should be so was a mystery to Michael. But as—
once again at her heels—he followed her down a tiny lane, he was
supremely conscious of an increasingly primitive urge to haul her back
and lock her up somewhere safe. She swept on, oblivious to anything
beyond her goal, leaving him to scan every which way for any potential
threats.

Which in this area were a distinct possibility. As he had all afternoon,
he carried his grandfather's swordstick in his left hand; Cleo had noted
the cane, asked to see it, but hadn't seemed all that impressed by the slender, very sharp blade concealed within the black case. Regardless, in their
present surrounds, having the concealed rapier in his hand made him, at
least, feel a touch more comfortable.

There was no pavement in the lane, just the ubiquitous cobbles. Cleo suddenly halted, then stepped back to look up at one of the narrow houses fronting directly onto the lane.

"This is it," she stated.

Jaw setting, Michael stepped in front of her and, with the silver head of his cane, beat an imperious tattoo on the door.

From behind him, he heard mutterings and felt a small, ineffectual shove, both of which he ignored.

The door was opened cautiously, and a worn and tired woman looked out. When she saw him and took in his clothing, she blinked, then nearly stumbled as she tried to curtsy.

When, straightening, she stared at him and uttered not a word, Michael curbed his impatience and said, "We'd like to speak with Mr. Fields. Is he in?"

The woman's expression soured, and her lips thinned. "No, he ain't. And afore you ask, I don't know when he'll be back." With that, the woman crossed her arms and braced herself as if to deny them entrance.

Understanding she thought they were creditors, Michael inwardly sighed. "My good woman, we have no argument with your husband. We simply want to ask him some questions about a cargo he may or may not have carried."

The woman's expression grew pugnaciously defensive. "He ain't done nothing wrong."

"We don't think he has. We just want to know—"

"You have one of them fancy cards?" the woman challenged. "If'n you do, you leave one with me, and I'll give it to him, and he can come and see you if he wants to have a chat."

Michael drew in a long breath.

The shove, this time, was a great deal more forceful—enough to have him shift to the side.

The woman's eyes went wide as she saw Cleo—who, Michael realized, had until then been entirely screened by his bulk.

The look on his equal-partner's face was almost as belligerent as the woman's had been; she all but glared at him.

Then she turned to the woman and, her expression reverting to one of sweetness and light, with commendable calmness said, "Ignore him. I am Miss Hendon of Hendon Shipping, and I—we"—she cast another black and warning glance at Michael—"merely want to ask your husband whether he moved a certain cargo we're trying to trace, or if he knows which of the carters on the guild list"—she held up the list—"might have moved it."

The woman's eyes fixed on the list, then she briefly studied Cleo's clothes and face. Eventually, she said, "You're not here to cause any trouble for him?"

"Not in the slightest. In fact, as we rewarded the last carter we spoke with for his time…" Cleo shot a look at Michael.

He reached into his pocket and fished out another half crown.

Cleo filched it from his fingers and offered it to the woman. "For your time."

The woman lifted the coin from Cleo's palm. As she studied it, Cleo added, "And there'll be another for your husband, although I suspect that will never make it home."

The woman barked a laugh. "You're right there." She looked at Cleo, briefly glanced at Michael, then returned her gaze to Cleo's face. "If you're set on speaking with him, you'll find him at the local." She stepped forward and pointed down the street. "Just go 'round that corner, and it's dead ahead. The Seven Keys—you can't miss it."

"Thank you." Cleo inclined her head and turned in the direction the woman had indicated—away from the street where they'd left the hackney.

Michael unclenched his jaw enough to add his thanks, then swung around and, in a few swift strides, caught up with his "partner." Having to let her take over the questioning of the woman and stand by while she succeeded where he had failed was bad enough, but… "You can't go marching into a workmen's tavern."

They turned the corner, and the tavern loomed ahead.

Cleo slanted him a glance. "Why not?"

"The fact you even ask…leaves me speechless." Abruptly he halted, and with a touch on her arm, halted her, too, and drew her to face him. "Look," he said, releasing her, "I'll walk you back to the hackney—you'll be safe enough there. I'll come back to the tavern, find Fields, ask our questions, then come and report." He looked into her eyes. "All right?"

Cleo stared at him for several seconds. How to explain? "You saw what happened with that woman." When he just blinked at her, she bit the bullet and said, "You frighten people. At least, people like this."

He straightened and frowned down his nose at her. "I didn't say or do anything intimidating."

"You didn't have to." When his expression hardened, and he looked increasingly dismissive, she cast about for some way to make him see... "In part, it's a function of class." And it was. The aura men like him effortlessly projected was instantly perceived by all around them, and it *was* intimidating. Yet it wasn't simply that they were scions of noble houses; some sons of the nobility were entirely unthreatening. But all the Cynsters she'd ever set eyes on, and men like Drake Varisey and others of their ilk, even her father and brothers, exuded intimidation without conscious thought. It wasn't purely their physical characteristics—their height, the broadness of their chests, their long muscled frames, and the predatory grace with which they invariably moved—but also their utter certainty that in any contest, be it of strength or will, they *would* prevail.

Born to rule. They grew up with that, were imbued with the concept from birth, until, by the age of thirty or so, it had sunk to their very bones. Until it manifested as an outwardly detectable, dominant strength, the sort that would always triumph.

How to explain to him that he didn't have to do anything other than be himself to convince others, male and female alike, that he was dangerous? Someone to be, if not feared outright, then given a wide berth?

Not that *she* felt the least bit threatened by him—which was a point she suspected she ought to ponder at some other time, but now...

She stared into his dark eyes and resisted the urge to clutch at the curls tumbling from her topknot. Instead, she drew in a careful breath and said, "People look at you, and even before you open your mouth, they recognize—at some level they can't even explain—*what* you are. Even though they don't know precisely who you are, they instinctively comprehend that you are the sort of man who wields power. And power frightens them. They don't understand it—and they certainly don't understand you. So they shut their mouths and try to make themselves as invisible to you as they can."

His frown darkened. He stared at her for several seconds, then said, "I'm trying to comprehend how being the sort of man others respect on sight is bad."

She shook her head impatiently. "I didn't say it was. I do, however, contend that when it comes to eliciting information from people like carters and their wives, I stand a significantly better chance of succeeding than you." An idea—a vision—blossomed in her mind, and she seized on the inspiration. "Consider this. You and I might move in similar social circles, but when people in this area look at me, they see someone they can relate to. That's why I keep telling people I'm a Hendon from Hendon Shipping—every carter and his family will have heard of us. We're a very large cartage customer, so my name and the company connection make me something of a known entity in their world. They'll treat me with respect, but not wariness, especially because I'm a woman. I don't threaten them."

His jaw had set and resembled granite. "You still can't go into that tavern."

"Not alone. Even were I here by myself, I wouldn't go in there without a male escort."

He muttered something she thought was "Thank God for that."

She ignored him and rolled on, "But in this case, you're here. And that makes things not just easier but well-nigh perfect. In terms of questioning Mr. Fields, it will smooth our way." She fixed her gaze on his eyes. "What I suggest we do is this. I will lead the way inside, but as long as you stay behind me, you may hover as close as you wish." She wasn't so sure of the wisdom of that, but if the concession won him over to her plan, she would grit her teeth and manage. "Mr. Fields, when we find him, will see me"—she put her palm to her chest—"entirely unthreatening, with you behind me as my guard." She waved her hand at him. "Your...*appearance,* so to speak, will not seem out of place because it will fit the role. Fields will see you, but he'll understand why you're there, and he won't feel threatened. He'll focus on me, and me having a guard, especially one like you, will only underscore how *unthreatening* I am. Then I will ask the questions, the initial ones at least, until Fields relaxes." She studied his expression, but it showed little of his thoughts.

Impulsively, she put out a hand and touched his sleeve. "Please—can we at least try it that way?"

His gaze shifted to her hand, barely brushing his sleeve; suddenly self-conscious, she withdrew it—but really? He could grip her arm, yet she couldn't touch his sleeve?

But his gaze had returned to her face. Then he nodded. Once. "All right. Let's see how your system works."

She managed not to let her jaw drop. For all her persuasiveness, she hadn't actually thought she'd get her idea through his thick skull... She whirled to face the tavern—before he changed his mind. She strode for the tavern door, noting the wooden sign swinging above it, showing seven golden keys on a dark-green background.

She wasn't surprised when she felt hard fingers grip her elbow.

He drew her to a halt and reached around her to open the door. "Move slowly and stay in front of me—don't dart anywhere."

He'd bent his head; his breath feathered over her nape as she stepped across the threshold.

She made no attempt to respond; she had too much to do quelling the riot of shivers tripping up and down her spine.

She halted two steps inside the large taproom. A bar ran along the far wall, and there were men of all trades sitting and standing at tables and leaning on the bar, all talking, each and every one with a mug or a tankard in his hand. Briefly, she scanned the heads, letting the cacophony—and the looks they were already attracting—wash over her.

"We should have asked Fields's wife what he looks like," her escort-cum-guard muttered.

She drew in a bracing breath. "No matter—we'll ask at the bar. It's his local, after all. The barkeep will know him."

"I'll speak with the barkeep." The growl brooked no argument.

She lightly shrugged and walked toward the bar. "As you wish."

She made for a gap that opened up at the long, polished bar as other patrons—as she'd anticipated—shuffled to either side to give them, mainly Michael, space.

The barkeep had seen them approaching. She smiled sweetly at the rugged man as he came to ask what they wanted.

Even as the unwisdom of allowing Michael to speak at all bloomed in her brain, she heard him say, "The lady has business with a Mr. Fields. His wife said we would find him here."

She blinked, then nearly grinned in appreciation. The man wasn't all brawn after all. He'd muted the autocratic command that resonated in his normal speech and had even managed to sound unaggressive; indeed, he sounded like some upper-level servant.

The barkeep studied him, then his gaze dropped to her. She brightened her smile and was rewarded when the barkeep started to smile in response. Then he raised his head, looked to their right, and nodded in that direction. "That's Fields there—in the green cap."

She couldn't see because of the men between, but Michael looked, then nodded to the barkeep. "Thank you," he said. Then his grip on her elbow tightened, and he steered her on.

She did her best to mute her awareness of the strength in his fingers, in his hand, but entirely unexpectedly—perhaps because of that inner wondering over why she, her senses, didn't perceive him as any sort of threat—a sense of safety, of being protected to the point that no danger could touch her, not ever, washed over her.

The sensation, the feeling, was so intense she would have mentally halted and examined it, but Michael guided her around a group of large men, and there was Fields, sitting with his back to her. He was of similar age to Joe Carpenter, perhaps a few years older, a touch smaller in build if a bit more rotund.

Michael halted her a respectful distance away.

She cleared her throat. "Mr. Fields?"

The man in the green cap swiveled on his stool. The instant he saw who it was, he came to his feet. "Yes, miss?" Fields's gaze darted to Michael, but then returned to Cleo's face.

She smiled reassuringly. "If I might have a word?"

Fields blinked, his gaze lifting again to Michael. "Are you sure it's me you want, miss?"

"Oh, indeed." She was still carrying the guild list in her other hand. She waved it. "Your name and address are on the list the guild gave me."

"Oh." The mention of the guild calmed Fields; he settled his gaze on her face. "Well, then—how can I help you?"

"I'm Miss Hendon of the Hendon Shipping Company..." She recited her tale of wanting to trace an order of gunpowder that had been brought into London by a carter on Wednesday. "We're looking to make an offer for those particular barrels, as they're especially suited for shipping to our client in Jamaica. As we don't normally trade in gunpowder, we're rather at a loss, and the guild suggested we ask around to see if we can trace the barrels through whichever carter handled the job."

Fields nodded. Her tale clearly made perfect sense to him. "Would that I could help you, miss, but I didn't do that job."

"Do you have any idea which of the carters on this list might have taken it?"

Fields shook his head. "Sorry, no—but perhaps I can help in another way. Mick Landry and Jack Grimsby should be on that list of yours."

She scanned the names, then nodded. "Yes, they are."

"Well, they're locals here, too," Fields informed her. "They should be here somewhere. Let's see if we can winkle them out for you. They might have heard something about that job."

The patrons around them had been shamelessly eavesdropping. Although the tavern was now even more crowded than when she and Michael had entered it, and seemed full of nooks and alcoves tucked away around corners, the word quickly spread that Fields was after Landry and Grimsby, and within a few minutes, two men, both a few years younger than Fields, mugs in hand, pushed through the crowd and presented themselves.

Fields introduced her as Miss Hendon of Hendon Shipping, which immediately made Landry and Grimsby regard her with professional interest, although both kept a wary eye on the looming presence at her back. Fields went on to explain that she was searching for the carter who had transported a load of gunpowder from Kent to London on Wednesday, and both Landry's and Grimsby's faces fell. Both shook their heads.

"Wasn't me," Landry said.

"Or me," Grimsby added.

Michael finally spoke, still working to mute his accent. "You haven't heard of any other carters taking that job?"

The men eyed him for a second, then transparently decided that if he was Miss Hendon's guard, he was acceptable company.

"I bumped into Joe Carpenter the other day," Landry said. "That was Wednesday morning, and we were both out to the mill at Islington, so it couldn't've been him."

Grimsby shook his head. "I haven't seen any of the others recently— not for the past few weeks. We three here"—he nodded at Fields and Landry—"tend to pick up from the more northern mills. The others live more to the south, closer to the river, which is why we don't run into them so often. But if the pickup was in Kent, then most likely one of them did the job."

Cleo smiled. "Thank you for your help."

Michael pointed to their mugs. "Your next round is on us—I'll tell the barkeep."

Three faces lit. All three chorused, "Thank ye, miss—sir."

With nods and smiles—at least from Cleo and the three carters—they parted. Michael gripped her arm tighter, steered her back to the bar, caught the barkeep's eye, flicked him a crown and told him to fill Fields's, Landry's, and Grimsby's mugs, take one for himself, and keep the change, then, guiding Cleo before him, he made a beeline for the door.

At least he'd contributed to their successful retreat.

They exited the tavern on a wave of goodwill and bonhomie. Despite that, he didn't draw a truly free breath until they reached the hackney and he helped her in.

He finally let go of her elbow; his fingers felt cramped. In retrospect, he was amazed she hadn't protested his continuing to hold her close once they'd left the tavern.

Just as well, because in the mood he was in, he wasn't sure he would have released her.

The shadows were deepening; it was late October, and night was not far away.

He looked up at the jarvey and was about to tell him to drive to Clarges Street when Cleo leant out through the open carriage door. She was frowning at the list, which she was holding between her hands. "Our next carter lives in Rosemary Lane." She looked up at Michael.

He hesitated. "It's getting late."

She glanced up at the sky, currently painted in shades of purple, then looked back at him. "It's not that late yet, and as I understand it, there's a clock ticking somewhere—correct?"

He couldn't deny that, but...

Before he could marshal further arguments, she stated, "Now we've worked out our strategy for asking questions, let's try at least one more."

He stared at her for several seconds, then set his jaw and looked up at the jarvey. "Rosemary Lane. Fast as you can."

"Aye, sir."

The encouraging smile his partner-in-adventure bestowed on him went some way—a very small way—to soothing the beast that seemed to be prowling just beneath his skin.

She drew back into the carriage, and he climbed up and joined her.

The instant the door shut, the jarvey cracked his whip, and they —*partners-in-adventure*—set off on the hunt once more.

He should have realized they would face the same situation in Rosemary Lane with Martin Carter as they had with Fields farther north.

More, he should also have realized that Rosemary Lane, being so much closer to the docks, would make the consequences, at least for him, infinitely worse.

They found Carter's house easily enough. This time, Michael stood behind Cleo's shoulder, and when the door was opened by Carter's mousy wife, he retreated even further behind his partner so she could question the woman without the patently timid soul being distracted by him.

He hadn't considered the effect he had on people—ordinary people not of his class—until she'd pointed it out, but he couldn't deny it. He knew it happened; he'd just never thought much of it before—it hadn't mattered.

The timid Mrs. Carter eventually volunteered that they would find her man in the Barrel and Spiggot in nearby White's Yard. Michael had actually been to the Barrel and Spiggot—in the wild and reckless days when he'd first come on the town. It had been a rough tavern then...

"Perhaps," he said, falling in beside Cleo as she strode briskly down the street, "we should defer speaking with Carter until the morning."

She cast him a swift, sidelong glance. "Nonsense. We're already here, and he's only around the corner."

They turned in to White's Yard. This was an area much closer to the docks, a warren of tiny lanes, alleyways, ginnels, and passageways in which all manner of vermin lurked. He reached out and took hold of Cleo's elbow while his eyes tracked movement in the shadows. The glow cast by the gaslights was dim and made murkier still by tendrils of mist rising off the river and seeping through the lanes.

"There's the place." As bold as brass, she made directly for the door.

He gritted his teeth and kept pace.

As they neared, the pub's door swung open, and three men, weaving on their feet and clearly the worse for drink, stumbled out, clinging to each other in an effort to remain upright.

Instinct kicked. He hauled Cleo against him, within his protective reach. They slowed, circling the drunken trio, who didn't even notice them in the pervasive gloom.

He halted to the side of the pub's door. She'd stiffened when her shoulder had connected with his chest. But she hadn't tried to pull away, nor had she made any protest. Just as well.

He hesitated, then lowered his head and murmured, "Are you sure you want to go in there?"

A second ticked past, then she turned her head and looked him in the eye. "You'll be with me. I'll be perfectly safe."

Something in him stilled. He blinked.

She faced forward and started for the door. "Come on. Let's find Carter before he drinks any more."

He couldn't argue with that, yet he kept her close—closer than before. As far as he was concerned, her earlier words gave him license to do whatever he felt necessary to ensure her safety.

Reaching past her, he pushed open the door and ushered her into the crowded public room.

Cleo halted just beyond the threshold and looked around. All of the carters they'd spoken with thus far had sported flat caps; she wondered if Martin Carter wore one, too.

But she couldn't see far; a wall of large male bodies blocked her view. More, her presence—and possibly that of the man at her back—was already drawing wary looks. She glanced at Michael. "Let's go to the bar and ask, as we did before."

All she received in response was a sharp nod. Rather than looking at her, his eyes were on their surroundings, tracking, assessing, evaluating—searching for threats. And if she was any judge, issuing blatant warnings. He eased them forward, guiding her through the throng. Despite the distraction of being held so close to him—so close that her senses felt overloaded—she had to admit that regardless of the horde of rough males surrounding her, she'd never felt so utterly confident of her own safety in her life.

That wasn't the way she usually felt when surrounded by rough men. Certainly not the way she was accustomed to feeling in the presence of a man like Michael Cynster. All the Cynster males were rakishly handsome, and it was commonly held that all were...rakishly inclined. Their reputations certainly painted them in that light. In the presence of such men, she was invariably stiff, very much on guard. Yet with Michael... she might have been guarded for the first few minutes of their acquaintance, but by the time she'd successfully pushed her way into his mission, she'd lost all wariness of him.

As they reached the bar, she realized that, although she'd known him for only a few hours, he'd somehow stepped inside her guard and now stood in a position similar to that of her brothers, although she definitely didn't view him in any sisterly light.

The barkeep was a dour-faced man; she smiled brightly at him while Michael asked for Martin Carter. After a measuring look for her and a wary glance at the presence at her back, the barkeep directed them to a table across the room.

They stuck to their previous strategy of her leading the questioning, waving the guild list and smiling sweetly; if anything, Carter proved to be even more easygoing than Fields, Landry, and Grimsby, but like them, he knew nothing of any barrels of gunpowder being ferried up from Kent. He confirmed that their group never loaned their carts to other drivers and said he hadn't loaned his even to one of his peers in an age.

Information secured, Michael again proposed a round of drinks for the table, which was well received, and they retreated in good order.

Cleo had expected to pause outside the door, if nothing else to tuck the list safely away, but Michael kept her marching rapidly across the cobbles.

Alerted by the grim tension still infusing him, she glanced right and left, then frowned. "It can't be much past six o'clock, yet it's as dark as night already."

"River mist. Overly spaced streetlights. Lots of shadows."

The shadows seemed especially dense, almost as if they were alive and reaching out from the alleys...

He was still holding her close; she decided she approved.

They reached the hackney, still waiting in Rosemary Lane; he helped her climb in, released her, and called up to the jarvey to drive to Clarges Street. As she sat and settled her skirts, she realized she actually missed the sensation of his hard fingers wrapped about her elbow.

The carriage rocked as he climbed up, then he sat beside her, swung the door closed, and the hackney lurched into motion.

Michael didn't say anything for several moments, too distracted by calming...whatever it was that had his guts in its grip. He couldn't recall ever feeling quite so exercised over any lady's safety before. Then again, he'd never escorted a lady to the Barrel and Spiggot before.

He glanced sidelong at her—at the list she was busily folding and tucking back into her tight-necked reticule. Given the tension he'd suffered—indeed, still felt—all of which she'd evoked...

After several moments, he raised his gaze to her face—and found her regarding him with a steady look that even in the dimness of the carriage felt far too knowing.

He watched as her eyes, locked on his face, narrowed.

"I believe you'll agree that in gaining the carters' trust, it's been my name—and the mention of my family's company—that was the critical factor." She raised her chin; her tone was decidedly tart. "And my tale of wanting to make an offer on those barrels for our fictitious client in Jamaica further paved our way—without that, it would have been difficult to ask the questions we needed to without raising suspicions, which in turn would have led to a lack of cooperation. As it is, we can cross five names off our list of fourteen. In addition, we've learned more about how the gunpowder carters run their business—we didn't know about the restrictions on loaning and borrowing carts before."

Evidently, she could read his thoughts loud and clear. She stared at him for a second more, then with a sound close to a sniff, her chin still high, she turned her head and looked out of the window.

He sighed and faced forward. "I take it there's no chance that, now I've learned"—he tipped his head her way—"from you what questions we need to ask, you'll agree to hand over the list and allow me to interview the rest of the men on it alone?"

"Not a chance in hell." The words were crisp and held a wealth of determination.

After a moment, she added, "I might also point out that without my knowledge and assistance, you wouldn't have any list at all. You had no idea a guild of carters existed, much less that they would have lists of members."

"Not even you knew they had a separate group of gunpowder carters."

She inclined her head. "That was a stroke of luck, but one we wouldn't have stumbled on if I hadn't known who to ask about carters."

There were too many things he couldn't deny. The hackney rattled on through the dark and darkening streets, the gloom of an October twilight fading rapidly to full night.

Finally, he stirred. "So we'll need to wait until tomorrow afternoon to speak with more carters."

"No." She turned to look at him. "Today is Friday, so tomorrow is Saturday, and one thing I do know about gunpowder is that the mills—the private ones, at least—don't send out barrels on Saturday or Sunday."

He studied her face through the gloom. "I thought Hendon Shipping didn't trade in gunpowder?"

"We don't, but our ships certainly carry cannons. I've been caught out before—long ago—trying to reprovision ships for a rapid turnaround over the week's end. We now hold several ships' worth of barrels in our own warehouse near the docks, but the mills deliver to us, so I've never had to engage a gunpowder carter."

He straightened on the seat. "So when—what time—can we start tomorrow?"

She shrugged lightly. "Nine o'clock, I imagine." Then she slanted a glance his way. "If you're up for it?"

He knew exactly what she was asking; it was generally assumed that gentlemen like him never saw the morning, never stumbled from their beds before noon. He couldn't justifiably be offended, but in accents every bit as acerbic as hers, he returned, "I'll call for you at half past eight."

She studied him for a moment, then inclined her head and looked forward. "All right. Eight-thirty."

In the deepening gloom, he wasn't sure, but he thought her lips had curved.

They reached Clarges Street. He helped her to the pavement, paid the jarvey, then escorted her to her parents' front door. The aged butler opened it and beamed upon them both.

She turned and gave him her hand. "Until tomorrow, then."

He grasped her gloved fingers, half bowed, then released her. Raising his cane in a salute, he turned away—saying at the last, "Eight-thirty. Don't be late."

He heard an unladylike snort, but at least, as he stepped onto the pavement and headed for Grosvenor Square, it was he who was smiling.

That, of course, didn't last long. Despite the hour, he'd elected to walk in order to give himself time to think. Unfortunately, his mind didn't want to cooperate. He'd assumed that once he was free of her distracting presence, his wits would resume their customary incisive function and lay everything—everything to do with him, her, and the mission—out clearly. Instead, much to his disgust, his faculties continued to be distracted by the tension still simmering beneath his skin. It wasn't precisely aggravating or irritating—it was more a sense of pressure building, of impulse edging into a compulsion to act.

To act in what way, to what end, he wasn't entirely sure, but the pressure was there—had been from the moment Miss Cleome Hendon had bullied her way into his mission—and it was steadily escalating.

Truth be told, he wasn't entirely sure why he'd allowed her to seize the baton as she had, but part of his reasoning had been an assumption that, by now, after a few relatively unproductive interviews, her interest would have waned. That she would have had enough adventure and be willing to hand over the list and let him get on with it.

Clearly, he'd misjudged her mettle. Indeed, however reluctantly, he had to admire the way she'd handled the interviews, and no matter his hopes, she was manifestly looking forward to continuing the hunt by his side on the morrow.

With the quiet, genteel clop of hooves on evenly paved streets in his ears, he paced along the spacious pavements of Mayfair and weighed the pros and cons of putting his foot down and—somehow—curtailing her involvement and wresting the list from her...yet the truth remained that she knew far more about the world of commerce, of carters and warehouses and factories, than he did.

And despite Drake's assurance that they had several days up their sleeve, Michael himself felt a very real sense of the mission slowly building in urgency—that they needed to locate the gunpowder as soon as possible.

That meant allowing Cleo Hendon to continue to investigate by his side.

He considered that conclusion as he turned up South Audley Street, walking steadily north toward Grosvenor Square.

There was no sense lying to himself; despite the tension she provoked, he was perfectly willing to have Cleo brighten a day spent rocking around in hackneys and talking to carters. They had nine more carters to speak with; he had no idea how many they might manage to interview in one day.

He might as well accept that he wasn't going to try to deny her patent wish to continue by his side because he had—entirely unexpectedly—enjoyed her company and wanted to see more of her rather than have her angry enough to shut all doors in his face. She was, on many levels, unique—an original, as the ton would no doubt label her.

Yet beneath the reason of needing her help, beneath even his liking for her company, ran yet another reason. An uncharacteristic reason; he wasn't a whimsical man.

Walking along the west side of Grosvenor Square, he noted that lights were blazing in the front hall of St. Ives House, suggesting his parents were in residence.

As he crossed the street on the last leg of his journey home, he recalled the eagerness that had lit Cleo's eyes, the triumph and real pleasure he'd sensed she'd felt over each of their small successes through the day.

Foolhardy, surely, to allow her to continue to assist him with the mission because of some idiotic impulse to keep that light in her eyes—to keep her happy.

That wasn't like him at all.

∼

Michael was in the front hall, shrugging off his greatcoat, when Sebastian descended the stairs and strolled to join him. Eyeing his brother's attire, Michael arched his brows. "Dinner with the prospective in-laws?"

Sebastian smiled. "Yes and no." He paused before the large mirror on the wall and tweaked a fold in his cravat. "Great-aunt Horatia. She got wind of our betrothal—how, I don't know—and comprehending that Mama will want to commence discussing details of the engagement ball and wedding immediately, Horatia has invited half the family to dine— the older half, of course."

Turning, Sebastian regarded Michael. "Are you sure you don't want to join us?" His smile broadened into a grin. "I'm sure our esteemed great-aunt would be delighted to see you."

Michael shuddered. Horatia was one who could be counted on to feel that, as Sebastian had finally taken the plunge, being the next in line, it was now Michael's turn. "Thank you, but I believe a tray in my room will suffice."

Sebastian chuckled.

Michael glanced up the grand staircase. "I take it the parents are in residence?"

Sebastian nodded. "They'll be leaving shortly. I'm off to Green Street first."

"Grandmama?"

"Had apparently gone to visit Lady Osbaldestone in Hampshire. Papa sent the traveling coach with the news, so I expect we'll see both of them here shortly."

Michael shook his head. "And once Louisa gets back, the triumvirate will be in residence."

"Heaven help us all," Sebastian murmured.

"The triumvirate" was the label their cousin Christopher had coined for the trio composed of their grandmother Helena, the Dowager Duchess of St. Ives, her bosom-bow and grandest of the older grandes dames, Therese, Lady Osbaldestone, and Louisa. It was undeniable that Louisa looked set to take up the social mantle the older ladies had carried for decades; she possessed the same remarkable—and rather scarifying— propensity for knowing everyone and everything that occurred within the upper echelons of the ton.

Sebastian stirred. He glanced at the stairs, then, his expression sobering, searched Michael's face. "Did you get anywhere regarding the gunpowder?"

"To borrow your words, yes and no." Briefly, Michael outlined his meeting with Cleo Hendon, how she'd inveigled her way into playing an active role in the mission—"she more or less blackmailed me into including her"—but that, through her, they'd obtained a list of the carters who ferried gunpowder around the capital.

"So," Sebastian said, "the names of the men who fetched the gunpowder from Kent have to be on your list."

Michael nodded. "From all we learned from the guild and also from the carters themselves, there's very little likelihood any other carter would have been able to do the job. The carts themselves and the horses—the rigs—are critical, and there are only so many of those. Fourteen, as it happens. We've already eliminated five, and we plan to continue the search tomorrow."

Sebastian nodded. After a second, he murmured, "It sounds as if Cleome Hendon takes after her mother."

Michael frowned. "How so?"

Sebastian regarded him in surprise. "Haven't you heard the tales?" When Michael looked his incomprehension, Sebastian went on, "Apparently, Lady Hendon—Kit—once led a smuggling gang operating on the north coast of Norfolk. I gather that was how she and Jack Hendon met. He was working covertly for the army, back in '12, I think it was, and he was leading a rival gang. I heard she—Kit—eventually got shot, but obviously, she lived."

Michael couldn't suppress a weak groan. *"Shot?"* Then he straightened; his features hardening, he shook his head. "That settles it. No matter how determined she is to see action, once we find the carters who collected the gunpowder, I'll return Cleo to her office and chain her to her desk if need be." The notion of her being shot...

Sebastian laughed. "Good luck with that. If she's anything like her mother..."

Michael set his jaw. "Regardless, one way or another, I'll manage it."

Sounds from above drifted down the stairs.

Michael murmured, "I believe I'd best play least in sight." He glanced at Sebastian and nodded. "Good luck."

"And you," Sebastian returned. "Both with the mission and the feisty Miss Hendon."

Michael snorted and strode to the stairs. He went up them quickly and silently. He managed to swing into the corridor to his room before his parents opened their door. He heard his mother laugh at something his father said, then she called down to Sebastian. Smiling, Michael opened the door to his room and walked into the quiet.

His quip about having dinner on a tray in his room had been intended as a joke, but as it transpired, that was exactly what he eventually did.

First, he spent over an hour sitting before the fire in his room, considering ways in which he might ease Cleo Hendon out of the mission—whether he could hold her to the wording of their agreement, which hadn't specified her actually participating in any action.

From what he'd already learned of her, combined with the information Sebastian had imparted, he didn't like his chances.

Eventually, he realized he was hungry, rang for Tom, and asked for a tray.

Later, he debated going out and hunting up his friends, but…the endless round of the clubs, the parties, visits to gambling hells, theatres and their green rooms, and all the other usual pursuits of a gentleman about town had paled. If he was truthful, they'd been losing their luster for some time.

In the end, a balloon of fine whisky cradled in one hand, he sat and stared at the flames in the hearth and found himself imagining what Cleo Hendon was doing at that time.

The Dog and Duck tavern at the northern end of Red Lion Street, just off the Whitechapel Road, was the haunt of honest laborers, hardworking navvies, and off-duty jarveys. Even clad in his oldest clothes, the man felt out of place, but he hadn't chosen the spot for his own comfort but that of the men he sought to suborn.

With his wide-brimmed hat once again pulled low to shade his face, he sat with his back to the wall, close by a corner of the taproom, a mug of ale on the table before him, and waited.

The four men pushed through the doors just before the stipulated hour of ten o'clock. They blended in with the local crowd far better than he, but in case they missed him, he raised his mug and, when they looked his way, saluted them.

They nodded and made their way to his table. With a wave, he invited them to sit. Dragging up stools, they did.

"Ale, gentlemen?"

The one who seemed to be the leader of the four glanced at the others, then nodded. "A pint wouldn't go amiss, sir."

The man smiled an ingenuously charming smile and signaled to the serving girl.

Once she'd taken their orders, then ferried four pints and an extra for him to the table and left, he leant forward and, one after the other, met the four men's gazes. "I know you've been ordered to assist me by your superiors, but I wanted to say that I—and O'Connor and the others—appreciate your willingness to be a part of an action that we hope will put the cause front and center in the government's mind again. I will definitely make sure that your names are made known further up the chain."

Unsurprisingly, the four Chartist militiamen looked pleased. "Happy to help," one assured him.

He smiled genially—conspiratorially. "Well, then. Let's get down to what we need you to do." He took them through the next steps of the plan as dictated by the old man. He felt reassured when the leader as well as two of the others asked questions about exactly how the barrels needed to be handled. Given they were talking about gunpowder, caution, to him—as apparently, to them—seemed wise.

To his relief, they appeared to grasp the intention of the ploy without him having to reveal any more details, and they were quick to suggest ways to accomplish the required tasks in complete and absolute secrecy.

Finally satisfied that, between them, they had a foolproof plan—one that would deliver to the old man's specifications without a single hitch—he nominated the date for the proposed action. "Do you think you can be ready to move on that night?"

Again, he was relieved that they didn't rush to agree but, instead, thought it through, discussing whether it was certain they would have this or that in place by then.

But at last, the leader met his eyes squarely and nodded. "Yes—we can manage that. We'll need to do a bit of finagling to get the transport arranged and get copies of the keys, as well as get all the barrels sorted, but you've given us enough time—we'll be ready."

"Excellent." The man allowed his approbation to show. "Another round?"

The four exchanged glances, then the leader grinned. "We could handle that."

The man signaled the serving girl, saw the four resupplied, then eased back from the table. "I need to leave, gentlemen, but before I do..." He picked up his almost-empty mug and raised it. "To our mutual enterprise! May all go well."

The four grinned, raised their mugs, and drank heartily.

The man drained his mug, set it down, and stood. He nodded to the four. "I'll meet you at the rendezvous at eleven o'clock that night—and don't forget to muffle the wheels."

"We won't," the leader promised. The other three nodded, eager and enthused.

Still smiling, with a last salute, the man left them.

CHAPTER 5

The following morning, Michael strolled into the front hall of the Hendon town house at precisely thirty minutes past eight o'clock. Despite having fallen into bed at what was, for him, a ridiculously early hour, he'd tossed and turned, and what sleep he'd eventually found had been filled with dreams.

Disturbing dreams.

At his age, certainly, he found the contents unnerving. It had been a very long time since he'd dreamt of a woman in that fashion.

Admittedly, his mind had already been filled with thoughts of her; how to deal with her was the subject that had kept him tossing and turning. Yet he would have sworn he was too old and surely far too experienced to have such vividly erotic dreams. Aside from all else, the last thing he needed was for his wayward libido to fixate on a lady with such termagant-like qualities.

The sound of light footsteps drew his gaze to the head of the stairs. He watched Cleo descend, stepping lightly, a bright, breezy smile on her face, her enthusiasm for the day—for continuing to pursue the mission by his side—brimming over and washing in warm expectation over him…

None of which helped—either in getting a handle on what he should do with her or in corralling his restless libido.

"Good morning, my lord. I trust you slept well?"

"Passably."

She smiled and spread her hands. "As you perceive, I'm ready to proceed." She shifted to allow the butler to drape a bright-blue mantle over her shoulders. The particular hue brought out the red glints in her hair and matched the color of the full skirt and fitted jacket she'd chosen to wear.

Michael stared at her. He'd met her only the previous day, yet there she stood, somehow effortlessly anchoring his world...

What the devil was this?

He managed to keep his frown from his face and let all her chatter about which carter they should try first slide past him.

Once she'd secured the ties of her mantle and set her reticule dangling from her wrist, he offered her his arm.

She paused, her gaze colliding with his, but then she smiled a touch shyly and set her hand on his sleeve. "Thank you," she said.

"Indeed," she continued, as he nodded at the butler, sending that worthy to open the door, "I meant to thank you for your protective escort last night." She looked down as they walked through the doorway and into the cool of a gray morning. "I would never have been able to go into those taverns without your support, and we would never have learned all we did if you hadn't been willing to protect me in that fashion."

He halted on the porch and, frankly dumbfounded, stared at her. She was *thanking* him for acting as he had? Regardless of the circumstances, most of the females in his family would have labeled his behavior presumptuous and overly possessive.

But Cleo glanced up at him and smiled, her gaze open and direct. "If you hadn't made me feel so safe, I would never have been able to manage those men and our questions so smoothly." Her smile brightened. "So thank you." She looked ahead. "Oh."

Again, she glanced up at him, this time arching a brow. "No hackney today?"

The question broke through his distracted daze. He looked at the small, anonymous, black town carriage waiting at the curb. "I decided having Tom along wouldn't hurt." *For extra protection,* but he left the words unsaid. He was still grappling with the notion that she didn't mind —indeed, even welcomed—the manifestation of his protective instincts.

He led her down the steps, across the pavement, and helped her into the carriage, then realized and asked, "The first address?"

She gave him the name of a lane, and Tom—a font of information on London's byways, which was another reason to have him drive them— informed them it was a tiny lane just north of the old Ratcliffe Highway.

Assured by Tom that he could find it, Michael climbed into the carriage and shut the door.

As he sat, Tom flicked the reins, and the carriage rolled smoothly off. Michael saw that Cleo had pulled out the list and was poring over it.

"With any luck," she said, "we ought to be able to get through the entire list today—or at least to the point of speaking with the carters who fetched those barrels from Kent."

He murmured a vague agreement and leant back against the squabs. Once they found the carters who had transported the barrels into London…what was he going to do then?

Tom pulled up at the entrance to the tiny lane. Michael helped Cleo down to the cobbles, then firmly took her arm and steadied her along the roughly surfaced ground.

Once again, he assumed the position of "my lady's guard," a role that, he had to admit, suited him to the ground, especially now he knew she didn't resent his more high-handed and overt actions.

Her acceptance of his protection had calmed something inside him, as if her attitude had pleased and placated some disgruntled and grouchy beast.

Cleo found the relevant door, knocked, and this time found herself dealing directly with one Walter Feeney. With Michael at her back, and the Hendon name to recommend her, she quickly got the answers they required.

Feeney hadn't been the carter who had ferried barrels from Kent into London on Wednesday morning. "I was off to the mill up by Wapping that day." He also had no notion which carter might have taken the job, nor had he loaned his cart in recent weeks.

They thanked Feeney, then carefully—with her having to rely on Michael's supporting grip on her arm—made their way back down the lane.

She remained exceedingly aware—hyperaware—of Michael's nearness, but the fluster of the previous day, while still present to some degree, was steadily giving way to…a certain curiosity.

Certainly, the temptation to experience and savor thrills and reactions that, to her, were altogether novel had grown to the point of compulsion.

She felt certain that the reason she felt able to indulge—to dwell on the thrills and sensual frissons—was because she was convinced, to her bedrock convinced, that with him, she was safe. That she would always be safe, no matter the situation.

He might be dangerous in that particular way that men like him could be dangerous to ladies, but she knew to her bones that he would never, ever, be dangerous to her.

They reached the carriage, and he helped her in. She drank in the aura of effortless strength that she sensed through his grip on her hand and, as she sat, allowed her gaze to linger on the clean lines of his profile as he spoke to Tom. She greedily absorbed the way he moved—so fluid and graceful despite being a large man—as he entered the carriage and sat beside her.

Her senses flared. Facing forward, she looked inside and confirmed that her lungs had seized again, restricting her breathing and leaving her nerves sparking and her wits oddly giddy.

"Cleo—the next address?"

What? She looked at him. "Oh—yes." Hurriedly, she consulted the list. "I don't think it's far." When she found what she thought was the nearest address, Michael relayed it to Tom, who confirmed it was close.

As they set off, she leant back against the seat and bludgeoned her wits into order. Then she glanced at the list again. "Six down, eight to go —and I believe several of the other addresses lie in this area."

When they alighted at their next stop, at Michael's suggestion, Cleo showed Tom the list, and the groom-cum-driver confirmed that all the carters they'd yet to interview lived in the areas on either side of Cable Street, between Well Street and Cannon Street.

Tom assured them they should easily be able to find all their marks that day, provided said marks were at home. Still, it was Saturday, a day of rest for the gunpowder carters, and so it proved to be. They found three more of the men on their list over the next hour and a half, but none of the three had any more information than the previous six.

As, her arm looped with Michael's, Cleo picked her way down the narrow lane that Tom had assured them would deliver them to their next port of call on Cains Place, she was less aware of Michael's physical presence than of a nagging worry that her brilliant idea to work their way through the list of gunpowder carters would somehow prove a false trail.

She glanced at Michael's face. "Could we have overlooked something? Some way in which barrels of gunpowder might have been moved without using any of the gunpowder carters?"

He looked down and met her eyes. In the rich brown of his, she could see that he, too, had started to question their assumptions.

After a moment, he grimaced, then looked ahead. "One has to wonder, but I keep coming back to the carts themselves. Anyone could, theoretically, drive a cart laden with gunpowder, but after hearing the descriptions and seeing Joe Carpenter's cart, while I can imagine it might be possible to transport ten barrels a short distance in an ordinary cart or two, I seriously doubt ten barrels could have been transported from Kent to London other than in properly reinforced carts drawn by heavy teams of horses."

"Which brings us back to our gunpowder carters, or at least, to their horses and carts—their rigs."

"Indeed. And on top of that, there are so many carters working in and around London, carting this and that down every street and lane, let alone along the highways, and they're all guild men and seem to know each other at least by sight, then if a non-guild man had been driving a gunpowder cart all the way from Kent into London, one of the guild carters would have noticed and reported him. That has to be the way the guild system works. By the sounds of it, they're rigid about protecting their turf, and the gunpowder carters are one of the most highly paid branches of the fraternity. I imagine the guild would act quickly and decisively to protect their monopoly."

She nodded. "True enough. And from all we've heard from the carters we've spoken to, none would even contemplate lending their carts to someone else—someone not of their number."

"Which is to say"—he looked down and caught her eye—"that our suppositions are sound, and we need to persevere and work our way through the entire list if need be. At least one of the men on it must have been the man behind the reins of a gunpowder cart that traveled from the Kent coast to London. Even if he doesn't immediately admit to taking the job, he'll react, and with him being a guild member, I'm sure we'll eventually persuade him to tell all."

She let herself absorb the confidence in his eyes, in his tone, then nodded and looked ahead.

They found the next address, which proved to be a lodging house. Michael raised his cane and beat a crisp tattoo on the dingy, faded door.

After a moment, heavy footsteps approached, then the door swung open to reveal a large woman with frizzy, pale hair, several chins, and a multitude of layers—a bodice, spencer, shawl, petticoats, heavy skirt, and apron among them. She was drying her reddened hands on a cloth, but her gaze as she took in the sight of them was shrewd and alert. Her eyes widened fractionally, then she focused on Cleo. "Yes, ma'am?"

"Good morning. I'm looking for"—Cleo glanced at the list to confirm the name—"Mr. Terrance Doolan. I understand he lives here?"

The woman slowly nodded. "Aye, that he does. I'm his landlady." The woman's gaze grew sharper. "And you are?"

Cleo was rather surprised at the question and its tone, but she trotted out her name, the company's name, and that she wished to speak with Doolan over a job he might recently have taken.

The landlady's features eased. "Sorry, ma'am, but I did wonder, you see…" Her expression turned openly anxious; her fingers clenched on the cloth, twisting the material. "I'd like to speak with Terry, too—he went off on a job four days ago now, and he hasn't returned, and that's just not like him."

Cleo's pulse leapt. "Four days ago…that would be Tuesday?"

The landlady nodded. "Odd, it was—he's usually off by first light to any job, but this one, he left in the afternoon. Tuesday afternoon." Her lips turned down. "Chipper and chirpy as usual, he went off with that apprentice of his up beside him, and I ain't seen hide nor hair of him since."

Cleo exchanged a look with Michael. Doolan had left for a job at the right time, and now, he was missing. Surely this had to be the connection they'd been searching for.

Michael dragged his gaze from Cleo's face and looked at the landlady. "The apprentice—do you have a name and address? Have you seen him since Doolan left?"

"No—I ain't seen Johnny, neither." The landlady shifted in the doorway. "Johnny Dibney, he is. Lives in Mrs. Hendrick's lodging house over on Cock Lane." The woman pointed west. "It's off Chamber Street over that way, just up from Rosemary Lane. It's not far." She twisted the cloth tighter and added, "If you do find Johnny and he knows what's happened to Terry, I'd take it kindly were you to get Johnny to come tell me straightaway." She paused, then her face fell, and she heaved a huge sigh. "I need to know what to do with Terry's things if he ain't coming back."

Michael nodded. "If we hear anything of Doolan, we'll let you know. One more question. Doolan—was he Irish?"

"Aye, that he was. Even though he'd been here in London since he was a mite, he still had all of the charm of those Irish beggars. Always had a twinkle in his eye, did Terry."

"Thank you." Michael shot a glance at Cleo.

She met it, then turned to the landlady and thanked her for her help. They left the woman standing in the doorway, slowly wringing the cloth between her hands.

"She doesn't think Doolan is coming back," Cleo whispered as they walked back down the lane.

"No, she doesn't." Michael scanned the streets, then nodded to their right. "This way." He tightened his grip on Cleo's elbow, and they set off in search of Doolan's apprentice.

They paused to consult Tom where he waited with the carriage drawn up by the curb in Church Lane. He directed them south to Rosemary Lane and recommended they follow that until they reached the southern end of Cock Lane. "Just past Leman Street. It's a tiny little lane runs between Rosemary and Chamber Street—you can't miss it."

Once they reached the tiny lane—and tiny was the appropriate adjective—by dint of asking passersby, they found their way to Mrs. Hendrick's door, midway up the street.

After rapping on the door, Michael murmured, "Let me lead this time."

He raised his head as the door swung wide and nodded politely to the short, buxom woman who stared at them in surprise. "Good morning. Mrs. Hendrick, I presume?" When the woman nodded, he continued, "We're making inquiries about the conditions of apprentices working under the carters' guild, and we were wondering if we might have a word with"—he pretended to glance at the list Cleo still held in her hand —"Johnny Dibney."

On their way to Cock Lane, Cleo had realized Dibney's name was on the list, indented beneath Doolan's.

"We understand," Michael smoothly rolled on, "that Johnny is apprenticed to Mr. Terrance Doolan."

Mrs. Hendrick nodded. "That he is, and a good lad, make no mistake." Her brow furrowed. "See here—Johnny's not in any trouble, is he?"

Michael widened his eyes. "Not that we're aware of."

"It's just that he hasn't been home the last nights—not since he went off to join Terry Doolan on Tuesday. Off on some job, Johnny said, but I did wonder, what with the timing."

"What she means"—a large man loomed behind Mrs. Hendrick; he put a huge hand on her shoulder and nodded politely to Michael and Cleo —"is that this job was starting in the afternoon, and Johnny said as he didn't expect to be back until the next day." The man glanced at Mrs. Hendrick. "We didn't rightly know what to make of that."

"And then Johnny never did come back." Mrs. Hendrick's face wrinkled in distress. She glanced up at the man. "I was thinking as perhaps I should go and ask at Terry Doolan's place, and see if his landlady has had any word."

"Sadly, she hasn't," Michael said. "We've just come from there." He paused, then said, "It's certainly rather troubling. I wonder—can you give us any indication of what, exactly, Johnny did in his work? Did he assist Doolan with loading, taking care of the horses, holding them, stabling them?"

"All that and more." The man leant against the doorframe. "Johnny was almost finished his training. He was cleared to drive carts, even those gunpowder rigs. Good bit of money in it once he'd got to journeyman, and Terry—he done well by the lad. He'd got him registered to drive, but of course, Johnny hadn't yet moved on to taking his own jobs."

"So Johnny and Doolan got along?" Michael asked.

"That they did," Mrs. Hendrick replied. "Terry was the master, of course, but Johnny was a hard worker, and Terry appreciated that."

The man nodded. "Aye—that were the way of it."

Michael exchanged an impassive glance with Cleo. Her eyes were just a touch wide. He turned back to the pair in the doorway. "Thank you. We'd best get on. We've other apprentices we must check on."

With a nod, he drew Cleo away—before Mrs. Hendrick or the man started asking awkward questions.

As they headed back to Rosemary Lane, Cleo murmured, "So Doolan's apprentice is missing, too." She looked up at Michael. "What now?"

"Now," he said, once more winding her arm with his, "I suggest we find a suitable place to discuss what this means, where it leaves us, and our next moves."

CHAPTER 6

*W*ith respect to a suitable venue for said discussion, when appealed to, Tom suggested the Queen's Head, which proved to be a snug public house at the corner of Queen Street and Rosemary Lane, literally in the shadow of the Tower. Michael instructed Tom to pull up in the tiny stable yard and consign the horses and carriage into the care of the ostlers; leaving Tom to take his meal in the taproom, Michael ushered Cleo to a table in the dining room.

The inn wife bustled up, beaming and ready to take their order. They both opted for portions of venison stew, and Cleo ordered a glass of cider, while Michael settled for a pint of ale.

After the inn wife left them, Michael studied Cleo's face. He wasn't at all happy with what they'd found—what it suggested; when she looked up as if to speak, he shook his head. "Let's wait until she comes back with the food."

Cleo nodded, apparently as ready as he to delay putting the inevitable conclusion into words.

But eventually, serving girls brought out their plates and drinks, set everything down, and left them in peace.

Michael quickly spoke first; if he could steer the conversation, so much the better. "Given Doolan and his apprentice left London on Tuesday afternoon supposedly on a job, then I believe we can safely conclude that they are the ones who traveled down to Kent, loaded up the ten barrels of gunpowder from the cave under Ennis's land, almost certainly meeting Connell Boyne in the process, then—as far as we can tell—they transported those barrels into London, presumably arriving sometime on Wednesday morning."

Her head bent, Cleo raised a mouthful of stew to her lips. She chewed, swallowed, then said, "Why did he—Doolan—take his apprentice? Did he always do that, or was it because he needed two drivers?"

"I imagine the latter, because of the ten barrels. Given their size, even if they'd been filled with sawdust, I don't think they would have fitted in one cart. So Doolan needed two carts, and he therefore needed Johnny to drive the second, and as we just heard, Johnny was registered to drive such carts." He frowned. "Do any of the other carters have apprentices? I wonder if that was behind Doolan being chosen for this job, rather than that he was Irish and might have been drawn in as a Young Irelander sympathizer."

Cleo drew out the list again; it was getting distinctly creased and worn. She ran her eyes down it. "Now I know that these subsidiary names are apprentices..." She reached the end of the list, then looked up. "Only one other carter—a Mike Oldham, who we've yet to speak with—has an officially listed apprentice."

"Hmm. Well, we can check whether Oldham was approached, but for my money, Doolan was most likely chosen because he was Irish, and whoever is behind the organization of this plot had reason to suppose he would work for the cause." Michael grimaced and reached for his ale. "That would fit with the plotters' methods thus far."

"What I would like to know," Cleo said, poking at the remnants of her stew, "is where Doolan got the second cart—the one for Johnny to drive. Doolan was, by all accounts, a guildsman through and through—he even trained apprentices. He wouldn't have broken the rules"—she met Michael's eyes—"so he would have borrowed a properly registered cart from one of the other gunpowder carters, wouldn't he?"

Slowly, Michael nodded. "You're right. And as we've asked all the carters we've spoken with whether they've loaned their cart to anyone recently and thus far drawn a blank, then the carter who loaned a cart to Doolan on Tuesday must be one of the four on the list that we've yet to interview."

Cleo glanced at the list, then tucked it back into her reticule. "It must be one of them, and presumably that other carter who has an apprentice— Mike Oldham—will know what a carter with an apprentice would do. Who he would turn to for an extra cart."

"We'll ask when we get to him, if we haven't already found out."

Cleo nudged her plate aside and reached for her glass. They'd danced around the subject long enough. "I understand what Doolan and Johnny Dibney must have done, and that as far as we can tell and must presume, they returned to London, but why are they missing?"

Michael raised his gaze to her face, hesitated for a moment, then he looked at his plate, slowly set down his cutlery, and pushed the plate aside.

Debating just how much to tell her; Cleo waited, wondering if he would come to the correct conclusion.

Somewhat to her surprise, he did; he raised his gaze and, across the table, met her eyes. "In your office, when I first told you of the plot, I mentioned that three people—two gentlemen and a lady—had already been killed because of it. Connell Boyne—the Irishman who arranged for the gunpowder to be shipped to London and stored in a cave on his brother, Lord Ennis's estate—killed his brother and sister-in-law after learning that Ennis planned to tell Drake of the plot. Subsequently, however, Boyne himself was slain—by whoever he had been working with."

Michael watched her take that in; murder was a gruesome subject at any time—generally considered unfit for a lady's ears—and in this case, there were overtones of betrayal as well, but better she know and appreciate the true dangers inherent in the mission.

Eventually, she tilted her head—something he'd noticed she did when especially curious or puzzled; her gaze on his face, she asked, "Why do you—and Winchelsea—think Connell Boyne was killed?"

"We had two reasons, not necessarily mutually exclusive. One, that because Boyne had murdered his brother and sister-in-law and was being actively pursued by the authorities, he had become too much of a liability. However, it's also possible that Boyne was killed on the principle that, as Drake puts it, dead men tell no tales." He paused, then continued, even as he followed the thoughts in his head, "Originally, why Boyne was killed didn't really matter—he was dead. However, with these latest disappearances..."

After a moment, she quietly filled in, "You think Doolan and Johnny Dibney have met with a similar fate."

He grimaced, then looked at her—took in the delicacy of her strawberry-blond, peaches-and-cream beauty, the fragility of her fine-boned frame, and felt protectiveness, deeper and more powerful than he'd ever felt before, rise and flow like a wave through him. "I can't see any other reason for them to have disappeared."

Her own gaze steady, she returned his regard, but after a moment, her gaze grew distant, and a frown gradually formed in her eyes. "That seems an odd way to manage a plot." She refocused on him. "Killing those who assist."

He nodded; even as he did, memory bloomed, and after a second's pause, he stated, "It's unusual, yes, but if there's something about this plot that those who are ultimately in charge of it want to—perhaps need to—keep from all those helping them, then killing people once their individual tasks are completed makes sense."

She frowned more definitely. "You mean, for instance, concealing from Connell Boyne that the plot isn't actually a Young Irelander plot?"

"That, too, but taking it a step further"—he recalled the possibility Drake had aired—"what if the true target of the plot, whatever they're planning to blow up, isn't something the Young Irelanders or any of those who've helped them, like Doolan and Johnny, would agree with? What if the target was something those people wouldn't support—wouldn't stand for to the point of going to the authorities?"

"That's…" She paused, then concluded, "Rather diabolical. If, through guile, you use someone to attack something that someone wouldn't want attacked at all…" She shivered slightly. "Only an astoundingly manipulative mind would think like that."

"Much less put a plot like that into action. But so far, this plot has all the hallmarks of a Young Irelander plot—even Doolan fits that bill—yet Drake has proved the plot has absolutely nothing to do with the movement. The Young Irelanders are being used—ruthlessly used. Not only are their sympathizers being drawn in and then killed off, had it been anyone other than Drake investigating, the Young Irelander movement would very likely be blamed for whatever the end result of the plot actually is, and *they* would suffer whatever retribution the authorities mete out." He paused, then went on, "And if the target is something sufficiently unthinkable that Young Irelander sympathizers would balk, then that retribution will be…dramatic."

She looked pensive. "It appears that whoever is behind this plot is no friend of the Young Irelander movement."

He blinked, then raised his brows. "Good point." He thought, then added, "I'd be prepared to lay odds that despite the latest rumors that Drake's off investigating, it won't be the Chartists behind it, either."

"Perhaps the Chartists are another group those behind this—the true perpetrators—want to damage."

He nodded, then restlessly stirred. "We'll know more once Drake gets back. Meanwhile"—he looked at where she'd set her reticule on the chair beside her—"I suggest we interview the final four carters. One of them must have loaned Terry Doolan his cart, and, pray God, Doolan might have said something that will give us some inkling of who he was dealing with."

"Indeed." She picked up her reticule and rose. "Let's forge on and see what we can learn."

He ushered her out of the dining room, summoned Tom with a look, and together, the three of them walked out to the carriage.

They found the next carter on their list at home in a house on a narrow lane off Lambert Street.

Although it was Cleo who stood before the door when it opened, Michael took one look at the dour-faced, heavyset man who filled the doorway, stepped forward to stand by Cleo's shoulder, and stated, "This is Miss Hendon of the Hendon Shipping Company. We are attempting to trace…"

Understanding her new role, Cleo did her best to appear haughtily superior as Michael went on, using her approach, but speaking in her name; she might have been inclined to take umbrage, except that she had a sneaking suspicion that if she had done the talking, even as Miss Hendon of the Hendon Shipping Company, even with Michael at her back, this brute would have dismissed her.

As it was, he listened long enough to growl, "Don't know anything about any job Doolan did in Kent. More than enough work for me hereabouts without going gadding into the country."

He reached for the door, and Michael asked, "One thing—if ten barrels had to be transported, would it require two carts?"

The man scowled, but nodded. "Aye. We can do up to six barrels per load, but no more. Not even our reinforced axles will take more'n six for long. So yeah, for ten, you'd need two carts or two trips. No one crams or stacks gunpowder, not even in good solid oak."

"And just supposing," Michael went on, "that a job was such that you had to use two carts, where would you get the second cart and driver?"

The man grunted; he fell silent, but appeared to be thinking. Eventually, he said, "If there was no other way than to run a second cart...I reckon I'd hire Terry Doolan's apprentice for the day and convince Terry to lend me his cart." The man looked at them and paused, studying them, then unbent enough to volunteer, "It has to be one o' the gunpowder carters' rigs, all registered proper with the guild, and one of the drivers the guild licenses to drive those rigs. There's only fourteen of us and the two apprentices that the guild's given the nod to, see?"

Michael glanced at Cleo, then said, "Thank you for your time." He held out half a crown. "Have your next ale on us."

The dour carter almost smiled. He took the coin and managed a bob that might, at a severe stretch, pass for a bow. "Happy to help you folks. Miss Hendon."

Clinging to her haughty role, Cleo inclined her head regally and allowed Michael to take her arm and lead her away.

Once they'd turned the corner, she let her spine and shoulders relax. "Well! It seems as if our thinking was correct. Doolan must have borrowed a cart from one of the other gunpowder carters, and there are only three to whom we haven't spoken." Drawing forth the list, she scanned it, then looked up at the surrounding houses. "According to Tom, our next carter"—she pointed to a small lane, little more than an alley, just ahead—"lives along there."

∿

The twelfth carter on their list knew nothing. The thirteenth, Mike Oldham, was the only other carter besides Doolan with a listed apprentice. Oldham lived in a tiny house in a lane stretching between Leman Street and Mill Lane.

Oldham's wife answered the door. When told of their errand, she pointed west. "He's gone to our daughter's to play with her two boys, but I can tell you where he'll be. Look for the bench near the chestnut tree in the fields—he'll be sitting there watching the young'uns play."

The "fields" to which she was referring had to be Goodman Fields, a large, parklike square surrounded by houses, shops, churches, and even a theater, which lay not far away.

"Thank you. We'll look for him there." Cleo glanced at Michael. He offered his arm, and she took it. Together they walked briskly back into Leman Street.

Goodman Fields was only a hundred yards or so north. They walked through a wide gap between two houses, and the expanse opened up before them.

They crossed a cobbled street and entered the park. Cleo looked around at the trees and eventually spotted a tall chestnut standing guard over a bench along a side path. "There." She pointed. Michael looked, and they turned their feet in that direction.

Sure enough, a grizzled older man with a flat cap similar to that favored by several of the other carters they'd interviewed was settled on the bench, his expression relaxed, unconsciously smiling as he watched two young boys of about six or seven kicking a round ball back and forth.

Cleo considered Oldham, then glanced at Michael. "You lead—I'll corroborate if necessary."

Michael shot her a faintly surprised look, but they were nearing the bench, and he had to face forward.

He halted them by the side of the bench, two feet from Oldham, who noticed and glanced up at them.

"Mr. Oldham?"

Oldham frowned. "Aye—who's asking?"

Michael smiled easily; he gestured to Cleo, who also smiled reassuringly. "This is Miss Hendon of the Hendon Shipping Company. We were wondering if Terrance Doolan borrowed your cart last Tuesday?"

Oldham's gaze was steady; his expression gave nothing away. After several seconds, he asked, "Why would you want to know that?"

Smoothly, Michael replied, "We're attempting to locate ten barrels of gunpowder brought into London, we believe by Terrance Doolan, on Wednesday morning, and we were wondering if Doolan, needing two carts for a cargo of that size, had borrowed your cart for the purpose."

Oldham studied them again, as if weighing them up; Cleo saw in his eyes when he decided to cooperate—not least, she suspected, because he was curious as to what was going on.

"Aye." Oldham slowly nodded. "Terry did borrow my cart for Tuesday night. And it was more than a little odd that it was a night he wanted it for, but that suited me as it meant there was less of a loss of business for me. Anyway, the two of us had an understanding—when Terry needed a second cart for his apprentice, Johnny, to drive, if possible, I'd let him have mine, and then when I got the sort of job where I needed a cart for my apprentice to drive, Terry would loan me his. Tit for tat. It's worked for us for some years."

Michael shifted fractionally; through their linked arms, Cleo sensed his increased focus, although nothing of that showed in his expression or his equable tone when he asked, "So you and Terry are mates?"

Oldham shrugged his heavy shoulders. "I wouldn't exactly say mates —we don't share a local—but we've both been in the business for a long time, and like I said, we had our understanding."

Michael inclined his head, accepting the qualification, but his gaze didn't leave Oldham's face. "Did Terry say anything at all about this job that required two carts?"

Oldham frowned slightly, his gaze growing distant as if recalling. "He said as he had a big commission to fetch barrels up from Kent and was being paid a nice slice extra to do it on the quiet-like...we both assumed the people hiring wanted to avoid the excise. Blood—" Oldham broke off and colored. He bobbed his head to Cleo. "Beg pardon, Miss Hendon. Very big lump of excise on gunpowder, and there were ten barrels after all..." Suddenly, Oldham looked up at them. His frown deepened. "But why aren't you asking Terry all this?"

Michael glanced at Cleo, then looked back at Oldham. "We would if we could, but Doolan hasn't returned to his lodgings since leaving there on Tuesday afternoon."

Oldham's face fell. He paled. "He never came back?"

"His landlady says not."

Cleo glanced at Michael, then softly said, "Mr. Doolan's apprentice, Johnny Dibney, hasn't returned to his lodgings, either."

Oldham swore beneath his breath. "Begging your pardon an' all, miss, but I *thought* there was something havey-cavey about that job."

"Can you think back?" she prompted. "Did Terry mention anything at all about who hired him or where he was taking the barrels?"

Oldham passed a hand over his mouth and stared unseeing across the grass. "He didn't say a word about who hired him, but as to where he was taking those barrels..." Oldham screwed up his face as if cudgeling his brains. "He did mention where he was headed—if only I can remember. I know it didn't sound odd—seemed a normal sort of run—which is why it hasn't stuck in me mind." He paused, then, jaw firming, continued, "Let's come at it another way. There's only so many places he'd be delivering to, and given it was on the sly, it wouldn't be to any of the munitions factories—tight as a drum, they are—and that goes for the explosives factories, too. So most likely he was delivering to one of the warehouses that supply the manufacturers..."

Abruptly, Oldham sat up. "That's it! I remember now. He was grumbling about having to get through the streets south of the river, about Johnny getting experience having to navigate a full load through the tight turns down there—because they'd be unloading in Morgan's Lane." Oldham looked at Cleo and Michael. "There's three firework supply warehouses in Morgan's Lane. I'd take an oath Terry was—or at least, thought he would be—delivering to one of them."

"Thank you." Cleo couldn't keep the excitement from her voice. At last, they had a trail to follow. "We'll check with the warehouses." She looked at Michael.

He met her gaze briefly, then looked at Oldham, who still seemed badly shaken. "One last point—can you tell us when Doolan asked to borrow your cart?"

Oldham glanced up; his gaze grew bleak. "He came around Monday afternoon after we'd knocked off. Asked if he could have the cart Tuesday at four o'clock and keep it overnight. Said he'd get it back to me by midday or just after. I agreed. He turned up in his cart Tuesday afternoon with Johnny beside him. Johnny took my rig, and they drove off."

Michael gentled his voice. "And that was the last you saw of them?"

Staring across the lawn, Oldham nodded heavily. "Aye."

"But you got your cart back?"

"I did." Oldham looked up. "And that was odd, too." His lips twisted, and he looked away. "I should'a known it wasn't Terry that left it."

"Why do you say that?"

Oldham heaved a weighty sigh. "Firstly, because I wasn't expecting to have the rig again until after lunchtime, but the missus saw it in the lane a few doors down when she came back from market—around eleven o'clock that was. I went and brought the cart an' horses into the mews—I couldn't fathom why Doolan had left 'em in the lane like that. Then when I got m'rig into the stable and unhitched the team, I found a packet of notes tucked under the seat. Well, that wasn't our usual way. We *traded* the use of the carts, and not to speak ill of the dead, but Terry was as tightfisted an Irishman as you'd ever find. Not that I wasn't grateful for the blunt, mind. I thought he must've come into a windfall with that load..." Oldham stopped, swallowed. His voice was smaller when he said, "I was thinking to meet up with Terry and stand him a round...guess that won't happen now."

Oldham suddenly looked up. "They're dead, aren't they? Terry, and Johnny, too?"

Michael met Oldham's eyes, hesitated, then said, "We don't know for certain that they're dead, but…" He didn't know what else to say. Oldham looked away. With his hands clasped tightly between his knees, he stared across the grass.

After a moment, Michael glanced at Cleo, then murmured, "Thank you for your help. If we learn anything about Doolan's or Johnny's fates, I'll let you know."

Oldham cleared his throat and, without looking at them, gruffly replied, "Thank ye."

Michael felt Cleo's fingers tighten on his sleeve. He covered her hand with his, stepped away from the bench, and turned them back along the path.

They'd gone ten yards when Cleo raised her head and halted. She stared along the path for an instant, then glanced at him. "One moment."

She released his arm, turned, and walked briskly back to where Oldham still sat on the bench. His grandsons had returned to him, and he was trying his best to smile and laugh and respond normally to their chatter.

Having turned to observe Cleo, Michael strolled after her. He caught up with her as she halted at the end of the bench and smiled reassuringly at the boys as, surprised, they stared up at her.

Then she shifted her gaze to Oldham's face. "In light of what we fear has befallen Mr. Doolan and his apprentice, you might want to let the other gunpowder carters know that whoever has those ten barrels might want to move them again—but those hiring for that job, no matter how much they offer, are clearly not to be trusted."

Oldham held her gaze as he sorted through her words, then his features hardened, and he nodded. "Indeed, miss. I'll pass the word."

Cleo managed another commiserating smile, then turned.

Michael offered his arm, and she took it, and they walked away. As they passed out of the fields, he murmured, "That was a stroke of genius —making certain none of the gunpowder carters assist in moving those barrels again."

Cleo grimaced. "I didn't think of that—I did it because this nonsensical killing of gullible innocents has to stop." She glanced at him. "And we've met virtually all the other gunpowder carters, and I don't want any of them to be hurt."

CHAPTER 7

*C*leo's warning to Oldham had clearly been prompted by recognition of the danger looming. Michael had hoped that she would, therefore, be amenable to retiring from the field...

He was starting to feel like a gullible innocent himself. Of course, she'd insisted on embarking on a reconnaissance of Morgan's Lane.

They'd agreed that finding and interviewing the last of the gunpowder carters would be a waste of time. However, as by then it was close to four o'clock on a Saturday afternoon and, Cleo had assured him, most ware-houses and the like would be closed, there was a limit to how much further in their investigation they could get that day.

Yet with the warehouses and factories shut and the area as quiet as it was likely to get in daylight, Cleo had argued that now was the perfect time to survey the warehouses in question and evaluate their approach for identifying to which of the three businesses Doolan had delivered the ten barrels.

Michael couldn't, in all honesty, disagree. In light of Drake's instruc-tions, he had broader reasons for familiarizing himself with Morgan's Lane and the siting of the three warehouses along it, but he wasn't about to share those reasons with Cleo, equal partner or not. Not after learning that Doolan and his apprentice had vanished, apparently immediately after delivering their cargo. If he and Cleo were getting closer to whoever was pulling the strings in this plot, he needed—needed in a way he wasn't about to question—to steer her away from that source of lethal danger.

With that goal in mind, he'd counseled himself that acquiescing to her presence now was the course of wisdom. Even in a lane in Southwark in the descending gloom of a late Saturday afternoon, with him by her side, she would be safe. More, including her in the initial reconnaissance would satisfy her curiosity, lull her into believing she was fully apprised of all that was going on, and divert her attention from the necessary subsequent actions, which had the potential to be significantly more dangerous.

The carriage rattled onto London Bridge. Michael glanced at Cleo's face. She'd grown quieter, more serious, since they'd learned of Doolan's and Dibney's disappearance, yet even through the dimness inside the carriage, he detected a certain heightened interest, an increased focus on forging ahead—a sense of suppressed expectation over what they might find in Morgan's Lane.

They reached the southern end of the bridge, and the carriage slowed as Tom turned left into Tooley Street. Within mere yards, they were surrounded by the meaner streets of Southwark.

Cleo swayed with the turn and the consequent jostling as the carriage wheels rumbled onto more roughly laid cobbles; her shoulder brushed Michael's arm, and she sensed the solid strength of him seated beside her. The flutter of her senses was growing familiar, less and less a true distraction and more a strange sort of comfort. Also becoming familiar was the feeling of being safe—unquestionably, indisputably safe—while in his presence.

Given his reputation, she still found that curious.

Nevertheless, she was grateful for the freedom that feeling of safety granted her. As she scanned the fading and often dingy façades as the carriage penetrated deeper into this area of commercial buildings and ramshackle lodging houses, she didn't think she would have felt at all comfortable getting out of the carriage had Michael not been there to accompany her.

As it was, when the carriage drew into the curb and Tom called down that Morgan's Lane was just a few yards back on the right, she was eager to alight. She waited impatiently as Michael descended first. He looked around, then stepped back and offered her his hand. She gripped it firmly and stepped out and down. Once on the pavement, she shook her skirts straight, then took Michael's proffered arm, and together, they strolled back along Tooley Street toward the top of Morgan's Lane.

There were other people about, both men and women, mostly alone, walking here and there with the determined stride of those going about their business. In this area, no one strolled to take the air. Smaller carriages and conveyances of every stripe rattled past in a regular, noisy stream.

They halted at the corner and looked down Morgan's Lane. It was wide enough to accommodate two narrow carts abreast. Scanning the façades she could see, Cleo felt buoyed by burgeoning determination. Doolan's and Johnny's disappearances—their presumed deaths—had only strengthened her commitment to exposing the blackguards behind the wretched plot, bringing the plot to an end, and seeing justice done.

Impatience prodding, she began to slide her arm from Michael's, intending to start down the lane, but he caught her hand, trapped her arm, and after a swift—warning?—glance at her face, indicated that they should stroll on. With a small nod, she acquiesced, left her arm twined with his, and side by side, they walked evenly down the lane. His behavior was, she decided, a small price to pay for the freedom his being near gave her.

He murmured, "The lane runs more or less straight down from Tooley Street to the Thames."

Drawing her gaze from the businesses on either side, she looked ahead. At first glance, a building extended across the far end of the lane, blocking the view of the river, but the building ended just short of the left side of the lane, and beyond the building's corner, they could see open space and a few thin masts rocking with the tide.

He nodded toward the spot. "Let's begin by walking all the way down. We'll note the firework supply warehouses as we pass, then take a closer look at them on the way back. First, I want to get some idea of the lane's relative position."

She pondered that as they passed the first of the firework supply warehouses—a substantial building, its bricks darkened by grime, squatting at the end of the first short block on the left. A narrow alley ran along the warehouse's side; it led into yet more lanes and alleyways. She glanced at Michael. "Do you think the location of the warehouse might mean something in terms of the plot? Of its purpose or target?"

His gaze scanning ahead, he eventually replied, "I think we can be certain that a warehouse in Southwark is not the ultimate destination for the gunpowder. As Drake emphasized, the real plotters have been very clever with their arrangements. It therefore seems likely that they chose a warehouse in Morgan's Lane not just because it was a place they could gain access to but also because, in some way, it facilitates their plans."

She "hmmed," and they walked on.

The second of the firework supply warehouses lay midway along the lane on the right-hand side. It was a much more prosperous-looking establishment with a stout paling fence and chained and padlocked iron-railing gates. A small paved yard lay inside the gates; a single-story structure to the left of the yard had a sign, "Office," on the wall beside the door, while across the yard and facing the gates stood a massive, high-roofed warehouse. The warehouse doors were bolted and padlocked.

Cleo took all that in as they paced past. They were walking steadily, fast enough not to attract any unwanted attention from the local populace. While most of the buildings fronting onto the lane appeared to be businesses—warehouses and factories of one sort or another—the smaller lanes and alleyways to either side led to lodging houses that in density of occupants seemed a bare step away from tenements. There might not be many people strolling the street, but the muted sounds of concentrated people—calls, arguments, the slam of doors, and the clash of pots—drifted on the dank air.

Those walking up the lane eyed them narrowly, but although their attire marked them as gentry at least, as this was a commercial district, their presence didn't immediately raise an alarm; it was possible they were meeting with some business owner.

They came across the third firework supply warehouse at the end of the lane on the left-hand side, on the corner beyond which lay the open space before the riverbank. That warehouse was run-down and shabby; the paint on the façade was peeling, and the lettering—once gold but now a grimy brown—that proclaimed it to be "Wallington's Warehouse, purveyors to the manufacturers of best quality fireworks" was barely legible. Nevertheless, the heavy double doors were firmly bolted and padlocked, and the windows all sported iron grilles as well as inside shutters.

After noting that security, as they walked into the open space before the river, Michael murmured, "I wonder if there are regulations about the structure of warehouses that store gunpowder." He paused, then arched his brows. "Given the control the authorities attempt to maintain over gunpowder brought into the city, I suppose that shouldn't be any real surprise."

They walked the short distance to the riverbank. Even though the light was rapidly fading, a multitude of small craft were still plying the pewter waters.

"This is more or less the middle of the commercial stretch of the Thames." Cleo waved across the gray, slightly choppy expanse. "There are stairs and wharves and piers everywhere on both sides, and that extends for quite a way both up and down the river."

Instantly recognizable, London Bridge lay to their left. "That's Billingsgate." Cleo pointed to the next section along the opposite shore. "Then comes the Customs House and its embankment"—she swung her arm to the right—"then Tower Stairs." Beyond that, still farther to their right, the gray walls of the Tower loomed over the river.

They both turned to survey what they could see of the bank on which they stood. To the left of the open space, a set of stairs led down to the water. When they looked right, they discovered a long wharf stretching the length of the building that ran across the end of Morgan's Lane. Five small craft and two flat-bottomed barges were moored along the wharf.

Cleo glanced up. "Look!" She pointed to a cornerstone on the building on which the words "Gun Wharf" had been carved.

Michael grunted. "So if one planned to move barrels of contraband gunpowder by water, a warehouse in Morgan's Lane is an excellent place to stash your illicit cargo."

Cleo shrugged. "It's also well placed for transporting barrels by road—north, south, east, or west, there's major thoroughfares close by."

He grimaced. "True." After a moment, he went on, "I agree that, target-wise, the choice of Morgan's Lane can't be said to point us in any particular direction. It does, however, stand as yet further testimony to the careful planning behind this plot. Someone spent a lot of time looking into every detail." He met Cleo's eyes. "For instance, thinking to hide their barrels of gunpowder in a warehouse that legitimately stores barrels of gunpowder. Once their barrels are inside, even if others see them, they won't immediately think the barrels out of place, as would happen in most other warehouses or stores."

She nodded and reached up to tuck back a lock of hair the brisk river breeze had tugged free. "Perfect camouflage, so to speak. But how long before the warehouse staff realize they have extra barrels?"

"I suspect the answer to that is long enough." He turned them back toward Morgan's Lane proper. "By which I mean long enough for the plotters' purpose, and according to Drake, that could mean anything up to a week."

"Doolan delivered the barrels here—to one of these three warehouses —on Wednesday morning." Cleo glanced at Michael's face; his expression told her nothing. "A week doesn't leave us much time."

He didn't reply, just urged her into motion. Still arm in arm, they walked back to the dogleg in the lane.

There, they paused briefly to run their eyes over Wallington's Warehouse.

She humphed. "Not even an unshuttered window through which we might peek."

Michael waved toward the rear of the building. "Does it have a back door?"

The answer was no; both rear wall and the other side wall abutted other buildings with not even a passageway between.

They returned up the lane and subjected the other two warehouses to similar swift examinations. The warehouse midway along the lane was hemmed in on all three sides; no chance of looking in, much less gaining entry, other than via the front gates and yard.

The first warehouse they'd passed, the one closest to Tooley Street, shared walls to one side and the rear, but the other side wall overlooked an alley. However, when Michael tried to peer through the small, high windows along the alley, he reported that they had grilles on the inside and shutters as well.

As they walked briskly back toward the carriage, Cleo shook her head. "You're right—all three warehouses are locked up tight. We'll need to come back when they're open."

Michael handed Cleo into the carriage, then after instructing Tom to drive to Clarges Street, joined her. It was time to bring this excursion to an end so he could get cracking on getting the necessary next steps into place.

From all he'd seen of the area as they'd checked around the warehouses, while Morgan's Lane itself was primarily commercial, it was hemmed in on both sides by warrens of tiny lanes and alleyways teeming with humanity. The humanity was neither here nor there, but the warrens were an issue, one he would need to plan around.

His partner—with whom he'd agreed to share all information received, but to his mind, "information received" didn't stretch to forward planning—had been sunk in her own thoughts, but as they rattled once more across London Bridge, she turned to him. "Can you think of any way we might locate the ten barrels before the warehouses open on Monday?"

He studied her face. "No." Then he admitted, "I haven't even thought how to approach the matter come Monday."

She waved that aside. "I'll just be Miss Hendon of the Hendon Shipping Company again. An extension of our earlier tale should suffice, and at least we can tell them that the particular barrels we're searching for were delivered on Wednesday morning."

He thought, then shook his head. "They—the warehouse staff—might not know they have any extra barrels. Not if they were somehow smuggled in and hidden."

"Indeed." Meeting his gaze, she smiled confidently. "But I assure you I can make each warehouse manager keen enough for our business for him to take us into the warehouse and show us all the gunpowder he has. He'll be working from his inventory, so any extra barrels will quickly become apparent."

Returning her smile, he inclined his head. "Very well. We'll try that come Monday morning. Until then"—he faced forward—"we'll have to have faith in Drake's prediction that they won't move the barrels yet."

From the corner of his eye, he saw her frown.

After a moment, she said, "I'm half expecting to find, come Monday, that there *are* no extra barrels in any of the three warehouses—that they'll already have vanished. Tell me again—*why* does Winchelsea believe our plotters won't move their hoard as soon as they can?"

"I admit I'm not that familiar with what might be involved in plots of this nature, but Drake was confident that the plot was being run in completely separate stages. The first stage involved getting the gunpowder and transporting it to London and, presumably, secreting it in one of the warehouses in Morgan's Lane." Through the deepening shadows, he met her eyes. "Drake believes that there'll be a break of some sort before the next stage gets under way—and the removal of all those involved to this point lends weight to his thesis. He thought it likely the arrangements for the next stage wouldn't have been made yet—that they wouldn't be initiated until after the first stage had been completed and all was confirmed as successful to that point. I can't claim to understand how Drake's mind works—"

She snorted softly. "Who can?"

"Indeed. But if I understood his reasoning, it was that the most cautious plotters, and he definitely classes this group among those ranks, will strive to keep each stage of a plot separate, so that they eliminate the risk of anyone or any element from an earlier stage interfering with the successful outcome of a later stage. Drake feels that's of particular importance in this case, but what that conviction is based on, I'm not sure I can explain."

He briefly scanned her face, then rattled on, "If I recall aright, it was the duplicity involved in using the Young Irelanders, and what Drake is sure is the likewise false implication of the Chartists, that led him to propose that the true target of the plot is—very likely—something neither group, and possibly any other such group, would want to attack. Hence, the target has to be concealed, even from those involved in the execution of the plot—calling for a gap between the stages."

"Hmm." Her frown didn't abate, but after several minutes of pondering, she mused, "That's an awful lot of supposing on Winchelsea's part, but as it is him…" She shrugged and looked forward. "I suppose we have to operate on the assumption that he knows of what he speaks."

Michael didn't reply. Drake's instructions had been clear. If they located the barrels, they were to keep a watch on the cache and, if and when the barrels were collected, follow them. They'd tracked the barrels to Morgan's Lane. Even if they didn't know the precise location, that was information enough to mount a watch.

Which was what he was planning to do.

If nothing occurred before Monday morning, they would inquire at the warehouses. He had no qualms over including Cleo in the Monday excursion; aside from all else, with her understanding of the commercial world, she would know which way to step in order to gain the information they needed.

But as to the action he intended to mount between then and now…he had no intention of mentioning a word of that to her.

Sitting back in the increasing gloom of the carriage, he fixed his gaze on the passing façades and gave his mind over to planning.

Cleo glanced sidelong at her companion—her supposed partner in this mission. She had three brothers; she knew what that absorbed, sunk-in-his-thoughts look portended. Her suspicions grew apace with his silence. She waited with feigned patience for him to stir and inform her of his plans; she felt certain she could guess what they would be.

She'd floated the idea of the barrels having already been collected to test the waters, but he'd simply fallen back on Winchelsea's theory that the barrels wouldn't be moved so soon—and volunteered nothing more.

As the carriage rolled through Trafalgar Square and on toward Mayfair, she debated broaching the subject directly, but if she did, she had a strong suspicion he would attempt to veto any involvement on her part, and they would end having one of those interminable arguments that led nowhere and achieved nothing.

And, after all, if she was wrong about his intentions, there would be no harm done.

CHAPTER 8

*M*ichael skulked in a recessed doorway not quite halfway down Morgan's Lane and listened as night laid its smothering hand over the surrounding area. After eleven o'clock, the noise level had started to fall, and as the moon sailed high with the approach of midnight, the last stragglers found their way to their doors, and moment by moment, the silence deepened, at least in Morgan's Lane. Further afield, he could hear voices, rumbling rather than raised. But even in Tooley Street, the main artery of the district, the carriage trade had faded to the occasional hackney clopping past.

The sky was relatively clear, with only a thin river mist trailing a translucent veil over the face of the almost-full moon and forming soft halos of light around the streetlamps—one near the river end of the lane and the other near Tooley Street. In this district, streetlamps were few and far between; rather than illuminating the pavements in any adequate fashion, the cones of weak light seemed to deepen the darkness beyond their reach.

From where Michael stood enveloped in shadows, he had an angled view of the locked gates of the second of the three warehouses—on the other side of the lane and a little to his left—while the doors of the first warehouse were only paces away to his right; if anyone came calling there, he would hear them.

The lack of suitable cover elsewhere along the lane had forced him to leave the watch on Wallington's Warehouse to Tom and two of his men.

He'd had a busy evening calling in and deploying his private army of watchers.

Nearly a decade ago—when he'd been watching a certain ladybird with a view to learning who she was favoring with her charms—through Tom, he'd realized that, as Lord Michael Cynster, he had a small army at his command. Virtually all the footmen and grooms at the Cynster town residences were the sort of males always up for a lark, ready to volunteer their free time to act as eyes and ears for him, especially as he paid well. As the butlers and housekeepers from all the houses knew him, there was never any fuss about the male staff being allowed to use their off-duty hours in such a manner. When the numbers drawn from all the many Cynster residences were added together, they formed an army nearly forty strong.

And in this season, when most of the families were in the country, albeit expected shortly to return, as the staff had no major ton events, dinners, balls, or soirees to assist at, he could call on almost the entire complement.

Tonight, he had twenty men circling the area around Morgan's Lane. As he'd seen that afternoon and had subsequently verified, the surrounding maze of tiny lanes—most just wide enough for a cart to pass through—made placing a tight cordon immediately around Morgan's Lane well-nigh impossible; there were simply too many ways a cart could go, and covering all of them would risk being spotted. However, the warren in which Morgan's Lane was situated was bound by three large streets and the river; the area was roughly an elongated triangle, with the long sides formed by the river and by Tooley Street, from where it led off the southern end of New London Bridge, then ran on into Fair Street and New Street, while the base of the triangle was formed by the western half of Dock Head and the eastern arm of Shad Thames, the street which ran parallel to St. Savior's Dock one block from the water.

Cynster footmen and grooms were presently stationed along Tooley, Fair, and New Streets, and along the relevant sections of Dock Head and Shad Thames, each with a clear line of sight to the next watcher. Michael had also stationed men all along the riverbank, overlooking every set of water stairs, every pier, dock, and wharf. Not a single boat would leave that stretch of the bank without him knowing—without those who were his eyes and ears seeing and, if there were barrels involved, following.

All the men in his army understood their purpose; he hadn't told them the whole story, but they knew they were watching for ten barrels of gunpowder as part of a mission with which Michael was assisting the Marquess of Winchelsea. Being Cynster staff, his army all knew who Winchelsea was and what he did; many were on good terms with the Wolverstone House staff. Michael felt confident that if the plotters attempted to move the barrels from Morgan's Lane that night, he and his men would see and follow.

Wrapped in an old greatcoat, he settled against the cold bricks beside the recessed door and prepared to wait until three o'clock. At that time, the rest of his irregular army would arrive to spell the first watch, and he would leave with Tom to catch a few hours' sleep. Groups of men in rotation would keep watch over the next day and through Sunday night, although if no one turned up to move the barrels tonight, he doubted they would be moved until Monday.

Assuming, of course, that the barrels were still somewhere in Morgan's Lane.

He was mulling over that when the sound of light footsteps reached him. He eased deeper into the shadows, pressing his back against the wooden door, even as he registered that there was something odd about the footsteps. They were furtive—a few rapid steps, then a pause, then a scurrying patter before halting again. And the steps were too light to be those of a man.

Some lad was flitting along the street, moving from shadow to shadow…a lookout? A youth sent to check all was clear?

Michael straightened. His men had orders to remain hidden and not tangle with anyone; they were there to watch and follow. As long as the youth didn't see him, he intended to do the same.

But was it possible the boy knew something about the plotters?

The footsteps pattered closer.

Michael told himself it was unlikely a lad would know anything about those pulling the strings, and if the lad disappeared, the plotters would be instantly alerted; they would grow suspicious and very likely abort any action tonight. They might even realize someone was hunting them—

His inner debate abruptly cut off as the lad appeared from Michael's right and paused directly in front of the recessed doorway. His back to Michael, the lad stared across the street—at the warehouse Michael was watching.

With a wide-brimmed hat pulled low to screen his face, the youth wasn't all that tall, his figure slight. More surprisingly, he was clad in clothes—a hacking jacket with breeches tucked into boots—that, even viewed through the gloom, seemed too good for the area; cut, fabric, and fit all suggested the other side of the river and farther west.

Michael tensed. If the lad was gentry or better, he was more likely to be connected to the true plotters rather than being a hired minion.

Should he seize the boy?

The decision was made for him. The youth suddenly tensed, then abruptly swung around and stared—

Michael surged out of the darkness, slapped his gloved hand over the lad's lips—already parted—seized the boy in a bear hug, and ignoring his struggles, hauled him into the recess. Roughly, he pushed the lad against the brick wall by the door—

Even as his instincts and his senses screamed at him—and the lad froze.

Michael's wits reeled. He stared through the dimness at the face before him.

As, wide-eyed, she stared back.

She.

He could barely credit what his senses were telling him, yet even as he grasped the undeniable truth, her eyes narrowed, and despite the shrouding shadows, he felt her glare.

Her glare?

Removing his hand from her lips, he leant close and, in a grating growl, demanded, "What the *devil* are you doing here?"

Every nerve he possessed was jangling, strung out and quivering.

Far from showing any signs of remorse, she tartly replied, "I suspect I'm doing exactly the same as you—keeping an eye on the warehouses in case our villains try to move the barrels tonight."

Through his teeth, he ground out, "You didn't need to come. You should have left it to me."

"*If* you recall," she replied in a frosty whisper, "you didn't mention anything about keeping watch over the barrels tonight."

Michael forced himself to straighten and ease back an inch; in the tight space before the door, an inch was the best he could manage.

As he did, she frowned, then moved to peer out of the dark alcove and down the lane; he caught her arm and held her back.

She trained her frown on his face. "What about the warehouse at the end of the lane?"

"I have men stationed all around." He drew in a breath, reached for calm, and forced himself to release her. "Please tell me that, even dressed like that, you didn't come here alone."

"Of course not." She raised her chin as if attempting to look down her nose at him. "My groom and coachman are with me." She flicked a hand up the lane. "We left the carriage a few blocks away, and they're waiting in Tooley Street just by the corner."

Too far away—*much* too far away—to render assistance should anything happen to their mistress.

He hauled in another slow breath, but before he could launch any further protest, she leant across and angled her head to peer out at the warehouse opposite, pressing against him and thoroughly distracting him.

"And it's just as I expected," Cleo forged on, keeping her voice low and her senses in as tight a grip as she could manage. "You might not have stated the obvious, but it was clear we would need to keep a watch on the warehouses. So you're here, and even better, you have men all around, so I am—as I expected—perfectly safe."

Admittedly, a lot of her expectation had been hope, but clearly, she'd correctly gauged his commitment to the mission.

Silence reigned. He was standing like an immovable pillar, and courtesy of the confines of the narrow space, she could feel the tension thrumming through him, emanating from him; a palpable aura, it abraded her nerves. She wasn't sure meeting his eyes, even through the shadows, would be a good idea.

She drew in a breath, one that felt too tight. "Perhaps," she murmured, "I should—"

He caught her arm in a viselike grip, his fingers biting into her flesh.

Startled, she glanced at his face, then she heard what he had—the *shush-scrape* of slouching footsteps.

Two pairs, and neither man was making any effort to conceal their approach.

"Could've sworn I heard some doxy sayin' summat," one rumbling voice said. "Did you hear her? Somewhere along 'ere."

"P'rhaps she's looking fer company, like," a second growly voice replied.

Aghast, Cleo focused on Michael's face. She saw his lips move in a barely breathed curse, then, faint as a breath, she heard him say, "Those aren't my men."

But the pair were coming closer.

"*We'd* be good company," the first man stated. Both men halted a yard or so away; from the sound of their feet shifting on the cobbles, they were turning this way and that, searching the shadows. "I'm sure I heard her—might be Jenny Quigley. But whoever she is, she has to be 'ere somewhere."

Then, "P'rhaps she's hidin' in the shadows before that door."

Cleo felt her eyes open impossibly wide. Through the dimness, she saw Michael's features turn stony.

She sensed more than heard his "Damn!"

Without warning, without a sound, he swung her so her back pressed against the door, then he bent his head, and his lips covered hers.

Then he kissed her—and her senses swam, and her wits deserted her.

Michael felt as if his mind had fractured. Literally split in half, with his wits, his senses, his very will ripped asunder by two equally potent forces.

One half of him was unwaveringly focused on the need to keep the woman he held safe. To protect her against all and every threat—especially that posed by the two thugs looming ever nearer.

The other half wanted to devour her, to seize and hold and know in the most blatant biblical sense, ultimately to make her his.

He was blindsided by the power behind both imperatives; both demanded his undivided attention.

Even as his lips captured hers, and with pressure and guile, he sought entrance to her mouth, half his senses were tracking the men as they lumbered up and peered into the shadows.

As his hands firmed about her shoulders and he held her steady as he angled his head and pressed the kiss into more heated territory, half of his mind was detached enough to be monitoring what the two thugs would see.

His back, with his old greatcoat hanging from his shoulders to his calves—a shield effectively screening her. But the angle of his head was a sign such men would not miss, and he took care to ensure he appeared fully engrossed.

Not that that required any acting.

Especially not when she parted her lips, and at the first touch of his marauding tongue to hers, all but melted against him.

The sensual half of him rejoiced and pressed on.

The still-rational and determinedly protective half considered the pair now making disappointed huffing sounds and decided it would be wise to make the situation even clearer.

He shifted one hand from her shoulder, pushed that hand under the side of her open jacket, and closed his palm and fingers firmly about one linen-shrouded breast.

Her senses leapt; so did his.

Yes, his sensual side demanded. *More of this.*

But his protective side was more interested in the soft moan she gave —a moan he drew back from the kiss enough to allow to escape.

One of the men watching muttered, "No use—she's taken."

The other returned a ribald comment along the lines of not having time enough to wait. "I might as well tup the missus."

His protective side remained on alert as the men turned and shuffled off down the lane.

Then, with the fading of the threat, his protective side calmed…and subsided.

Leaving the sensual side fully in command.

Finally able to register, to evaluate—to understand…

That she was kissing him back every bit as passionately, as unreservedly, as he was kissing her.

That wasn't what he'd expected.

He wasn't sure what he'd assumed—how he'd imagined she might react—but he hadn't expected such unalloyed heat, such unrestrained passion.

He was an expert in both, a past master on the subject of ladies' responses to kisses such as his—demanding, commanding, and openly possessive.

She'd frozen at the first touch of his lips to hers—a shock that had lasted all of two heartbeats. Then she'd breathed in, and her lips had all but attacked his—hungry, greedy, yearning.

In some distant corner of his mind, he knew he could stop kissing her —that he *should* stop kissing her now the need for their camouflaging performance had passed—but all of his senses and most of his will were swept along on an inexorable tide of wanting to know.

To know more of this, of her. To explore and seek out and learn.

To test, to experiment, to define what most pleased her—and him.

Ultimately, to see where this would lead…

He could now admit—could hardly deny given the evidence of what was raging inside him—that he'd been slavering to kiss her in just such a comprehensive way for the past two days. Ever since he'd first laid eyes on her.

Lust at first sight.

Lust and more—there was curiosity and a different level of interest twining through what he felt for her.

Regardless, he was greedy for more, and given her encouragement—and her blatant enthusiasm—he felt not the slightest qualm in deepening the kiss and allowing his hunger full sway.

Cleo had lost touch with the world. All she knew was the solidity of the man before her, the rock-steady body behind the coat she clutched with both hands. All her senses truly registered was the heated fire of his lips and the molten hunger behind his kiss.

Passion wasn't something she'd ever encountered, not within herself. The surge of desire, of hunger and need that had poured through the inner door his kiss had opened was stunning, fascinating, and enthralling.

She knew who he was; she knew she was safe—knew that with a certainty that could not be gainsaid—and that left her free, free to seize a freedom she'd never known before and explore...*this*.

This landscape, this power, this hunger, this wanting.

Nothing seemed more important.

His lips were firm, forceful, so male; her lips molded to them, cushioning and enticing.

Their tongues tangled, stroked, and provoked. His hand on her breast lay hot and heavy, no longer squeezing or kneading but, purely with that touch, awakening a desire to feel...more.

She knew what she wanted; deliberately, she moved into him, pressing the fullness of her breast into his palm.

Michael felt his world rock. Abruptly, he realized control was sliding from his grasp and, in instinctive reaction, seized his reins and clung... even as his mind woke to the reality that the desire she'd evoked, the need she'd provoked in him, was far more powerful, more primitive, than anything he'd felt before.

Before her.

The realization shocked him—and opened his mind to where they were. To the night, to the shadow-filled recess, to the cold bricks surrounding them.

It took effort, but he willed himself to end the kiss—gently; he didn't have it in him to cut the engagement off too sharply. Yes, he was shocked, but...he wanted to continue this. Just not here, not now.

At last, their lips, clinging until the very last second, parted. Their breaths mingled for a moment, then slowly, he raised his head.

He stared into her face.

Her lashes fluttered, then rose, and she stared back.

The darkness was too dense for him to read her eyes; he could barely make out her features. Yet he knew to his soul that she was as shaken and as stunned as he—as shocked at what had transpired.

At what they'd discovered.

Exactly what that was, he didn't yet know—and he was fairly certain she wouldn't be any the wiser.

In this sphere, he had far more experience; of that, he was sure.

He saw her blink. Saw her chest rise as she drew in a deep—and still deeper—breath.

It would be wise to take charge before she regained full command of her wits. He lowered his hand from the soft warmth of her breast, locked his fingers about one of her hands, and forced himself to take a large step back, then to turn and look up and down the lane. It was deserted. He glanced back at her. "We should go."

He tugged her forward and fervently hoped she was still too dazed to argue.

When she fell in beside him, he released her hand, and they walked side by side up the lane.

Cleo found herself striding toward Tooley Street without having made any conscious decision to do so. Despite that, she couldn't seem to care; far more dominant in her mind was the way her lips were tingling, how the curves felt hot and swollen. Almost throbbing. She fought down an urge to raise her fingers to her mouth.

She'd been kissed before, but she'd never known—hadn't even dreamed—that a man could kiss like that.

His kiss—Michael Cynster's amazing, eye-opening kiss—consumed her. Still all but overwhelmed her, even though, with Tooley Street fast approaching, she knew she would soon have to make rational decisions and string together coherent sentences.

Focusing on the here and now—pushing that remarkable kiss to the edge of her mind—took every ounce of willpower she possessed.

He halted on the corner and looked both ways along Tooley Street. Then he lowered his gaze to her face. "My men can handle anything that might happen here—assuming anything happens at all. I'll escort you home." He raised his head and scanned the shadows. "Where are your groom and coachman? I thought you said they were here."

"They are." She gestured to the opening of an alley across the road.

"They're over there, where they could see down the lane. The carriage is farther along that side."

There were a few people on the larger road, but at that hour, everyone had their heads down, hurrying home. She stepped off the narrow pavement and started across the street. If he was going to return to Mayfair with her, then presumably he'd concluded that, as nothing had thus far occurred, the barrels, assuming they were still in Morgan's Lane, would most likely remain there for the night.

In two strides, he loomed by her side. She felt his fingers brush her elbow as if he intended taking her arm, but then he must have remembered her disguise, and his hand fell away.

Michael gritted his teeth and strode beside her. In the aftermath of that kiss, with the added complication of her unexpected attire, he felt as if, inside, he was being buffeted by an emotional storm. Sebastian's warning echoed in his head; if Cleo's mother had once led a smuggling gang, then presumably she'd worn male clothing. Evidently, Cleo had felt no more reluctance over doing so than her mother—not when adventure beckoned.

Given what was roiling inside him, that did not bode well.

They reached the opposite pavement, and in response to a hand signal from her, two men materialized from the alley's shadows. Michael sized them up—a grizzled older man, presumably the coachman, and a groom Michael judged to be in his late twenties. Neither man looked the sort to be swept away by a giddy lady's plans; both looked sound and reliable. Michael compressed his lips and said nothing. Yet.

"We're calling it a night," she whispered to the pair.

They nodded in acknowledgment. The coachman took the lead, and the groom waved his mistress and Michael to precede him. They walked quickly and quietly along the street to where a small black carriage stood by the curb.

Two ragged urchins had been holding the horse. While the coachman paid them off, Michael opened the carriage door. Before he could give her his hand, his partner scrambled in. Her jacket rode up as she did, and the sight of her shapely rear encased in breeches reminded him—forcefully— that she was dressed as a lad. He drew in a fortifying breath—then he paused, let the door swing almost shut, and walked to where the coachman was about to climb up.

Michael lowered his voice and decidedly sharply asked, "What the devil did you think you were about, assisting your mistress in a start like this?"

The coachman regarded him stoically, then replied, "Beggin' your pardon, my lord, but have *you* succeeded in saying no to the young lady?" His lips setting, Michael cast his mind back over their interactions. He couldn't claim to have done so.

The coachman nodded. "When you manage it, let us know how it's done, because we haven't figured it out yet, and we've known her since she was a nipper."

Michael thought he heard an amused snort from inside the carriage.

"Howsoever," the coachman went on, "as to why we let her go off down the lane, we ran into some of your men. They told us you were along down there, and more of your men were at the end. When she vanished into that alcove, we realized that's where you must be. Figured you'd have it covered." The man nodded toward the body of the carriage. "Looks like you did."

Michael followed the man's gaze. He'd had her lips covered, certainly. If his inner demons had had their way, he'd have—no. He wasn't going to think of that. "Back to Clarges Street," he ordered, and the coachman nodded and gathered the reins.

Michael returned to the carriage door, opened it, and climbed inside. The carriage tipped as the coachman climbed up. After shutting the door, Michael dropped to the seat beside his partner and wondered—in the wake of that revealing kiss—what she was thinking now.

As the carriage rattled off, he glanced sidelong at her face. The dim light from a streetlamp briefly illuminated her profile, the curve of her chin, the corner of her lips...

Looking forward, he dragged his mind from wallowing in memories of that kiss. He didn't regret it in the slightest—how could he? The simple act had opened up a prospect he'd had no inkling existed...and he wasn't, when all was said and done, averse to further exploration. But not now. Any venturing into unknown territory required careful consideration, and while in the throes of a mission, he didn't have time to plot appropriate strategies.

Later. All that should be left until later.

Meanwhile, however, between then and now...

He waited until the carriage reached the next streetlamp and, in the pale glow, studied her face. From what he could see, her expression remained haughtily self-assured, but the curve of her lips had softened; he got the distinct impression her gaze was distant, her mind far away...as if she was still thinking about their kiss.

He definitely didn't want to discuss that, to raise that issue between them—not yet. But that kiss made it even more imperative that he steer her away from any further active involvement of the more dangerous sort —the sort that required her to traipse around in breeches.

Facing forward, he said, "This afternoon, after seeing you home, I called at Scotland Yard." He hadn't intended to inform her of his late afternoon's discoveries, deeming them too gruesome for her ears, but that was before she'd appeared in Morgan's Lane—in breeches; if his findings served to frighten her into leaving the dangerous skulking to him, he'd be a fool not to share them. "I used family connections to ask if they'd discovered any unidentified bodies recently—since last Wednesday morning."

She'd turned her head; he could feel her gaze on his face. He had her full attention.

"They have a register, including whatever details they've been able to glean." His tone detached, he continued, "Early on Thursday morning, the bodies of two men were pulled from the river down toward Rotherhithe. One was middle-aged, the other about twenty years old. Both had been struck down, then garroted, and their bodies tipped into the river—the surgeon says they went into the water most likely the day before." He paused, then went on, "The use of a garrote marks the murders as unusual, but other than that, the details give us no further clue."

Silence reigned for several seconds, then in a quiet voice, she asked, "Did you identify them—Terrance Doolan and Johnny Dibney?"

"No. Not as such. Aside from all else, I've never actually seen them, and the bodies are at the River Police's morgue farther down the river. But I gave the Yard the names and addresses, and they'll pass them on and get the formal identification done."

Cleo nodded. She fitted the details of the deaths into the picture she was building in her head of what had happened with the ten barrels. Eventually, she sighed. "We already suspected Doolan and Johnny were dead."

His gaze had drifted to the street beyond the window. "I suspect that Doolan accepting the job of transporting the ten barrels was the action that, ultimately, ended their lives. Once he'd agreed, there was nothing anyone could have done to save them."

If her resolution to expose the villains behind the plot had needed any bolstering…

Her jaw firming, she looked at Michael; she waited until he glanced her way and trapped his gaze. "All we can do for them and the others killed as a result of this plot is to do everything we possibly can to bring the blackguards behind it to justice."

He searched her eyes, her face; she waited while he read her commitment, her resolution, in her expression and in the unwavering steadiness of her gaze.

His lips tightened, as did his jaw. With a brief, rather stiff dip of his head, he turned to look out at the streetscape.

Michael resisted the urge to thunk his head against the carriage window. If all he'd seen in her face was any guide—and he felt certain it was—then his telling her of Doolan's and Dibney's murders had only strengthened her determination to forge ahead with the mission. And he didn't doubt that, in her mind, that meant active involvement—active participation whenever possible.

He stared out unseeing at the familiar streets. And inwardly admitted that the confirmation of the carter's and apprentice's deaths—of their ruthless removal by the plotters once their part had been played—had only heightened his own determination to see the villains in the dock to answer for those and all their other crimes.

Given her background, given all he'd learned of her, he shouldn't have expected her—couldn't expect her—to react in any other way.

Retreat wasn't an action a Hendon would be easily driven to, any more than a Cynster would. That she was a lady and not a gentleman... given his own female relatives, he really should have known better.

Still, their agreement had been that he would share all information; at least he'd kept faith with that—one thing over which she couldn't take umbrage.

Mentally, he looked ahead, evaluating the possibilities that lay between then and Monday morning. He wondered what she planned to do tomorrow—how she intended to fill her Sunday. But he wasn't going to ask. Wasn't going to start any discussion of watching the warehouses in Morgan's Lane.

When the silence stretched unbroken and the streetscapes of Mayfair started to roll past, he decided that, if she didn't say anything about the next day, it would behoove him to leave well alone.

CHAPTER 9

"My lord?"

Michael woke with a grunt, then rolled over and blinked blearily at Tom, who was standing by the side of the big four-poster bed. "What time is it?" He glanced at the window, which was now uncurtained. Muted light and a cloudy sky informed him it was at least after dawn.

"It's just gone half past seven, my lord. You said you wanted to be woken at this time. Shall I ring for your shaving water?"

Recalling all that had happened the previous night, Michael pushed himself into a sitting position and rubbed a palm over his bristly chin. "Yes. And what news have we had from Morgan's Lane?"

Tom crossed to the bellpull and tugged it. "Tully got back just before I came up. He said to tell you it was quiet as a grave for the rest of the night, with no sign of activity at any of the three warehouses or any of the other businesses, either. The next crew have taken over and will stay until two o'clock as arranged."

Michael nodded. "Are any of the family up and about?"

"No. The duke and duchess, and the marquess, are all expected to sleep late, given they didn't get home until three."

"I see." Michael could imagine the never-ending conversations and excitement engendered by the news of Sebastian and Antonia's betrothal. The diversion they were, however inadvertently, providing for his own activities was welcome. He raked his fingers through his hair, then swung his legs over the side of the bed and reached for his robe. "As that's the case, no one will miss me—I've decided to go out for breakfast."

"Indeed, my lord. With friends?" When Michael grunted an assent, Tom responded, "I'll lay out appropriate clothes."

Leaving him to it, Michael rose, shrugged on the robe, belted it, then padded across to the window. He'd fallen asleep with the thorny problem of what to do with Cleo Hendon—how best to protect her from her own enthusiasm regarding the mission—revolving in his head. As so often happened, he'd woken with a plan—a sound and simple strategy—crystal clear in his mind.

He looked out of the window. "Carpe diem." Despite the clouds, with any luck, the day would afford him the perfect opportunity to seize the reins and reassert control.

Cleo sat in her usual place at the breakfast table and absentmindedly nibbled a slice of toast liberally slathered with marmalade. For the umpteenth time since she'd awoken, she mentally sighed and—once again—hauled her mind from whence it had wandered.

That kiss still held the power to command her thoughts to the exclusion of all else. Which wasn't at all helpful. After finding her bed last night, she'd spent hours telling herself not to read too much into the interlude. That he'd kissed her purely to excuse their presence in the alcove in the lane; there was no reason to suppose the exchange had meant anything more to him.

For all she knew, he kissed all the many ladies with whom he no doubt dallied like that.

As if he wanted to—*gah!*

She had to stop thinking about it or she'd go mad!

The mission—she needed to think about the mission. She needed to find some way to learn if anything had happened in Morgan's Lane overnight. Or that morning.

Determined to keep her mind on that point and her wits from wandering, she debated sending a message to St. Ives House, inquiring whether Michael, or more pertinently, his men, had learned anything. Then she realized she didn't know who else was presently residing under the same roof; very likely his brother was there, perhaps even his sister and his parents. The notion of someone else being near when Michael received her note...she didn't want to raise anyone's curiosity over her involving herself in Michael's part of the mission.

"So how else?" She reached for her teacup and sipped.

Sounds in the front hall wafted to her ears. She hadn't heard the doorbell, but Morris, the butler, had crossed the front hall and opened the door; it was the rumble of male voices that had interrupted her reverie.

Distantly, she heard the front door shut.

A second later, the breakfast-parlor door opened, and Michael Cynster strolled in.

Lowering her cup, she stared at him.

He smiled genially at her; was she wrong in thinking there was an element of intentness lurking in his dark-brown gaze?

"Good morning." He walked to the place opposite hers and drew out the chair there.

Her eyes had widened; they remained locked on him. "What...?"

He glanced at the open door, then sat. "I hope you don't mind, but I've invited myself to breakfast. We need to confer, and we may as well do that over the teacups."

At that moment, Morris rushed in with a silver pitcher of coffee.

Michael smiled his thanks. "Or coffee cups, as the case might be." Morris poured him a cup of the dark brew. "Thank you." Michael raised the cup and, meeting her still-stunned gaze, sipped.

She wrestled her wits into order. Having him suddenly appear in the flesh had brought far too many memories surging to the forefront of her mind, thoroughly distracting her. He and she hadn't discussed the kiss in any way—hadn't actually referred to it at all; as Morris quit the room, presumably to fetch appropriate sustenance for her unexpected guest, she fervently hoped that they weren't going to discuss that incident now. She needed to focus. She arched her brows. "Has anything occurred in Morgan's Lane?"

Michael studied her. He'd sensed her sudden...not exactly nervousness but more a shying away and could guess the cause. But he could see no benefit in even alluding to the kiss they'd shared—they both knew it had happened, had both been very much involved—and to his mind, courtesy of that moment, he now knew all he needed to on that score. Bringing up that subject would only tangle them in all sorts of awkward talk—witness her entirely sensible unease at the prospect. Instead, he proposed to leave all discussion of that and associated subjects until later —until after they'd completed the mission and had had a chance to get to know each other better.

So he wasn't there to discompose her; quite the opposite. He was there to reassure her. Consequently, smiling easily, he replied, "My men —those who were there when we were—were relieved at three o'clock. The second crew returned not long ago and, as with the first group, reported no action of any kind in Morgan's Lane."

He was, he realized, entirely amenable to sitting there, sipping excellent coffee and letting his gaze feast on her. Today, instead of the jacket, blouse, and skirt outfits she seemed to favor for business, she was garbed in a neat, gold-colored walking dress. The bodice hugged her curves and drew in to a tiny waist; the sleeves were tight and fastened with a row of tiny gold-bead buttons that ran from elbow to wrist. There was a single row of narrow white lace adorning the edge of the dress's collar, the sides of the bodice's front placket, and the edges of the sleeves. With her strawberry-blond curls in their usual artless knot on the top of her head, with tendrils already escaping to form a gilded frame for her face, she was... his version of Aphrodite.

The realization was a trifle unsettling.

Especially as she was regarding him with a steady gaze behind which lurked a soupçon of suspicion.

It was time to redirect her thoughts. "Given the lack of action in Morgan's Lane, which might well extend until tomorrow morning, I wondered whether there was anything else we might do to advance our cause between now and visiting the warehouses tomorrow."

The distraction worked. Her gaze turned pensive; her brow furrowed slightly as she thought.

The butler appeared with an array of breakfast dishes. Grateful for the additional diversion, after his hostess had absently waved the offerings aside, apparently preferring to stick with her toast and jam, Michael helped himself to scrambled eggs, sausages, and ham. Leaving his partner to her cogitations, he applied himself to the meal.

Eventually, she stirred. "I can't see any way of gaining access to those warehouses—not in any way that will allow us to identify barrels of gunpowder delivered on Wednesday last—other than via some form of commercial inquiry." She set down her teacup and, across the table, met his gaze. "Given how tightly the movement of gunpowder is controlled, I think we're on solid ground in assuming the ten barrels we're after will be from a private mill in Ireland and will be branded accordingly."

With his mouth full of ham and eggs, he nodded.

"But even if we broke into the warehouses and found ten barrels with an Irish stamp, we couldn't be sure those are the barrels we're after—that the barrels we're after haven't already been spirited away." She wrinkled her nose. "I have no idea how common it is to find gunpowder from Irish mills in London, but I suspect it wouldn't be all that rare. London is, after all, the hub of many industries, including the fireworks manufactories— those factories supplied by our three warehouses."

He grimaced and swallowed. "Sadly, I agree. Your analysis seems sound."

She studied the tablecloth between them for a moment, then raised her gaze and met his eyes. "So in answer to your question, no—I can't think of anything we might do to advance our cause between now and tomorrow morning."

Slowly, he nodded, as if reluctantly accepting that conclusion. He glanced at his cleared plate, then set down his cutlery, patted his lips with his napkin, and laid it aside. "Given that"—he returned his gaze to her face and finally asked the question he'd come there to ask—"what are your plans for the day?"

Cleo felt her eyes widen, but although she searched, she could see nothing beyond mild interest in Michael's dark-brown eyes. Feeling slightly silly for imagining there might be anything else behind what was doubtless merely a polite social query, she replied a touch more acerbically than she intended, "As I spent all Friday assisting you, I need to go into the office to check over any orders I need to sign or decisions that need to be made." And to confirm there was nothing pending that might need her attention over the next several days.

Somewhat to her disquiet, at her words, Michael smiled. "Actually"— if anything his smile grew more charming, more beguiling—"I wonder if I might accompany you. Once you've dealt with anything requiring your attention, I'd like to pick your brains about the basis of the business." His smile turned winning. "I've been thinking for some time about getting into the investment side of importing and exporting, and I would appreciate gaining a deeper insight into the area."

She blinked. A stern voice in her head reminded her of his reputation; if half the tales told of him were true, he was a past master at seduction—

and of course, a man who professed an interest in the import-export business would be alluring to her. Much in the way of a rare and fascinating species. But he was making that up, wasn't he?

No matter how keenly she studied his eyes, his no-doubt-deliberately distracting smile, and his hopeful expression, she honestly couldn't tell.

Should she risk it or...?

But this was her adventure—not just the mission but all of it.

Her eyes still locked with his, slowly, she inclined her head. "Very well. If you wish to come along, by all means do, but I warn you, the first hour or so while I deal with correspondence is likely to be hideously boring."

His smile appeared to be entirely genuine. "I assure you I'll survive." His eyes gleamed. "Tales of my abysmal attention span have been greatly exaggerated."

She couldn't stop a disbelieving snort. She knew exactly to what he referred—the gossip among the young matrons of the ton that his interest was exceedingly hard to hold; even she had heard it. Repressively, she replied, "We'll see," then pushed back her chair and rose.

Michael came to his feet. He was comprehensively pleased with the outcome of his new tack with respect to her. It was plain she didn't believe he had any real interest in the import-export business, no doubt assuming his assertion to be a ruse; he was looking forward to correcting her misapprehension. His interest in the area had been growing for some time, and he suspected he could learn quite a lot from her. Being a female had likely meant she'd had to prove her knowledge to a higher level than her brothers or other males. She'd had to excel to claim the position she held. Who better for him to learn from?

He felt sure he would enjoy her lessons, and aside from all else, the endeavor would keep them both pleasantly occupied during this day of enforced inactivity on the mission front.

He had little confidence in her ability to readily accept inactivity, enforced or otherwise. Consequently, satisfying his aim of keeping her safe had translated to finding a way to stick by her side while ensuring her hours were filled with non-threatening pursuits.

Feeling smugly satisfied with his achievements of the morning thus far, he walked beside her into the front hall.

He waited patiently in the hall while she went upstairs to fetch her cloak and bonnet.

The butler, who Cleo had called Morris, hovered, waiting to see them out. When Michael glanced his way, Morris cleared his throat. "If you will permit, my lord"—Morris glanced swiftly up the stairs, confirming his young mistress had yet to reappear—"on behalf of the household, I would like to tender our thanks for your actions in…er, extricating Miss Hendon from her foray last night. Her excursion had been preying on our minds."

Michael raised his brows. After a moment, he murmured, "I understand that it must be difficult to rein her in."

Morris primmed his lips as if to smother a laugh. When he could manage it, he replied, "Indeed, my lord. It wasn't easy when she was a slip of a thing, and now, given her age, that's quite beyond our reach."

"How old is she?" Michael knew she was younger than he, but he'd given no real thought to her actual age.

"Twenty-eight, my lord. Lady Hendon hasn't quite given up hope, but as we all know, Miss Hendon will go her own road."

"Indeed." The sound of a door closing above stairs, followed by the patter of light footsteps, put an end to their exchange, one Michael had found both encouraging—as he was quite sure he was meant to—and entertaining. Did Morris and the Hendon staff but know it, he needed no encouragement when it came to Miss Hendon.

He stood in the front hall and, expectantly, gazed up at the head of the stairs.

Then she appeared; a shaft of weak sunlight struck through the skylight in the hall ceiling and bathed her in a gentle glow. She saw him and smiled—an entirely innocent, looking-forward-to-a-day-spent-in-his-company, ready-for-adventure smile. With her cloak over one arm, her bonnet dangling by its ribbons from one hand, and her reticule swinging from her other wrist, she swept gracefully down the stairs.

And with his eyes and mind filled with the sight of her, he couldn't understand why he hadn't seen her for what she was in the first instant he'd laid eyes on her. He must have had some sort of veil restricting his vision.

As she halted before him, he smiled and reached for her cloak. "Allow me."

With a regal tip of her head, she let him drape the heavier fabric over her shoulders. With that done, she stepped to face the large mirror hanging above a side table.

He watched her don her bonnet and fuss with the ribbons, tying them, staring at the lopsided result, then, making a frustrated sound, yanking the yellow ribbons free and tying them again—and still the result wasn't up to scratch. He'd noticed on the previous two days that, when it came to her coiffure or her bonnet, she seemed peculiarly sartorially challenged. Hiding a grin, he reached out, grasped her arm, and turned her to face him; he brushed her hands aside, ignored her frustrated humph and irritated frown, straightened her bonnet, then tied the ribbons in a neat bow just below her left ear.

By that time, she'd narrowed her eyes at him, but when he stepped back and waved her to the mirror, she whirled, looked, raised her fingers to the bow, then humphed again.

Turning back, she cast him a glance from beneath her lashes. "Thank you."

His grin deepened into a smile. "It was my pleasure."

He heard the snort she couldn't quite smother, but when he offered his arm, she didn't hesitate to take it.

Morris, his features commendably impassive, leapt to open the door.

Michael escorted Cleo down the steps, paused on the pavement to—under her curious gaze—instruct the young groom he'd left waiting by the railings that, should there be any word from Morgan's Lane, he could be found at the Hendon offices and gave the direction. The boy saluted and took off to convey the message to St. Ives House.

Tom had been walking the horse and now brought the carriage to a halt by the curb. Michael helped Cleo in, then glanced up at Tom. "The Hendon Company office on the corner of Fenchurch and Lime."

Cleo settled in the chair behind her desk and wondered how on earth she was to keep her mind on business while faced with the distraction of the sprawling masculine figure currently subsiding into the chair on the opposite side of the desk.

Luckily, Fitch had stacked all the letters and orders she needed to read and sign, together with the ledgers she needed to check and approve, on her blotter. The task before her was simply a matter of starting at the top and working her way through the pile.

She hauled in a silent breath and, with ruthless ferocity, focused her mind on the first letter.

Somewhat to her surprise, her business mind took over. It was, apparently, less easily distracted...or perhaps it was because he, definitely to her surprise, made no move to reclaim her attention.

Steadily, letter by order by ledger, the pile reduced, until an hour and more had passed in a silence broken only by the scritch of her pen and the turning of pages, and she found herself shutting the last ledger.

Even before the ledger fell closed, he shifted in the chair, swinging to face her. "Done?"

She looked up and met his eyes. "Yes."

"Good." He fixed her with a direct, almost challenging look. "I wanted to ask—"

He proceeded to ply her with questions that, very quickly, proved that his interest in import-export trading was no sham. She found herself pressed by the undeniably insightful questions to put aside her reservations and rise to the challenge of sharing her knowledge of her world with him.

"The safest ventures," she replied to one leading question, "are undoubtedly those seeking to supply an established market that is currently experiencing, or likely to shortly experience, a significant undersupply. Tea is one such commodity—we've yet to achieve oversupply, and it's doubtful we will any time soon. However"—she paused to lend her words weight—"as in most areas of business, the safe investments are rarely those with the highest returns."

"So how does one identify less-safe investment opportunities— meaning those involving products that, imported or exported, are likely to deliver richer rewards?"

Lips curving, she replied, "If I knew that, I'd be richer than that fellow Golden Ball ever was." She waved dismissively. "That said, there are certain...I suppose one might call them qualities, that indicate—"

Michael found himself hanging on the talented Miss Hendon's every word. He had seriously underestimated the breadth of her knowledge, the depth of her understanding and experience. He'd expected to feel quietly smug over having so efficiently arranged to kill two birds with one stone —to claim her time so she wouldn't find any way into danger while simultaneously expanding his knowledge of an area of investing he'd started to think held the promise of engagement and the sort of intellectual return he'd been seeking; he'd expected to be genuinely but only mildly interested.

He hadn't expected to be swept off his feet, to find his mind awhirl with dozens—nay, scores—of ideas and possibilities, all conjured by the information she so readily and unselfconsciously imparted.

The office clock finally interrupted them, chiming melodiously to mark twelve o'clock.

She looked surprised.

He was, too. They'd been talking, engaged and deeply absorbed, for well over an hour. He caught her eye. "Is there a tavern nearby? One we might lunch at? The least I can do while so determinedly picking your brain is to feed you."

She chuckled. "Yes—all right. The Pig and Whistle is just around the corner in Church Street. We can continue our discussions there."

They didn't stop talking—he asking, she explaining—as they went down the stairs. He broke off only to tell Tom where they were going and to recommend he find someone to hold the horse and get a bite himself, then Cleo and he strolled arm in arm along Fenchurch Street, with her explaining the relative risks of trading across the Atlantic versus the Baltic or nearer-European routes.

It was Sunday; although the tap of the Pig and Whistle was crowded, the dining room held only two other couples. Michael escorted Cleo to a table for two in one corner, and over an excellent steak-and-kidney pie, they continued their exploration of import-export trading unabated.

Eventually, Cleo couldn't contain her curiosity any longer. They'd pushed aside their empty plates, and she was cradling a half pint of cider while he was sipping from a pint of ale. She raised her glass and took another sip, studying him over the rim. Regardless of their surroundings, just a glance would be enough to inform anyone familiar with the species of his station in life; the quality of his clothes, the commanding way he held himself, and the controlled and oddly graceful strength that invested his every movement all screamed that inescapable truth.

She would never have imagined—had never in her wildest dreams considered—that a gentleman-nobleman would have any real interest in the ins and outs of the world she inhabited. That he might be sincerely interested in, to the point of being fascinated by, the scope of the deals and the mechanics of the enterprise she managed. Yet Michael's interest —and his enthusiasm—were patently genuine. His questions had ranged over a wide swath of that sector of the business world with which she was deeply familiar, but in particular, he'd delved into the investment side of both import and export. She studied him for a moment more, then fixed her eyes on his and asked, "Why are you so interested in the business of import-export trading?" She waved briefly, indicating his appearance. "You're a duke's son. You don't need to involve yourself in such things, yet I accept your interest is real. I just don't understand from what it springs."

His lips twisted in a wry grin. "A duke's son." He saluted her with his glass. "You—and most of society—would be surprised to learn just what that entails, even for sons such as myself, who are not the direct heirs."

She set down her glass, crossed her forearms on the table, and opened her eyes wide. "So what does being a second-or-worse duke's son entail?"

He grinned, sipped, then set down his glass. "For many, but certainly for all Cynster men, we're expected to make our mark in some way. Those who succeed to the title bear the responsibility for all the entailed lands and the family coffers. Most people understand that. For the rest of us, though…" He paused, his gaze on his fingers, still clasped about the glass, then went on, "The best way to explain it is to consider the Cynster males of my father's generation. Not counting my father, there's five of them—technically, six, but I'm not going to count Simon Cynster, as he's much younger, a son from a second marriage. Of the older five, Richard Cynster manages his wife's estate in Scotland—that's almost as big an undertaking as managing a ducal estate. Vane Cynster runs a very large holding in Kent, and his primary interest is all things farming, especially crops and orchards. Anything to do with such things, we all know to ask Vane. Demon Cynster runs a hugely successful horse-racing stud. Gabriel Cynster is the family's investment specialist—he deals with all the usual financial investments. Lucifer Cynster is an expert on antiques and antiquities, especially jewelry and old books." He looked up and caught her eye. "Each and every one of them has a particular field they've made their own."

His lips curved, and he raised the glass. "So that's what's expected of us second-or-worse sons."

She watched as he swallowed a long draught of ale. When he lowered the glass, she said, "So you're thinking of making investing in the import-export trade your specialty."

It wasn't a question, yet he nodded. "Investing has always called to me. I've worked alongside Gabriel on and off for years, but some… element was always missing. He invests primarily in stocks and bonds, and that's always seemed too theoretical—divorced from real life —for me."

She nodded. "I know what you mean. It's harder to be excited about the deemed value of a piece of paper as opposed to the price you'll get for a particular cargo."

"Yes." His eyes lit. "That's it exactly." He hesitated, then leant forward. "What do you think of—"

Another hour passed, and Cleo started to feel her head spin. Not only was Michael serious about establishing an import-export investment firm but he also had ideas. Some of them wild—just the sort to appeal to her. And, she realized, to him, too. Some she felt compelled to dismantle and deem unworkable, but others, such as exploring the possibilities inherent in the Baltic amber trade, had, she judged, very real potential—and he had the wherewithal to make such a business work.

Indeed, he had wealth to invest, connections to exploit, and a passion that seemed to have grown wings.

As she listened to him extoll the possibilities, she felt an inner glow at knowing that it had been her information that had helped to stoke his burgeoning commitment.

Finally, the hovering serving girl brought them to a sense of the time. Cleo gathered her cloak and prepared to stand.

Michael tossed coins on the table, then looked at her. "What now? Back to Clarges Street?"

She blinked and recalled the necessary appointment she had to keep. Yet she hadn't enjoyed herself this much in…forever. Not ever. She didn't want to lose his company—and how very strange that seemed. And…

She met his gaze and took the bull by the horns. "No, actually. I'm due at my mother's cousin's house for afternoon tea. It's an absolute condition of my remaining in Clarges Street with only the staff and no chaperone—I have to attend Cousin Maude's Sunday afternoon tea." She paused, then added, "Maude is the wife of my mother's cousin, Geoffrey Cranmer."

Michael frowned. "Geoffrey Cranmer. I've heard that name, I'm sure."

"Very likely. Geoffrey is the head of a highly successful import-export firm." Cleo drew in a breath and said, "If you like, you could come with me and meet Geoffrey. I'm sure he'd be happy to share his experiences with you."

Although he'd kept his gaze on her face, Michael hadn't missed the way her fingers had tightened on her reticule, or the way her chin had—challengingly—risen. But the challenge wasn't directed at him. He studied her expression, the greeny-hazel of her eyes, then quietly asked, "Will it bother you, or your Cousin Maude, if I accompany you?"

She'd already shared so much with him that day—far more than he'd had any inkling she might, or that she even could—and now she was offering him more. But he wouldn't accept if his presence might in any way make life difficult for her.

Cleo stared at him. Evidently, he could see that she was in two minds. On the one hand, much as a committed mentor, she felt an odd responsibility to do all she could to further his evolving passion. It was a passion that spoke to her, that enthused her, too, and meeting with Geoffrey would keep that passion burning and, more, might well steer it in productive directions.

Against that, she could readily envision the reactions of all the family members present if she turned up at Geoffrey and Maude's house with Lord Michael Cynster in tow...

It took only an instant to weigh the two issues. She wasn't such a coward, and this, after all, was still a part of her adventure.

She smiled and firmly stated, "No. It won't bother me." She wouldn't allow it to. "You're very welcome to accompany me, and I know Geoffrey and Maude will be delighted to meet you."

They would be, too; she could guarantee that.

Michael searched her eyes; all he saw was resolve and certainty. And the chance to meet Geoffrey Cranmer was too good an opportunity to unnecessarily pass up. "If you're sure, then yes, I would like to accompany you." He rose and held out a hand.

After an instant's pause, she laid her fingers across his palm. Closing his hand—not too tightly—he helped her to her feet. He held her cloak for her, then—again—assisted her in settling her bonnet.

Her grin was rueful, but "Thank you" was all she said.

As he escorted her from the tavern and down the street to where Tom waited with the carriage, Michael marveled at the turn his day had taken. From the moment he'd elected to drop his reserve and share his hopes and dreams with her...they'd taken off. And now, they were heading to... He turned to her. "The address?"

"South Audley Street—the southern end."

He relayed the information to Tom, then handed Cleo up and joined her in the carriage. As they started off, he returned to his interrupted thought: Now, they were heading to a meeting that held the potential to transform his nascent ideas into reality.

He settled against the squabs and slanted a glance at the lady beside him.

Who would have thought Miss Cleo Hendon would prove to be such an inspired and inspiring choice?

She'd insisted on claiming the position of his partner. He smiled and faced forward. He no longer had the slightest interest in arguing that point.

CHAPTER 10

*A*n hour later, Michael stood beside Cleo in the drawing room of the Cranmers' fashionable town house and watched her chat with two of her cousins. On arriving, he and she had done the rounds, and between them, she and Maude had introduced him to everyone there. The gathering appeared to be comprised primarily of family members of varying degrees of connection, leavened by longtime family friends. Somewhat to his surprise, males and females were present in roughly equal numbers, while the ages ranged from early twenties to two older ladies he judged to be of his grandmother's generation.

Everyone was talking, but in polite, well-modulated tones; it was a pleasant, relatively informal gathering.

That said, he hadn't missed the implication that Cleo was present more or less under duress, her attendance being a mandatory requirement of her living in Clarges Street unchaperoned. Yet she'd been welcomed warmly by Geoffrey and Maude Cranmer and seemed genuinely relaxed and at ease in their company and that of most of the others there. But if he wasn't mistaken, beneath her outward equanimity, there was a thread of tension; over what, he had no idea.

"What-ho!" Anthony Cranmer, a youthful third cousin who, along with his sister, Georgia, had been chatting amiably with Michael and Cleo, looked across the room. "Looks like tea's being served." He glanced at Michael. "Shall we fetch the cups?"

"By all means." With a smile, Michael waved Anthony on; after exchanging a quick glance with Cleo, he followed.

Seated behind a tea trolley, Maude was dispensing cups and saucers to the gentlemen who had dutifully gathered. Michael and Anthony chatted with others as they waited in line.

He and Anthony were returning, each bearing two cups and saucers, when a pair of middle-aged matrons swept down on Cleo. That she was their target was obvious; the pair barely noticed Georgia.

Even though he was several yards distant, Michael sensed Cleo stiffen. Nothing about her demeanor changed, yet she'd tensed.

"Well, my dear Cleome." The woman in the lead—a Mrs. Herbert, if Michael recalled correctly—was built like a battleship and had a voice like a drill sergeant. "Dare we hope that your presence in town in this season is due to some social engagement, and you are no longer wasting your time in your father's office?"

"On the contrary, ma'am." Cleo's tone was admirably even. "I'm in town because this is where the office is, and I am in charge." She turned to Michael as he regained her side and offered her a cup and saucer. She accepted; balancing the saucer in one hand, she raised the cup and sipped.

Anthony handed Georgia her cup with an arched brow—clearly asking if she wished to move away—but Georgia's lips set; she took her cup and determinedly held her ground.

Anthony, a small smile on his lips, settled beside his sister to observe whatever was to come.

Unhurriedly, Cleo lowered her cup and returned her attention to Mrs. Herbert. Michael was relieved to see both matrons already had saucers in hand; he didn't want to have to offer to fetch them tea and miss the exchange.

He, too, sipped, aware that Mrs. Herbert was eyeing him and Cleo with faint puzzlement. The second matron, a Mrs. Winston, appeared a milder, less aggressive sort, but from the avidness in her gaze as she sipped and watched, she was likely to be the greater gossip.

Eventually, Mrs. Herbert said, "I had rather thought..." Then she rallied and, determined, swung her gaze to Michael. "Lord Michael, I'm sure you have an opinion on young ladies involving themselves in business affairs."

He smiled and lowered his cup. "Indeed, I do, Mrs. Herbert. In this modern age, with a queen on the throne and her consort so interested in new developments, the world has changed, and much of what was once frowned upon is now a new frontier." He glanced smilingly—approvingly —at Cleo. "For myself, I'm beyond grateful that Miss Hendon was at the helm of the Hendon Shipping Company when I walked through the doors, seeking information. With her understanding of the commercial world, she has been and continues to be of invaluable assistance." He looked at Mrs. Herbert and beyond her to Mrs. Winston. With his genial façade firmly in place, he stated, "You and Miss Hendon's wider family must be proud to count such a talented lady among your number."

Mrs. Herbert blinked owlishly. "I...well—yes, of course." Her brow furrowed. "I hadn't quite thought of things in that way."

"Would you say, my lord," Mrs. Winston put in, "that gentlemen with an eye to, as you put it, new frontiers might, indeed, prefer young ladies whose interests, at least broadly speaking, parallel their own?"

Michael decided he approved of Mrs. Winston. "I believe, ma'am, that that's increasingly likely to be a consideration going forward. If a lady is to support a gentleman's endeavors, then that's going to be much easier and more effective if the lady understands what the gentleman's business is about." Smiling slightly, he inclined his head. "My family has always prided itself on being at the forefront in such matters—we've found it pays."

Mrs. Winston nodded in apparent seriousness, even though her eyes were twinkling. "That is certainly the Cynsters' reputation, my lord." She swung her attention to Georgia and Anthony, directing several questions their way, then she tapped Mrs. Herbert's arm. "Come, Edna—let's leave these young people to get on with their modern lives."

With a surreptitious wink for Michael, Mrs. Winston towed a rather deflated Mrs. Herbert away.

Anthony and Georgia grinned and excused themselves.

As they moved away, Cleo sighed and glanced at Michael. "Thank you. Some, like Winnie—Mrs. Winston—are supportive, but most feel my interest in business, and even more my active involvement in running the company, is...well, not to put too fine a point on it, faintly disreputable. Very definitely unladylike and, of course, largely to blame for my unwed state."

He shrugged. "As I said, times have changed, and such perceptions need to be updated. Progress, as the Prince Consort so frequently declares, is upon us." A footman approached, collecting the empty cups and saucers. "Here"—Michael reached for hers—"let me relieve you of that."

Cleo wasn't surprised when, in groups of two and three, more of the ladies descended on her and Michael. She tensed, expecting the usual disapproving comments about her chosen occupation, but—whether distracted by Michael or alerted by Winnie—today's queries were more curious and far less judgmental than usual.

Of course, they were also wondering why Michael—Lord Michael Cynster, no less—was there, by her side. His glib response that she was assisting him with a matter of business was accepted, but, she suspected, not actually understood. She had to admit she found that amusing.

All in all, as the minutes rolled by, she discovered she was enjoying herself—or at least, she was finding the ordeal much less trying than usual. And it was obvious who she could thank for that.

From beneath her lashes, she glanced at him, standing by her side and, with easy affability, deflecting the almost-impertinent questions. She wondered how much of what he'd said earlier reflected his personal view.

She seized a moment between interrogations to ask, "You said it was the done thing in your family for the males to find their own niche occupation-wise. What about the females? Are they encouraged to pursue interests of their own? What about your sister? What are her interests?"

He looked down, met her eyes, and allowed her to see the amusement in his. "The females of my family need no encouragement to forge their own path. They ask for no permissions, but simply claim such freedom as their birthright. As for my sister, Louisa has carved out a niche of her own choosing. She's widely regarded as the true successor to the mantles my grandmother, the dowager duchess, and her bosom-bow Lady Osbalde-stone have carried for the past forty or more years."

When she opened her eyes wide, requesting further clarification, he grinned. "Among the haut ton, at any given time, there are ladies who are considered the final arbiters of all things, because they are ultimately the repositories of all knowledge. Of all the rumors and whispers and private dealings—everything that happens within the ton, they know and, largely, understand. They are the ultimate controllers of the machine that is the haut ton—theirs the hands on the levers. My mama, as Papa's duchess and Magnus Anstruther-Wetherby's granddaughter, is definitely a grande dame, but neither she, nor even Drake's mama, the Duchess of Wolver-stone, quite reach the pinnacle of power that my grandmama and Lady Osbaldestone long ago attained."

"Yet Louisa does…whatever that means?"

He nodded. "I don't understand it myself, but it's something along the lines of 'knowledge is power.' You need a certain type of mind to absorb everything—every current and past fact—about the haut ton, and then keep everything clear in your mind, ready to be accessed and used as needed." He paused, then said, "Knowing Grandmama and Lady Osbaldestone, and knowing Louisa, it's as plain as day. She will be— perhaps already is—as powerful within the ton as they." He met her eyes. "Although it's possible not everyone has realized that yet."

"So that's her…chosen occupation, as it were?"

"Yes. And it's one she'll do very well with."

"That seems rather appropriate for a duke's daughter."

"Indeed. Just as your chosen occupation is appropriate for you. It's founded on and builds on your inherited strengths—just as with Louisa. Just as with my cousin Lucilla, who has taken over her mother's position as Lady of the Vale in Scotland, and as for Prudence Cynster, she sees herself as her father's natural successor, running his stud outside Newmarket—and trust me, no one is about to argue with her over that, not even her father."

She held his gaze for an instant, then smiled. "No wonder your views are…updated."

He grinned, then others joined them, including Maude, and Geoffrey strolled up with several of the older men. Gradually, the group split into two—the men talking business and the ladies, somewhat to Cleo's irritation, concentrating on upcoming family events. She would much rather have been with the men. Much rather have been by Michael's side, gaining a better understanding of his business ideas and facilitating his interaction with Geoffrey and the others, all of whom she knew well.

The enforced separation chafed, but there was no opportunity for her to relocate, not without calling too much attention to herself.

Eventually, people started to leave. As the company thinned, Cleo found herself standing by the bow window, for an instant alone with their hostess.

Maude leant closer. "My dear," she whispered, "I'm so thrilled for you, and your parents will be, too." Maude's eyes, alight, were fixed on Michael, standing with Geoffrey and several other men, all apparently engrossed in some detailed discussion.

Cleo inwardly sighed, but she'd known Michael's presence would inevitably lead to such speculation. "He came because he was interested in meeting Geoffrey." She made her tone definite, faintly insistent. "Michael wants to learn more about Geoffrey's area of business." Maude looked at her—searched her eyes, her expression. Then Maude gripped her arm. "My dear, if furthering his understanding of the import-export business was his *only* interest, then a gentleman such as Lord Michael Cynster would have made an appointment to speak with Geoffrey at his club. I don't deny Lord Michael has such an interest, but to brave a family afternoon tea for no other reason...?" Maude briefly shook Cleo's arm, then with a twinkle in her eye, released her and said, "I think you underestimate the scope of his interests, my dear."

So saying, Maude swanned off, leaving Cleo staring across the room at Michael. *Hmm.* While one part of her insisted Maude was being fanciful, her more rational side observed that Michael had spent most of his time by her side, deflecting any implied criticism of her rather than pursuing Geoffrey; it had been Geoffrey who had approached and drawn Michael aside.

More, there were Michael's comments about gentlemen such as himself finding ladies with shared interests more supportive of their life's ambitions, as well as his family's acceptance that ladies, too, needed to find their own purpose in life. And, now she thought back over the recent exchanges, although he'd discouraged any queries about him having a personal interest in her, he hadn't denied having such an interest.

Unbidden, memories of the kiss they'd shared in the dark of the previous night rose inexorably and filled her mind. Her lips tingled. She recalled the powerful, dominant emotions—the passion, the desire, the outright lust—that had captured them both and driven them...she felt the echoes even now and fought to quell a shiver.

To her, that kiss had been eye opening in its depth, its power, its promise. Had it struck him in the same way?

She couldn't believe it had. She knew his reputation; he was an aristocratic hedonist, an experienced lover of high-born ladies. With all the ton's beauties to choose from, why would he fix his eye on her? She really couldn't compete.

Even if she wanted to.

Yet there he stood, having readily endured an entire afternoon of her family's curiosity.

Was Maude right? Was she—Cleo—being willfully blind?

Perhaps. Perhaps not. But Maude was undeniably correct in one respect: Michael had to have had some reason other than his interest in business to have been moved to accompany her and willingly spend his Sunday afternoon being quizzed by her family.

Before she could dwell on what his ulterior motive might be, he and Geoffrey stepped away from the others in their group. Still chatting with each other, they strolled toward her.

Both smiling, they halted before her, and Michael said, "Mr. Cranmer —Geoffrey—and Maude are entertaining an investor acquaintance, who is visiting from Philadelphia, for dinner this evening, along with his wife and two children. Geoffrey has suggested that you and I should join the company."

"It would be a great favor if you could manage it," Geoffrey put in. "Mr. and Mrs. Hepworth are older than Maude and I, but that's not the problem. It's their children I'm concerned about—a son and daughter in their later twenties. Closer to your age than to our brood, who I would prefer not to have at the dinner table." Geoffrey and Maude's children were still in the schoolroom. "I confess I'm at a loss as to how to properly entertain the younger pair. However"—Geoffrey glanced at Michael—"as Cynster here is especially interested in the prospects for import-export trade with our ex-colonies, I was hoping to entice the pair of you to come to our aid."

Michael's brown eyes held an almost boyish plea. "It really seems too good an opportunity to pass up—to get a feel for such trade from the other side, so to speak."

She fully understood his reasoning. In her mind, she heard again his comments regarding the benefits of ladies who knew enough to comprehend their gentleman's business interests. Both men were waiting in transparent hope; it was clearly her decision to make. She nodded. "Yes, of course. I'm happy to assist and…" She glanced at Michael.

"And of course, I'll escort you here tonight." The quality of his smile, the way it lit his eyes, suggested unalloyed satisfaction.

Cleo studied that smile and had to wonder if, as Maude had suggested, he had more than one motive—more than one goal in play. He was clearly seeking insights into trade with the Americas; what other insights might he be hoping to gain?

An unanswerable question; she was quite sure he wouldn't tell her even if she was so bold as to ask.

The others had all left. They were the last guests remaining.

Geoffrey had turned to inform Maude of his good news—that Cleo and Michael would be dining with them that evening and would assist with the younger Americans.

Cleo was still studying Michael's face, and he was still returning her regard.

His expression altered slightly, growing more serious—his gaze more intent. Memories of that illicit kiss swirled, rising in her mind.

She blocked them out and forced herself to glance away. Her gaze fell on the clock on the mantelshelf. "Heavens—it's almost five-thirty!" She turned to Maude. "What time?"

"Given the season and that our guests are Americans," Maude replied, "I've said seven in the drawing room, and we'll go in at seven-thirty."

Cleo nodded and glanced at Michael. "We need to go if we're to dress for dinner and get back in time."

His smile returned, and he half bowed, waving her to the door. "Our carriage awaits."

Cleo touched fingers with Maude, then stretched up and planted a kiss on Geoffrey's cheek; of all her many relatives, she liked them the best. "Until later."

As on Michael's arm she walked out of the town house and down the steps to where his carriage waited, she hoped that an hour or so away from him would allow her senses to properly settle, enough for her to gain some clearer perspective on whether he might, in fact, now harbor some romantic interest in her—and, if so, what her response should be.

"No, not that one." Cleo frowned at the mauve silk evening gown her maid, Jilly, was displaying for her approval. "That's too…"

Uninspiring. Not me. It was a lovely gown, but she would never feel confident in it.

Jilly just looked at her; the mauve creation was the third gown Cleo had vetoed.

She stood in her corset and petticoats and mentally cataloged her wardrobe. As a lady who rarely went to balls and dinners—who rarely gave a thought to her appearance at all—her choices were limited.

"The green figured silk," she eventually decided. *Yes, that will do.*

Jilly pulled a face and returned the mauve silk to the wardrobe. The mauve gown was new and in the latest fashion; the gown in green was more than a year old. "Are you sure, miss?" Jilly asked from the depths of the wardrobe.

Was she?

She was supposed to entertain foreigners; the Hepworths' daughter was, very likely, far more au fait with the latest fashions than Cleo would ever be—so no point trying to compete on that score. Cleo set her chin. "Yes, quite sure." She'd rather feel confident than fashionable, especially with Michael present.

Especially if he had a non-business—and obviously non-mission—motive for spending more time in her company.

Jilly drew the figured silk gown from the wardrobe, shook out the skirts, and held it up for Cleo's approval.

She nodded. "Yes—that's the one for tonight." To appease Jilly, she added, "I need to hit just the right note."

After Jilly, still disapproving, helped her into the gown and did up the dozens of small jet buttons holding the gown closed at the back and also down the outside of the tightly fitting sleeves, Cleo carefully sat on the stool before her dressing table and watched as Jilly took down her by-then rather straggly topknot, brushed out the heavy fall of her hair, then proceeded to refashion it into a much tighter, sleeker knot, once again anchored on the top of her head.

She spared a thought for her constant wish that she could risk a bun further back on her head, or even the looser coiffures that were currently all the rage, but her hair was heavy and silky and inevitably slipped from all such moorings and ended in an unacceptable mess. A topknot balanced properly and anchored well was more or less the only safe hairstyle for her.

A glance at the clock on her mantelpiece told her it was almost half past six. Michael had brought her home in his carriage and, as the distance between Clarges Street and the Cranmer town house wasn't great, had said he would call for her at a quarter to seven.

The thought of him brought to mind her earlier cogitations regarding his motives. It had occurred to her that his secondary, non-business motive might have been to keep her away from Morgan's Lane; when he'd first arrived at the house that morning, she'd certainly suspected his primary intent had been to ensure she didn't climb into a hackney and go into Southwark to assure herself that no action involving the barrels had taken place. But if keeping her away from Morgan's Lane had been his aim, he hadn't needed to accompany her to the afternoon tea to achieve it. Once he'd heard of her destination, he could simply have dropped her off in South Audley Street and gone elsewhere to amuse himself—but he hadn't. Of course, he'd been interested in meeting Geoffrey with a view to learning more about the import-export business, but as Maude had said, it was passing strange for a gentleman of Lord Michael Cynster's ilk to have volunteered to endure a family afternoon tea if that had been his only goal.

While Jilly fluffed out a few locks, teasing them into hanging in corkscrew curls on either side of her face, Cleo stared at her reflection, then pressed a hand to her midriff—as if she could thus calm the rising flutter of butterflies in her stomach.

It was so silly, really. She, who never bothered about what she looked like, was fretting over her dress, over her hairstyle, over what shawl and reticule she should carry.

When Jilly stepped back with a "There you are, miss! Quite a picture, if I do say so myself," Cleo barely glanced at her maid's latest effort; she was too busy debating what jewelry to wear.

"My pearl bobs and the long strand of pearls, I think."

Jilly nodded in approval and hunted in her jewelry case.

While she donned the earrings Jilly handed her, Cleo thought again of that kiss. Thought of the morning, of all they'd shared over lunch, thought of that afternoon and of her less-than-settled state—and of what the evening might bring.

The butterflies fluttered more furiously.

She wasn't sure the reaction attested to anything about him or his motives, but she was increasingly concerned as to what that reaction said about her and hers.

～

Cleo walked into Geoffrey and Maude's drawing room on Michael's arm. This was not her milieu, but it was, most definitely, his, and his ineffable confidence, his social ease as he guided her to greet Geoffrey and Maude by the fireplace, in some strange but wonderful fashion seemed to infect her.

The way his face had lit when he'd seen her on the stairs in Clarges Street as she'd walked down to meet him hadn't hurt, either. His patently genuine reaction had confirmed beyond question that her decision to opt for the green silk gown had been the right one.

Buoyed and fortified by his nearness, by his relaxed assurance, she smiled and greeted the Hepworths as Maude introduced them.

On hearing Michael's title, Mrs. Hepworth's eyes grew round. "*Lord* Michael? Doesn't that mean...?"

"Lord Michael is the second son of the Duke of St. Ives," Cleo explained.

"Well!" Miss Andrea Hepworth exclaimed. "Fancy that! A real duke's son." Miss Hepworth eyed Michael measuringly.

To Cleo's amusement, Michael edged fractionally closer to her.

"I say—is it true," Robert Hepworth, the Hepworths' son, asked, "that all gentlemen like you—the aristocrats—are members of White's Club?"

Michael smiled. "Our fathers—who are all members—tend to propose us as members when we come on the town."

"That's when young gentlemen are around twenty or so—after they come down from, meaning graduate from, university," Cleo explained.

Michael's swift smile warmed her. "Indeed." He returned his attention to the younger Hepworth. "So generally, we're all proposed and accepted into White's, so yes, most of us are members. However, for our generation, other clubs are more likely to enjoy our regular patronage."

"Which other clubs?" Robert inquired.

"Boodle's, Brooks, although both are rather tame." Michael went on, "The current favorite is Arthur's in St. James Street."

"Never you mind," Mrs. Hepworth told her son. "We're not here for you to go gallivanting about."

What Robert might have said to that, they were destined never to learn, as Geoffrey, who had been talking with Mr. Hepworth, turned and asked Cleo, "My dear, Mr. Hepworth is seeking to acquire good quality hardwood—the sort for furniture makers. Where in London would you suggest he look—or is there some other port that might be preferable?"

Cleo promptly replied, "The vast bulk of furniture-grade timber comes into the Pool of London. Most is placed in warehouses in the East End." She smiled at Mr. Hepworth. "I don't carry the list in my head, but I'd be happy to have our office send you the names and addresses of the better suppliers."

Mr. Hepworth blinked. "Your office?"

Still riding on the wave of Michael-bolstered confidence, Cleo had no trouble keeping her smile in place. "Yes. My family owns and operates the Hendon Shipping Company. You might have heard of us."

Mr. Hepworth's eyes widened. "Why, indeed, I have. I believe I met one of your brothers recently—in New York."

She nodded. "Jarred. All three of my brothers are currently on the other side of the Atlantic, pursuing various deals. That's what they do. Meanwhile, I remain in London and manage the firm." Before they could ask, she added, "My parents are at our estate in Norfolk—in the country. They prefer the country to town."

Mrs. Hepworth glanced at her daughter, then said, "But when your brothers come home, I take it they will resume control and you will retire from the office?"

Cleo laughed; so did Maude and Geoffrey. Even Michael smiled at the absurdity of that suggestion.

"Oh no," Cleo assured Mrs. Hepworth. "Running the company—managing its affairs—is my agreed role, and none of my brothers has the requisite skills to juggle all the details involved."

Mrs. Hepworth's confusion was writ large on her face. "I'd rather thought..." She glanced at Michael, then looked back at Cleo. "We'd assumed that young ladies of the ton were forbidden to...well, *work* in any capacity. To be involved in *trade*."

Michael inclined his head in acknowledgment. "In our parents' day, that was true for young ladies and all the aristocracy, male and female alike. However, these days, there's a distinction drawn between managing an asset and working as such, or being involved in a trade. Managing investments and business is entirely acceptable, but actually working with one's hands or drawing a salary remains beyond the pale."

He glanced at Cleo and smiled. "For example, as I was explaining to Miss Hendon earlier today, every one of the males in my family is expected to choose some business to invest in." He nodded at Mr. Hepworth. "Which is what's behind my interest in the import-export business. My brother, who will inherit the title, has to learn to manage the estate—that's his role—while I'm expected to find a similar role investing in some other sphere. Most of the younger aristocracy these days have some role in investment or business, or are actively engaged in managing some asset. That's not only acceptable now but also financially desirable, of course. And in some instances, those roles in business management are, indeed, being claimed by our young ladies—as is the case with Miss Hendon."

All four Hepworths had been listening avidly. Michael smiled easily. "Times have changed, and the English aristocracy have a very long history of successful adaptation."

Mr. Hepworth exchanged a glance with his wife. "Well! I have to say that's an immensely enlightening piece of news."

"Indeed." Mrs. Hepworth turned to Maude and asked about Almack's and whether there was any chance of visiting while they were in town.

Miss Hepworth tugged Cleo's sleeve, and when Cleo glanced her way, asked, "Was there anything special you had to learn to take charge of your family's business?"

Cleo arched her brows. "Arithmetic. And a sound understanding of geography helps, but…why do you ask?"

Miss Hepworth looked at Robert, who volunteered, "I'm dreadful at sums, and anything to do with finance goes straight over my head. Of course, Papa wants me to take over after him, but I'd much rather do what it sounds like your brothers do—travel and meet people and negotiate business. I'm good at that."

"And *I'm* good at sums and finance," his sister put in. "And I don't mind staying home in Philadelphia." She glanced at her parents, who had drawn a little away and were talking to Geoffrey and Maude. "But until now, Mama—and Papa, too, but mainly Mama—wouldn't hear of me even helping out at the office, much less learning how Papa manages things."

Miss Hepworth's eyes lit, and she beamed at Cleo and Michael. "I can't tell you how helpful and encouraging learning of your roles—both of your roles and all you've described—has been. Now…" She glanced at her brother.

Robert Hepworth nodded decisively. "Now, we'll go to work on them. Clearly, if it's socially acceptable for both of you to engage in managing investments or a business, then it's time Philadelphia society adapted, too." Robert grinned. "I can just imagine using that notion as a lever. If the English can see the sense, then…"

Michael chuckled. "I haven't yet visited America, but from all I've gathered, that should go a long way toward winning your point."

The butler appeared at that moment to announce that dinner was served.

Geoffrey offered Mrs. Hepworth his arm, and Maude accepted Mr. Hepworth's, and in congenial vein, Cleo and Michael followed behind with Miss Hepworth—"Please, call me Andrea"—and Robert.

The rest of the evening was largely spent in a broader and more varied discussion of business interests than Michael could possibly have hoped for. Andrea and Robert were as eager as he to elicit their father's and Geoffrey's insights, and although he suspected Cleo already knew much of what was discussed, she nevertheless drank in every word and was frequently instrumental in steering the conversation in new and revealing directions. Between the four of them, they questioned and interrogated the older men as course followed course.

Later, when they were once more in the drawing room and the teacups were handed around, while Mrs. Hepworth and Maude sat and chatted about social matters, the rest of the company congregated before the hearth and continued their exploration of the current state of the import-export trade and touched on various possibilities for the future. It was plain that all six of them—Geoffrey, Mr. Hepworth, Robert, Andrea, Cleo, and Michael—were enjoying themselves to an extent and in a way none of them had anticipated when they'd first walked into the room.

When it finally came time to call an end to the evening, Mr. Hepworth looked at his children and, without any prompting, humphed and said, "Well, you two—when we get back to Philly, we'll see."

Robert beamed. Andrea looked as if she'd just been handed her dearest wish on a platter.

With sincere thanks all around, the Hepworths took their leave. Michael, with Cleo beside him, walked into the front hall with Geoffrey and Maude to see the Americans on their way.

With his coat on and his hat on his head, Mr. Hepworth turned to Michael. "If you're ever in Philadelphia, my lord, please do call on us. I'd be happy to introduce you"—Hepworth paused to raise his hat to Cleo and smile benignly—"both of you to the gentlemen of my circle."

Michael grasped and shook Hepworth's proffered hand.

Then the older man took Cleo's hand and bowed surprisingly elegantly. "A pleasure, my dear. I've learned a lot tonight—and not all of it about import-export."

Cleo laughed. "Indeed, sir." She glanced at his family. "I believe we've all taught each other quite a lot."

After the Cranmer carriage had rumbled off, ferrying the Hepworths to their hotel, Michael and Cleo took their leave. His thank-yous to Geoffrey and Maude were heartfelt. "I haven't enjoyed myself so much in an age."

Geoffrey clapped him on the back. "The pleasure, my lord, was ours."

Geoffrey met Michael's eyes. "I believe I'm correct in stating that we all benefited in unexpected ways this evening."

Michael held Geoffrey's faintly challenging gaze, then wryly smiled, inclined his head, and followed Cleo, now wrapped in her cloak, out of the door and down the steps.

~

Clarges Street wasn't far; Cleo had opted to walk home, and after they'd arrived in South Audley Street, Michael had sent Tom and the carriage back to Grosvenor Square.

Now, beneath a cloud-screened sky, they ambled along well-lit streets, through soft shadows and into successive cones of light cast by the street-lamps. By Mayfair hours, it was relatively early. Carriages rattled past, and there were others, like them, taking advantage of the clement weather to stretch their legs.

"That was"—Cleo raised her head—"a surprisingly pleasant evening. I hadn't expected the Americans to be such good company—to be so open-minded. Or for them to have such…parallel interests."

Michael smiled and paced beside her. "Learning of your role with Hendon Shipping seems to have galvanized Andrea and Robert into pushing for and seizing the sort of life each of them wants. And Mr. Hepworth seemed ready to recalibrate his expectations."

Cleo flashed him a grin. "Mrs. Hepworth wasn't so pleased, but I suspect she'll come about." She looked ahead. "If I ever visit America, I'll be interested in learning how they've all managed."

You could travel there with me. Michael didn't utter the words, but the thought more than appealed. "I wouldn't mind observing that myself—in a few years, once they've had time to settle into their new roles."

"Hmm."

They paced on; although they continued to exchange comments on various business matters—something he couldn't imagine discussing with any other lady—with every yard they walked from South Audley Street, the pleasant ambiance of the evening receded, and eventually, the mission resurfaced, reclaiming their minds.

After several seconds of silence, Cleo glanced his way. "If anything had happened in Morgan's Lane, would your men have come to find you?"

He nodded. "Tom knew where I was, and I gave orders to be informed immediately." He met her gaze. "So we can conclude that the evening has passed quietly in Morgan's Lane, and the barrels are still in one of the three warehouses."

"Will you—or rather your men—continue to keep watch?"

He looked ahead. They were walking along Curzon Street; the corner of Half Moon Street lay to their right. The intersection with Clarges Street wasn't far away, and the Hendon town house was only a few doors from the corner. "Yes, we'll continue our watch. But as I mentioned before, my men reported that the entire area has been very quiet all day." He'd filled her in on the lack of activity during the drive to the Cranmers' house. "And given it's already past eleven o'clock and it is Sunday night, I think it's unlikely any attempt to move the barrels will be made before tomorrow morning."

"Assuming that the barrels are, indeed, still in Morgan's Lane."

He nodded. "Assuming that."

When they reached the pavement before the Hendon house, they halted and faced each other.

Cleo looked into Michael's face. Despite all her questions regarding him and her, as her eyes met his, the dominant feeling that assailed her was, put simply, connection. Something far deeper, broader, and more solid than mere attraction, although that remained, steady and strong. They'd both avoided mentioning the kiss—that stunningly revealing kiss they'd shared twenty-four hours before. Throughout the day, they'd both held back—reined in—the resulting reactions, but now, as they stood a foot apart on the pavement in Clarges Street, reaction surged, pushed free of all restraint, and bloomed.

Between them, that ineluctable connection snapped taut.

She managed to find her voice. "Thank you for escorting me home."

As if I could have done anything else. Michael looked at her and scrambled to find his usual debonair façade. He tipped his head and, his eyes still locked with hers, attempted a rakish smile. "The pleasure, I assure you, was all mine."

Her lips curved at the glib words; she thought them superficial, insubstantial—just polite verbiage. He was conscious of a sudden urge to assure her—vehemently—that the sentiment was entirely sincere. Then to taste that smile, to cover her lips with his and sip...

He was drowning in her green-and-gold eyes. He felt a tug—from his heart to hers.

As if she felt it, too, she swayed toward him...but then caught herself.

She tried to pull back, to step back—he saw that in her eyes—but she couldn't seem to manage it.

He dragged in a breath, but with his gaze still captured, with his entire being still focused on her, despite knowing he should, he couldn't get his feet to step back. To move away from her.

They were on the open street, with carriages passing and others on the pavement not that far away. They couldn't give in to the sudden compulsion that had clearly seized them both.

His protective instinct came to his—their—rescue. He heard himself say, "I don't suppose you'll agree to leave investigating the warehouses to me, even if I promise to keep you apprised of any and all developments?"

She blinked, and the spell was broken. She refocused on his face, her gaze direct and determined. "No." She breathed in and eased back, now-familiar stubbornness investing her expression.

He felt the heightened tension between them subside—and just for one instant, he considered throwing caution to the winds, hauling her into his arms, and kissing her... Then reality impinged, and regretfully, he jettisoned the notion; God alone knew what might happen, but regardless, she wouldn't be dissuaded from further participating in the mission. He felt his features set. His voice hard, he said, "Very well. I'll pick you up at nine o'clock."

Her gaze grew distant, then she shook her head. "No—better make it half past eight." When he arched his brows, she added in explanation, "The sooner we find out if the barrels are still there, the happier we'll both be."

He couldn't deny that.

Cleo read acceptance in his eyes, then he dipped his head.

"Eight-thirty, then."

He raised his head, and their gazes met.

Again, she felt a welling compulsion to step forward—into his arms, into the unknown. The impulse surged inside her; her eyes widened as, looking into the dark chocolate brown of his eyes, she realized the same impulse was riding him, too. Equally strongly.

But then he slid his hands into his pockets, angled his head in farewell, and stepped back. "Until tomorrow."

She forced herself to straighten, to hold her head high and draw in a breath, then incline her head in response. Then she turned and climbed the steps to the door. She rang the bell, then looked back.

He was standing on the pavement, watching her.

"Good night," she said. Then Morris opened the door, and she went inside.

Michael watched the door shut. He stared at the glossy panel for several seconds, then turned on his heel and started walking northward, toward Grosvenor Square and his bed.

The October night wrapped cold about him, yet even so, given the fevered nature of his prevailing, persistent, and insistent dreams, he seriously doubted that enjoying a "good night" lay in his immediate future.

CHAPTER 11

*T*his time, Tom drove the small black town carriage Michael had commandeered from the St. Ives House stable for the duration of the mission into and down Morgan's Lane.

Tom drew the carriage up outside the first warehouse—the one on the left closest to Tooley Street. The hour was just nine o'clock; Cleo could hear the city's bells pealing on the other side of the river.

Attired in his usual clothes—fashionable enough to mark him as a gentleman, but also sufficiently austerely styled to avoid drawing unnecessary attention—Michael stepped down to the cobbles. After a comprehensive glance up and down the street, he reached into the carriage, gripped her hand, and assisted her down.

She was garbed in her customary business style, in a fitted jacket and matching full skirt in a rich, warm brown worn over a white blouse adorned at the throat with a lace-edged mock cravat. A distinctly unfrivolous bonnet capped her head; she hoped the firmly fitting bonnet would restrain her wayward hair. Her cloak was a paler brown, as were her leather gloves and half boots. She'd selected each article with a view to strengthening the image she wished to project. She'd already decided on her story and the part she would play to induce the warehouse managers to reveal what she and Michael needed to know. Luckily, just being Miss Hendon of the Hendon Shipping Company was really all she needed to be.

A frown in his eyes, Michael was looking up and down the street.

"Either the barrels are still here, in one of the three warehouses, or they had already been moved before Saturday evening."

She opened her mouth to remind him of Winchelsea's theory that the barrels would remain in place for a time... Instead, she said, "You mean that unloading the barrels here was just a staging point?" She studied his face. "That they were moved on more or less immediately?"

Continuing to glance about, he grimaced. "Put it down to the thoughts of a fevered brain in the small hours. Drake stressed how cautious these villains have been, to the extent that what passes for normal procedures—such as not killing your own helpers—are not being followed, so we can't rely on anything being as one might think." He met her gaze. "Knowing that the barrels were delivered somewhere here on Wednesday morning and that they haven't been moved since Saturday evening doesn't mean they're still here."

She considered that, then shook out her skirts and determinedly raised her head. "Against that stands the fact that our villains took the trouble to arrange for the barrels to be stored in a warehouse where the presence of such barrels, hidden among lots of similar barrels, wouldn't be readily detected."

He inclined his head. "There is that."

"Indeed. They brought the barrels here, to what ranks as possibly the best hiding place they could find. If, as Winchelsea maintains, there's a reason to have a pause between one stage and the next, unless they had a still-better place to secrete the barrels—and that's hard to imagine—why run the risk of moving them again?"

He gripped her elbow. "Your reasoning is sound. I just no longer have faith in our ability to predict what these villains will do." His expression set, he tipped his head toward the warehouse outside which they stood. "Let's see what we can find."

She faced the warehouse. "Indeed." She took a step forward, only to have Michael halt her.

He eyed the façade. "How are we going to approach this?"

She smiled confidently. "You aren't. I am." She cast a swift glance over him. "Just back me up and look guard-like." She met his eyes. "As you usually do."

Michael stifled a grunt. He gentled his hold on her arm, steadying her over the cobbles to the warehouse door. He pushed it wide, then released her and followed as she swept—frigate-like—into the rather dim space.

She halted a few yards inside the door, in a cleared area that appeared to be some sort of receiving bay. Michael halted by her elbow, his expression impassive.

Directly ahead, two large laborers were manhandling crates onto a handcart. They barely spared a glance for Michael and Cleo.

But through a dusty window, a clerk in an office to the left saw them. He put down his board and came hurrying out.

The clerk halted before Cleo. His gaze darted from her to Michael, then back again. "Yes, ma'am?"

Her voice firm, her tones ringing, Cleo stated, "I am Miss Hendon of the Hendon Shipping Company. I would like to speak with the manager, if you please."

The clerk's eyes had widened at the mention of the Hendon name. He bobbed repeatedly. "Yes, of course, Miss Hendon." The clerk gestured behind him and started to back away. "If you'll wait just a minute, I'll fetch him."

Cleo regally inclined her head, and the clerk scurried back into the office.

In significantly less than a minute, a small, round man, his jacket straining to cover his paunch and with strands of greasy hair combed over his balding pate, hurried out of the office. Clasping his hands, rubbing them together, with his eyes alight, he came to stand before Cleo and bowed. "An honor, Miss Hendon." He straightened. "How can we help you?"

"My family's company has a long-standing client in Jamaica who has appealed to the firm for assistance in fulfilling an order for ten barrels of gunpowder." Cleo held up a finger to stay the manager's obvious exuberance and eagerness to launch into a sales spiel. "I should stress that this is not normally something our company does, but this is a special client. Consequently, we've made inquiries and have discovered that the local gunpowder mills have a waiting list. As our client's need is urgent, I am making inquiries at those warehouses—such as yours—that supply various factories with gunpowder in one-hundredweight barrels."

The manager was so eager to speak he was all but bobbing on his toes, but Cleo continued to hold up a restraining hand. "While I know you —and, very likely, several of your competitors—will be able to supply me with ten barrels of gunpowder, there is another stipulation. I will need to inspect the barrels to ensure they are suitable, especially with respect to the quality of their construction. As I'm sure you understand, the journey to Jamaica is a very long one, and from experience, we know that the barrels must be of a certain quality for us to be assured the gunpowder will still be useable when it arrives."

"Of course, Miss Hendon." The manager's expression had grown calculating, as if he was running through a mental inventory of the barrels he had in his warehouse.

In distinctly superior accents, Cleo continued, "In the circumstances, we are prepared to pay a premium to secure suitable barrels. We are looking for barrels that have been delivered recently—within the previous week, if possible. The shorter the time they've been sitting in a warehouse, the better for our client."

"Indeed, Miss Hendon." The manager waved to a bench seat set before the office wall. "If you would consent to wait just a moment, I'll consult my inventory, and then you may inspect our stock."

"Thank you." With a faintly arrogant, rather haughty air, Cleo allowed Michael to take her arm and steer her to the seat.

There, with a soft shush of skirts and petticoats, she sat.

Michael sat beside her. As soon as he did, with her head high and her gaze fixed across the warehouse, Cleo murmured, "While the manager shows me the barrels on his inventory, you'll need to search for any barrels that aren't on his list."

He nodded. Before he could add anything, the manager reappeared.

"Here we are!" He brandished several sheets. "We had a delivery early last week—Tuesday, I believe it was." He squinted at the top sheet. "Twelve barrels, all told." He looked hopefully at Cleo as she rose. "If you'll come this way?" He waved toward a narrow path that led deeper into the warehouse.

With a haughty nod, Cleo followed the manager along the path. Michael prowled at her heels. Piles of stacked merchandise towered to either side—crates of split bamboo, others trailing cotton fuses, still others stuffed with printed sheets, as well as large rolls of paper in a rainbow of colors.

The manager babbled, "We store our barrels toward the rear. They're easier to move than the crates, you see."

"Indeed," Cleo replied repressively.

After one faintly startled glance back at her, the manager hurried on.

Amused—and greatly impressed by her invention of the persona of the haughty Miss Hendon and her execution of the role—Michael leant closer to her and, lowering his head, murmured, "I think I'm in love."

Even as the words left his lips, as their import registered, something in him seized. He'd meant...

She glanced up, startled.

Almost equally off-balance, he met her wide-eyed gaze and saw the slight shiver she failed to suppress.

And understanding dawned.

She dragged in a tight breath. Her eyes narrowed, and she glared, then she faced forward and swept quickly on in the warehouse manager's wake.

Leaving Michael...facing the truth.

The words he'd uttered had bypassed his brain. They'd gone from some point deep inside him straight to his lips.

Yet as he followed, more slowly, in Cleo's wake, it seemed pointless to deny that, unsettling though the realization was, the sentiment he'd expressed was accurate.

Decidedly accurate, and a truth he—his inner self—had, apparently, already embraced.

They finally reached the area toward the rear of the packed warehouse where barrels—not just of gunpowder but also of materials such as fine sand and oil—were stored. He let Cleo and the manager go ahead and started searching. Given the two laborers steadily working in and out of the stacks of goods, he suspected that any barrels left elsewhere in the long building would have been quickly found and moved into the correct area.

The manager started pointing out large barrels to Cleo, the remainders from earlier deliveries of gunpowder, at which she turned up her nose.

Michael scanned all the barrels they passed. Most were smaller. The three he spotted of the right size were stamped and labeled as gypsum. There was no place he could see inside the warehouse walls where barrels might be hidden out of sight.

He caught up to Cleo as the manager was proudly displaying a stack of hundredweight barrels five wide and two high, but there were only four barrels in the upper row.

The manager was consulting his sheets. "We did have twelve. All delivered last Tuesday morning." The manager looked hopefully at Cleo. "Perhaps you might take these nine, and then you would have only one more to find."

Cleo didn't immediately reply. She was peering this way and that at the barrels, then she pointed to a mark on one. "This brand—what does it signify?"

The manager perched a pair of spectacles on his nose, looked, then smiled. "That means these barrels hail from the Camfrey mill down Rochester way. And these"—he pointed to two dates stenciled on the barrel's side, one above the other—"give the date the barrel was filled and the date we received it. Tuesday last."

Cleo stood back and regarded the barrels, then turned to the manager. "If we fail to find ten barrels of a more recent delivery, we might come back."

Michael was standing close again. With an effort of will, she blocked her awareness of his warmth, his strength, and put her mind to sweeping the manager before her, up along the other arm of what had proved to be an elongated horseshoe-shaped path through the warehouse.

She did her best to distract the manager with questions, yet most of her attention was focused behind her—on Michael. A swift glance behind showed he was, indeed, checking the other barrels stacked at the end of the warehouse.

When she and the manager reached the cleared area inside the warehouse doors, she filled the time until Michael joined them by inquiring as to the other warehouses nearby and asking which the manager thought might have received a recent delivery of gunpowder.

Not wanting to lose a potential sale, the manager professed to have no notion.

From the corner of her eye, Cleo saw Michael nearing the end of the path. She pasted on a superior smile and graciously thanked the manager for his time.

The poor man all but deflated as she turned away. With Michael once again assuming his guard's position at her shoulder, she led the way out of the door and into the lane.

Michael reached past Cleo, opened the carriage door, and handed her up. He followed.

As he sat beside her, she asked, "No other barrels hidden away?"

He shook his head. "The closest I found were four barrels of flash powder. No gunpowder other than the barrels he showed you." He glanced at her. "But at least we've now seen what barrels of gunpowder look like, and that was interesting about the stamp—the brand."

"Yes. It seems that the barrels we're after should carry a stamp from some Irish mill." She glanced briefly his way, but didn't meet his eyes.

"So that's one warehouse searched." She peered out of the carriage window. "Should we try the one across the lane next?"

He hesitated, then said, "No. Let's drive to the end of the lane and check the place down there." When she arched her brows in question, he explained, "It's closer to the river and appears to be a more disreputable enterprise. It seems more likely to be the place we're seeking."

She sat back. "You mean because it looks run-down, it's more likely to have been chosen to provide a hiding place for items involved in an illegal plot." She cast him a distinctly superior look. "I should warn you that in business, more than in any other endeavor, looks can be and often are deceiving."

He humphed. "Let's see."

He leant out and told Tom to drive to where the lane made a dogleg into the area before the riverbank. Tom eased his horse forward and, a minute later, drew up before the front of Wallington's Warehouse.

Once again, they approached with Cleo in the lead and Michael hovering behind her shoulder. She prayed that, this time, he kept his lips firmly shut. She couldn't afford to be distracted by silly, ill-considered remarks.

To her relief, he obliged and remained silent as she swept into the warehouse. Outwardly shabby it might be, with its peeling paint and run-down air, but inside—as she had warned him might be so—Wallington's Warehouse was a hive of well-organized activity.

It was easily three times as busy as the first warehouse; aside from all else, there were two other customers waiting to be served ahead of them. Rather than make any push to be served immediately, she joined the queue and patiently bided her time while both she and Michael surveyed the scene.

Crates and containers of all sizes and shapes were stacked literally to the rafters. Several heavy ladders mounted on wheels were being moved by pairs of men; they positioned the ladders beneath certain stacks, then climbed up and brought down various goods—for the waiting customers in some cases, but to Cleo's experienced eye, the men also appeared to be filling orders.

This was a warehouse with a large clientele. She suspected the goods they stocked would turn over rapidly—probably too rapidly to allow any barrels to sit undetected for more than a few days.

Michael nudged her shoulder. When she glanced his way, he tipped his head toward the side wall. Cleo looked and saw barrels of the right size to be the ones they were seeking neatly stacked along the wall as far as she could see.

When she finally reached the head of the line, she found herself fronting a raised counter behind which a young woman, neatly dressed and with a pencil perched behind one ear, waited to serve them.

Cleo smiled. Although she trotted out the same tale she'd used at the previous warehouse, she delivered it with much less haughtiness.

The young woman confirmed they supplied gunpowder in hundred-weight barrels. However, they brought in only five barrels at a time. When Cleo inquired whether they had any barrels currently available, the young woman—clerk or manager, Cleo didn't know—consulted her inventory, which was kept in a set of neat ledgers of which Cleo approved. "We had five barrels delivered last Friday, but there's only three of them left." The woman glanced commiseratingly at Cleo. "I'm afraid that's all we have at present, Miss Hendon. We could order more in, but if you're in a hurry…"

They needed to search for barrels hidden in the warehouse. "Actually," Cleo said, "would you mind if we examined your barrels? The three of them left? Given our client's requirements, the only way we might be able to assemble ten barrels quickly is by orders to more than one warehouse." She glanced at the three people now behind her, waiting to be served, then looked at the young woman, who was very conscious of the queue. "We're happy to look at the barrels ourselves." Cleo pointed to the side wall. "They're just down there, I take it?"

The young woman looked relieved. "Yes, they are. And if you don't mind, Miss Hendon, that would be a great help. I'll be here if you need any further information or wish to purchase the barrels."

With a nod, Cleo stepped away from the counter. With Michael at her shoulder, she walked to the side wall and down the narrow avenue that ran parallel to it, leading deeper into the building. Although most of the barrels along the wall were of other goods—flash powder and different types of mineral sands presumably used in manufacturing fireworks or explosives—they found the three barrels of gunpowder easily enough. Tipping her head to one side, she read, "The Rochford Mill, Gravesend."

She stood and pondered the barrels, while Michael strode swiftly down the narrow avenue.

He returned in just a few minutes. When she looked at him, his expression set, he shook his head. "Other than what's along this wall, there are no barrels anywhere." He glanced around. "This place is so neat, they would stand out like..." He looked at her and improvised, "Masts on a ship."

A smile much like a smirk curving her lips, she refrained from saying "I told you so" and headed for the door.

As she drew level with the counter, she saw the young woman farewelling the last of the previously waiting customers. Although two others were approaching, Cleo paused to say, "I noticed you sell bunting." The customer who had been before her had left with a large parcel of crepe-paper ribbon. "We use quite a lot when our ships are involved in celebrations. I'll let my head clerk know we can purchase more from Wallington's."

The young woman beamed; getting an order, any order, from the Hendon Shipping Company, certainly in this area, would be something of a coup. "Thank you, miss. I'll be sure to warn my father to look out for it."

Happy to have made the day of another young woman working in a family-run business, Cleo smiled and led the way out into Morgan's Lane. "Well," she said, pausing to resettle her gloves, "that leaves the warehouse in the middle."

Halting beside her, Michael looked to where the largest of the three warehouses squatted midway down the lane on the opposite side. With its solid fence and iron-railing gates protecting the inner yard and the doors to the warehouse, it was the most impressive of the three establishments, but having now seen the activity behind the peeling façade of Wallington's, he had to admit that business-wise, appearances could, indeed, be deceptive.

He glanced down to find Cleo regarding him quizzically. "Let's walk while Tom turns the carriage."

After instructing Tom to turn the carriage in the open area by the river and then follow them to the warehouse, Michael took Cleo's arm, and together, they picked their way over the cobbles across the street and walked on to the larger warehouse.

They reached the gates, now standing open, as Tom drew the carriage to a halt beside them. Michael glanced at Tom. "Wait here." Then he looked at Cleo. "Shall we?"

She smiled and swept into the yard.

The doors to the huge warehouse were propped wide, but a sign directed them to enquire at the office, and an arrow below pointed toward the low building that filled the space between the warehouse and the front fence on the left side of the yard. A sign declaring the building to be the "Office" was fixed to the wall by the door. Two drays were pulled up on the opposite side of the yard, and several men trooped back and forth from the warehouse, loading small crates and parcels. Both drays bore signs identifying them as the property of one of the city's fireworks manufactories.

Michael paused for a second, taking in the activity, then lengthened his stride and caught up with Cleo as she made for the office door. He reached around her and opened it, and she walked in, head high, the haughty Miss Hendon to the fore.

The sight that met their eyes stopped them both in their tracks.

There were two customers heatedly arguing with two clerks over the raised counter. Farther back, in the area behind the counter, another older clerk and a red-faced man, rather better dressed than the three clerks, were conferring in frustrated and exasperated tones. Taking in the scene, with a hand at her back, Michael eased Cleo forward and to the side of the somewhat crowded area before the counter. When he pulled the door shut behind them, a bell tinkled, and the older clerk and the harassed-looking man glanced up.

Both blinked; the sight of Cleo and Michael, dressed as they were, was guaranteed to make the heart of any merchant in that area leap, and so it proved. The red-faced man pulled a handkerchief from his pocket, mopped his brow, then, tucking the handkerchief away, he came forward. "Yes, ma'am? How may we help you?"

Cleo introduced herself and repeated the tale of her client in Jamaica; this time, Michael noticed, although she wasn't as friendly as she had been with the woman at Wallington's and her delivery remained reserved and precise, she didn't assume any arrogant, haughty, or demanding attitude—judging, no doubt, that the harassed-looking man needed no further drama.

In that, she'd guessed correctly. When she reached her summation— her requirement for ten barrels of gunpowder, recently delivered and in excellent condition—the man groped for his handkerchief again. Then he realized where he was and to whom he was speaking and, with an attempt at dignity, offered Cleo a small bow. "Miss Hendon, we would be honored to fulfill your order..." The man's gaze slid to the older clerk, who had followed him and stood nearby. "Indeed, I daresay we can, but you see"—he looked at Cleo almost pleadingly—"my foreman has failed to arrive, and we're rather at sixes and sevens."

Michael closed his fingers around Cleo's elbow and lightly pressed, but she'd already realized; from the corner of his eye, he saw her open her eyes wide.

"Your foreman has *failed to arrive*? Where had he gone?"

"That's just it, miss. He shouldn't be anywhere else. Not to put too fine a point on it, he appears to have vanished." He hurried to add, "Not that I hire any wastrels here, which only makes this all the more puzzling. Ellis"—he indicated the older clerk—"called me as soon as he arrived, and the gates and the warehouse were still locked. I'm the owner—Mr. Shepherd at your service, miss." He bobbed again. "But as to the foreman, we've no idea what's happened to the man, but of course, to you that's neither here nor there."

"Indeed." Apparently deciding that searching for their ten barrels took priority over learning more about the missing foreman, Cleo fixed Ellis with a commanding eye. "I'm sure your inventory will allow you to show me all the barrels of gunpowder you have in stock."

"It will?" Shepherd turned a questioning look on his clerk.

Ellis nodded. "Indeed, sir. If you'll just allow me to find the lists…?"

Shepherd waved him off. Ellis scurried toward the rear of the office and pulled out a drawer in a cabinet. In less than a minute, he returned, waving two sheets. "These are the recent deliveries, sir—over the past two weeks."

Ellis proffered the lists. Before Shepherd could take them, Cleo reached over the counter and plucked the sheets from the clerk's fingers. "Perfect." She scanned the pages; Michael glanced at them over her shoulder, then left her to it.

Eventually, she raised her gaze from the lines of tiny writing and smiled at Shepherd. "You appear to have quite a large stock of hundred-weight barrels, Mr. Shepherd—exactly what we're looking for. But I will need to inspect them." With the lists, she waved toward the warehouse. "If we may?"

"Yes, of course, Miss Hendon." Shepherd was only too ready to fall in with her suggestion. He peeked at the lists she still held. "I'm fairly certain I can locate our stock of gunpowder."

With an encouraging nod, she gestured him on.

Shepherd led them into the courtyard just as one of the two drays pulled out of the gate.

The two men who had helped load it saw Shepherd and stopped. "Sir?" one asked.

Shepherd waved them to the other dray. "You continue with that. I'll take care of this."

"Aye, sir." The men trooped back into the warehouse, heading down the far alley of the three that led into the depths of the huge building.

Shepherd led them down the middle alley; as at Wallington's, crates, parcels, packages, and containers of all sorts were piled to the rafters. Michael spied many smaller barrels, but Shepherd led them on toward the rear of the vast space, to where another path ran across the warehouse, joining the ends of the three long alleys.

"Here we are." Shepherd turned and halted before a quite shocking number of hundredweight barrels of gunpowder. The stacked barrels filled the rear-facing space between the ends of two of the long alleys.

Cleo consulted the inventory, then looked at the towering pile. "According to your inventory, you have twenty-eight barrels here."

Shepherd was rapidly counting. "That seems to be the case." He looked quite pleased. "We have an excellent relationship with a number of mills. I'm sure some of these will meet your client's needs."

Cleo studied the barrels. "Let's see if we can identify which came from where and when."

Michael stood to one side and watched as, under her direction, Shepherd verified the brand and dates stamped on every barrel.

When Shepherd reached the last barrel and turned to them in something akin to triumph, Cleo met Michael's eyes. "So all the barrels delivered last week arrived on Tuesday or on Thursday, regular shipments from the normal mills, and all those barrels are present and accounted for."

Michael held her gaze. Had they got it wrong? Had Doolan delivered the barrels somewhere else?

But if he had, why was this warehouse's foreman mysteriously missing?

Coincidence?

Michael shifted closer to Cleo, lowered his head, and whispered, "Keep him busy. I'm going to search."

She nodded infinitesimally and turned to Shepherd. "I would also like to look at some fuses. I assume they're nearby?"

"Yes, indeed." Shepherd stepped back and ushered her up the right-hand alley. "They're this way. We have quite a selection…"

Michael turned and scanned the stacks of goods. He didn't believe in coincidences. Lips tightening, he surveyed all he could see, trying to spot suitable places where ten barrels might be hidden. This warehouse was enormous, but most of the stacked containers—crates, parcels, packages, drums, tins, and the like—were too small and varied to easily conceal ten barrels.

Except for the rear wall; it was covered in widely spaced shelving on which were stacked open crates of tarpaulins of every size, color, and weight.

He started at one corner, poking and peering behind the stacked material. When he came to a heavy tarpaulin draped over some crates, he flicked it back—and there they were.

The barrels—all ten of them—were lined up beneath a shelf in the middle of the rear wall, concealed behind the heavy tarpaulin which had been artfully arranged to look as though it was covering nothing more than more crates of tarpaulins.

Michael stared at the barrels, then he let the tarpaulin fall and walked to the end of the alley into which Cleo had gone. She and Shepherd were a little way along, examining fuses of various sorts. "Miss Hendon?"

Cleo's head snapped up, and she looked at him. "Yes?"

"It was ten barrels you wanted, wasn't it?"

"Yes." She was already poking the fuses back onto the shelf.

"In that case, you might want to take a look at these other barrels."

Shepherd frowned. "What other barrels?"

Cleo strode swiftly down the alley. Shepherd, puzzled, trotted behind her.

Michael walked back to the barrels, once more concealed. When Cleo and Shepherd joined him, he reached down, gripped the tarpaulin's corner, flung the covering back, and waved to the barrels. "Ten. All from the same source."

Cleo immediately crouched and checked the brand and the date stamp.

Shepherd's eyes had grown round; they threatened to pop from his head. "But—but…I have no idea where these barrels come from. I don't recognize that brand, and there's no date for arrival into the warehouse." He fished out the sheets of inventory Cleo had returned to him. In a furious flurry, he searched through the pages. "These barrels are not on our inventory."

"No matter." Cleo straightened and met Michael's eyes, then she turned to Shepherd. "These barrels are from an Irish mill, quite a good one. We'd had word that such a shipment had been brought into London last week, and we've been trying to find anything half as good. I'm so glad we've located these—I know these barrels will be just perfect for our client's needs."

"Yes, but…" Shepherd stared at her; he wanted to make the sale, yet wasn't sure he could. "I have no idea how these barrels came to be here." He looked down at the pages in his hands. "There has to be a supplier…"

"Indeed." Cleo gently took the pages from Shepherd, straightened them, then folded them and handed them back to him. "I suspect you'll discover your errant foreman accepted the barrels and forgot to note them down. No doubt the supplier will eventually invoice you, and then you'll know to whom to pass on the payment. Meanwhile, Hendon Shipping will take these barrels off your hands, and you can sit on the payment until whoever you owe it to claims it."

Shepherd blinked.

Cleo took the man's arm and inexorably turned him back up the central alley. "Meanwhile, if you don't mind, I'll have one of our gunners stop by and check the contents for quality."

Michael took a last look at the barrels, then flicked the tarpaulin down. He checked the barrels were once more concealed, then followed Cleo and Shepherd.

He caught up with them in time to hear Cleo say, "Now, you will put a firm hold on those barrels for Hendon Shipping, won't you?"

Shepherd was still blinking, but Michael wasn't surprised to hear him reply, "Of course, Miss Hendon. I'll let Ellis and the others know."

"Excellent! Now"—Cleo glanced at Michael while smoothly continuing to Shepherd—"just when did your foreman disappear?"

"We haven't seen him since he closed up on Wednesday," Shepherd replied. "I hoped he'd be here this morning, but no…"

Wednesday. Michael met Cleo's eyes. The foreman had been here to accept the barrels, then once he'd left the warehouse…

Cleo refocused on Shepherd. "Could I trouble you for your foreman's name and address? We'd like to check, just in case he's ill. He might be able to tell us from which supplier those barrels came."

Shepherd eyed her for an instant, as if he was starting to suspect that something was seriously amiss. Then he licked his lips and waved toward the office. "Ellis has the address, but we have sent around, of course. His wife says she hasn't seen him since he left for work on Wednesday morning…but maybe you, being a woman, will have better luck with her."

They all returned to the office. Shepherd directed Ellis to supply the name and address of the foreman, then brightened as he informed his clerks of the hold the Hendon Shipping Company had placed on the ten barrels of gunpowder sitting along the rear wall.

From the blank looks on Ellis's and the other two clerks' faces, they had no knowledge of the ten mysterious barrels, either.

Ellis handed Michael a folded piece of paper carrying the foreman's name and address.

Cleo thanked Ellis and farewelled Shepherd, then Michael ushered her from the office and shut the door behind them.

They walked to the gates and halted.

Cleo nodded at the paper. "What's his name, and where does he live?"

Michael unfolded the scrap, read, and felt his lips tighten. "He lives in Webb Street, which I assume is not far away—Tom will know." He drew in a long breath. "And as for the man's name—he's an O'Toole."

Cleo's brows rose. "Another Irishman."

"So it seems." He waved her to the carriage and followed.

CHAPTER 12

*W*ebb Street was only a few blocks away down Bermondsey Street; Tom had, indeed, known the location. He drew the carriage to the curb in the larger street, just past the corner with Webb Street.

Cleo waited for Michael to hand her down. Once on the narrow pavement, she straightened her skirts, then looked around. The area was solidly working class, the buildings an eclectic mix of shops, small factories, and row houses. From the smell in the air, the leather market with its associated tanneries wasn't far away.

She turned and looked down Webb Street. Narrow and cobbled, the street curved west. Michael took her arm, and they started along it, scanning the houses. The southern side of the street was occupied by a long row of workers' terrace houses, each no more than twelve feet wide, built cheek by jowl with their front doors opening directly onto the cobbles. They found O'Toole's door midway along the street.

Michael knocked on the panel. Halting beside him, Cleo noted the gravity of his expression. Neither he nor she held out much hope for O'Toole, but they had to check. Had to know.

Light footsteps approached. A bolt grated as it was slid aside, then the door opened, just a little way. A woman of similar age to Cleo looked out. Pale and wan, through red-rimmed eyes, she stared at them. "Yes?"

The fearful expectation carried in that one word was enough to tell them that O'Toole hadn't returned home.

Cleo stepped forward, drawing the woman's gaze. "Good morning. Are you Mrs. O'Toole?"

The woman nodded. "Yes, ma'am."

Something pushed against the woman's side, and she shifted, releasing her hold on the door. It swung wider, revealing a small boy who had flung himself against his mother's legs. Clutching her skirts, he looked up at Cleo and Michael with big, wide eyes.

Cleo smiled at the boy, then raised her gaze once more to Mrs. O'Toole's face. "We've just been to the warehouse, and we're trying to find out what's happened to Mr. O'Toole. I take it he's still missing?"

Mrs. O'Toole nodded, her anxiety easy to read. "I told Henry—the man Mr. Ellis at the warehouse sent to ask. Eddie didn't come home last Wednesday. Normally, he'd be home to tuck Joe here into bed, but...he didn't come back." The woman's gaze had dropped to the boy. With one hand, she smoothed his hair. "I know something's happened." Her voice had lowered; it sounded raw. "Eddie wouldn't not come home to me and the young ones—he's not that sort of man."

Cleo's heart contracted. O'Toole had been missing for five days; there was little likelihood of him turning up hale and whole, and Mrs. O'Toole knew it. She was trying to manage—to cling to normality for her children. Cleo glanced at Michael.

His voice gentle, he asked, "Mrs. O'Toole, did Eddie ever mention working for someone else on the side?"

Mrs. O'Toole blinked. She raised her eyes to Michael's face, her expression puzzled. "No. He never said anything about working anywhere but at the warehouse."

Michael felt as if he was treading on eggshells, but he had to ask. "I don't know if this has any connection—and it certainly wouldn't reflect in any negative way on Mr. O'Toole—but it might give us some idea of where else we might seek information. Was Mr. O'Toole ever involved with—or was he a sympathizer of—the Young Irelanders? We noticed his name is Irish."

Mrs. O'Toole frowned as if she was thinking. "Yes, Eddie's Irish. And he does talk sometimes about the movement and the government and all that, but as far as I know, it's never been anything more—just talk." She focused on Michael's face. "If it was one of my brothers or most other men, I'd say you should talk to his drinking mates, but Eddie isn't a big drinker—just the odd one on a holiday or in celebration. Most of his time outside work he spends here with us." She paused, then added, her voice low, "But there are a few old mates of his—Irish from the old days. They occasionally meet up, but I've never met any of them. I don't know who they are—well, other than that two are called Mick and one's a Pat." Her lips lifted in a sorrowful smile. "That's not much help."

"It might be more help than you know." Michael inclined his head. "Thank you for speaking with us."

"Here." Unobtrusively, Cleo had opened her reticule and found several shillings among the pencil ends and pins. She held them out. "For your time."

Mrs. O'Toole stiffened, but her eyes had locked on the shiny coins.

Then, from behind her, came a thin, reedy wail; she had a baby as well as the young boy.

Michael searched in his coat pocket, fished out a guinea, reached out and took the coins from Cleo's fingers, and held out the combined sum. He met Mrs. O'Toole's eyes. "Please, take them. Although I can't explain, you have helped us, and this is little enough in return. Whatever your resources, this will help until things sort themselves out."

At first hesitantly, then with greater determination, Mrs. O'Toole reached out and accepted the coins. "Thank you." Her voice was gruff.

She slipped the coins into her apron pocket, then gently pushed the boy inside, stepped back, and reached for the door.

Michael inclined his head in farewell, and Cleo murmured, "Good luck."

They were about to turn away when Mrs. O'Toole gripped the door and said, "If you find out anything…"

Michael met her eyes and nodded. "If we learn anything about what has befallen your husband, we'll make sure you're told."

"Thank you," Mrs. O'Toole whispered, then she closed the door.

Michael took Cleo's arm, and they set out at a brisk pace for the carriage.

A few seconds later, Cleo said, "I can't imagine what her life will now be like—the struggle it will become."

"Neither can I." Michael glanced at her face, saw the open concern and also the rapid calculation. "But we can't rescue everyone."

Slowly, she nodded. "No—but I can do something about rescuing her, and the little boy and the baby. I can ask around to see if any of our acquaintance have a place for a woman with two young children. She spoke well—she could easily be a housekeeper or a companion. Especially if she was willing to move to the country—better for her and for the children as well." As they neared the carriage, Cleo raised her head and drew in a deep breath. "I believe we should do all we can to…mitigate the impact on the innocents arising out of this dastardly plot. We might not be able to rescue everyone, and we can't erase the pain, but making bad better is something we can and should do."

Michael saw no reason to argue. "I agree we should do whatever we can." They reached the carriage, and he opened the door. He met Cleo's now distinctly militant gaze. "I'll send O'Toole's name and address to Scotland Yard. I'll suggest they get a description from the warehouse in case his body turns up in their morgues."

She nodded crisply and decisively. "Beyond that, our way forward is obvious—we need to push on and stop this plot. And bring to justice whoever is behind it and all the misery it has caused." She paused, then added, "When it comes down to it, exposing the perpetrators and seeing justice done is the only way we can avenge all those they've killed— O'Toole, Doolan, Johnny Dibney, and the Boynes, too."

"Indeed." His jaw setting, Michael helped her into the carriage.

They repaired to a coffee house on the Strand to appease their appetites and review all they'd learned. All they'd uncovered.

Any excitement over finally locating the barrels of gunpowder had been effectively doused by their concerns for the missing O'Toole. But as they sat in a corner booth and consumed an excellent fish stew, gradually, a sense of quiet triumph, of achievement, rose and eased their mood.

"I almost can't believe we were right, and the barrels were just sitting there, under that tarpaulin, waiting to be found." Michael pushed aside his empty plate and reached for his coffee cup.

Cleo had already finished her meal. She'd been sitting, sipping delicately at the rich brew and, he feared, thinking too much while waiting for him to clean his plate.

"Indeed." Over the rim of her cup, she met his eyes. "We should certainly take a moment to pat ourselves on the back, but now we have… what comes next? Should we organize for the barrels to be seized or, perhaps, replace the gunpowder with something else?"

He arched his brows. "That's not a bad idea." He considered, then amended, "Actually, that's a brilliant idea if we could manage it without raising any suspicions of the barrels having been tampered with." He paused, then went on, "Drake was very clear—insistent, in fact—that if we found the barrels, we were to leave them in situ, exactly as we found them, essentially as bait to trap whoever comes for them."

"I can see his point," Cleo said. "We all want to catch these villains. But replacing the gunpowder with something of similar weight—a mixture of sand and other powders, perhaps—would eliminate the risk posed by the gunpowder, yet still allow the barrels to be used as a lure."

Michael frowned. He turned his cup between his hands as he weighed the various possibilities. "While I would prefer to replace the gunpowder, that will be difficult to do without Drake's authority, and I hesitate to tamper with the barrels' contents without him knowing." He met Cleo's eyes and grimaced. "He might appear to share all with us, his irregular recruits, but there are always issues he plays close to his chest. There might be some reason we know nothing about that makes replacing the gunpowder a risk." He shrugged. "Albeit a risk of a different sort."

"Hmm." Cleo didn't look impressed, although Michael suspected her attitude was directed not at him but at Drake. "So we just sit and watch the barrels and wait?"

Lowering his cup, Michael nodded. He swallowed his mouthful of coffee and hastened to add, "And that's already in hand. My men are stationed all around Morgan's Lane."

She frowned. "I didn't spot any of them—are you sure they're in place?"

"Quite sure. But they can't watch from in the lane itself—precisely because, as you just pointed out, they would be spotted. If the barrels are to act as bait, then whoever comes to fetch them mustn't see the watchers. We can't afford to scare the villains—or their pawns—off." He hesitated, but if it helped to keep her away from Morgan's Lane… "The upshot is that we have to watch the area rather than the specific spot. I have men stationed in Tooley Street, and also…" Post by post, he described the cordon he'd placed around the warren surrounding Morgan's Lane. "The end result is that whoever comes for those barrels won't be able to take them anywhere without being seen and followed."

She was still frowning, but not as deeply; she now knew enough of the area to appreciate his strategy.

He wanted—very much wanted—to lay down the law and forbid her to return to Morgan's Lane, but he was well aware that any such attempt could, and most likely would, prove entirely counterproductive. He plowed on, "Now we know the barrels are there, I'll send word to my men—the confirmation that the ten barrels are, indeed, in Shepherd's warehouse will ensure that my army of watchers stay alert." He paused, then continued, "And as you so cleverly placed a hold on the barrels, the warehouse staff won't let them be removed during the working day. That will make things easier—we only need to maintain a strict watch during the hours in which the warehouse is shut."

"And the lane more or less deserted." Cleo met his eyes. "Did you notice that, although the streets around are packed with lodging houses and the like, and taverns, too, none of those fronted onto the lane? There weren't even any shops with living quarters above."

He nodded. "From our villains' point of view, a warehouse in Morgan's Lane really is the perfect place to store their barrels. Assuming they plan to remove their hoard at night, there's no chance of someone glancing out of a window and seeing them."

He looked across the table at her—and was visited by a vision of her in her boy's garb, skulking around Morgan's Lane in the dark. The thought shook him. Ruthlessly keeping his expression impassive, he set down his cup and slid along the seat. "Come on—let's go and see if Drake's back. If he is, we should report."

And if Drake was back, Michael would ensure Drake exerted some of his undoubted authority and forbade Cleo to lurk about in dark lanes. Either that or performed one of his amazing feats of manipulation to the same end. Or at the very least, came up with some way to distract her.

Blissfully unaware of his thoughts, Cleo nodded, collected her reticule and gloves, and rose.

～

"Unfortunately not, my lord." Hamilton, the Wolverstone House butler, continued imperturbably, "The marquess has yet to return, although he is expected soon."

"Soon, when?" Cleo inquired, not the least bit cowed by Hamilton's majesty.

Hamilton eyed her and decided it would be politic to reply. "We expect to see him within the next twelve or so hours, miss."

Cleo nodded. "In that case, I expect we'll be back tomorrow."

"Thank you, Hamilton." Taking Cleo's arm, Michael steered her out of the Wolverstone House front door.

Hamilton shut the door quietly behind them.

They halted on the porch. It was the middle of the afternoon. Michael cast a sidelong glance at his partner's face; she was thinking too hard again. "There's nothing more we can accomplish at the moment. Would you like me to drive you to your office?"

She considered, then shook her head. "No. There's not enough time left in the day to accomplish anything worthwhile."

"Clarges Street, then." Michael steered her down the steps to where Tom had the carriage waiting; he had things to do—men to see and brief, and deployments to review—but she didn't need to be involved in that.

They settled side by side in the carriage, and it moved off, into the traffic circling the park in the center of Grosvenor Square. The trip to Clarges Street wouldn't take long; Michael was aware he needed to make every moment count—in the right way.

He looked toward the window as if idly watching the façades slip past. "I've been revisiting what Drake said about the way this plot is being run, and in light of that, his prediction that the villains will be in no hurry to reclaim the barrels seems sound." *As far as it went.* As if thinking aloud, he went on, "He suggested we might well have a week's gap between the end of the first stage—the barrels arriving in London—and the beginning of the next, when presumably the barrels will be collected." *At the outside.*

He skated over that and rolled on, "If we accept that as the most likely scenario—the one Drake believes will eventuate"—*who knows what Drake believes?*—"then as the barrels were delivered on Wednesday, there's no reason to suppose they'll be moved tonight and possibly not even tomorrow night."

His partner arched her brows. After a moment, she said, "I suppose that's true."

Michael stretched out his legs and stared at the toes of his boots. "Of course, I'll keep my men in place, maintaining their surveillance." To further propagate the appearance of sharing all, he added, "I'll drop by later in the evening to check that all's well, but I don't anticipate seeing any action." He managed a faintly disaffected snort. "And as Drake will be home tomorrow, I daresay he'll take over, and we can leave the rest of this mission to him. If he behaves as he usually does, we'll have no choice—he's something of an autocratic dictator." He was perfectly willing to slander Drake in a good cause; indeed, given that cause, he doubted Drake would mind.

He wondered if he should further stress the lack of need for her to concern herself about the barrels that night, but decided that would be over-gilding his argument. The more he pressed, the more he risked provoking her resistance. Ladies, he'd long ago learned, possessed a contrary and powerful reactive streak.

Cleo swayed as the carriage took the turn into Curzon Street. The brush of Michael's shoulder against hers brought a sense of comforting reassurance. She'd heard everything he'd said, had taken it in, but her mind had been whirling with thoughts, not of the barrels but of the bodies. Of the people the villains seemed to have, with chilling cold-bloodedness, left strewn, dead, in their wake. And there was not only the dead to weigh in Justice's scale, but also those left behind—the potential disaster visited on Mrs. O'Toole, having to fend for and bring up her children alone. The innocents so carelessly harmed along the way.

What on earth could be worth doing so much damage to so many?

Or didn't the villains care?

She suspected it was the latter. And her commitment to seeing the blackguards brought to book hardened to granite.

"I assume you would like to accompany me when I report to Drake tomorrow?"

Michael's question jerked her back to the real world—to the carriage slowing outside her home.

"Yes." She glanced out of the window, then turned to him and frowned. "Of course."

His smile suggested he'd realized she'd been woolgathering. He reached to open the carriage door. "I'll come for you at eleven. We'll call on Drake and inform him we've exceeded his wildest expectations and located the barrels. Thereafter, the next steps will be his to define."

She nodded, waited for him to descend, then allowed him to help her to the pavement. He walked her to the door, waited until Morris opened it, then very correctly took his leave of her, bowing over her hand.

"Until eleven tomorrow." He released her and, with a smiling salute, turned and went down the steps to the carriage.

Cleo retreated into the front hall. She turned to the mirror and untied her bonnet. She heard the rattle of wheels as the carriage pulled away, then Morris shut the door.

"Your cloak, miss?"

"Please." Cleo let Morris lift the weight of the cloak from her shoulders.

"Will you be home for dinner, miss?"

"Yes. It'll just be me tonight." As it often was. She started up the stairs, idly swinging her bonnet by its ribbons, conscious that the quietness of the house—the certainty that she was alone and free of the company of all other members of her family—which had previously seemed such a boon, now felt...uninspiring. Unenlivening. There would be no reason for her to exercise her wits over the dinner table tonight. Instead of the relief she had previously felt over that situation, a sense of disaffected boredom hovered.

Her steps slowed as she pondered that.

She reached the half landing, turned to ascend the next flight, but then her feet halted, and she stared unseeing at the stairwell wall as her mind —having moved on to the question of what Michael would be doing tonight—replayed his comments on that subject.

He would be going to Morgan's Lane later, even though he believed —as did Winchelsea—that the barrels were unlikely to be moved that night.

She understood his and Winchelsea's reasoning; although she didn't know enough about how plots like this were conducted to evaluate their thinking, she was prepared to trust in their judgment. She could see no reason not to accept Michael's assessment on that score.

But...

He'd told her of the disposition of his men, and now that he had, she recalled enough from her visits to the area to appreciate his strategy. However, if he did "drop by" as he'd said he would, then he would secrete himself in the same shadowy alcove halfway down the lane. It was the only possible hiding place in the lane—at least for a man of his size.

She paused to consider the notion that he might simply check with his men as they maintained their cordon around the area and then depart for some club or the theater or some soiree...and dismissed it. Over the last days, she'd seen enough of the real Lord Michael Cynster, the man behind the reputation, to be absolutely certain that, when he reached Morgan's Lane, he would slip through the shadows and take up the only position from which anyone could be certain of getting a good look at whoever came to retrieve the barrels.

What if, contrary to all expectations, the villains came to fetch the barrels tonight?

Michael would be there, hidden in the alcove before the single door; he would be able to see anyone who approached the warehouse gates, and once the gates were open, he would be able to see anyone moving in the yard before the warehouse. He would see it all.

He would watch them leave...but what if he, or his men, unversed as they all were in the nuances of the commercial world, missed some vital clue? And because of that, lost the barrels' trail?

They'd worked hard to locate those barrels, and following them was the only avenue that might lead to the villains behind the plot in time to stop the gunpowder being used.

And they hadn't yet had a chance to replace the gunpowder.

Premonition didn't just tickle her nape; it rose and swamped her.

The barrels would be collected tonight; regardless of any oh-so-rational arguments to the contrary, she was suddenly immutably convinced that was so.

Then she thought of Michael, alone in the lane, very possibly the only one of the watchers who might get a clear view of any of the villains' faces.

And she thought of the villains who had so callously murdered everyone who might identify them.

She thought of the men who would come to fetch the barrels—men who had, to that point, proved so very cautious and canny. She tried to imagine being in their shoes.

They would check the lane, wouldn't they? As Michael had noted, Morgan's Lane might have been chosen because it contained the right sort of warehouse to temporarily hide the barrels, but it was also perfect in the sense that no room where people might be at night overlooked the lane.

If the villains thought to glance around to make sure that no one had seen them—not well enough to be any threat—they would see that alcove.

They might not realize anyone was in it, but if they were as careful and cautious as they had thus far proved to be, they would check.

And alone in the shadowed space, Michael would be trapped. The only one of his men who might see the villains approaching his hiding place would be the man he'd said would be stationed at the head of the lane—far too far away to be able to help Michael.

If the villains found Michael and realized he'd seen them, that he'd been watching them, for why else would he be there...

They'd already killed other aristocrats. Being a duke's son wouldn't save Michael.

But having someone else around might. Someone strolling in the lane, someone no one—Michael or the villains—would think twice about. Someone the villains wouldn't see as any threat. Someone slight enough to slip into the two smaller shadowed nooks she'd noticed.

Premonition transformed into compulsion.

Her chin firming, determination welling, Cleo refocused on the stairs and continued her upward climb.

~

After returning Cleo to her home, Michael had directed Tom to drive straight to the mews behind St. Ives House. Consequently, Michael entered the mansion via the rear garden and the kitchen door.

He paused by the side table in the front hall to pick up several envelopes addressed to him—invitations by the look of them. On hearing a door open, he glanced around and saw Crewe coming out of the library, a tray balanced on one palm.

Michael had spent the drive home contemplating his options regarding one over-adventurous lady. Impulse prompted, and he asked, "Is my father in?"

"Yes, my lord."

"And the duchess?"

"I believe Her Grace is closeted upstairs with her modiste."

Perfect. "Thank you, Crewe." Pocketing the invitations, Michael crossed to the library door. He opened it and went in.

Devil Cynster, Duke of St. Ives, sat behind the massive desk. He looked up as Michael shut the door and smiled affably. "We'd wondered where you'd got to. Sebastian said you were helping Drake with this latest mission."

Michael strolled across the room. "It's been…absorbing, to say the least."

His father watched with amused interest as, on reaching the desk, Michael subsided into one of the twin armchairs facing the mahogany expanse. When he failed to launch into speech, His Grace arched a black brow. "Can I help you with something?"

Michael met his sire's pale-green eyes. "As it happens, I hope you can."

When his father simply waited, Michael cudgeled his brains for the right words, then mentally threw his hands in the air and stated, "In order to locate some barrels Drake—and Sebastian and Antonia before that—have been searching for, I enlisted the aid of Miss Cleome Hendon."

His father's brows rose—both of them. "Jack and Kit Hendon's daughter?"

His lips firming, Michael nodded. "That's her. I needed her help, and there was no viable alternative, but in return, she insisted on…"

The essential elements of his dilemma—at least as he saw it—tumbled from his lips.

His father listened; after a time, he set down the letter knife he'd been wielding and sat back in his admiral's chair, the better to take in Michael's plaint.

"So, you see"—Michael raked his fingers through his hair—"I can't deny that she's fulfilled her part of the bargain, and although I could fall back on the letter of our agreement and insist she no longer actively participates in any action, knowing how much she longs for adventure—and I don't think it's only that, but that she wants to be involved in this sort of mission, contributing to something important and meaningful—then…" A moment passed, then he looked up and met his father's eyes. "I feel as if I'm skewered on the horns of a dilemma. I don't want to shut her out of things—I want to give her what she wants. But even more, I need to ensure that she's safe, and she won't be if she continues to involve herself in this mission."

His expression impassive, as it usually was, his father studied him for several seconds, then said, "And…"

Confused, he frowned. "And what?"

"And…why do you want to please her? To give her everything she wants? I assume that's what you're really saying."

He felt faint color seep into his cheeks. He held his father's gaze…but he knew he wasn't hiding anything from those far-too-perceptive eyes. He drew in a breath, felt it fill his chest, then forced himself to state, "I want to please her because I think she's the one for me, and when this is over—and assuming she's still speaking to me—then I intend to pursue her and, eventually, ask her to be my wife."

His father's lips slowly curved into a smile. "Excellent. I'm relieved to hear you've worked that much out."

He humphed. "Much good will it do me."

"Let's see if I can help." His father's gaze remained steady on Michael's face. "From what you've said and from what I know of her family, I take it Miss Hendon—"

"Cleo."

His father inclined his head. "Cleo is, in general parlance, a lady one might describe as being her own woman."

Michael nodded. "Very much so."

"And she knows where the barrels are?"

"She was instrumental in locating them."

"In that case, even if you intervene and—unwisely, I'm sure you'll agree—attempt to rein her in, how do you envisage preventing her from turning up and assisting with the surveillance?" Devil paused for only a second before going on, "The critical questions in such matters are these. First, is it in your power to stop her doing whatever she wishes? And second, regardless of whether you can, regardless of whatever you feel, is it in *her* best interests to do so?"

Silence lengthened as Michael digested that.

Eventually, his father continued, "When it comes to shielding them, as we feel compelled to, on some occasions, in some circumstances, our role becomes a matter of simply doing the best you can, coping in whatever way you can, protecting her however you can—meeting the challenge as well as you can—rather than attempting to constrain her." He paused, then, his deep voice lower, said, "You have to allow her the freedom to choose and act on her choice, because ultimately, you want her to choose you and to act on that choice."

Michael sat and let that wisdom sink in, then he heaved a huge sigh. He met his father's eyes and grimaced. "So it's as I thought." He pushed to his feet. "I was starting to fear that was the case."

His father grinned. With a chuckle, he waved Michael away. "Go and face your music. And good luck."

Michael paused; meeting his father's eyes, he inclined his head. "Thank you."

Devil smiled. "My pleasure."

With a resigned salute, Michael left the room.

CHAPTER 13

*W*ith his shoulders propped against the door in the darkness of the alcove in Morgan's Lane, the only way Michael could track the time was to strain his ears for the peals of the bells on the other side of the river. The nearest bell was in the Chapel of St. John in the Tower. The great bass *bong* reverberated over the water, penetrating the rising river mist to bounce off the stone walls all around.

After circling the area and checking the positions of all his men, Michael had walked calmly down the lane and stepped into the recessed doorway. Tom, tonight stationed at the head of the lane, had assured him that not even a rat had stirred over the previous half hour.

And not even a rat had stirred since.

As best Michael could judge, it was close to half past eleven.

Angling his head, he glanced up at the sliver of sky he could see. Tonight, the clouds were fitful, sometimes completely blocking the moon, at other times streaming over it in shreds and banners. Regardless, a perpetual veil remained, weakening what moonlight there was to a sullen glow. As for the streetlamps, they were too distant to shed much illumination on the warehouse gates. Still, with any luck, if someone turned up to fetch the barrels tonight, there would be light enough for Michael to see them in the lane before the gates, both when they arrived and, later, as they quit the scene.

It was the river fog that posed a greater concern; initially just a fine mist, it was gradually thickening. Even as he stared across the lane at the section of the warehouse he could see, a thicker tendril of fog drifted past.

Michael shifted and risked a glance down the lane and inwardly swore. Closer to the river, the visibility was already down to twenty or so yards.

All in all, it was an excellent night for illicit doings.

Regardless of his comments to Cleo, he'd had a sneaking suspicion that tonight would be the night. More, after hearing her brilliant suggestion of substituting something non-explosive for the gunpowder, suspicion had converted to conviction. Admittedly, his certainty wasn't based on any facts but rather on instinct, albeit informed by experience.

If the barrels remained in the warehouse until tomorrow, he had every confidence Drake would seize on Cleo's brilliant notion, and the barrels would no longer be a threat.

To Michael's mind, it was the likelihood of the barrels being rendered harmless provided they remained where they were until tomorrow that made the barrels being collected that night such a certainty.

In his experience, Fate never played fair.

Consequently, he was tense, on high alert, with his thumbs pricking and some primitive primal voice whispering a warning that, any minute now, the action would commence.

Ruthlessly, he quashed the temptation to lean out and scan the rest of the lane. He knew from where that temptation sprang; he was worried that, despite his careful words and her apparent agreement, Cleo would turn up. But his men had orders to keep their eyes peeled for a slight youth and, if they spotted one, to ascertain who said youth truly was, and if he proved to be her, to keep her back in relative safety with them. He'd set Tom at the head of the lane specifically for that purpose. If Cleo did arrive, he felt certain she would guess that he was in the alcove; he could rely on Tom to stop her before she entered the lane and came to join him.

Such arrangements, he felt, fell within the bounds of doing the best he could to protect her without constraining her. Constraining her would have been arranging with Morris, her coachman, and her groom to ensure she didn't leave Clarges Street. He felt he'd done reasonably well in adhering to his father's advice.

The minutes slid by. It was a cold night, but thankfully not yet freezing; his breath wasn't condensing in telltale puffs before his face.

Then a figure blocked out the faint moonlight. He nearly started and shifted, but the short, cloaked figure sauntered smoothly past, heading up the lane.

He blinked. A streetwalker. He hadn't expected to see a lady of the night in this area; as Cleo had noted, there were no taverns or even lodging houses fronting the lane. But from what little he'd seen in that fleeting glimpse—gold satin skirts and a froth of lace beneath an enveloping cloak with a hood—the woman belonged to one of the higher levels of the sorority; perhaps she was merely on her way home after a stint in the better streets over the river.

That made sense. Crossing the river by boat and walking up Morgan's Lane was a relatively safe route given there was no one around to accost her.

He wondered if she'd seen him; regardless, she hadn't paused, for which he was grateful.

The cold started to penetrate his greatcoat. He crossed his arms and settled his shoulders once more against the door, looked out through the shadows at the warehouse gates, and tried to tell his overstretched nerves that nothing was happening.

Not yet.

In an effort to make the minutes go more quickly, he conjured up a vision of Cleo in his mind and let his thoughts wander into imagining what she was doing, where she was, and what she was wearing at that very moment.

If nothing else, the distraction went some way toward alleviating the chill.

∼

The man wore the same hat he'd worn in the Dog and Duck tavern when he'd first met these men. Once again, he'd tugged the hat low over his face, but tonight, he was dressed in a greatcoat over a hacking jacket, breeches, and boots. The greatcoat, jacket, and breeches had seen better days—he had no idea where his man had found them—but when it came to the boots, he'd refused a shoddy pair and insisted on wearing his own.

There were some levels to which a gentleman could not be expected to stoop. Not even for the old man's plans.

As stipulated, he found two of the men in Black Lion Court, a block to the east of Morgan's Lane. At this hour, the lodgings and tenements were largely silent; no one paid any attention to the two empty drays drawn up to one side, the drivers waiting patiently with their huge horses semi-somnolent, heads hanging.

Quietly, he trotted his horse forward. He'd muffled its hooves and was pleased to note that the wheels of the drays and the heavier horses' hooves were likewise swathed with cloth.

He drew up beside the drays and nodded to the drivers. "Are the others in place?" He kept his voice low.

The man on the forward dray nodded. "Aye. They're waiting to help us unload and store, like you wanted."

Given they'd got the drays, there was no need to ask if they'd gained entry to the required yard.

The other driver confirmed that, assuring him, "And we've everything we'll need ready in the yard."

"Excellent," the man murmured.

"So where're we headed?" the second driver asked.

The man couldn't help his grin. "Just around the corner." He hadn't divulged their destination, deeming that a secret best kept until the last moment. "The barrels are in a warehouse in Morgan's Lane."

The man on the first dray frowned. "All the warehouses in Morgan's Lane are locked up tight of a night. How're we to get in without making any noise?"

"I have the keys." The man turned his horse. "Let's get going. Follow me." He was suddenly keen to see the barrels, to take possession and unerringly steer the old man's plot through this stage. Success would mean...a great deal. Especially if he performed well enough for the old man to grant him management of the final stage.

Somewhat to his surprise, he felt excitement mounting. Nevertheless, he kept the pace slow, walking his horse so that the drays' horses plodded slowly and ponderously behind, and the carts made only the slightest of rumbles as they rolled out of Black Lion Court, turned west into Tooley Street for just one block, then turned right into Morgan's Lane.

He drew rein outside the gates of the warehouse midway down the lane. A swift glance around confirmed the lane was deserted; all was still and as silent as the area ever was. Even better, fog was drifting up from the river; with any luck, it would soon blanket the area, providing an additional screen.

Reassured—indeed, heartened—he dismounted before the gates. The key slid into the hole in the padlock and turned smoothly; he was careful to catch both padlock and chain before they fell. After draping them on his saddle, he returned to the gates and pushed them wide, then he grabbed his horse's reins and led the beast into the yard. The drays followed.

After tying his horse to a ring near the office door, he returned to the gates and glanced—again—up and down the street, but there was no one in sight.

The man smiled, tugged his hat more firmly over his brow, then turned and walked quietly to the locked warehouse doors.

The second key slid home. He turned it, and the padlock disengaged. The two drivers were already beside him. At his nod, they opened the doors, and he led them down the central aisle.

And there the barrels were, exactly as the guardsman had described.

All was progressing smoothly—perfectly. While he oversaw the barrels' removal, he could, he felt, start composing his report to the old man.

~

Michael stared across the lane at the activity in the warehouse yard. His premonition had proved correct; he gave mental thanks he'd paid it due attention.

He'd now seen enough of registered carters' carts, especially those of the gunpowder carters, to know that the two carts presently being loaded with the barrels of gunpowder weren't of that type. The men who had driven the carts weren't any of the carters they'd met, either. Who the drivers were was a mystery.

As for the man who had led the pair into the yard and into the warehouse, Michael was certain he wasn't the missing foreman.

Aside from all else, he rode too well and walked with an arrogant assurance Michael recognized as inherent to the aristocracy. More, the man's horse was of a quality impossible to imagine as coming from any jobbing stable, and even in the poor light, his boots marked their wearer as a gentleman of the upper echelons. A foreman's annual wages wouldn't be enough to buy those boots.

Michael hadn't missed the implication of the man opening the gates and the warehouse with keys—presumably the missing foreman's keys— either; that he was watching one of the principal villains seemed certain.

That realization made it harder to resist the impulse to take advantage of those moments when all three men were in the warehouse to slip through the shadows and get closer—close enough to get at least a glimpse of the leader's face.

With every barrel brought out and loaded onto the carts, that impulse grew more insistent. More urgent.

From across the lane, the man's face was too shadowed by the low brim of his hat for Michael to have any hope of recognizing him.

Among his peers, both family and friends, Michael's nickname was "the huntsman," a moniker earned not just because of his almost uncanny ability to stalk game over hills and moors but also because of his exploits in the ton with a different sort of quarry. The impulse to hunt the villain he could see before him was well-nigh overwhelming, but…Drake's directive rang in his mind.

If the villain or his men caught the slightest glimpse of Michael, he—his type—would be as instantly recognizable to them as the social status of the leader was to him. They wouldn't allow him to slip back into the shadows, and in the resulting melee, if Michael failed to hold the leader—perfectly possible given it would be three to one for too long—the entire plot might go to ground. Drake and the rest of them would lose the trail and never know when or where it might surface again—and there was no saying that the ten barrels being loaded into the carts were the only explosives the villains had at their disposal.

The perpetrators, all of them, had to be caught—now, in the next days, before the plot came to fruition.

No one would thank him for any overeager misstep now—not when they'd finally sighted the bastards.

Holding his position and contenting himself with what little he could see from across the street required the exercise of significant will, but Michael grimly clung to the concealing shadows and watched.

And waited.

On hearing the muted thuds of horses' hooves approaching, Cleo had taken advantage of a swirl of fog to slip across the lane, trusting the wafting cloud to hide her from Tom's sharp eyes, and had squeezed into a tiny space between two buildings. Her hidey hole—it was no more than that—was on the same side of the lane as Shepherd's warehouse and closer to Tooley Street, out of Michael's view; he would have to step out of the recessed doorway to look in her direction.

She'd left her carriage, along with her coachman and groom, in a street off Tooley Street; they'd approached the area from the south, outside the cordon of Michael's watchers. She'd walked onto Tooley Street almost opposite the mouth of Morgan's Lane and had spotted Tom tucked beneath an overhang. She'd turned and walked the other way. Pulling her cloak tight about her, she'd walked purposefully across Tooley Street and then along it, crossing the mouth of Morgan's Lane to turn down the next lane to the west. Grateful for the rising fog and the lateness of the hour, she'd picked her way through the shadows and had eventually reached the open area by the river at the end of Morgan's Lane.

From there, ignoring Michael's men who she assumed would be watching, she'd more overtly assumed her guise of a lady of the night and had sauntered up Morgan's Lane. She'd wanted to confirm that Michael was, once again, watching from the recessed doorway; just the barest glance into the shadows there and she'd seen his darker figure in the gloom. She'd walked on without pause; when he hadn't stormed out and seized her, she'd breathed easier, had smiled a small smile, and more confident in her disguise, had loitered in the mouth of the narrow alley beside the first warehouse they'd visited, until she'd heard the approaching hoofbeats, and the fog had given her the opportunity to slip across the lane.

Surreptitiously, she'd watched a rider, followed by two drays, clop past. She'd cautiously peeked along the lane and watched as, with his hat pulled low, shielding his face, the rider had opened the gates of Shepherd's warehouse with keys. He'd gone into the yard, and the drays had rumbled in after him.

She'd waited, then had held her breath when the rider returned to the gates and looked up and down the lane, but he hadn't spotted her.

After he'd retreated, she'd waited a full minute before stepping out of her refuge. With her eyes trained on the open gates, she'd hugged the front of the buildings, edged as near as she'd dared, then paused to review the situation.

She could hear soft grunts and the clink of shifting harness as, presumably, the men heaved the barrels onto the drays. From where she stood, courtesy of the paling fence, she couldn't see into the yard; she would have to walk right up to the gates to get a clear view. Michael, on the other hand, would be able to see what was going on before the warehouse doors, but from across the lane, with the rider wearing his hat pulled so low, Michael would have no chance of getting a decent look at the villain's face.

She, on the other hand, might.

She hadn't joined Michael in the shadowed alcove for precisely this reason; he would never have allowed her to get closer to the men—close enough to the rider to see his face.

And Michael couldn't risk being seen himself; no matter how he was dressed, one look at him and all three men would know they were in trouble, and there was no saying what might happen then.

It was the rider they needed to know more about; he wasn't a local, nor was he a carter or anyone like that. She felt sure he was a gentleman, and given he'd had the keys, which she assumed he must have taken from the presumably dead foreman, then for her money, the rider was likely to be one of the principal villains. One of the killers behind the plot.

She wasn't reckless; she'd taken precautions. Yet now the moment for action had come, she was conscious of the hollowness of fear, a cold, empty feeling in the pit of her stomach. But she'd wanted adventure and now wanted even more to help bring the villains down; this was her chance.

She stepped away from the wall, rearranged the fall of her cloak so the front of her was exposed, then she squared her shoulders and started walking toward the open gates.

Her office was in the City; while traveling there and back from Mayfair, she saw ladies of the streets promenading on a daily basis. She mimicked their way of moving, the insolent sway of their hips and their almost languid saunter; she'd always been excellent at charades.

By the time she reached the open gates, she was deeply immersed in her role.

She paused in the opening, to one side, and waited.

The two drivers were carefully settling a barrel on the back of one dray; they glanced at her, but thereafter ignored her. Three of the barrels on the dray had their brands turned her way; she recognized the shape of the Irish mill's stamp. The men were, indeed, taking the barrels brought up from Kent.

As the pair turned back to the open warehouse doors, the rider emerged from the dimness. "Make sure every barrel is secure—we don't want any unnecessary accidents."

Swiftly, Cleo scanned the man's face—what she could see of it below the shadow cast by his hat's brim; his accents confirmed that he was well born.

"Don't worry," one of the drivers replied. "We've roped them in, and they're heavy. They ain't going to shift about."

The rider nodded, then he saw Cleo—or rather, her alter ego.

She immediately tipped up her chin and shifted her shoulders back and forth, then she raised one hand to her hip and tilted her head in invitation, as she'd seen the ladies of the streets do, posing their age-old question.

The rider's gaze raked her. For an instant, he seemed to actually consider...then, curtly, he shook his head.

Cleo's lungs had seized; she tentatively eased in a breath, then shrugged lightly. Resuming her hippy saunter, she walked on down the lane.

∼

The rider watched the woman walk off. He hadn't noticed any whores plying their trade nearby, but then, he hadn't been looking.

That said, the woman had seemed unusually appealing, with a glow still in her cheeks. Perhaps she was a high-class ladybird making her way home.

He humphed and turned to the drays. If his current job hadn't been so important, he might have been tempted.

Perhaps later...if not her, then some other appealing wanton. He knew of a few who would be happy to accommodate him, and he wouldn't even have to pay.

The first dray was fully loaded with its five barrels. He tested the lashings, found them secure, then returned to the warehouse to supervise the removal of the rest of the load.

∼

Cleo kept to her lazy, lady-of-the-night stroll. Her heart was thudding—pounding—and her nerves were taut as bowstrings as she waited to see if the rider came after her.

But no sound of footsteps trailed her.

She drew in a deeper, still-shaky breath.

She hadn't seen all of the rider's face, but the moonlight had illuminated his chin—and the fine scar that ran from one corner of his lips, angling back to the point of his jaw.

She would know him when she saw him again.

Albeit muted by the prevailing danger, triumph welled; she'd achieved that much.

Distinctly pleased with herself, she glanced toward where she knew Michael would be watching and smiled.

Then she drew level with the tiny ginnel she'd spotted earlier and marked as a possible place to hide. She glanced back at the still-open gates, but no one had yet emerged.

Swiftly, she pulled close her skirts and cloak and stepped into the ginnel. She had to wriggle to fit, then she reached back and tugged the cloak's hood further forward, so if she ducked her head, her face would be hidden.

Then she settled to wait. The rider and the drays would come out into the lane and trundle up it—away from her position—to Tooley Street, where Michael's men were waiting to follow them. Once the rider and drays turned into Tooley Street, Michael would emerge, intent on following them as well, and she would go out and join him.

All perfectly safe. She—and he—just had to wait.

◆

Michael gawped; he couldn't seem to get his mouth to shut as he stared across the lane.

He'd half expected Cleo to turn up—dressed as a lad.

It had never occurred to him—never would have—that she might saunter into the heart of the action in the guise of a whore.

A whore! Good Lord! Even his mental voice was weak with shock.

He could barely believe that she'd walked right past him—within arm's reach—and he hadn't known it was her. Until she'd looked his way —looked directly across the lane to where he stood hidden—and smiled, he hadn't recognized her.

Some small part of his brain pointed out admiringly just what a feat that was—what a testimony to her histrionic skills. She'd fooled him, his senses, at every level; at no point—not until that swift smile—had she dropped the mask she'd chosen for the night.

Sadly, that small center of appreciative calm was submerged beneath a raging tide of clamoring emotions, powerful and roiling and battering his mind to the point he could no longer think.

He could barely breathe.

Finally, he snapped his mouth shut; his lips settling into a grim line, he forced air into his lungs and exhaled—then did it again.

He had to regain control of his wits; this was too important to cock up, and with Cleo's arrival, the importance quotient had escalated to infinity.

Yet his protective instincts were on a rampage; did she have any idea what might have befallen her in this area, dressed like that? If he could have reached her, he would have shaken her. What if that damned villain had fancied her and tried...? He—Michael—would have stormed across the lane and blown their surveillance to kingdom come.

His fists clenching, he dragged in another breath and fought to steady his whirling head, to cool his overheated emotions.

He had to refocus. Now. Before anything further occurred.

By angling his head, he could see Cleo's position, although he couldn't any longer see her. But from the way she'd backed into the tight spot, he assumed she was still there, facing the lane and waiting for the rider and carts to move out.

She was safe enough for the moment. And from that smile she'd sent winging his way, he assumed she'd seen something potentially useful about the rider or the carts.

His overwhelming fear for her receded somewhat, and his mind calmed.

He shifted his gaze to the warehouse. The doors were still open. The drivers were busy lashing barrels on the second cart. Michael swiftly counted; all ten barrels were now loaded, five on each cart with their weight distributed as evenly as possible. Although the two carts were sturdy, they didn't have the extra supports built into the gunpowder carters' carts.

Then the rider emerged from the warehouse. He glanced at the carts, then turned and closed and locked the doors.

Rapidly, Michael reviewed his options. Seizing the barrels wouldn't be good enough; they had to learn who was behind this before more people wound up dead and the plotters succeeded in advancing their plans all the way to attacking their target.

He understood the reason for Drake's directive, but with his protective instincts in full flight, offended to their core, it was damned hard to rein them in enough to clear his mind and assess where they—he, Cleo, and the mission—now stood.

This, a small voice whispered in his mind, was what his father had meant. *"...on some occasions, in some circumstances, our role becomes a matter of simply doing the best you can, coping in whatever way you can, protecting her however you can—meeting the challenge as well as you can..."*

And then the part that had truly hit home. *"You have to allow her the freedom to choose and act on her choice, because ultimately, you want her to choose you and to act on that choice."*

He had to make the right decision—for the mission, for her, for himself.

According to his father's wisdom, he needed to follow his preordained plan, hold his position, and allow Cleo to contribute as she would.

He could protect her. He couldn't block her.

Across the lane, the rider had fetched his horse, and the drivers had scrambled up to their benches.

The rider said something, and as the drivers picked up their reins, the rider waved them to precede him out of the warehouse gates.

Michael set his jaw, watched, and waited.

And told his still-pacing protective self that the carts would soon rattle away up the lane, and the rider would follow, and Cleo would remain safe in concealment until rider and carts had vanished.

On that score at least, the worst was over. Once the rider had gone, she would be safe.

The drays lumbered out of the warehouse gates and turned north, toward the river.

The drivers held their horses to a slow plod, no doubt hyperaware of the weight of the barrels at their backs.

The man watched the drays set off, then drew the gates closed and locked them. Through the fog, he heard the city's bells toll midnight— plenty of time in hand for his four helpers to accomplish the rest of the night's work. He tucked the keys into his breeches pocket, then mounted and nudged his horse in the drays' wake.

Within a few paces, he had to rein in to a plodding amble at the rear of the second dray. Then he and the second dray came to a halt as they waited for the first dray to carefully negotiate the tight turn to the right, into the even narrower lane that led to the northern end of Black Lion Court.

Initially, he'd been puzzled by the old man's plan—the barrels had surely been safe where they were—but once he'd learned of the next and final act in this second stage of proceedings, all had made irrefutable sense, as everything the old man planned always did. In his earlier life, before he'd become chair-bound and had worked within the government, he'd been a force to be reckoned with. Clearly, he hadn't lost any of the acumen with which he'd long been credited. It was almost a pleasure to follow such carefully crafted plans.

The rider glanced ahead to the left, to where the lane joined the open area before the river. The fog lay thicker there. Nothing moved in the gloom.

The first cart had cleared the corner. The second cart jerked into motion again.

The rider faced forward and nudged his horse to keep up. As he started moving again, to his right, from the corner of his eye, he glimpsed a flash of brightness.

Gold satin. A sliver revealed—just for a second—as the clouds scudded overhead and moonlight briefly shone through.

He had the presence of mind not to turn his head and look. As the second cart slowed again to negotiate the turn and he kept his horse close, he tried to fathom what the damn female thought she was doing, wedged into that nook in the dark.

Was she spying on them?

But how could she have known they would go that way? Admittedly, she'd seen them loading up, but if she'd decided to follow them—why, he couldn't imagine—wouldn't she have assumed they would go up the lane, not down?

Regardless, she'd been there and had seen them leave.

Perhaps she was simply curious.

Or perhaps she was a spy.

As he steered his horse toward the corner, he reflected that, if she continued following them, it would be easy to find out.

～

Cleo had held her breath when, instead of going up the lane and away, the two drays had rumbled down the lane and past her position.

She hadn't dared breathe when the horse had walked past, and the rider had pulled up just a yard farther along from where she stood. With her cloak wrapped about her, her head down, and her hood well forward, shielding her face, she'd told herself he wouldn't see her even if he looked.

She had no idea if he had glanced her way; she'd been able to see only his horse's legs and hadn't dared raise her head and risk looking directly at him.

Finally, after what had felt like agonizing minutes but likely had been less than two, the drays had rolled on, and the rider had followed without any worrying pause. Without any sign whatever that he'd spotted her.

She raised her head, breathed deeply—and wondered why the drays had gone the wrong way. The unexpected way.

Michael's men were stationed all around the area, so the drays couldn't leave it without being seen and followed, but why were they taking such a route? One that led deeper into the warren of narrower lanes and alleyways.

Drake's comment, repeated by Michael, replayed in her mind—that so much about this plot hadn't followed any predictable pattern…

What if they lost sight of the barrels inside the warren? What then?

Was there some other way of transporting barrels they hadn't thought of and so hadn't blocked?

She could hear the slow, muffled clop of the rider's horse—he was still in Morgan's Lane and hadn't yet turned the corner. She didn't dare lean forward and peer out; as he went around the corner, if he glanced up the lane, he would see her.

For the moment, she was stuck, but the instant the rider was around the corner, she would be free to slip out and creep along the buildings on this side of the lane until she could peek after the drays. Michael, in the doorway on the other side of the lane and much farther from the corner than she, would be forced to remain where he was until the rider was a good deal farther along the secondary lane—just in case the man glanced back.

If the rider and drays turned this way or that before Michael reached the corner…

The tone of the muffled hoofbeats changed. Dragging in a breath, she eased forward and looked out of the ginnel—and through the thickening murk, saw the rear of the rider's horse pass slowly into the narrower lane.

She didn't wait to think further; she slipped out and, holding her cloak tightly about her, quickly crept along the front of the buildings.

They—she or Michael—had to keep the barrels in sight.

And he would come after her the instant he could.

He was going to lose his mind.

His heart in his mouth, Michael watched the dim figure that was Cleo reach the end of Morgan's Lane where, a block back from the river, a narrower lane led east.

From scouting the area, he knew the lane led to the north end of Black Lion Court—a place notorious because of the many ways in and out; thieves on this side of the river regularly used its mazelike qualities to lose pursuing constables.

He had no idea why the villain had chosen that as his route, but at that moment, he really didn't care.

What he did care about was Cleo, but the damned rider was moving so very slowly, still keeping at the rear of the second cart, that even with the distraction of the fog, Michael didn't dare risk breaking from the shadows.

His gut tightening and tying itself in knots, he watched Cleo inch to the corner, then carefully peer around.

He could still see the rider—just. The man didn't turn, didn't glance back—didn't see her.

Finally—*finally!*—the rider moved on, farther down the lane, and Michael could quit the alcove.

With swift strides, he crossed the lane and headed for Cleo. Courtesy of the uneven cobbles, he didn't dare run. His men were well positioned; he could leave watching and following the barrels to them.

He would follow Cleo; she was his to protect.

CHAPTER 14

*T*he lane the drays had taken wasn't that long. Cleo peered through the increasingly dense, sulphurous fog and watched the second dray lumber to the right around the next corner—turning toward Tooley Street, although that thoroughfare was quite some way away. The rider followed without glancing back.

Cleo turned her head, looked up Morgan's Lane, and saw Michael striding toward her. Reassured he was following and accepting it was critical that they kept the barrels in sight, she turned and hurried around the corner and on along the short, narrow lane.

Somewhere ahead along the next lane, she could hear the low-pitched rumble of the drays' muffled wheels. With so many alleys and lanes leading this way and that, they couldn't afford to allow the little cavalcade out of their sight—or at least, out of their hearing.

There was no streetlamp in the narrow lane. What moonlight there had been had largely been obliterated by the thickening clouds and the fog.

She reached the next corner and paused. She could still hear the wheels rumbling, but the sound was fading. Were the drays turning again? She glanced back along the lane, but Michael hadn't yet appeared.

Increasingly dense, the fog was funneling up from the river, finding its way through every space; the chill dampness brushed her cheeks with icy, clammy fingers, but it would give her some cover until Michael reached her.

She drew in a breath and quietly edged around the corner. Hugging the front of the buildings along that side of the slightly larger lane, she crept forward. Dimly through the fog, she could see the rear of the second dray fading into the murk.

She quickened her pace. Farther along, a single streetlamp glowed a faint, sickly yellow; all its light seemed to achieve was to turn the shadows a deeper shade of dark.

Where was the rider? The fog was dense enough to obscure shapes, but she didn't think he was following the dray—perhaps he was now between the drays or even leading them.

She blinked. The drays seemed to be vanishing up ahead. She hurried on.

An arm snaked out of a gap between two buildings, circled her waist, and yanked her off her feet—clamping her against a rock-hard body. She opened her mouth, but before she could scream, a gloved palm slapped over her lips.

She flung her head back—connecting with a hard shoulder—and caught a glimpse of the brim of a hat. The rider! She struggled furiously, fighting to get free.

A deep, low chuckle sounded in her ear. "You can scream all you like, my lovely, but trust me, in this place, no one will come to your aid."

That's what you think.

But given help was near, and she knew it...

Slowly, she stilled—until she stood unmoving in his hold.

"Good to see you're not without intelligence. So"—the hand covering her lips lifted away—"you may now tell me who you are and why you're here. Who are you working for? My cousin, perchance?"

His cousin? Cleo frowned. "I have no idea who your cousin is."

The rider sucked in a breath. Then his every muscle tensed.

The arm about her waist tightened, and in the next blink, his other hand returned, this time brandishing a knife. He laid the blade against her throat as he snarled, "Tell me—*who sent you?* Who knows about...our little enterprise?"

Her head pressed against his shoulder in an instinctive effort to get away from the knife, Cleo struggled to breathe. She could hear the panic reverberating in his voice. Her accent! He'd realized she wasn't some doxy happening to wander by.

The blade of the knife felt cold and sharp. Carefully, she swallowed and, with her pulse thundering in her ears, managed to get out, "I'm not working for anyone. Women like me don't work for others."

The words had tumbled out without any real thought, a simple statement of fact.

The rider cursed. Abruptly, the arm at her waist vanished, and instead, he grabbed the top of her hood, his fingers sinking into her hair beneath. Shifting the knife from her throat, he used his grip on her hair to swing her around so he could look into her face.

Cleo forgot about the knife he still held. Her lips setting grimly, she stepped forward and kneed him hard between his legs.

Her aim was slightly off, but the blow was sufficient to make him freeze and suck in a tortured breath. His grip on her hood eased.

She jerked free and quickly took several steps back.

Teeth gritted, he raised his head. His gaze pinned her, and with a low growl, he came for her; the knife blade flashed in his right hand.

She didn't have time to scream before she was shoved aside, and Michael was there.

He caught the man's wrist and twisted it sharply. The man uttered a harsh sound, and the knife clattered to the cobbles.

The man swung a fist at Michael's face—which he half dodged. Then Michael struck back with a punishing blow to the man's stomach.

But the man wasn't going to go down without a fight. He swung again, and Michael blocked the blow.

Cleo stepped back, giving them space. Through the wreathing fog, she watched as they traded punches. To her educated eyes—she had three brothers—Michael definitely had the upper hand, but the other man wasn't a novice, either. He got in a succession of blows that forced Michael to regroup.

The man seized the moment to step back—but not to flee. Instead, he reached beneath his greatcoat and drew out a sword.

Cleo's eyes grew round. Her father had a sword like that—a long, curved, cavalry saber.

The man grinned evilly and slashed.

Michael leapt back.

Cleo remembered that he always carried his cane-cum-swordstick. Always; he'd even had it in the lane the other night. Against a saber, it wouldn't be much, but it would be better than nothing. He must have set the cane down. Frantically, she searched the cobbles where he must have paused before pushing her aside...*there*!

The cane lay on the ground on the other side of the two men.

The villain was grinning from ear to ear and making a great show of slashing his saber through the air. He advanced one step, still limbering up. "I'm going to enjoy slicing you to ribbons."

Michael, his gaze locked not on the swinging blade but on the man's face, retreated a step. His expression was set, graven. Without glancing at her, he grated, "For God's sake, Cleo—*run*, damn it!"

There was no way she was leaving him. She'd never reach Tooley Street in time to summon his men to help him; he would be dead long before she got back.

She set her jaw and did as he'd ordered.

She grabbed up her skirts and ran straight toward the pair of them.

Her sudden rush shocked them both; both shifted back—and she pelted between them.

She skidded to a halt on the slimy cobbles and, her back to both men, scooped up Michael's black cane. A quick twist of the head and she pulled the concealed rapier from its sheath—in the same instant, she smoothly turned and flung the hard sheath directly at the villain's head.

Instinctively, he ducked.

She continued her pivot and tossed the rapier, hilt first, to Michael.

Michael could barely believe what she'd done, but he didn't have time to roar at her. He seized the hilt, settled his hand about the stag's head, and before his opponent could recover and launch an attack, lunged straight for his chest.

The man got the saber up just in time to parry the thrust.

Michael inwardly swore. That had been his best chance to do serious damage. Now...

He feinted and thrust, parried as best he could. Although he'd carried his grandfather's swordstick for years, who the devil fought with a sword these days?

Cavalrymen. He would take an oath this man had been one—hence the sword and the ability to use it.

He was in deep trouble. A rapier against a saber was not a winning proposition. He had to find some opening or some way to tip the scales. The only reason he'd managed to hold the man at bay thus far was his years of no-holds-barred sparring with Sebastian.

He spared a fleeting thought for this unanticipated benefit of having an older brother who was a touch taller, had a longer reach, and happened to be an expert fencer. In order to hold his own, Michael had learned every underhanded trick in the book.

He used them shamelessly. Kicking, lashing out, and doing everything he could to keep his opponent off balance.

But he didn't know for how long he could keep the dance going, not without sustaining major injury. He'd already taken several cuts, but as far as he could tell, none were yet bleeding badly.

He knew Cleo was somewhere near, but he couldn't take his eyes off his opponent long enough to find her in the gloom. He knew she hadn't run; he hadn't heard her footsteps retreating.

He wished she would go; this wasn't going to end well, and if he had to die, he didn't want her dying, too—

A silver flash whizzed past him.

The man's face registered shock, and he pulled back. His left hand rose toward his upper right arm—to the slash that had appeared there.

Damn—she'd thrown a knife! And she'd nearly pinked the bastard, even though he'd been moving at the time.

What other weapons did she have?

Michael launched a fresh strike, pressing whatever advantage he might now have even though he didn't expect that to be much, but it was soon apparent that Cleo's strike had done enough damage for the man to have lost telling strength in his sword arm—although he retained enough to keep Michael at bay.

Gritting his teeth, Michael searched for an opening, found it, and tossing caution to the winds, closed, and ran the rapier's blade beneath the saber's hilt until the rapier's hilt hit the saber's blade—then quick as a thought, he twisted the stag's head and locked it over the edge of the other blade, stepped back, and with an almighty wrench, hauled the saber from the man's grasp, and with a flick of his wrist, sent the saber flying into the darkness.

Michael sucked in air; he was close to winded, and so was his opponent.

But the man flashed a sickly smile, and as Michael straightened, the bastard stepped back, reached into his coat, and pulled out a pistol.

Cleo already had her fingers wrapped about the ivory grip of the American pistol concealed in her skirts. She whipped the gun out and pointed it at the villain.

From the corner of her eye, she saw Michael's hand clearing his pocket, a pistol gripped tightly.

The man had his barrel leveled on Michael's chest. The man's trigger finger was already flexing.

"No! Here!" Cleo fought not to close her eyes as she pulled the trigger.

Three shots rang out, virtually simultaneously. The combined sound was deafening in the enclosed space, ricocheting off the walls all around them.

The fog swirled as if in reaction, suddenly thickening to the point that they were only shadowy figures to each other.

She peered through the murk and saw their adversary slowly crumple, then he collapsed in a heap on the cobbles.

Then Michael loomed beside her. His face a graven mask, he took one raking look at her, then he hauled her into his arms.

He clutched her to him. "Tell me you're all right." The harsh demand was muffled in her hood.

"I'm entirely unharmed." She tried to pull back to examine him, not that she could see much in the foggy gloom, but he hugged her tight, tighter, then he eased his hold, raised his head, and put her from him.

She looked at his face, then followed his gaze to the figure on the cobbles.

They approached cautiously.

Michael bent and removed the man's pistol from his now-lax grasp and slipped the weapon into his own pocket. Inside, he was still reeling, feeling hot one minute and chilled the next, with more emotions than he'd known he possessed buffeting him, desperately clamoring for release.

Straightening, he looked down at his erstwhile opponent. The man's hat had tipped back, revealing features that declared their owner was probably English and, almost certainly, well born. His greatcoat had fallen open during the fight; two holes, both dark with blood, decorated the left side of his chest.

Cleo crouched by the man's other side. Gingerly, she brushed the man's spotted neckerchief aside and pressed two fingers to the side of his neck. A second later, eyes widening, she glanced up at Michael. "He's alive."

He wouldn't be for much longer. Michael crouched and gently patted the man's cheek.

A frown formed between the man's brows. He shifted his head slightly, then his lids fluttered.

Cleo leant closer.

Michael did, too. As the man's eyes opened, Michael asked, "Who are you?"

Cleo spoke over him. "Who are you working for?"

Across the dying man, Michael met her eyes, then looked back at the man. "Where did you send the barrels?"

The carts were long gone, vanished into the fog with not even the faintest rumble in the distance remaining.

The man's eyes had opened wide; even though they were both all but hanging over him, his gaze wasn't focused on them but on something far distant, something only he could see. Then his lips moved.

Michael held his breath the better to hear.

"Damn," the man whispered.

Then his lids fell, and his head lolled to the side.

A second ticked by, then slowly, Michael straightened.

Cleo rose, too. He looked at her. Her face was paper white, leached of every last vestige of color, her expression shocked, stunned.

Without conscious thought, driven by impulses too powerful to resist, he stepped around the body.

Cleo shifted to face him. He halted before her, raised both hands, and framed her face. He paused for only an instant to look into her eyes, then he bent his head and covered her lips with his.

He'd intended it as a reassuring kiss—a kiss to remind her that he was there, that she was, too, that they were both alive. A kiss to anchor her —and him.

But her lips moved under his, then she raised a hand and closed her fingers about one of his wrists—not to prise his hand away but to hold him. To grip and hold tightly as she parted her lips and boldly returned the kiss—as she stepped closer and kissed him with passion, with desire, with unrestrained ardor. With a challenge and a blatant demand that provoked and incited, and everything he was leapt to meet her and engage.

In a flash, the kiss transformed into a heated exchange of consuming, unrelenting, near-desperate hunger. The fires of mutual desire raged, fierce and undeniable, cindering every last rein, unleashing all their demons.

Want, fear, and need whirled and swirled, laced with shock, with the lingering panic of protective instincts abraded to rawness, all subsumed by the inevitable aftermath of a physical fight that had threatened their lives. And come far too close to taking them.

He felt as if he'd aged ten years in minutes. Driven by an impulse too powerful to gainsay, he lifted his lips but a whisker from hers and groaned, "I've only just found you—I can't lose you now."

She sank the fingers of one hand in his hair and clutched. "You're never going to lose me—I'll never let you go." Then she came up on her toes, pressed her lips to his, and whirled them back into the flames.

Her words—her belligerent, defiant, stubborn tone—rang through his mind, and the raging beast inside calmed, soothed.

Cleo clung to the solidity of him, to the strength, the warmth, that to her, to her senses, meant Michael, meant safety. She clung to the reassurance that he was still with her, that he'd survived and was still there—still her partner.

The partner of the heart she'd never thought to find.

That he wanted her—that he transparently needed her as much as she needed him, and in the same way that she needed him—was a beacon beckoning them to a bright future, but for now, in this foggy lane, she needed to hold on to him. To him and their kiss.

A sound—indiscernible in the fog, but possibly that of a bolt being drawn—jerked them both back to the here and now.

To the chill clamminess of the fog-drenched lane.

To the dead body at their feet.

Easing back from the kiss, both as yet unwilling to let the other go, they raised their heads and listened.

No further sound disturbed the smothering stillness.

She glanced at Michael's face and whispered, "Those shots sounded like cannon fire. Lots of people live around here, yet no one's come to investigate."

He was scanning their surroundings, plainly once again on high alert. "Not yet." Apparently satisfied they were, still, alone in the lane, he looked down at the body sprawled on the cobbles. "We need to get out of here, and we need to take him with us."

Although reluctant—on so many counts—to leave his embrace, she forced herself to step away from him. "What about your wounds?" She'd seen the saber's blade strike his arms several times; she peered at his sleeves, trying to locate the cuts. "They must be bleeding."

He raised one arm and examined a ragged slash in his greatcoat sleeve, then humphed, lowered both arms, and wriggled both sleeves. "He mustn't have sharpened his saber. None of his slashes cut through to my skin."

She blew out a breath. "Thank heaven for small mercies." She glanced around. "Should I pick up the weapons?" That seemed a wise move.

"Yes." He bent and wrapped the fallen man's greatcoat about the man's body, then glanced up at her. "That pistol of yours. Is it a single shot?"

"No." She spotted her knife and bent to pick it up. "It's one of the new American guns. Jarred brought it over for me. It has six shots, and it was fully loaded."

His lips tightened, but he nodded. "Keep it in your hand, just in case. See if you can find the saber and the sheath for my rapier."

She hunted over the cobbles, looking this way and that, and felt lucky to locate both. She returned the black cane to Michael, and he resheathed his rapier. He handed the swordstick to her, then took the saber and slid it home in the scabbard the dead man had worn beneath his greatcoat and fastened the tie, holding the blade firmly in place.

"Right. Help me get him up."

Michael hauled the man more or less upright. Cleo braced the body as Michael stooped and hoisted the man over his left shoulder. Michael clamped his arm around the man's legs, straightened, and resettled the weight. His expression grim, he looked into the dark shadows and fog that obscured the rest of Black Lion Court. His features like granite, he shook his head. "Not that way—back the way we came. It might take a little longer, but it'll be far less dangerous."

He turned and waved her toward the narrow lane that would lead them back to the end of Morgan's Lane. Her pistol in her hand, she led the way, constantly scanning the area ahead of them, then turning to make sure Michael, burdened with the body, was still close and that no one was sneaking up on him.

They reached Morgan's Lane unaccosted. The trudge up the lane was slow, but Michael paused only once to resettle the body, then plodded on.

Three quarters of the way to Tooley Street, Tom came racing down with two more of Michael's men. All three looked stunned when they realized it was Cleo who was with him, but wisely, they made no comment.

Michael relinquished his burden. Using the man's greatcoat like a huge sling, Tom and the other two lugged the body on.

Falling in beside Cleo, Michael reclaimed his swordstick. Her quick thinking in grabbing it and tossing him the rapier had arguably saved them both, but the risk she'd taken in running between him and the man... He drew a deep breath and battened down his mental hatches. Forcing his voice to evenness, he asked, "Where's your carriage?"

The question reminded him of her costume—her act. Her propositioning of the now-dead man. His control wavered.

"It's just along that side street." They stepped into Tooley Street, and she pointed to the opening of a street on the opposite side and a little to the left.

Outside the cordon of his watchers—a cordon he'd described in detail to her so she wouldn't feel the need to join him in Morgan's Lane. He grunted, faintly disgusted at his susceptibility regarding her, and directed Tom and his helpers to take the body that way.

They found her carriage and, after some deliberation, stowed the body in the well between the bench seats. Michael noted that her coachman and groom did not seem overly perturbed over being asked to ferry a dead body around town. But before they could leave, there was one last matter to clarify.

He closed the carriage door on the body and turned to Tom. "Have we had any sightings of the carts with the barrels yet?"

Tom shook his head. "Before they got the barrels, we saw the rider and the carts come out of Black Lion Court. The odd thing is, as far as I've heard, none of us saw those carts come into the area. But they trundled out of the court and then around into Morgan's Lane." He grimaced. "We couldn't see well, what with the fog, but you must've seen them at the warehouse."

Michael nodded. "I"—he glanced at Cleo and amended—"we did. They loaded all ten barrels, five in each cart, and then they headed off."

Tom bobbed his head. "We heard them go, but we couldn't see well enough to be sure of which way they went. We just know they didn't come back this way."

"We followed them down the lane and around into Black Lion Court." Michael stifled a sigh and looked at Cleo. "I lost sight of the carts when they left Morgan's Lane. Did you see which way they went?"

She shook her head. "I was trying to keep them in sight when he"— she tipped her head toward the carriage—"caught me. The carts were quite a way ahead—I don't think they knew anything of our fight." She grimaced. "All I know is that the carts rumbled on into the fog, and then they were gone. Whether they turned into a side street or went on to Tooley Street, I can't say."

Tom shook his head. "They definitely didn't come back into Tooley Street."

"No matter." Michael resettled his greatcoat across his shoulders. "That's why we have men stationed all around. Someone will have seen the carts, left word, and followed." Except no such word had yet reached Tom, Michael's designated center of command. Michael exchanged a glance with Tom, whose increasingly grim expression confirmed that.

Inwardly frowning but keeping the expression from his face, Michael glanced at Cleo. "You should stay with your carriage. I'll do a quick circuit and check with my men, then join you."

She held his gaze for a long moment, then simply said, "I'll come with you."

No argument; no suggestion she would entertain any discussion.

She pulled her cloak around her and looped her arm in his. "Come on. The sooner we find where those wretched carts have gone, the happier we'll both be."

He fell back on his father's wisdom, and in truth, as long as she was by his side, she would be adequately protected and safe.

Indeed, as they returned to Tooley Street and started walking east to where the next of his watchers was stationed, it occurred to him that, while she was with him, he didn't have to worry over what she might be doing—what she might involve herself in. If the carts suddenly trundled out of Black Lion Court, would she meekly leave Tom and his men to follow the carts, or would she take the lead?

Silly question. As he paced along the foggy street, he concluded that his own peace of mind would be best served by allowing her to remain with him.

The first of his watchers had seen and heard nothing, not since the carts had turned down Morgan's Lane.

They heard a similar tale from every man, including those watching the riverbanks. Over the last hour—since the bells had tolled midnight—there'd been no carts transporting barrels sighted anywhere.

Finally, now hand in hand, they walked back along Tooley Street. They joined Tom at his post at the top of Morgan's Lane.

Michael halted. They were all tired; they were all worried. They might have killed the villain—one of them, at least—but the gunpowder was still out there. Presumably in the hands of someone who knew the plotters' plans and had agreed to carry them out.

He scanned what they could see of the buildings across the street. "All

ten barrels have been moved, but they're still somewhere in this warren."
He looked at Cleo, then transferred his gaze to Tom. "I'm going to take a
small group and comb the area." It was the last thing he wanted to do, not
at this hour with fog all around and Cleo intent on sticking by his side,
but if he didn't, he would always wonder if a vital chance had been
missed.

Given Tom and the two others had returned to their posts and maintained the watch down Morgan's Lane, and two burly footmen stationed
in the open area by the riverbank at the very end of Morgan's Lane had
also reported no sign of any carts, both carts and, more importantly, the
barrels must still be somewhere in the maze of lanes filling the area
between Morgan's Lane and St. Saviour's Dock to the east, and between
Tooley Street on the south and the river to the north.

It took them more than an hour to search through the streets from
Morgan's Lane all the way east to Shad Thames and St. Saviour's Dock.
With seven of his army drawn from the now-likely-to-be-irrelevant
watching posts to the west, and with Cleo stubbornly maintaining her
position by his side, Michael walked every lane and went down every
alley along which a cart might have passed. His men poked into any yard
or space to which they could gain access. At that time of night, with the
cold intensifying, not even cats were creeping about.

He'd resigned himself to finding nothing, and he wasn't disappointed.
The carts with their ten barrels were no doubt still there, but must have
been locked away in some building or inner yard.

Returning with the men and Cleo to the top of Morgan's Lane, at
Tom's questioning look, Michael shook his head. "Winchelsea's right.
This plot isn't following any rational course." He turned and thanked
his men, adding, "We'll need to keep a tight watch on the area until
further notice. I expect to be able to reassign posts and schedules later
today."

Tom shifted. "I've already sent Fred back to Mayfair to tell the next
shift they'll be needed."

"Good." Michael thought, then continued, "Once your relief arrives,
turn in for the night. Keep to our earlier rotation, and I'll send word later
today about what changes we'll need to make."

The men drifted off to join others about their redefined area of
interest.

Michael clapped Tom on the shoulder, then retaking Cleo's icy hand
—few ladies of the night wore gloves, and she hadn't missed that point—

he walked with her around the corner to where her coachman and groom still waited with her carriage and the dead body of their foe.

He handed her into the carriage; it was awkward, sidling around the dead man. Once she'd maneuvered around and sat in the far corner, he looked up and told the coachman, "Head back to Mayfair. I'll give you an address when we're closer."

The coachman saluted. "Aye, my lord."

Michael climbed into the carriage, closed the door, and dropped to the seat beside Cleo.

She was still fussing with her full skirts and the voluminous folds of her cloak. Eventually, she made a sound suspiciously like a snort, raised her legs, and propped her half-boots on the seat opposite. That left her slightly slouched in the seat.

Michael considered, then followed suit, stretching his legs over the body. Then he raised his arm, set it about her shoulders, and tugged her against him. He was grateful when she not only permitted it but also wriggled and settled against his side.

She'd pushed back her hood. He leant his cheek against the softness of her hair as the carriage rolled evenly and unobtrusively on.

I've only just found you—I can't lose you now.

You're never going to lose me—I'll never let you go.

Words uttered under pressure, their true feelings without doubt. Now they'd been said, regardless of what issues rose between them, they both now knew—had both acknowledged—the essential, underlying, funda-mental truth.

Little more need be said.

Unfortunately, because, thanks to all the feelings still roiling inside him and the crushing vise about his heart that had yet to ease its grip, it seemed he couldn't *not* ask, he straightened his head and, as nonjudgmen-tally as he could, said, "What possessed you to come there tonight dressed like that?"

Under his arm, she stiffened, but before she could reply, he barreled on, "When I realized that the whore propositioning that villain was *you*, I…" The feeling of utter shock, the inability to move, to function at any level rolled over him again; his voice was harsh as he grated, "You might as well have taken a rock to my head. I was frozen. I couldn't move—I couldn't even *think!*" His tone hardened. "Do you have any idea what it felt like to be forced to watch and know that if anything happened, I couldn't reach you in time? That I wouldn't be able to protect you?"

That last question, and the emotion close to anguish reverberating in his voice, saved him from verbal annihilation; Cleo tightened her lips and swallowed her initial blistering response. After several seconds, in what she felt was a commendably even, if distinctly chilly, tone, she stated, "I didn't go there dressed as a lady of the night intending to proposition anyone." *Not even you.* Her tone added "obviously," but she held the word back—then changed her mind and stated, "Obviously." With men in the throes of protective rage, there was, her mother had often informed her, no point in being subtle.

With rather awful patience, she went on, "I chose the disguise as the one most likely to allow me to get close enough to whoever came for the barrels. Men have a tendency to dismiss women—they don't see us as threats. And so it proved—I did get close enough to see his face, well enough to note that he had a scar that ran from the corner of his lips to below his ear. If he'd later escaped us—and we were, after all, supposed to let him go and just follow—I would have been able to recognize him." She glanced down at the body below their legs. "Now he's dead, of course, that's no longer of much use, but it would have been had things gone as they were supposed to."

The breath he drew was beyond tense. "I never before understood what the phrase 'being beside oneself' meant, not until I saw you with his knife at your throat."

Crisply, she shot back, "I wasn't thinking too clearly at that point myself."

From the corner of her eye, she saw the hand he'd rested on his thigh tighten into a fist.

After several fraught seconds, he said, still speaking very precisely as if measuring each word, "I *thought*, when we parted earlier in the evening, that I had convinced you—that we *agreed*—that there was little likelihood the barrels would be moved tonight."

She snorted and folded her arms across her chest. "Clearly, we were both wrong—and both of us realized that."

He nodded tersely. "But what changed your mind?"

She hesitated, then asked, "What changed yours?" He'd said he would "drop by," yet he'd been secreted in the alcove, ready and waiting for the barrels to be moved.

It was his turn to hesitate, but eventually, plainly reluctantly, he replied, "Your suggestion of replacing the gunpowder meant that, very likely, we would have nullified the threat the gunpowder posed by…later today. If the gunpowder remained in the warehouse until today, there would be no more immediate danger from the plot." He paused, then said, "Call it superstition if you like, but I'm too old to trust in Fate's benevolence. Especially given the way this investigation has run thus far, with us always arriving just too late, I decided that, come today, the barrels would be gone from the warehouse, leaving us with no further lead to pursue."

She inclined her head. "My reasoning was...not quite the same. I suspected you would be there, in the alcove, waiting. And it occurred to me that, if our villains came calling, Morgan's Lane was too deserted to be safe, even for you. But there was nowhere else any others could hide, not close enough. But a lady of the night could be openly about, and I would have my knives and my gun, and as you saw, I'm tolerably good with both." She paused, then said, "He must have glimpsed me while I was tucked away in that ginnel and wondered why I was there. That was what he asked when he caught me. But if he and the carts had gone the other way, to Tooley Street, as we all assumed they would"—she glanced down at the body—"there would have been no danger to me, and he would still be alive."

Michael dragged in a breath. It was as he'd feared. "So...you came to protect me."

She hesitated as if thinking, then nodded. "Yes."

He took time to consider his next words, but again, they had to be said. "Don't think that I don't appreciate the sentiment, but I really, *really* would rather you didn't try to help or protect me—not if doing so puts you in harm's way."

She took her own time in thinking over her response. Finally, she said, "If you meant what you said earlier, in the lane—and for the record, I certainly meant each and every word I said in reply—then I regret to inform you that I will never, ever, be the sort of lady who sits quietly at home, embroidering by the fire, while you go off to face God knows what threats. If you go into danger, you may be very sure that I will be by your side. Or at least lurking about, armed and in disguise."

The qualification drew a bark of a laugh from him.

At the edge of her vision, Cleo saw the hand he'd fisted fraction by fraction relax. Then with that hand, he reached across, tugged one of her hands free, and to her surprise, raised her fingers to his lips and pressed a gentle kiss to them. "Yes," he said. He turned his head, and his eyes met hers as she lifted her gaze to his face. His expression turned wry, and he admitted, "I know. But I had to say it."

That was all right, then. She felt her lips curve. As long as they understood each other...

She shifted her gaze across the carriage, considered, then added, "Just to be clear, although I've developed a definite liking for adventure, I find I'm not so enamored of danger. You may rest assured I won't go seeking it out." Turning her fingers, she gripped his hand. "And I would appreciate it if you didn't go out of your way to engage in dangerous exploits, either."

She looked up and saw him grimace, but then he met her gaze, and his lips curved wryly. "It seems my hedonistic career is at an end. No more phaeton races."

She laughed.

The painfully tight tension had fallen from them both. They'd survived the night, and at least between them, they recognized in which direction they wished to go.

Onward, hand in hand, into a future they had yet to define.

More immediately, however...

She looked at the body beneath their legs. "Where are we taking him?"

Michael relaxed against the squabs. "Wolverstone House. The staff there will know what to do."

CHAPTER 15

*A*s Michael had predicted, Hamilton, the Wolverstone House butler, didn't turn a hair on being informed that the body deposited on the tiles of the front hall was very definitely dead.

"Of course, my lord. Leave the matter with me" was the extent of Hamilton's perturbation.

Somewhat to Michael's amazement, despite it being four o'clock in the morning, the butler and the two footmen he summoned to remove the body, and Drake's man, Finnegan, who came hurrying down the stairs, were all wide awake and fully dressed.

On seeing Michael's puzzlement, Hamilton explained, "We are expecting the marquess to return at any moment, my lord."

"Ah." Michael nodded. "I see." The Wolverstone House staff were utterly devoted to the family, but most especially to Drake now that he'd stepped into his father's shoes, government intrigue-wise.

Finnegan, a short, slight Irishman who looked a great deal more youthful than he actually was, hurried to peer into the bundle as the footmen hoisted it. Looking at the man's face, Finnegan's eyes went wide. "A body! And a gentleman at that." He cocked his head. "Possibly one down on his luck." Finnegan looked at Michael. "Do we know his name, my lord?"

"Sadly, no." Michael knew Finnegan was entirely in Drake's confidence; Drake frequently used him for this or that inquiry. "However, your master and I and all concerned in this latest mission need to learn his name as quickly as possible."

Finnegan nodded. "I will endeavor to discover it, my lord." He murmured something to the footmen, then led them into the nether regions of the mansion.

Michael glanced at Cleo. With the fingers of one hand interlaced with his, and her gaze taking in the magnificence of the ducal front hall in a mildly interested fashion, she'd stood quietly beside him, absorbing the interplay between him and the staff.

They'd sent her carriage back to Clarges Street, bearing a message that she would remain in Grosvenor Square with Michael until after their meeting with Drake, whenever that might be. Michael had told coachman and groom that he would see their mistress home in due course, an assurance they'd accepted without apparent qualm.

As he watched, her gaze shifted to Hamilton, who she'd met the previous afternoon, and she smiled tiredly. "Good morning. I rather think the marquess will want to speak with us as soon as possible. Indeed"—she waved in the direction in which the body had been taken—"we certainly need to speak with him urgently. I wonder if there's somewhere we can rest until his lordship arrives. We've been up all night and would appreciate a chance to refresh ourselves."

Hamilton didn't exactly smile, but his features eased, and he bowed low. "Miss Hendon. The marquess would consider me quite remiss not to offer you and Lord Michael all the comforts this house can provide. None of the family bar the marquess are currently in residence. It would be our pleasure to provide you with rooms and beds and every other amenity."

Michael hid a grin and watched Cleo try to disclaim the need for quite that degree of hospitality, but as he could have told her, turning Hamilton from such a tack was something few had ever managed.

"But you said the marquess was likely to arrive at any moment," Cleo protested. "There's no sense putting your staff to such trouble for us to gain just a few minutes of rest."

"Well, as to that, miss," Hamilton explained, "while we are holding ourselves ready to welcome the marquess home, there's no saying when he will arrive. It's quite likely he won't grace this hall until closer to noon, and then you and Lord Michael will have wasted a good seven hours you might have spent regrouping."

Cleo narrowed her eyes on Hamilton's face, but the butler met her suspicious look with an air of complete and utterly unshakeable certainty.

She surrendered with what grace she could muster. "Very well. As you insist, you may show us to rooms for the rest of the morning. But you will inform the marquess that we are here the instant he arrives."

"Indubitably, miss." Hamilton bowed, then straightening, waved to the grand staircase. "If you will follow me, I will show you to suitable chambers." He nodded to another footman who had taken up a position in the hall. "Jeffreys will alert one of the maids to attend you, miss, and will arrange for hot water to be brought up for you both."

Jeffreys immediately sped away to do so.

Michael walked beside Cleo up the stairs. He was still suffering from a species of inner turmoil in the aftermath of the action in Morgan's Lane and, even more, the clash in Black Lion Court. That they had somehow, out of that, managed to come to some sort of amenable understanding without railing at each other was, he felt, nothing short of amazing. Yet when they'd both been forced to witness the other waltzing one step away from death, their reactions—and the words that had subsequently tumbled from their lips—had established a truth it was impossible to step back from, much less suppress.

That didn't make the roiling feelings, the impulses denied, any easier to bear. But as his father had intimated, he'd just have to manage it.

Hamilton led them to the guest wing. Michael was relieved to note that the rooms to which the butler showed them were close, with only two doors between. His protective instincts were still a trifle raw; even in such safe and secure surrounds, knowing Cleo was close soothed his inner guardian.

Michael halted closer to the main stairs, at the door to the room that Hamilton had indicated would be his, and watched as the butler guided Cleo to the room three doors along. A little maid came hurrying up, still tucking strands of hair under her cap.

Cleo glanced back along the corridor, caught his gaze, fractionally shook her head in resigned surrender, then followed the maid into the room.

Michael opened the door and went into his allotted chamber. He'd already declined the offer of Finnegan or a footman to help him to bed; on that score, he needed no help.

The bed was a large tester much like Michael's own. He shrugged out of his greatcoat; on registering the weight of his pistol and that of the villain's in the pockets, he reminded himself he would need to clean his pistol later. He would offer to clean Cleo's pistol—her revolver—too. He was curious to examine the gun; he rather thought he should get one of his own.

If his wife had such a gun...

He stilled. Then he straightened and eased off his coat. It was the first time he'd attached that label to any woman, even in his mind, yet it fitted the woman he'd chosen to a T.

Cleo, his wife.

He smiled and unknotted his cravat, then he turned down the lamps and opened the curtains over one wide window before sitting on the side of the bed and easing off his boots. After setting the boots aside, he weighed the notion of removing the rest of his clothes, but who knew when Drake would arrive?

Deciding he didn't need to strip to get some sleep, he tipped backward, brought his legs onto the bed, then settled his head on the pillows.

He clasped his hands on his chest, closed his eyes, and waited for sleep to claim him.

Cleo lay on the big, wide bed and stared up at the canopy. It was blue. Royal blue. Everything in the room was in some shade of blue. Which was an interesting observation, no doubt, but in no way contributed to her finding her way into slumber.

She'd washed, grateful for the warm water, and had allowed the maid to let down her hair and ease out the tangles. Then she'd dismissed the girl, doused the lamps, lay down on the bed, closed her eyes, and tried to relax.

After ten minutes of relaxing, she was still wide awake. Keyed up, with a certain tension thrumming along her nerves.

She knew what the problem was. She'd made a decision—prompted by the heat of the moment, perhaps, yet she'd stepped over a line, decisively and with intent. In her mind, that decision was settled, sealed, accepted, and was now a part of her. She'd recognized and acknowledged where her future lay, and now, she wanted to get on with it.

Now, she wanted to seize it.

She wanted to seize him, be seized in return, and see what came next.

On top of that, there was a compulsion building inside her, fed by some need, some yearning far deeper and more compelling than any rational argument.

Restless, she shifted onto her side.

Ten seconds later, she rolled once more onto her back. "This is hopeless."

She sat up, swung her legs over the side of the bed, and stood. She glanced down at her skirts as she shook them straight. She'd disguised herself as a high-class lady of the night; if seduction was her goal, that wasn't a bad start.

Should she do this?

Could she?

Would she?

She raised her head, straightened her spine, and with great deliberation, walked to the door. She was her mother's daughter; she was perfectly capable of seizing the moment and acting decisively to secure the future hovering before her, hers if she dared to claim it.

Patience had never been her strong suit; she wanted that future now.

She opened the door and paused to check the corridor. Although lights burned in the front hall, all seemed quiet and calm downstairs—awaiting the arrival of the house's junior master. On this level, the mansion lay slumbering, blanketed in the pervasive stillness that signified unoccupied rooms. Reassured, she stepped onto the runner, quietly closed the door behind her, then walked—quietly but not surreptitiously—to the door three doors up the corridor. The door to the room into which Michael had gone.

Pausing outside the door, she debated whether to knock or not, then with a mental shrug, she grasped the knob, opened the door, and calmly walked in. She shut the door behind her, then looked toward the large bed.

He, too, had turned down the lamps, but he'd opened the curtains over the window to the side of the bed. There, in Mayfair, the fog was no denser than a wispy veil, allowing moonlight to wash over the bed, illuminating the expanse in a silvery radiance while, by contrast, making the shadows swallowing the rest of the room darker, more impenetrable.

She wasn't interested in the rest of the room, only in the man stretched out on the bed. He lay with his head cushioned on the pillows, his hands, fingers interlaced, resting on his chest, his legs straight, his stockinged feet crossed at the ankles. He still wore his waistcoat, shirt, and breeches, but had dispensed with his cravat, leaving the strong column of his throat exposed between the points of his collar.

She was visited by a sudden urge to set her mouth to the bare skin of his throat, to lick and taste. Quelling the impulse—reserving it for later—she fastened her gaze on his face. His eyes were open; no more than she had he fallen asleep.

Incapable of completely hiding her satisfaction, she allowed her lips to curve just a little as she walked to the nearer side of the bed. She watched him track her approach and noted the faint signs of the heightening tension that laid siege to his muscles. Recognized, too, the stirrings of something more primitive, more primal, as, with his features hardening, his gaze remained unrelentingly locked on her, and something darkly powerful stared at her through his eyes.

Steering this clash—for she felt sure it would be a clash of sorts—in the direction she wished it to go would require retaining control of the reins, at least at the start, and the only way she might achieve that ambition was to keep him off balance.

She reached the bed, met his gaze for a long second, then she turned, sat, swung her legs up to the coverlet, and lay down.

Michael watched her settle beside him. Her expression calm and open as it generally was, she lay staring up at the canopy overhead—exactly as he'd been doing when she'd come in. Unable to even collect his wits, much less think with her so close—in the dark of the night, in the same bed, no less!—he stared at her for a good minute, then, because it seemed the only sentence his brain could muster, asked, "Why are you here?"

The single most important question as far as his inner warrior-guardian was concerned.

She turned her head and, across the pillows, looked at him. Unhurriedly, her gaze traced his features, then she met his eyes. "I couldn't sleep. Trying was futile." Through the silvery moonlight, her eyes searched his, then she arched her brows. "What about you?"

Her tone had turned sultry, loaded with feminine invitation. The sort of invitation that made his pulse leap. But...he needed to go carefully here. He needed to stay in control—of himself as well as her.

Ruthlessly clinging to impassivity, he straightened his head and, once again, gazed at the canopy. "The same." After a second's pause, in a somewhat diffident tone, he added, "It's the aftermath of the action." He felt it was important he mention that; he doubted she'd lived through such excitement—such danger—before.

"The inability to sleep? Perhaps. However, as that does seem to be our mutual state, I thought we might seize the moment to address..."

When her voice trailed tantalizingly away, he set his jaw and counseled himself to wait and not show his very real interest…but she seemed to have lost her train of thought. Eventually unable to stand not knowing, he prompted, "Address what?"

As if she'd been waiting for the words—for that invitation from him —she drew in a deep yet distinctly tight breath, then she rolled toward him, came up on her elbow by his side, looked into his face, and succinctly stated, "This."

Before he could stop her, before he could react, she bent her head, pressed her lips to his, and kissed him.

With fervor, with passion, with desire unleashed.

Firm and warm, deliberate and certain, her lips moved on his in a blatant incitement that exploded across his senses. That reached straight through his defenses and connected directly with the warrior-guardian inside.

The kiss lured, powerful and potent, laden with the promise of making his most immediate and urgent dream into reality, and he couldn't not respond. Couldn't not reach for her. He'd grasped her shoulders and drawn her to him, into his embrace and deeper into the kiss, before his whirling mind caught up with his actions.

And by then, it was far too late.

Too late to haul on any reins and pull back.

He cupped her nape and held her head steady as he took control and deepened the kiss. Her lips had parted, luring him in; he took full advantage, thrusting into the honeyed warmth to plunder and claim.

But she wasn't about to surrender so easily.

Stoked by the ensuing duel, the exchange flared into a blaze of heat, hunger, and escalating need.

Her free hand traced his jaw, then trailed down to rest, palm down, on his chest; her fingers curled, and she clutched his shirt, braced her arm, and supported her weight as she leant over him the better to engage. The better to press the reality of her need upon him.

Not that he needed any instruction. His senses had expanded; even while engrossed in every nuance of the kiss, in the passionate duel it had become, he was acutely aware of every element of her—of the alluring feminine curves pressed against his side, of her legs brushing and threatening to tangle with his, of that evocatively clutching hand on his chest. Of the warmth of her breasts that hovered so tantalizing mere inches above him.

As his warrior self, that guardian who she alone truly touched, who she alone truly commanded, that inner self for whom protection of his woman—this woman—was a compulsion impossible to resist, vied with her for control, through the now-blazing kiss, through the insistent, persistent message of her lips, through her blatant caressing of his tongue with hers, he sensed her purpose.

One part of him—that warrior part—thought: Why argue? As long as he scripted the play, there would be no danger. Wasn't this—her surrendering to him—what he wanted?

Against that, his rational, cautious side pushed him to slow their onward rush—long enough, at least, to determine that she really did intend them to thunder down this particular road.

That she understood where the road ended.

That seemed a sound idea on several fronts. With an effort, he drew his awareness from the kiss—and from where her busy fingers had opened his waistcoat and were currently engaged on a quest to slide every last button down the front of his shirt free.

Breaking from the kiss—battling his own urges, primitive and powerful as, when it came to her, they were, while simultaneously countering her and her always-flagrant incitements—wasn't easy. In fact, it rated as one of the hardest things he'd ever done. But finally, he closed his hands about her shoulders, lifted her more fully across him, then held her high enough to press his head back into the pillows and force their lips apart.

Apparently accepting the change, she hung in his hold, her gaze falling to her fingers and a recalcitrant button. By relying on his support, she could use both hands and eagerly did—rushing ahead in her usual impetuous fashion. Further compounding his problems, she shifted and slid one sleek thigh, still screened by gold satin, thank heavens, across his hips, and swung to sit astride his waist.

He drew in a deep breath and fought to block the sensations of her warm weight across his stomach, of the firm pressure of her inner thighs gripping his hips, fought to block his awareness of the softness that lay at the apex of those widespread thighs… For him, that was a losing battle.

Clenching his jaw, battling the impulses she was inciting, the flames she was so deliberately stoking, in a voice that desire had roughened to a low growl, he managed to say, "Cleo—you do know where this leads, don't you?"

She glanced briefly at his face; her eyes fleetingly touched his. "Yes. Of course." Immediately, her attention shifted to tugging his shirt from the waistband of his breeches. Triumph infused her features as, succeeding, she hauled the halves of the shirt wide, baring his chest.

The look on her face as she stared down at what she'd uncovered—the open delight and blatant covetousness that gleamed in her eyes and stroked him like some invisible flame—made him literally groan. From the brightening of her expression, the sound delighted her even more. Ignoring the tensing of his fingers on her upper arms, she eagerly spread her hands and set her palms and fingers to his chest. To skin that flamed at her touch, to heavy muscles, already hard, that her evocative caresses turned to iron.

The trail of her fingers over his skin shattered his concentration; the tripping of her fingertips through the wiry hair that adorned his chest vaporized his ability to think. The intensity of her gaze as she visually drank in his body, her focus as, like a cat, she sank her fingertips into the muscles she'd claimed, testing their resilience, felled his good intentions and left him awash on a sea of conflicting emotions, of clashing impulses.

He wanted her—beyond thought.

And it was perfectly obvious that she wanted him. In the same physical, sensual, earthy way.

He caught his breath as she found the flat disc of one nipple and artfully circled the sensitive skin. Closed his eyes as she threaded her slim fingers through the coarse hair on his chest and gently—very gently—tugged.

He opened his eyes, read the truth she made no effort to hide in her gloriously open expression, and knew without question in which direction she was—with her usual deliberate impatience—heading.

But he—they—had to get this right. He had to be sure they were walking the same path. He could assume...but he needed to know. With her, he needed to be certain.

From where such unexpected vulnerability sprang, he had no idea, but this was her—and she was different. She was the only woman he had ever wanted to—yearned to—wake up with after, in the stark light of morning.

When she sat back and, hands stilling, fingers splayed, on his chest, stared as if memorizing the landscape, the contours she'd conquered, he seized the moment. He steadied wits rendered giddy by barely leashed desire, hauled in a breath, and stated, "Just to be clear, if we go any further with this—you and me, together in this bed tonight—there can be only one possible outcome, and that's marriage."

Cleo raised her gaze to his face. It took an instant for her brain to shift from its preoccupation and replay his words. Her immediate impulse was to flash him a quick smile and say: Yes, of course. But something—instinct of a sort—made her hold both smile and words back.

She stared at his face, at his set expression. Simply agreeing—as if to a formal proposal—with a man like him...would mean that later, she would have no leverage when it came to discussing the aspects they would need to agree on to make any marriage between them work. Such as her work with the company. And her need for independence, at least to a point.

For her, tonight was supposed to be a step toward commitment—a vital step, but still just a step. Tonight wasn't—or at least, hadn't been—about any final and unalterable declaration, not on her part. Only after she was sure on all fronts...

Yet looking into his eyes, she could see that there was nothing flippant about his stance; he was in earnest and intent on getting an answer—the answer he wanted—from her. It struck her that, compared with the way she'd always heard such conversations went, they seemed to have switched roles. It was she who murmured, as seductively as she could, "We can discuss that later."

Immediately, before he could tighten his grip on her shoulders, she gave in to her earlier impulse, swooped, and set her lips to the long, strong, lightly tanned column of his throat. She pressed a hot, damp, open-mouthed kiss to the warm skin, then licked up, then down to the hollow at the base of his throat. There, she laved, tasting his skin, feeling even such minor muscles tense at her touch.

He groaned softly, the sound plainly escaping despite his best efforts to stifle it.

A sense of power hummed beneath her skin as she drew back just enough to survey her playground.

"Damn it, woman!" His voice was a low, grating rumble. "Listen to me."

The for-him-distinctly-weak command made her smile. "Why?" She was too absorbed, too intent, to meet his eyes. "Do you have any particular requests regarding what you would like me to do?"

"Yes—*no!* What?"

His confusion was music to her ears. "How about this?" She bent and, with her teeth, grazed the taut tendon at the side of his throat. His entire body tightened beneath her; excitement surged through her.

"And this?" She nipped, and various muscles spasmed, and his lower body jerked.

He sucked in a breath, then softly swore. He released her shoulders, swept his hands between them, and seized her wrists. Holding them together, he pushed her up and held her above him.

Balanced there, still straddling him, she looked down into his eyes—and saw something close to desperation in his bitter-chocolate gaze.

"No," he gritted out, his eyes searching hers. "Answer me...please. Tell me you understand—that you accept." He hesitated, his eyes locked with hers. For a second, he held back, then more quietly added, "Because for me, this—with you—is...*it*. Everything. The end of one life and the beginning of another."

The sincerity in his eyes, the need in his tone, floored her. That she mattered that much to him, enough for a man of his ilk to find the words and the courage to tell her, to in unambiguous terms reveal to her how much he now saw his life as being dependent on her...with three brothers, with a father like hers, she knew the value of that.

She found a need of her own rising in response. Easing one wrist from his hold, she reached down and laid that hand, gentle and caressing, against his cheek. She hadn't shifted her gaze from his eyes—couldn't have even had she wished to. Drowning in his gaze, she found the right words waiting on the tip of her tongue. "I have no intention—none whatsoever—of backing away from this, from you. I harbor no thought of not committing to a life with you—marrying you is my shining goal."

His eyes searched her face, and he seemed to breathe again.

She trapped his gaze and went on, "But if you feel that way—and I accept you do—then before we go further, I need to hear a declaration from you, too."

Lost in his eyes, with her senses steeped in him, wrapped in the warm confines of the bed with the pale glow of the moon washing over them both, she looked into her heart, found her own vulnerability residing there, and forced herself to enunciate that critical fear—as he had. "I want nothing more desperately than to marry you—to be your wife and your partner in all things, to share a life and a future with you. But I need to know that you'll accept me as I am in that role—that claiming you, and you claiming me, and us going forward thereafter hand in hand isn't contingent on me changing. On me no longer being me—being the lynchpin at Hendon Shipping, being a lady more interested in managing an enterprise than in ton balls."

She held his dark gaze and went on, "I know there'll be adjustments on both sides—of course, there will. But if becoming Lady Cynster means I need to fundamentally alter who I am—"

"Hush." He'd raised his free hand and laid a finger across her lips. In the poor light, his eyes seemed impossibly dark, his gaze impossibly intense. But his expression had eased, the hard angles and planes softening; his lips curved, his smile openly affectionate—openly loving—as he gazed up at her. "I don't want you to change. The lady I want to take as my wife is you—exactly as you are at this moment. The lady who refused to run away and leave me to my fate in Black Lion Court. The lady who came to Morgan's Lane tonight because she felt I might need her help."

He paused, then, his voice low yet resonant, his eyes locked with hers, continued, "You, Cleo Hendon, exactly as you are, are my perfect other half —my perfect partner. *You* are the lady I've been waiting to meet, and now I've found you, I will never let you go. And for the record, to have you as my wife, having you by my side, in my life, is all I truly want or need. However you wish to fill your days, whatever undertaking makes you happy, whatever adventure next strikes your fancy, know one thing—as your husband, I will be at your back, supporting and protecting you every step of the way."

She felt her lips curve in a smile that mirrored his. Her heart swelled, filled to overflowing. She let every last shield fall and, with complete confidence, let her joy at his words shine through. "Thank you. That is all and everything I needed to hear." Their fates, their future, were well and truly sealed. Her eyes on his, she tipped her head, her brows arching in question. "So...as you mentioned adventure, there's a particular area of personal interaction I'm rather keen on exploring. Might I tempt you to join me?"

He laughed, then grinned at her. "Nothing"—he reached up, cupped her nape, and drew her down until their lips were separated by less than an inch—"would please me more." He closed the gap and kissed her— and she kissed him back—with passion, with desire, with a hunger too long held at bay.

That hunger roared, erupted, and surged through them; it seized and ruthlessly commanded them.

He rolled and brought her down to the silky coverlet.

She wrestled with his shirt and waistcoat; he obliged by rearing back on his knees, stripping his arms from the sleeves, then flinging the garments into the shadows.

Before he could do more than lower his arms, she halted him by the simple expedient of spreading her hands over the magnificence of his chest and breathing the words, "No—let me look."

He stared at her, but although his hands fisted, he remained kneeling and allowed her to explore.

When, emboldened, she eased upward and, pulling her full skirts out from under and around her legs, came to her knees the better to reach, the better to caress, his lids fell, and he tipped his head back, his jaw setting, for all the world as if he was battling some ferocious force.

She suspected he was.

Smiling to herself, she bent her head, set her lips to his heated skin, and traced...

His muscles tensed even more. Without opening his eyes, he ground out, "You're not going to make this easy, are you?"

After a moment during which she licked her way around one pearled nipple, she murmured, "I can't see the point in rushing."

In those words, delivered with sultry intent, Michael saw, if not his salvation, then at least a viable way forward. He straightened his head, raised his lids, looked at her, then opening his hands, he raised them, gently gripped her waist, and murmured, "If you want to take things slowly..."

Predictably intrigued, she drew her lips from where she'd been branding his chest and glanced up.

He swooped and covered her lips with his, took possession of her mouth, her tongue, her senses, and calling up every ounce of his long-established expertise, waltzed her—slowly—into the dance.

A dance of which he knew every step, every dip and whirl, every variation and version. Clinging to a slow, regimented beat was guaranteed to heighten awareness—his as well as hers—and would ratchet the inevitable tension by several degrees, draw out expectation and anticipation to an almost-excruciating extent, and finally, augment the intensity of the crucial moments by an order of magnitude.

But she'd wanted slow, and as they danced—as their hands swept and caressed to the steady beat, and their pulses pounded to the arousing rhythm, as their breaths came in increasingly shallow drafts, and he helped her from the froth of her skirt and petticoats and, later, still clinging to the slow beat, unlaced her light corset, then ultimately, drew her fine chemise off over her head—she clung to him, to their kisses and increasingly arousing caresses, to the moment, and to that unrelenting beat with a fervor and a determination to match his own.

His partner.

Even in this.

Even when he eased her down against the pillows and feasted on her breasts.

Even when he trailed his knowing hands over her heated skin, watching the fine, creamy silk flush a delicate rose as he traced every curve and hollow.

Cleo had lost touch with the world beyond the bed. Lying naked amid the rumpled sheets with him hovering over her, a dark shadow so intrinsically male, she'd discovered a universe ruled by sensation. He'd led her there, shown her the way—opened her eyes and all her senses to the pleasures and delights.

To the heat that steadily grew to furnace-like proportions, to the glorious tension that tightened nerves until they leapt at even the most delicate touch. To the slow, driving compulsion that steadily grew within them both to eventually rule their minds.

Between them, desire burned and passion raged, yet their adherence to the steady beat that resonated in their hearts held strong, held firm, and let her, let them, absorb each moment of scintillating pleasure to the full before being forced by that compulsion to move on.

She'd wanted to take sufficient time so she would remember the way, but she now knew she would never forget. Every new sensation he offered her—from his attentions to the full, swollen mounds of her breasts to the long, sweeping caresses that had her arching against his hard, so very male body—seemed to etch itself into the bedrock of her psyche.

She'd never imagined lovemaking would involve such a close communion, that it would involve layers of herself and of him that lay far beneath the surface of their conscious minds—far deeper than speech or touch, more in the realm of feelings. She opened her senses, her mind, her soul, and embraced it all—embraced him as he patently embraced her.

They opened their hearts, and with thoughts exchanged via soft gasps and the touch of their gazes through the moonstruck shadows, through the stroking of their hands, reverent yet sure as they progressed along the route they'd chosen, they anchored the other deep within.

Each to be forever a part of the other.

As the engagement spun on and the beat intensified, he touched her, caressed her, and drove her wild with desire, with passion and hunger and wanting. His lips traced her curves, leaving damp trails on her overheated skin, then he parted her thighs and touched her most private flesh and found it swollen, soft and slick. Then he dipped his head and set his mouth to that slick softness, and for several heated moments, she was quite sure she would lose her mind.

But then he disengaged, drew back and away.

Panting, she sprawled on the coverlet, naked and heated, and waited and watched as he shed his breeches and stockings and, finally naked himself, joined her on the bed.

Their control held, even then. Even as he lowered his hips between her widespread thighs and, with the moonlight gilding his tensed and straining muscles and her sleek curves, they discovered just how well they fitted, how perfectly, despite her momentary discomfort, they matched in this way, too, the beat thundered and pounded through their blood, through their hearts, and bound them.

And into the dance they plunged, with that beat still driving them, still constraining and compelling them. Not in her wildest dreams had she imagined the sensations could be so acute, so intense; never had she guessed at the indescribable impact of feeling the hard, heavy weight of his erection buried so snugly, so deeply, inside her.

The intimacy of the moment—the closeness, the shattering togetherness—flooded her mind.

And with every long, slow thrust, her gasps of wonder, of delight and burgeoning pleasure, filled the soft shadows engulfing them.

The power of his body, repetitively driving into hers, pleasuring her senses to her very fingertips in so very many ways and taking her soaring beyond this world, thrilled and fulfilled her. The physical reality of the act was so much more compelling, so much more consuming than she'd ever dreamed.

She clung and rode with him, her body instinctively matching his—partnering his. Yielding and taking, absorbing and clutching.

This, she dazedly realized, was what she'd been born for. Not just being all she could be in her daytime life, but forging this connection, participating in this communion—*this* completed her.

This, surely, was the greatest adventure that would ever come her way.

She was gasping, clutching, striving with him to reach some peak of pleasure she only vaguely perceived when, finally, they lost their guiding beat. The forces they'd harnessed to that point snapped their fraying leashes and broke free—and overwhelmed them.

Both of them, for he was with her, as he'd promised, every step of the way; she heard it in his tortured breathing, in his guttural groan—he was as swept away as she.

They had no choice. They clung and surrendered and gave themselves up to the fury of the moment—and together, they raced.

Flat out for that beckoning peak.

On that non-corporeal plane, she reached through the driving, pounding desperation and put her hand in his, and when they reached the pinnacle, together they leapt—

They soared.

And reality shattered.

A supernova of sensation burst across her mind, searing through her awareness, crystal clear and sharp, an eruption of her senses etched in golden glory as he drove into her one last time, then held still, quivering as his own release ripped through him and emptied him...then ecstasy, powerful and unstoppable, rose and flooded them.

Delighted to her toes, still floating on that plane far removed from the world, she turned this way and that, bathing in that sea of coruscating glory.

Gradually, the sensation faded.

She sighed and let go, and he slumped upon her, and something inside her eased; she reached as far around him as she could and held him, claimed him, too, and let oblivion's tide float them into slumber.

Michael woke, he had no idea how much later. The moon had sailed on across the sky, and the room now lay in darkness. Nevertheless, as he cautiously levered himself up and looked down at the woman sprawled boneless beneath him, quietly sleeping, he could see well enough to appreciate the sight.

To see and rejoice.

To remember and feel compelled to bend his head and brush a feather-light kiss to her forehead.

Carefully, he lifted from her. She seemed dead to the world and didn't stir even when he slumped beside her, then, unable to resist, gathered her to him, settling her against his side, within the circle of his arms.

His.

He closed his eyes and felt that truth resonate through him.

He'd been dubbed "the huntsman" for many years, but now, his hunting days were over. His new role was as a protector—her protector, hers and any children they were blessed with—and that role suited him to the ground. More, such a role would satisfy and fulfill him in ways the hunter's role never had and never could.

The woman sleeping within his arms was his new future personified. The future he'd been unconsciously searching for, at least for the past decade. The future he'd now claimed.

She was now his, and he was hers, and no power on earth would ever put them asunder.

Such was the magic, such was the power—the power that now linked them.

CHAPTER 16

*M*ichael was still sunk in sleep when the sound of a brief tap at the door penetrated the pleasurable fog shrouding his mind.

His senses immediately informed him that Cleo still lay snuggled, safe and warm, by his side.

He raised his lids; squinting over the tousled red-gold mass of Cleo's curls, he saw the bedroom door open.

Even as Michael tensed, Drake swanned in, his gaze downcast as he settled the sleeves of the coat he'd apparently just shrugged on. "Get up, you lazy beggar. If I'm awake, so should you be, and"—Drake halted and raised his gaze—"I understand you have something urgent—"

Drake's gaze collided with Michael's—over the top of the rounded, coverlet-covered lump that was Cleo, now shaking as, having woken and realized what was happening, she tried to control her laughter. Sensibly, she kept her head down.

"Ah." Drake blinked rather owlishly. Then he swung on his heel and headed for the door. "Obviously, I didn't see what I just saw." He reached for the doorknob. "When you're ready to emerge, I'll be downstairs."

He walked out and closed the door—gently—behind him.

Cleo raised her head and looked at Michael, hilarity bright in her eyes.

He met her gaze—and started to laugh.

So did she.

They rolled onto their backs and laughed uncontrollably, in Cleo's case, until tears slid from the corners of her eyes. "Oh," she eventually gasped. "What a way to meet the man. And we've not even been properly introduced."

Michael was still struggling to rein in his laughter. "You didn't see his face." The memory temporarily robbed him of speech. When he regained control, he managed to get out, "I've never in all my life seen him so blank-faced with astonishment. If we'd taken a club to his head, he couldn't have looked more stunned."

Gradually, although amusement lingered, the impulse to laugh faded. Her lips still curved, Cleo met his eyes. "I suppose we'd better get up and face the day."

Michael searched her eyes and saw her understanding that, for them, today would not simply be a continuation of their yesterdays. Today would be the first day of their future, the day that would usher in their tomorrows.

Through the events of the night, both in Southwark and there in Grosvenor Square, they'd acknowledged the power that now linked them by word and by deed, yet neither of them had uttered the critical word; they hadn't put a name to that power.

He found her hand amid the rumpled sheets; he raised it to his lips and, holding her gaze, pressed a lingering kiss to her fingers. "I haven't yet stated this, but regardless of whatever today and our tomorrows bring, I love you. And I always will."

Cleo hadn't needed to hear the words, but was grateful nonetheless. She smiled with all the joy welling in her heart and replied, "And I love you—now and forever."

After a second during which they gazed besottedly at each other, she inwardly sighed, forced herself to glance briefly at the door, then returned her gaze to his eyes. "And given we routed Winchelsea, clearly, together, we'll be able to handle anything life throws our way."

Michael chuckled, kissed her soundly, then rose from the bed. "Come on—we shouldn't keep the man waiting."

Cleo grinned. She lay relaxed for a moment, cataloging the odd twinges and savoring the strange sense of contentment that permeated her body all the way to her bones. Until the past few days, she hadn't understood the attraction of physical intimacy—had never understood why other ladies seemed to lose their heads over the activity. Now, however, she had to own to being completely won over—to the extent of wondering why she'd taken so long... Her gaze had fixed on Michael as, untroubled by his nakedness as men usually were, he'd walked across to the washstand. And there lay her answer. She hadn't, until the past few days, met him—the critical factor. For her, intimacy wouldn't be the glory it was without him.

She spent a moment reflecting on that, then, smiling still, rolled to her side of the bed. After sliding from beneath the covers, she hunted for and found her chemise.

They used yesterday's chilly water to wash, which, aside from anything else, had the benefit of rendering them fully awake.

She needed his help with her corset; his nimble fingers made short work of her laces, testifying to his experience in that arena, which only left her feeling even more smug at the thought that she—Cleo Hendon, the unmarriageable businesswoman—had succeeded where all those other ladies had failed.

Of course, her gold satin lady-of-the-night gown wasn't what she would have chosen to make her first appearance as Michael's fiancée, but when she mentioned it, he pointed out that once Drake or anyone else learned the purpose of her disguise, they would appreciate and, indeed, approve of her appearance.

Once they were dressed and she'd reanchored her curls in a passable knot, he offered her his arm. His gaze captured hers as she laid her hand on his sleeve. "Are you ready to face whatever comes?"

She smiled. "As long as you're by my side."

He raised her hand to his lips, kissed her fingers, set her hand on his sleeve, and together, they walked to the door.

As they left the room, Cleo recalled her thought of the small hours—that the act of intimacy was the greatest adventure that would ever come her way.

But that wasn't and wouldn't be so; what lay before them would trump even that.

Marriage, with all its many facets, would be the greatest, most consuming, most rewarding adventure of their lives.

With her head high and her gaze firmly fixed on their joint future, on Michael's arm, she descended the stairs.

∾

Hamilton came into the front hall just as they reached the bottom of the stairs; he led them to the breakfast parlor.

Drake, seated at the head of the table, rose. His gaze on Cleo, he bowed. "Miss Hendon, I believe?"

Her hand on Michael's arm, Cleo curtsied. "Lord Winchelsea."

Drake met her gaze as she straightened and smiled wryly. "Please, just Drake. After our earlier encounter, that seems more appropriate."

Calmly, Michael stated, "Cleo has done me the honor of agreeing to be my wife."

Drake's smile was genuine, if faintly amused. "Congratulations to you both." He shook hands with Michael, then claimed Cleo's hand and bowed elegantly over it. Releasing her, he glanced at Michael. "So another Cynster falls courtesy of this mission. Your parents should be pleased with me."

Michael grinned. "I'm sure Mama will be in touch with your mother to convey her appreciation."

Drake sent him a mock-sour look, then waved them to the well-stocked sideboard. "I daresay you both have an appetite. Do join me."

Michael couldn't stop grinning. He glanced at Cleo and, at her nod, led her to the sideboard. Once they'd served themselves from the array of chafing dishes, Hamilton seated them beside each other on Drake's right, then inquired whether they wished tea and coffee. On being informed they did, he departed to fetch fresh pots.

Drake looked up from his plate, fixed an inquiring gaze on them both, and arched his brows.

Michael sobered and opened his mouth, but before he could say anything, the front doorbell cut him off. The peal was followed by voices in the hall. Seconds later, Sebastian ushered Antonia into the room.

Michael and Drake rose, as did Cleo.

Drake murmured, "I sent for them. I thought they'd want to hear all we've discovered."

Smoothly, Michael introduced Cleo to Antonia and then Sebastian.

Sebastian clapped Michael on the shoulder and smiled welcomingly at Cleo. "I understand you've been Michael's partner in this mission."

Cleo inclined her head and cast a glance at Michael.

The moment was too good to pass up; he took her hand and faced his brother. "As I've just told Drake, Cleo and I have decided to extend our partnership into wider fields, including marriage. You three are the first to know." He looked pointedly at Sebastian and Antonia. "And that also means you two had better hurry things along, because we"—he glanced at Cleo and smiled with prideful intent—"are prepared to wait only so long before fronting the altar ourselves."

"Wonderful!" Antonia stepped forward and hugged Cleo with transparent warmth and undeniable delight. "It will be a relief to have someone with whom to share the inevitable ton limelight."

Despite her smile, Cleo managed to pull a face. "I'm not sure about the limelight. I rather fancy dodging it as much as possible."

"That's a dream unlikely to come true." As Antonia turned to Michael, Drake met Cleo's eyes and smiled warmly. "Again, my very real felicitations, Miss Hendon."

She smiled back. "Please, just Cleo."

Still smiling, Drake inclined his head. His gaze shifted to Michael, currently accepting Sebastian's and Antonia's wishes, along with what appeared to be a ribbing; lowering his voice, Drake said, "He's a good man."

"He is." Cleo waited until Drake's strangely penetrating—almost piercing—golden gaze returned to her face to state, "And a warning for the future—he and I will always be a team."

Drake's smile faded. "Antonia informed me of much the same thing. I'm unsure if that means my list of agents has expanded or contracted."

Cleo arched her brows. "I suspect that will depend on the missions—and on you."

"Hmm." Drake moved aside as Sebastian came to congratulate Cleo.

Grinning delightedly, Sebastian squeezed her fingers, then bent his head and kissed her cheek. "I can't begin to tell you how pleased I am." He released her and glanced at Michael. "At least now someone else will be there to keep him in line."

Michael made a scoffing sound, but as his gaze returned to Cleo's face, he smiled and didn't disagree.

Drake had returned to the head of the table. "Perhaps," he said, pulling out his chair, "we should get back to the business that brings us all here."

Cleo and Michael returned to their places, while Sebastian seated Antonia opposite Cleo, then took the next chair along, the one opposite Michael.

Hamilton arrived with a large pot of coffee and another of tea. After pouring cups of tea for the ladies and setting a rack of fresh toast between them, he poured cups of coffee for the three men, then glanced at Drake.

Drake nodded. "Thank you, Hamilton. That will be all for the moment."

Hamilton bowed and withdrew. The door quietly shut behind him.

"Right then." Drake set down his coffee cup. He looked at Michael and Cleo. "What have you two learned?"

They shared the honors, allowing one of them to eat while the other spoke. Michael started, reminding everyone that his task had been to find the missing gunpowder. After he'd related how that had led him to Cleo, she took over, explaining the existence of the Worshipful Company of Carmen and the register of carters and carts. Between them, they described their pursuit of the fourteen carters registered to move gunpowder, culminating in the discovery that a carter named Terry Doolan and his apprentice had fetched the barrels from Kent, delivered them to a warehouse in Morgan's Lane, and then disappeared.

Michael explained how he'd exploited family connections at Scotland Yard and, through them, confirmed that the bodies of Doolan and his apprentice had been pulled from the river, and that they'd been murdered, most likely soon after delivering the barrels to the warehouse.

"Doolan," Drake murmured. "I assume he was Irish. Did he have any connection to the Young Irelanders?"

"Possibly a sympathizer," Michael replied. "But no one knew him to be actively involved."

Michael outlined the situation they found in Morgan's Lane, with the three warehouses that might have taken in the barrels, and went on to describe the cordon of men he'd subsequently placed around the area to guard against the barrels being moved.

Cleo stepped in before he mentioned her appearance as a lad and leapt ahead to give a condensed version of how they had called at the three warehouses. "When we walked into the third warehouse, the one midway down the lane, we discovered the office in chaos because the foreman hadn't been sighted since Wednesday—the day on which the barrels were brought into London and, as we later confirmed, stored at that warehouse."

Michael flicked a glance at Drake, then looked across the table at Sebastian. "The dead bodies are piling up. I'm sure we'll discover O'Toole, the foreman, among their number. Along with a few more besides. O'Toole was an Irishman, but again, not known to be actively involved with the Young Irelanders. In his case, he's left a young family to which it seemed he was devoted."

Her expression set, Cleo nodded. "He wouldn't have left his family, so it seems likely he, too, has been murdered." She drew in a breath, then continued, describing how they'd gone into Shepherd's warehouse and found the barrels sitting under a tarpaulin along the rear wall.

Drake's eyes opened wide. "So you've found them?"

Michael exchanged a grim glance with Cleo. "Yes, but they've vanished again."

"What?" came from three throats.

Michael sipped his coffee, then pushed away his empty plate, sat back, and, step by step, detailed the events of the past twenty-four hours. He explained how Cleo had put a commercial hold on the barrels—and what that meant—but that a rider with two carts driven by two men who weren't gunpowder carters had turned up close to midnight. This time, he didn't shy from describing Cleo's presence in the lane.

"Ah." Drake nodded. "That's why you're dressed as you are. I did wonder at your...sartorial elegance." Approval glimmered in his eyes, and in Sebastian's.

Blushing slightly, Cleo lightly shrugged. Across the table, she met Antonia's gaze. "Men always disregard women, and a lady of the night proved to be a sight none of the men involved thought particularly noteworthy."

Her eyes met Michael's, and he smothered a grunt; at least she hadn't mentioned that *he* hadn't recognized her until later. He quickly resumed his recitation of events. After explaining what happened once the barrels had been loaded and the carts had moved off again, surprising them all by going in what they'd deemed the wrong direction, he admitted, "If Cleo hadn't been there, closer to the end of Morgan's Lane and on the same side as the lane the carts took, as I couldn't reach the corner in time, we would have lost sight of the carts and barrels at that point. But because Cleo was there, we know the carts went at least partway up Black Lion Court, but the court opens into a veritable maze, and where they went after that, we don't know, because"—he broke off to draw in a deep breath; just thinking about what had happened next still made him tense —"we ended up tangling with the man directing the carts—the rider."

Drake regarded them impassively. "Am I to take it his is the dead body currently residing in one of the outhouses?"

Michael nodded. Briefly, he ran through the action from the moment the rider had seized Cleo.

"A cavalry saber!" Sebastian exclaimed. "Was he a cavalry officer?"

Michael shook his head. "Other than the sword, and him knowing how to use it, there was nothing to say he was. However, it's certainly possible that he was in the cavalry at some time in the past."

"I checked the body," Drake said. "He was older than us by at least a few years, so yes, that's entirely possible."

Michael briefly outlined the fight. Sebastian and Antonia hung on his words. At the head of the table, Drake listened with hooded eyes.

When Michael came to the point of the rider drawing a pistol, he blandly added, "I did the same. His shot went wide—mine didn't."

Cleo turned her head to look at him and smoothly added, "I had my revolver—I shot him, too. And I didn't miss, either."

Drake's lips curved slightly. "That explains why our villain has two bullet holes in his chest, entering from two very different angles." He met Cleo's, then Michael's eyes. "For the record, either shot would have proved fatal."

Both Cleo and Michael grimaced.

Drake continued imperturbably, "While it would have been nice to have captured the man alive, I suspect that was never on the cards. Given how indefatigable our villains have been in silencing all possible sources of information about this plot, I seriously doubt our rider would have allowed himself to be taken alive. And even if we'd managed that feat, he wouldn't have talked." Drake's features hardened. "As I think we all agree, there's a clock ticking somewhere in the background, and there's only so much time before this mission ends—one way or another. This man, I suspect, was of the inner circle. He would have known that—known he only had to keep quiet for just so many days, and his group, whoever they are, would succeed."

After a moment of considering that prospect, Drake looked at Michael. "So what happened with the carts?"

Michael explained how the carts had vanished into the fog and described their subsequent search. "All futile, I'm afraid."

"But it's not a complete loss," Drake said. "Although you lost sight of the carts, we know the barrels are still within a specific area of Southwark, and you have men keeping a close watch over the borders of that area."

Michael glanced at Sebastian. "It's the footman army—they won't let anything escape them."

"Good thinking," Sebastian said. "I can't imagine that our plotters' intended target is in that area." He shifted his gaze to Drake. "Which means we—or rather, the plotters—are still at least one step away from the gunpowder being used."

Slowly, Drake nodded. "I agree. So we have at least a little time yet, and a decent hope of preventing the eventual deployment of the barrels." He sat straighter. "And losing one of their number—a number that, I'm certain, won't have been large to begin with—will have thrown a spanner in their works. It'll take them at least a few extra days to sort themselves out—possibly even to realize the rider is missing, let alone dead."

Antonia looked at Cleo. "You said all carts were registered. Is there any way of tracing the carts used to take the barrels from the warehouse?"

"Carters' carts are registered, but the two carts used were drays..." Cleo paused.

"What?" Michael asked as she stared into space.

"I *think*," she eventually said, "indeed, I'm fairly sure that the carts, which, incidentally, were definitely drays—they had lower sides and backs—might well have been brewers' drays." She glanced at Michael. "There are several breweries in that area, aren't there?"

He grimaced. "Yes, but there's no saying, even if those carts were brewery drays from one or other of those breweries, that the brewery was the destination for the barrels."

"Given how busy brewery yards are, that's unlikely," Drake said. "The risk of the gunpowder being discovered would be unacceptably high." He glanced at Antonia. "I can't imagine any way of identifying a dray that's been used to move barrels of gunpowder, not once the barrels are no longer on it." He looked at Michael. "We're more likely to discover the men involved—the drivers—by trawling the morgues."

Grimly, Michael nodded. "I'll speak to the officers at Scotland Yard and ask to be informed of any unidentified bodies they pull from the river. That seems to be these villains' preferred method of disposal."

Drake humphed. He leant his elbows on the table, interlaced his fingers, and rested his chin on his hands. After a moment of staring down the table, he said, "So the barrels are somewhere in that area. Could we mount an effective search?"

"We searched the streets and all accessible yards and found nothing," Michael said. "But as for searching the buildings...the area's exceedingly densely populated. Ten barrels of gunpowder could be hidden in a single room, or in an outbuilding, warehouse, stable, cellar —the possibilities are endless. You would need to turn people into the streets and go through the entire area with the equivalent of a fine-toothed comb. You'd need a regiment to do it, and the populace might well riot."

Drake grimaced. "I thought you'd say that." He stirred, then straightened. "So searching for the barrels is out, and looking for the carts isn't likely to get us anywhere." He looked around the table. "Where does that leave us?"

Frowning at the tablecloth, Sebastian tapped a finger on it. "One question—why have they bothered to move the barrels at all?" He glanced at Michael. "Shepherd's warehouse was a relatively safe location, at least for some time. Why not leave the barrels there? Yet they've moved them, but only a short distance. As far as I can see, that move wasn't occasioned by anything we did—they didn't know you were close, that you'd discovered the barrels. They didn't know you were watching." He looked at Drake. "Moving the barrels from Shepherd's warehouse to somewhere else in that warren has to be a part of their careful plans. But why?"

A silent second elapsed, then Cleo lowered her teacup and sighed. "It's possible someone—the rider, for instance—inquired at the warehouse yesterday afternoon, much as we did, just to make sure all was well with the barrels. The staff would have informed him that someone had put a commercial hold on the lot—and he would then have known he had to move the barrels quickly to some other spot." She glanced at Michael, then looked at Drake. "Our interest in the barrels might have caused them to be moved."

Drake weighed the notion, then shook his head decisively. "No. In order to have discovered your hold on the barrels, for no reason he could have known, he would have had to show his face—which is something these people have thus far been very careful to avoid—and, more, admit to an interest in gunpowder and those barrels in particular, specifically calling attention to barrels that, as far as he knew, no one left at the warehouse was aware existed, which was the whole point of secretly delivering the barrels into the warehouse, then removing the foreman. The rider knew the gunpowder was there—there was no reason for him to break with their careful habits and call attention to the hoard, and risk being identifiably associated with it. On those grounds alone, I can't see him making inquiries and learning about your interest.

"But on top of that, these people do not move quickly—their cautiousness and deliberation have remained unwavering. Every little step in their plot has been carefully crafted and planned well in advance. For the rider to have learned of your interference in the afternoon, and by night, have organized two suitable carts with drivers prepared to work in secret and transport the barrels to some new place he'd organized...that would constitute a massive change from their modus operandi to date. At no time have they moved quickly. They haven't changed plans. They've never moved without very carefully choosing the people to draw into their plot." Again, Drake shook his head, if anything even more decisively. "No—Sebastian's right. Moving the barrels last night featured in their plans all along. And therefore, it tells us something, if only we can figure out what."

Another silence descended. This time, Michael broke it. "The carts rolled on." He met Cleo's eyes. "Even though, when all was said and done, we remained with the rider in the lane for ten or more minutes, the drivers didn't come back to ask which way to go. And when we searched the lanes an hour or so later, we didn't find the drivers or anyone else searching for the rider."

Slowly, Cleo nodded. "It was all arranged—the drivers knew where they were going. The rider didn't need to tell them anything else. Not that night."

"Perhaps," Antonia said, "that's why the barrels are still in the area. With the rider gone, no one knows where next to send them."

They all pondered that scenario. Eventually, Drake said, "We can but hope. That might give us a few more days, but eventually, whoever is ultimately directing this plot will realize they've lost the rider, and they'll send in someone else."

He paused, then went on, "That the barrels are currently somewhere in that area of Southwark means we still have a chance to follow them on. However, I have to admit that I'm growing uneasy over continuing with that tack. Given the proximity to so many potential targets, the next stage is likely to encompass moving the gunpowder into its final position..." He grimaced. "We'll have only one more chance to intercept the barrels and catch the plotters—or at least learn enough to identify them. Time, indeed, is running out."

Drake sat back and looked at Michael. "Can you keep your army of watchers in place?"

"At this time of year, that shouldn't be a problem."

Drake drummed his fingers on the table, then glanced around at the others. "No matter how tight a watch we keep on the area, we have to accept that there's a finite possibility that the gunpowder will be disguised in some fashion and successfully moved on to the target. These people have planned carefully, and so far, they've planned well." He paused, then frowned. "This is such an abnormal plot, I can't feel confident in predicting how it will unfold. However"—his tone grew more definite —"I don't believe we should rely on foiling the plot purely through keeping an eye on that area of Southwark."

Sebastian grunted. "So what did you learn up north? Any clues there?"

Drake's expression turned grim. "It's as I suspected—whoever is behind this plot, it's not the Chartists. I spoke to O'Connor. He swore that after '48, the movement had committed to pursuing its agenda by entirely peaceful, law-abiding means."

Michael snorted. "He's a politician now. Of course, he would say that."

Drake inclined his head. "True. But in this case, he wasn't lying. He all but tripped over his own feet to give me an introduction to London's Chartist militia leaders and invited—nay, encouraged—me to contact them." Drake sipped from his coffee cup, then lowered it. "Which I will do, but more on that anon. So that was O'Connor, but given I was up there, I scouted around among the general membership. I heard a lot of mutterings from the more militant members, but nothing of the ilk of using gunpowder to blow something up in London. Erecting a barricade and making a noise in the local town square is more their plane of operations."

He looked down at his coffee cup, cradled between his hands. "I weighed things up and decided it was worth rolling the dice and making contact with the other Chartist leaders. O'Connor might be the head, but the others are still there and are rather better connected with the general ranks. They know me as a local—and therefore know enough to suspect that I might have the Home Secretary's ear." Drake's lips twisted cynically. "That said, they have a fairly realistic view of their organization's standing, and I hoped—believed—that in a matter like this, they would tell me the truth."

He looked up and met the others' gazes. "And I think they did, as far as they knew it. They denied—vociferously and with convincing force— that the organization had any involvement in a gunpowder plot in London or anywhere else. However, I got the distinct impression that they were uneasy over speaking for the London militia, and they, too, urged me to use O'Connor's introduction."

"So," Michael said, "although the heads of the Chartist movement haven't authorized any such plot, they acknowledge there's a possibility Chartists from London might be involved?"

Drake nodded. "From what we already know, someone very clever has used Young Irelander sympathizers as foot soldiers in the first phase of this plot—namely for purchasing, transporting, and secreting the gunpowder in London. I suspect that the next phase—which I assume involves facilitating the deployment of the gunpowder to the target and possibly even detonating the stuff—is slated to be performed by members of London's Chartist militia, under the guidance of the plotters, of course. However, the militia members will believe their orders are coming from O'Connor and the committee in the north."

Drake drained his coffee cup, then set it down. "I'll approach the local militia leaders, but I suspect that will get us nowhere, at least not quickly —not in time. If, as we suspect, the local leaders have allowed themselves and their members to be drawn into this...once they learn it isn't an approved plot and they've been hoodwinked, the implications of ten barrels of gunpowder is so serious, they will be far more likely to deny all knowledge rather than assist me and risk being blamed and bringing the movement, O'Connor and all, crashing down." Drake shook his head. "Despite talking to me being in their best interests, I expect to get nothing more from them than horrified stares followed—a few seconds too late— by protestations of complete and utter innocence. At least at first."

Sebastian pulled a face. "Given the government's heavy-handed response last time, in their place, we'd probably do the same."

Drake humphed. "Which, again, testifies to the cleverness of whoever is behind this damned plot. You can see it, can't you? If the plot succeeds and something major is blown up, there will be public outrage, and everyone will be searching for a scapegoat. And of course, once the gunpowder blows, it won't be so hard to trace the plot backward—first to the Chartists, if, as we think, they're the ones involved in this second stage, and subsequently to the Young Irelanders who brought the gunpowder into London." He paused, then his lips quirked in reluctant, if grim, acknowledgment. "It's ingenious, really. There will be so much outcry and fury, all directed at the Chartists and Young Irelanders, that no one will think of looking for who actually directed the plot."

"Whoever they are," Antonia dryly remarked, "it appears they bear no love for the Chartists or the Young Irelanders."

"True." Drake tipped his head her way. "And that's something, ulti-mately, to bear in mind. But for now..."

When he didn't immediately continue, Cleo crisply stated, "For now, as of this hour, we have ten hundredweight of gunpowder that's gone to ground, so to speak, in a circumscribed area of Southwark. And we know that the instructions directing this plot aren't coming from either of the obvious suspects, namely the Young Irelanders and the Chartists." She raised one hand and ticked off her subsequent points on her fingers. "We don't know who is behind the plot. We don't know the motivations driving it. We don't know what the next move will be. Most troubling of all, we have no idea what target the gunpowder is destined to blow up."

She looked around the table. "Did I miss anything?"

"Clearly, having a business mind comes in useful in other spheres," Drake remarked. "But no, that was a masterful listing of the major points we don't know. I can't see any important point you omitted." He paused, then went on, "But one corollary of your last point is that, having no idea of the target, we also have no way of telling who or what needs to be protected. With that sense of time running out intensifying, it's that point that exercises me most."

"What about the rider?" Sebastian looked at Michael. "You said he was a gentleman. Do we know who he is?"

Michael grimaced. "He carried no cards, but Finnegan seemed confident he would be able to trace his identity." Michael looked at Drake, who appeared sunk in consideration of some unappealing prospect. "You saw the body—did you recognize him?"

Drake looked up; after a second, he shook his head. "Never seen him before."

"Has Finnegan had any luck in learning the man's identity?" Sebastian persevered.

Drake glanced at him. "No. The man's clothes weren't his own—Finnegan's sure of that. But his boots, on the other hand, were. Finnegan's off chasing the bootmaker."

Drake glanced at the clock on the mantelpiece, then, with evident reluctance, bestirred himself. "I need to report to Whitehall." He gripped the carver's arms, preparing to rise. "We have ten barrels of gunpowder in the hands of unknown plotters secreted in an area that's effectively impenetrable to the authorities and also far too close to any number of strategic political targets. I will, of course, urge Greville to alert the constabulary and the various regiments guarding such places, *but*"—Drake's lips thinned; his expression was grimly mutinous—"I seriously doubt Greville will authorize even an advisory."

"Good God!" Michael said. "Why not?"

"Because," Drake said, cynical impatience dripping from his tone, "Greville, while at heart a good man, is an excellent politician, and given the current climate—meaning the public uncertainty lingering after the upheavals of '48—he and his government colleagues will do everything possible to avoid alerting the public to anything of this nature. In Greville's and his colleagues' eyes, such news becoming public is certain to further erode confidence in the government, and that, they will not risk."

Cleo frowned. "But if the plot succeeds and something is blown up...?"

Drake's cynicism deepened. "That will be a disaster, and they will happily deal with it then—and paint themselves as decisive, active, and bold defenders of the people while they're at it. And as we've already noted, courtesy of the mastermind behind this plot, they'll have the perfect scapegoats to hand—scapegoats the public will readily accept."

Aghast, Antonia stared at Drake as he pushed back his chair and rose to his feet. "You mean to say that Greville—and the government—will happily sit back and allow this plot to succeed? That they'll allow some monument or public building to be blown up?"

Drake looked down at her, then quietly said, "Not happily." He paused, then glanced around the table, meeting the others' eyes. "What I'm trying to instill into your heads is that Greville and his cohorts will sit on their hands and pray that something will happen and this plot won't succeed—that will be their preferred outcome. But while they'll hope for the best, they will refuse to do anything that might weaken or in any way damage their current position with the public, and meanwhile, they'll prepare for the worst." His voice weighted with world-weary cynicism, he concluded, "While an explosion of that size in central London might be the end of the world for some, it won't be the end of the world for the government."

The other four stared at Drake as his words sank in.

After several silent seconds, Drake grimaced. "I need to go."

Sebastian shook himself. "Yes, go—and see if you can't convince Greville to see sense. Meanwhile, we"—he glanced at the other three—"will go over the things we do know and work out what avenues we might pursue to get the answers to our burning questions."

Drake nodded and started for the door. "I suggest we reconvene later this afternoon. It'll take me that long to deal with Greville and his secretaries." On reaching the door, Drake paused and glanced back. "However, we shouldn't meet here." A ghost of a smile touched his lips. "A group of individuals will be calling this afternoon to remove the body to a helpfully discreet private morgue, and I make it a point to never be in when that particular group calls. Better for them, and better for me as well."

Michael shrugged and glanced at Sebastian. "No reason we can't meet at St. Ives House. The parents might be around, but the back parlor's out of everyone's way."

"I was given to understand," Sebastian said, "that Mama expected to be out all morning, possibly all day, consulting with the countess and our numerous female relatives regarding our engagement ball. Papa mumbled something about retreating to White's and playing least in sight, along with the earl, so we should have the house to ourselves."

Drake hesitated, then asked, "What about your sister?"

"Apparently, she's not expected until tomorrow." Sebastian glanced at Antonia, who nodded.

"Very well." Drake opened the door. "As soon as I return from Whitehall, I'll join you at St. Ives House."

The others murmured farewells and "Good luck."

With a salute, Drake departed, leaving the door open.

Michael rose and drew out Cleo's chair. On the other side of the table, Sebastian performed the same office for Antonia. In a group, they walked out of the breakfast parlor. Hamilton and a footman were waiting in the front hall to assist them into their greatcoats and cloaks.

Drake had already quit the house.

The four emerged onto the front porch. Michael and Cleo paused to take in the pewter skies, brisk breeze, and the bustle and sounds of late morning.

Antonia linked her arm in Sebastian's, and they walked down the steps.

Michael offered Cleo his arm. When she looked up at him, he smiled. "Shall we?"

Cleo read the invitation in his eyes and knew it extended to far more than just a walk along the pavement, that it encompassed their future and all yet to come, of which this short walk was merely the first step. Their first public action as an affianced couple; she felt a smile unlike any she'd ever smiled before curve her lips. "Indeed." She linked her arm in his, and together they descended the steps and set off in Sebastian and Antonia's wake.

CHAPTER 17

*C*ontrary to Sebastian's understanding, the Duke and Duchess of St. Ives were at home.

At Sebastian and Antonia's heels, Michael and Cleo walked into the front hall to discover the duke in earnest discussion with the duchess at the foot of the stairs.

The ducal couple glanced briefly at the newcomers—then both looked again, their gazes fixing on Cleo, on Michael's arm and still gowned in her gaudy lady-of-the-night finery.

She blushed vividly, although even she could tell that Michael's parents looked intrigued rather than shocked.

Michael and Sebastian shrugged out of their greatcoats and handed them to the waiting butler, then lifted the cloaks from their respective ladies' shoulders.

By that time, the duke and the duchess had approached—the duke with a long-legged prowling stroll, the duchess with bustling, maternal intent.

Cleo braced herself, then dropped into a regulation curtsy—at least her full skirts were useful for that.

Michael stepped to her side. Taking her hand, he drew her up. "Papa, Mama—allow me to present Miss Cleome Hendon, the lady who has agreed to be my wife."

"Really? Excellent!" The duke's delight could not have been doubted;

it shone in his green eyes and lifted the lines of his somewhat harsh-featured face. He smiled at Cleo. "Welcome to the family, my dear. We know your parents well, and an alliance with the Hendons of Norfolk is wonderful news."

"Indeed." Beaming unrestrainedly, the duchess pushed forward to envelop Cleo in a warm, welcoming embrace. "My dear," she murmured in Cleo's ear, "quite literally, I could not be happier."

As the duchess stepped back, Cleo could see the sincerity of that statement in her face.

The duchess glanced at her husband. "This calls for a celebration—even if it is just an informal one over luncheon."

The duke had offered his hand to Michael, along with his enthusiastic best wishes. "Indubitably." He turned aside to speak to the butler, who, it appeared, was struggling to maintain a properly impassive demeanor in the face of an overwhelming impulse to beam, too.

The duchess had tugged Michael down to kiss his cheek. "Well done," she said as she stepped back. She glanced at the duke and the butler, still conferring. "Luncheon will be served virtually immediately." She turned and surveyed Cleo's gown. "Meanwhile, my dear"—with a gesture, she indicated the gown—"am I allowed to ask…?"

Cleo met Michael's eyes briefly and opted for the truth. If the Duchess of St. Ives was to be her mama-in-law, anything less was unlikely to be wise. "I knew Michael was watching for some villains in Morgan's Lane—that's in Southwark—last night, and that although he had men around the area, none could be anywhere in the lane, and I decided that was too dangerous, and if I went in disguise"—with one hand, she waved at the tawdry gown—"then none of the men who came were likely to pay any attention to me, but just by being there, I would be able to help…" She shrugged. "And so it proved."

The duchess regarded Cleo for several seconds, then looked at Michael. "Clearly, you've chosen well." Smiling delightedly again, the duchess swung about and linked her arm with Cleo's. "Let's go into the dining room. Antonia?" The duchess collected her other soon-to-be daughter-in-law with a glance, and in high good humor, led the way to the luncheon table.

The footmen had scurried to lay the table for six. The duke sat at the head, the duchess at the foot, with their prospective daughters-in-law on either side of the duke and their sons flanking their mother.

A delicate chicken broth was the first course. As they supped, the duke studied Cleo. "I understand you, too, have been recruited to assist Drake with this latest mission of his."

When she nodded, the duke smiled. "Did you know that, in years past, your parents have joined with us"—the duke nodded down the table at his duchess—"and Drake's parents, and Antonia's, too, in various missions?" The duke glanced at Sebastian and Antonia, including them as he said, "Just as you four are doing now."

Cleo thought of all she'd heard of her parents' past adventures. "I know they were involved in various intrigues, but I've never heard all the details." She met the duke's pale-green eyes. "I've never heard much of the others involved."

The duke rolled his expressive eyes. "How like your father. Well, let's see."

He proceeded, with assistance from the duchess when his memory proved selective, to entertain his sons, Antonia, and Cleo with a recitation of numerous instances when her parents had worked hand-in-glove with the Cynsters and with others of the fabled Bastion Club to right various wrongs and, mostly, to expose and capture villains and wrongdoers of various stripes. "And then there was the incident of the Black Cobra. That was quite a lengthy exercise."

After the duke described that action, the duchess told them of the West African scandal that had occurred twenty-five years ago. Cleo and Antonia were fascinated to hear of the role a fabulous blue diamond necklace had played in the unmasking of the villains.

"I've seen that necklace," Cleo put in. "Mrs. Isobel Frobisher wore it to a ball when the Frobishers were in London a few years ago." She paused, thinking, then offered, "The Frobisher Shipping Company is a major competitor, but there's always seemed to be some closer connection—as if they're a sister company of sorts. Now I've heard that story, I suspect that explains it."

The duke looked down the table, met his wife's eyes, and smiled the sort of smile only married couples could share. "It's one of the great strengths of the British aristocracy—the way our generations connect and reconnect."

The younger generation glanced around the table and grinned; they were, it seemed, living proof of that.

As the meal drew to a close, Michael mentioned his firming interest in investing in the import-export trade and his meeting with Geoffrey

Cranmer and, through him, the Hepworths of Philadelphia. That started another round of discussion, which continued as they repaired to the back parlor, the room the family used for relaxation.

Taking possession of the longer sofa, the duchess drew Antonia and Cleo to sit on either side of her; all three ladies were soon engrossed in an enthusiastic discussion of engagement balls and weddings. The duchess appealed to her husband on some point, and the duke sank into the armchair opposite, the better to hear what was demanded of him.

"And," Sebastian murmured, taking in his father's delighted expression, "because he appreciates the view."

Standing beside Sebastian behind the sofa, safely out of their mother's and their intendeds' line of sight, Michael smiled and nodded. "That—telling them—went a lot easier than I'd expected."

"That's because I did all the hard work," Sebastian said. "Antonia and I broke the ground—or the ice, or whatever the appropriate analogy is. For them, it's like a domino effect—I fall, and so you follow." Sebastian slanted a sidelong glance at Michael. "After all, it's always been that way."

Slipping his hands into his breeches pockets, Michael snorted, but was too content to take brotherly umbrage. "I really don't care how it came about or what anyone else thinks—Cleo is the right lady for me, and to me, that's all that matters."

His gaze resting on Antonia's dark head, Sebastian murmured, "It's strange how it happens. I was thinking of marriage, but never thought of her. You, on the other hand..."

"I wasn't thinking of marriage at all—at least not until you and Antonia raised the prospect in my mind."

"Still, don't you find it strange that, one minute, you're not thinking of them at all, and the next, they stand at the center of your universe, the fulcrum about which your life revolves? From complete unawareness to..."

"A connection so deep you can't imagine how you lived your life without them in it?"

Sebastian grinned. "You've obviously been bitten by the same bug."

Michael shifted. "The only part of it I don't appreciate is that feeling of impending doom when they're not where they're supposed to be—safe beside you."

"And even then," Sebastian somewhat grimly added. After a moment, he sighed resignedly. "I fear we're going to have to get used to that feeling. They're not going to allow us to keep them safely locked away."

"No." His gaze on Cleo's tumble of curls, Michael realized that, regardless, he was smiling. That contentment had slid deep and now circled his heart. That the simple happiness he now felt, and the eagerness to go forward and, with Cleo by his side, make of life what they could was a very long way from the ennui that had assailed him a mere five days before.

What a difference love makes.

At that moment, with him regarding Cleo with, he suspected, a besotted look on his face, she turned on the sofa and, spotting him, said, "Your mama has raised a very valid point—we need to inform my parents with all speed, before they hear our news from someone else. Despite the season, there are still a lot of people in town who are acquainted with Mama and Papa."

Sebastian murmured, sotto voce so only Michael could hear, "And you don't want Jack Hendon learning you've been dallying with his only daughter *before* you tell him your intentions are honorable."

Michael glanced at his father, who arched his brows as if to say the challenge was Michael's to meet, then Michael returned his gaze to Cleo's face. "I suggest you and I write a suitably informative letter, and we'll send it by courier direct to Castle Hendon."

"We should include the promise to visit there as soon as we can," Cleo added, "or else they'll be in Clarges Street tomorrow, and we really need to concentrate on helping Drake."

He nodded and glanced at his parents. "We haven't told you the details, but we definitely need to continue to assist Drake with this mission."

Standing shoulder to shoulder with Michael, Sebastian added, "The threat is now very real, and by all measures, this plot, if successful, will be dire for England as a whole." He, too, met his parents' gazes. "We—the four of us—need to work with Drake to get to the truth of it, put a stop to it, and expose those behind it as soon as may be."

The duke looked at the duchess as, suddenly entirely serious, she turned to him. Their gazes held for a moment in that indefinable communion of those who have shared all for many years, then the duke looked at his prospective daughters-in-law before raising his gaze to his sons. "It's your generation's turn to carry that torch. Do what you need to do—your duty to queen and country—and leave it to us to deal with society." Devil

Cynster grimaced. "That's now our milieu. Pursuing traitorous villains and their foiling plots now rightly falls to you."

∼

The Home Secretary, Sir George Greville, received Drake in his inner sanctum, deep within the hallowed precincts of Whitehall. Drake had consulted Greville's secretary and made the appointment for three o'clock, then had gone to Arthur's. He'd fallen in with several acquaintances, enjoyed a pleasant lunch, and had still had time to review his approach to Greville before returning to Whitehall.

In selecting three o'clock for the meeting, Drake had hoped to avoid the presence of the minister's principal private secretary, Sir Harold Waltham. Sadly, as Drake entered Greville's office, the first obstacle his gaze fell on was the rotund figure of Waltham, ensconced in a chair on the far side of Greville's large desk. Waltham had been scheduled to attend a briefing elsewhere, but clearly he'd checked the Home Secretary's appointment book before departing and had elected to remain at his post, the better to shield his master from Drake's influence.

Drake had a natural appreciation of and a healthy respect for those civil servants who were, so often, the ones who got things done. Waltham, in contrast, seemed to have made it his personal mission to ensure as little as possible was ever done; he frequently and forcefully spoke against Greville taking action of any sort, regardless of the pressure to act.

Regardless of what was best for the country.

Waltham had a habit of using the adjective "radical" when what he actually meant was the rather more cowardly "politically risky."

Consequently, Waltham viewed Drake in much the same way as Drake viewed him—as a necessary evil to be worked around.

Inwardly resigning himself to failure, at least in terms of getting Greville to issue any warning to the constabulary or guards, and that had been an outside chance at best, Drake returned Greville's greeting, shook his hand, then sat in the armchair angled before the desk. The angle allowed Drake an excellent view of his nemesis's already disapproving countenance.

Greville, whose family's ancestral estate shared a border with the principal seat of the Dukes of Wolverstone and who might therefore be classed as a neighbor of Drake's, leant his forearms on the desk, clasped his hands on his blotter, and fixed Drake with a genuinely earnest regard.

"I take it that threat you mentioned, the one involving gunpowder, has proved to be real."

Drake inclined his head. Without emotion, he described the bare bones of the action to that point and outlined the salient facts—namely, that after investigating various rumors, and courtesy of an alert from Lord Ennis, who had consequently been murdered by the villains, they had uncovered a plot involving ten barrels of gunpowder, enough to destroy a large building. Furthermore, that cache of gunpowder was currently secreted in a section of London just across the river, unfortunately an area into which the authorities couldn't effectively penetrate. He concluded, "The barrels are there, far too close. My agents are maintaining a watch over the area, but given the proximity of the river, it's entirely possible the gunpowder will be moved, one way or another, to the intended target."

He paused, then evenly stated, "I would strongly urge you to issue an alert to Scotland Yard and the constabulary, and also the various regiments responsible for guarding government buildings and the royal family, to be on the lookout for any suspicious activity. If the gunpowder is successfully brought over the river, the constabulary and the guardsmen will be the last line of defense. If they're warned, they'll be watching, and there's a decent chance they'll be able to foil the plot at the very last gasp."

Predictably, Waltham was frowning. "I heard about Ennis's death—I thought he was killed by his younger brother."

"He was," Drake replied. "Connell Boyne was a Young Irelander sympathizer and believed he was acting for the cause, and that his brother had betrayed both him and that cause."

Waltham's frown deepened, and he directed a confused look at Greville. "But I thought you said you'd checked with your contacts in Ireland, and this *wasn't* a Young Irelander plot."

"It isn't." Drake paused to reinforce his hold on his temper; he'd already explained the Young Irelander connection in simple and unambiguous terms. "Several Young Irelander sympathizers, like Connell Boyne, were hoodwinked into believing they were acting for the cause. But they weren't. Someone else is behind this."

"Yes, but"—Waltham leant forward, an expression of earnest confusion on his round face—"what I can't quite see is why, whoever this nebulous person is, it couldn't simply be a matter of them seeing a good way to have someone else smuggle ten barrels of gunpowder into the country."

That's the point. Drake forced himself to draw in a breath. Then he tried another tack. He caught Greville's gaze. "Ten barrels of gunpowder. One thousand, one hundred, and twenty pounds of the stuff. I agree with Waltham." From the corner of his eye, he saw Waltham blink. "The vital question is: Why did this person—the one actually behind the plot—want that much gunpowder smuggled into the country?"

Greville knew very well what answer they should assume and act on, yet after a moment of holding Drake's gaze, he glanced at Waltham, inviting his input.

An invitation Waltham grasped with both hands. "Well, who's to say?" He gestured as if to indicate that the possibilities were endless. "Perhaps...he's an explosives manufacturer and is running close to the wind and wanted to avoid the excise?"

Drake had to hand it to Waltham. Pushed to it, he'd come up with a scenario that wasn't impossible. It just wasn't the right one.

Greville now looked at Drake as if this was a debate—first one side, then the other.

Keeping his voice rigidly even, Drake said, "Thus far, every man drawn into assisting with this enterprise has been murdered. No matter how hard-pressed a manufacturer might be, killing man after man just to avoid excise is stretching the probabilities beyond breaking point." He paused, then went on, "And the rider who attacked my agents last night and was subsequently killed was a gentleman, possibly an ex-cavalry officer." In his earlier recitation, he'd withheld that little tidbit; he knew better than to share everything he knew, even with his supposed master.

Before Greville could comment, Waltham, his pasty brow furrowed once again, said, "I don't know where that gets us. Are you sure the Chartists aren't involved?"

"Quite sure. O'Connor and his lieutenants know nothing about this." Drake omitted to mention the possibility that some of the local members might have been drawn into the plot; no need to give Waltham further rope to tangle them in.

"Yes, but...perhaps the local branch might have decided to forge their own path." Waltham looked at Drake. "Several gentlemen—younger sons —flirted with the cause, you know."

That was a dig at Drake's own inclinations. Waltham didn't like Drake's political leanings, either.

Drake could see where Waltham was leading the conversation. If Drake said this was a Chartist plot, then Greville would feel forced to take action. But then potentially draconian retribution would rain down on the remnants of the Chartist movement—which would suit Waltham down to the ground. Drake calmly stated, "This is not a Chartist plot—that much is certain."

"So it's not a Chartist plot, and it's not a Young Irelander plot, either." Waltham looked with feigned puzzlement at Greville. "But who else is there who would undertake such a plot? This makes no sense—are we even sure there is a plot?"

Waltham sat back and regarded Drake as if having suddenly seen a light. "Perhaps this is, as we hypothesized earlier, a simple case of smuggled gunpowder, and some other beggar has seen a chance and stolen it. That's why this gentleman ex-cavalry officer was involved—he was a mercenary some other manufacturer hired to steal his competitor's smuggled goods, hoping to put his competitor, the one who needed the untaxed gunpowder, onto the ropes so he could buy him out."

Drake stared at the now-almost-genial Waltham and felt a faint—very faint—stirring of respect. The civil servant had managed to conjure an explanation that covered most of the facts in such a way as to render the whole innocuous. No threat.

Finally, Greville spoke. "Could that be it? That this is all just a harmless—or at least relatively harmless, speaking from a government perspective—case of commercial subterfuge gone wrong?"

Drake studied Greville. He knew the man, even liked him on a personal level, but there was no doubt he was a canny politician, and after the suppression of recent years, Greville had very little stomach for being forced to act in any way that implied weakness or vulnerability. With a sharp eye to his own political future, Greville didn't want this to be a political plot. More, he would cling to any fiction that cast the plot as being of no real threat to the population in general—that it somehow wasn't the sort of action that fell within his remit. And in that, he would have no more ardent supporter than his principal private secretary.

"The way I see this," Drake said, hoping to lead Greville into widening his view, "is that someone—at the most a very small group of people acting together, but almost certainly under the orders of a single person—has succeeded in arranging for ten barrels of gunpowder to be smuggled into London and secreted very close to the centers of government and of society. As yet, I have no evidence as to who that person is or what their target is. There is nothing to say that this plot has anything to do with politics in the usual sense—only that whoever is behind it has an excellent grasp of current political realities."

Greville shifted, uncomfortable with that subtle prod.

Smoothly, Drake went on, "But in my view, the critical point, as of this moment, is that those ten barrels of gunpowder constitute a strong, credible, and potentially quite urgent threat to the realm. Against the scenario of commercial misdemeanor so eloquently outlined by Sir Harold must be weighed the reaction of the public should Sir Harold's proposed scenario not be true, and ten hundredweight of gunpowder is detonated somewhere in the capital."

The light was behind Greville, yet Drake thought he paled. After a second, Greville glanced at Waltham. "Perhaps we might try an unspecific warning...?"

Waltham's eyes flared wide; his concern was unfeigned. "Mr. Secretary, I'm not sure that would be wise. Can you imagine the panic if word got out—as it undoubtedly would? Why, *especially* with an unspecific warning, the man on the street would be looking in every direction in terror." Waltham glanced at Drake. "The city might well become paralyzed by fear, with people imagining death lurking everywhere."

Drake couldn't dispute that, but if it were left to him, to ensure no word got out, he would issue a detailed warning under absolute secrecy directly to those responsible, ignoring the normal chain of command. Unfortunately, Greville was a different sort of man. He played by the official rules.

That was the reason Greville was behind the desk, and Drake—as his father had before him—chose to face it.

When politicians failed, the likes of the Variseys and Cynsters stepped in. For queen and country. That was the creed they'd been born to, an inalienable part of the mantle of nobility.

Greville knew well enough what he faced in Drake; aside from all else, he'd been the one to recruit Drake to fill his father's shoes. Now he studied Drake, trying to feel his way toward what would placate his most dangerous of subordinates—dangerous because Drake was only *nominally* subordinate.

Finally, Greville ventured, "If I understood correctly, you cannot—at this moment in time—point to a specific target. Nor have you yet found evidence of who is behind this, hence their motives remain obscured."

Curtly, Drake nodded.

Greville drew in a breath, then let it out in a resigned sigh. "In that case, my lord, I fear we cannot oblige you by authorizing any alert at this time. Until you can produce irrefutable evidence of an active plot targeting the government or the realm via a specific target, our hands are tied." From beneath his lashes, Greville glanced sidelong at Waltham, then continued, "However, I wish you to continue to investigate this matter with your usual thoroughness and to pursue it to its conclusion. One way or another, this office will wish to know what transpires."

Drake didn't smile, especially not wolfishly, but that statement was the one thing he'd wanted and needed to take from this meeting—a clear directive to pursue the matter under his usual terms. He would have continued to pursue the villains—and the gunpowder—regardless, but with official standing, he could call on greater resources and was more likely to succeed.

For Waltham's benefit appearing to be reluctantly resigned, Drake inclined his head. "As you wish."

Fleetingly, Greville met Drake's eyes and faintly grimaced. He recognized what he'd done; if Drake failed and the gunpowder was used and the threat Drake believed existed materialized... All responsibility for preventing that outcome now rested squarely on Drake's shoulders.

When he'd walked in and seen Waltham, he'd known and accepted that that was the best he could hope to achieve.

With his customary grace, he rose and inclined his head to Greville. "Mr. Secretary."

Greville rose and nodded back. "Lord Winchelsea."

Drake flicked a glance at Waltham, who had more ponderously got to his feet. Sir Harold smiled a trifle smugly and half bowed.

Unsmiling, Drake regarded him for an instant, then turned and walked from the room.

On the steps of the building, he paused to look heavenward and draw in a cleansing breath. He considered the task that lay before him; he wasn't in the habit of appealing to any deity, but if ever there was a mission for which invoking divine aid seemed appropriate, this was surely it. He was going to need all the help he could get.

Whoever was behind the plot was the epitome of a malignant intelligence. They—whoever they were—had thus far been at least one step ahead of Drake and his supporters, dangling the distractions of political movements and conspiracies and slowing and deflecting the investigation; the killing of their pawns had furthered that aim, creating a succession of literal dead ends. But if the recent interview had added anything to Drake's perspective, it was that the malignant intelligence behind the plot knew a very great deal about what was and wasn't possible in the political sphere, in government and civil service.

Drake shook his head and muttered to himself, "Despite not being a Young Irelander or a Chartist plot, this still feels as if there are political overtones of some sort involved."

He wished he could define what they were, but regardless, ten barrels of gunpowder suggested the perpetrators intended to make a very public statement.

One it now fell to him to silence.

With a twist of his lips, he stepped down to the pavement. He'd always enjoyed a challenge. Seeing a hackney trotting past, he hailed it. With his boot on the step, he called to the jarvey, "Grosvenor Square. North side."

~

At the same moment that Drake was speculating on the motive behind the plot, the ageing man who spent his days in the parlor of a manor house in Berkshire was fretting and fuming. His gnarled fingers picked restlessly at the blanket draped over his now-useless legs, the palsy afflicting his right hand distinctly more pronounced.

The light was starting to fail, the weak sun sinking behind a bank of clouds to the west, and *still* no one came. Specifically, the gentleman the old man considered his second lieutenant hadn't reported as he'd been instructed most stringently to do, and now he was late.

For the fourth time in the past half hour, the old man reached for the bell on the table beside his Bath chair, intending to ring for his manservant, Reed—if only to have someone on whom to vent his frustrated agitation—when the sound of hoofbeats approaching stayed his hand.

Slowly, he released the bell, then he withdrew his hand and settled back in the chair. "At last! About time."

He hunched, vulture-like, and waited to hear his lieutenant report that all had gone as planned.

But when the door opened, it was Reed who entered. A studiously blank expression on his face, he approached the Bath chair bearing a salver on which lay a sealed note.

"What's that?" the old man barked.

"It's a note from Badger, sir."

Badger? Badger was his second lieutenant's manservant. Through his man-of-business, the old man had established a connection with the manservant, just in case.

Just in case something happened to his second lieutenant.

The old man scowled. Cursing his weakness, he ignored the irritating shaking of his hand, reached out, and after two abortive attempts, succeeded in picking up the note. Carrying it to his lap, he fumbled and broke the seal. Unfolding the single sheet, he held it up before his face and, steeling himself, read the few lines scrawled across the paper.

His scowl deepened. His expression grew puzzled.

He reread the message. On reaching its end, he slapped the paper with his crabbed fingers and snarled, "Damn it! The fool tells me nothing beyond that his master didn't return last night. What am I supposed to make of that?"

Unmoving, and apparently unmoved, Reed remained by the chair and, exercising prudence, said nothing.

After reading the missive yet again, the old man grunted and let the note fall to his lap, then, as if as an afterthought, he crushed the paper between his fingers. For several seconds, he stared unseeing across the room at the wide window that overlooked the dying garden.

This was the first hiccup in his carefully orchestrated plot—the very first stumble. The only step that, thus far, hadn't gone precisely as he had planned. As he had instructed—as he had decreed.

A tremor of uncertainty rippled through him. For a moment, he couldn't think. For a moment, he was simply an old man who wasn't certain of anything anymore, who had lost control of his life and now felt the reins of his greatest enterprise slipping from his grasp…no! *No!*

He set his jaw and forced in a long, slow breath.

He wasn't going to allow this setback—if it even was a setback—to rattle him. He couldn't—*wouldn't*—give up his revenge. Not now. Not when he knew he wouldn't have any other chance—that this was his moment to seize, and he wouldn't get another.

The plot would proceed—it had to. So he could die avenged. So that he could go knowing the satisfaction of having struck a mighty blow that ensured his country was, once again, ruled as it should be.

Knowing that he, through his bold actions, had changed history.

He let the rousing thoughts and the expectation of success infuse him and bolster him. For all he knew, whatever had happened was no more than a minor reverse; he could and would come about.

Gradually, the panic that had shaken him subsided, and his wits— those sharp and agile elements of intelligence that had served him so well throughout his long career—rose to the fore.

What was the current situation? His second lieutenant had, apparently, ridden out to attend to the action planned for the previous night, that of moving the barrels from the firework supply warehouse. Why would his second lieutenant not have returned home and, today, ridden out to report as arranged?

The old man had chosen his lieutenants carefully. He'd given them incentives to perform to his expectations; he knew both well enough to be certain that neither would fail him—not unless they had no choice.

It seemed likely, therefore, that his second lieutenant had fallen.

In his mind, the various players he, through his lieutenants, had drawn into his plot figured much as chess pieces on a board—albeit a board of his own devising for a game played by his rules.

As in any serious game, several pawns had been sacrificed—such was the nature of pawns. But in this instance, it was one of his knights who had, it seemed, been taken.

He considered that. While it wasn't an outcome he had wished for, it was an outcome he had to accept. There was no point railing over something that couldn't be changed.

But his knight's removal raised a red flag. It meant some opponent had taken a hand in his game. Someone else was playing now.

He could guess who it was. He'd hoped to avoid engaging that particular person, but...to some extent, the reality of having some opposition would only add spice to the game—to his eventual victory.

He did not doubt that he would win—that his plot would reach its terrible apogee, and for that one second, the world would stop spinning, and the multitudes would look up with a collective gasp.

Buoyed by the thought, he turned his wits—still incisive, still up to the task—to a review of his plot's progress. He made a mental list of the questions his fallen knight would have answered, the arrangements he would have confirmed had he been able to report. There were, in fact, only two.

Did the barrels reach their destination last night without interference?

And equally importantly, had the necessary steps been taken to facilitate the next stage?

He evaluated what he knew and what he didn't. Clearly, he lacked the vital information necessary to give the orders to proceed.

He glanced at Reed, still standing, mute, by his chair. "Get the writing desk!"

Reed hurried to obey.

The old man knew a moment of intense frustration; courtesy of the wretched palsy, he could no longer write. But he still had his wits and the wherewithal to command others. As soon as Reed settled at the nearby table with the writing desk before him, with paper on the sloped surface and ink on his pen, the old man said, "Address this to the captain. Dear sir, my other lieutenant left for his scheduled appointment late yesterday evening. We have just received word that he has not returned home, nor has he reported here as instructed. As we have heard nothing else to the point, we believe he must have fallen, but without revealing anything substantive regarding our endeavor. You are therefore my sole remaining lieutenant and, as such, will reap the full reward as discussed. However, as you are aware, that is contingent on our enterprise succeeding. I therefore require you to ascertain whether our barrels did, in fact, reach their arranged destination last night. It is fortunate that I made you privy to my other lieutenant's planned actions—you already have the details you require to step into the breach. Once you have learned all you can regarding the current state of our cargo, naturally without alerting anyone of your interest, I ask that you report to me here with all speed. As ever, I am not in favor of precipitate action and look forward to reviewing the next steps and the execution of the final stage of our enterprise with you at that time. Yours, etcetera." The old man focused on Reed, still rapidly scribbling. "And you may sign my name as well."

As soon as Reed looked up, the old man waved his hand for the sheet. Reed carried it over.

The old man scanned the missive, then nodded and handed it back. "Get that off by courier immediately."

"Yes, sir."

He waited for Reed to leave the room, then sank back in the chair. He stared into space while he envisaged, yet again, the culmination of his careful planning. There was no point in rushing, after all—everything ultimately hinged on the date. Thanks to his foresight and his cautious step-by-step advance, and to the instinct that had prompted him to share the instructions he'd given his second lieutenant with his first lieutenant as well, he had plenty of time to overcome the minor setback of losing one knight to the forces that, apparently, were finally mobilizing against him.

He wasn't frightened of them. They didn't know who he was, and he had time up his sleeve to maneuver around them should it prove necessary. He seriously doubted they would comprehend what he was about.

What his target was.

What—and who—he intended to bring down.

CHAPTER 18

*T*he gathering in the St. Ives back parlor broke up shortly before four o'clock.

Michael's mother, still smiling delightedly, declared she was off to spread the glad tidings that she and the female half of the family now had *two* engagement balls to plan, with two weddings to follow. With hugs and kisses all around, his mother departed in a cloud of exuberant joy.

His father, also smiling but in a rather different way, rose and informed Michael and the others that he would be in his study and that, as he was expecting a visit from the family's man-of-business, Montague, he would undertake to inform that worthy that there would be a second marriage settlement to arrange. With nods and that subtle, not-quite-cynical smile playing over his harsh-featured face, he followed his wife from the room.

As his father's footsteps faded, Michael exchanged glances with Cleo, Sebastian, and Antonia, then they resettled on the two sofas that faced each other across the hearth—Sebastian and Antonia on the longer one, Michael and Cleo on the other. Relaxing on the damask beside Cleo, with her hand wrapped in his, her fingers lightly entwined with his, Michael felt settled, focused, and strangely complete, with their joint life stretching before them—an adventure on which they had already embarked.

He and she had agreed to leave writing to her parents until after the meeting with Drake, when they hoped to have a better understanding of how the next phase of the mission would play out. After learning of their parents' shared past endeavors, they had no doubt that Cleo's parents, like Michael's, would understand their need to put dealing with the mission before all else.

Helping Drake end this mission was the most immediate next stage in their adventure.

Once settled, as Sebastian had intimated to Drake, the four of them spent some time revisiting the events of the mission thus far, evaluating what they could deduce with any degree of certainty. But when it came to defining what actions they should take, very little discussion was needed to illustrate the futility of proceeding in the absence of Drake and his various insights.

Seeking distraction, they turned to exchanging views on the few details of their engagement balls to which they'd thus far been made privy. The clock ticked on, and they segued to sharing somewhat light-hearted visions of their weddings.

Michael glanced at Cleo, then at Sebastian and Antonia. From the way all their gazes strayed again and again to the door, their interest in their weddings was, at that point, distinctly perfunctory; they were all waiting for Drake to join them.

Despite all matrimonial distractions, the mission—the need to find the damned gunpowder and expose whoever was already responsible for too many murders—still ranked uppermost in all their minds.

They were arguing the merits of the small church in Brancaster over St. George's for Michael and Cleo's nuptials when they heard voices and footsteps in the front hall—both indistinct given the distance between the front hall and the back parlor. They broke off their discussion and turned to look expectantly at the door, but no one appeared.

"The doorbell didn't ring," Sebastian pointed out.

Michael shrugged. "Must have been some household matter."

They returned to their discussion of atmosphere over size, of comfort over style, and the likely impact of the weather.

Finally, the doorbell pealed. They fell silent, not, this time, swinging about to look at the door, yet waiting nonetheless. They heard the distant murmur of voices in the hall.

Several seconds later, Drake strolled in.

Drake had thought his expression inscrutable, yet after one searching glance, Sebastian arched his black brows. "No luck with Greville?"

Drake turned and shut the door, then walked to the armchair placed beyond the end of the shorter sofa. He allowed himself a resigned grimace. "No." He tugged the armchair around so it faced the hearth, thus allowing him an unobstructed view of the occupants of both sofas, then sank into the well-padded comfort. "But I didn't really expect to prod him into action, and the instant I saw Waltham was present, I knew the best I could hope to gain was permission—more accurately, formal authority— to continue with the mission. That, at least, I managed to secure."

Antonia stared. "Do you mean to tell me that Greville refused to put out an alert?"

Her tone, Drake noted, was definitely in the same league as his mother's or Sebastian's—appropriate for a duchess-in-waiting. He waved with dismissive elegance. "Greville—and even more Waltham—are exceedingly leery of any situation that might panic the populace, especially if that situation has political overtones, as this plot has—" He broke off, then tipped his head slightly. "Or at least has been made to appear to have." After a moment, he added pensively, "Given the current political climate, I'm not sure we can blame them."

Again, he considered just how accurately the malignant intelligence behind the plot had read the politics of the day—not just read but understood the implications, the ramifications and impact on those who inhabited the corridors of power. "Indeed," Drake mused, "I'm starting to suspect that the villain behind this plot—our opponent, as it were, and I'm increasingly inclined to think said opponent will prove to be singular, just one man—has crafted the Young Irelander involvement and any Chartist involvement we might yet discover precisely in order to effectively tie my hands, at least with respect to having any formal warning issued to the constabulary and the guards. After the retribution visited on both Young Irelanders and Chartists in recent years, neither Greville nor I would move against either organization without irrefutable proof that they were the instigators of the plot."

Cleo humphed. "I can't see how putting out a quiet warning to the right individuals is going to cause a panic. What *will* cause a panic is ten barrels of gunpowder exploding in the City or in Trafalgar Square."

Antonia shuddered.

"Actually"—Drake pulled a face—"the more I think of it, the more I can see Greville's point. Were I in his place, I would have issued the warning and used a degree of intimidation to ensure it wasn't spread beyond those who need to know. However, on reflection, even doing that much would inevitably raise questions inside the government, the civil service, and the military, and it's the answers to those questions—namely that the Young Irelanders *might* be involved, or the Chartists, or even worse, some group we know nothing about—that Greville doesn't want to have to give." He paused, then, jaw firming, went on, "And none of us would be happy were there to be fresh witch hunts mounted against the Young Irelanders and the Chartists because of this plot when, in fact, they know nothing about it."

Sebastian grimaced, as did Michael, while both Cleo and Antonia sniffed in a disparaging way that suggested they thought the world would be a better place without politics.

"When it comes down to it," Drake said, "we have no actual evidence of any specific plot."

Michael snorted. "Other than ten missing barrels of smuggled gunpowder and numerous associated and otherwise unexplained deaths."

Drake told them of Waltham's thesis of some manufacturer attempting to avoid the excise and the barrels subsequently being stolen by a competitor.

Even Cleo was stunned into silence; she opened her mouth several times, but ultimately, could find nothing to say.

"Indeed," Drake dryly concluded. "You have to hand it to the man— he had to invent that on the instant, and he managed to account for everything we've found in a way that rendered the whole unthreatening."

After a moment, Sebastian caught Drake's gaze. "But Greville didn't suggest there was nothing to investigate? That in light of Waltham's explanation, you should let things lie?"

"No. He's not such a twit. I'm free to investigate with my usual thoroughness and pursue this matter to its conclusion."

It was Michael who first saw the implication. "So...if things go *boom* before you can prevent it, it's on your head?"

Drake inclined said head. "If not publicly, then certainly in my own estimation."

"Good Lord!" Cleo exclaimed. "How unfair!"

"Whitehall." Antonia's tone dripped with contempt.

"Politics," Drake stated. "Sadly, in this instance, there's no way of avoiding that." Courtesy of the cleverness of whoever was behind the plot.

After a second, Sebastian stated, "Well, we're here to help."

"Exactly," Michael affirmed. "So what do we do next?"

Drake studied their expressions; Sebastian's and Michael's determination, he'd expected, and in truth, he wasn't surprised to read a warning not to discount them in Antonia's and Cleo's faintly narrowing eyes.

After a moment, he suggested, "Let's recapitulate. Then we can define the questions facing us and the most promising avenues we might pursue." Settling his shoulders against the comfortable cushions, he fixed his gaze forward and tipped his head back. His gaze fell on the mirror above the mantelpiece. In its reflection, he noticed the door to the corridor was fractionally ajar; he'd thought he'd closed it. Yet given the position of the parlor and whose house this was, there seemed little reason to bother rising and shutting the door firmly; there was nothing to fear with respect to anyone overhearing their words.

He refocused on the plot. "The essential points are these. A group of Young Irelanders of the lower ranks, mistakenly believing themselves to be acting as part of an officially approved action, secured ten barrels of gunpowder from an Irish mill and successfully arranged to have said barrels transported by ship to a cave under the grounds of Pressingstoke Hall, Lord Ennis's estate in Kent. That stage of the plot relied on Connell Boyne, Ennis's younger brother. Expecting Ennis to be glad to support the cause to which he was no doubt sympathetic, Boyne told his brother about the gunpowder. Ennis agreed to pay for the delivery, but when Ennis insisted that the gunpowder go no farther and arranged to speak with me, Boyne panicked. Before Ennis could speak with Sebastian, who was acting as my proxy, Boyne killed Ennis, then, fearing that Ennis might have shared his concerns with his wife, Boyne killed her, too. With Boyne's connivance, by night, the gunpowder was loaded onto two legitimate gunpowder carters' carts driven by Terrance Doolan and his apprentice, Johnny Dibney, and conveyed into London. The following afternoon, Boyne himself was murdered, presumably by the man behind the plot or his proxy—his lieutenant." He paused, then added, "Let's keep that man —Boyne's killer—in mind.

"Subsequently, we now know that Doolan and Dibney delivered the ten barrels to Shepherd's warehouse in Morgan's Lane in Southwark. They would have arrived on Wednesday morning, perhaps about nine o'clock, and the barrels were accepted into the warehouse by the foreman, one Eddie O'Toole—very likely another Young Irelander sympathizer hoodwinked into believing he was playing his part in some official plot."

"Whoever's been recruiting these men must have been quite persuasive," Antonia observed.

Drake nodded. "He had to have known precisely which carrots to dangle to best appeal to them. Whoever he is, he's also exceedingly cold-blooded. Wednesday was a busy day for him—by all accounts, Doolan and Dibney were killed and their bodies slipped into the river sometime on Wednesday, most likely soon after they completed the delivery. Boyne was shot on Wednesday afternoon. O'Toole's body has yet to be recovered, but he was last seen on Wednesday evening when he locked up the warehouse. He hasn't been sighted since, and I doubt there's any other explanation than that he, too, is dead."

"Especially as it was almost certainly O'Toole's keys our rider used to gain entry to the warehouse last night," Michael said.

"Indeed." After a moment, Drake went on, "At this point, I'm assuming that the murders on Wednesday were carried out by one man. Given the distances and the timing, that's possible, but of course, there might have been more than one man involved. At this point, we can't say. However, moving on, the barrels were left in the warehouse until last night, when a rider, accompanied by two drivers with unidentifiable brewery drays, used the foreman's keys to gain access to and retrieve the barrels, locking up afterward and leaving no sign that the barrels had ever been there."

Drake shifted his gaze to Michael and Cleo. "If you two hadn't found the barrels, no one would ever have known they'd been there. I think that's an important point, at least from our villains' perspective, and, I believe, that explains what happened next. Meaning the barrels being moved to somewhere in the same area—moved, but not taken far."

Drake paused, then went on, "When working with groups like the Young Irelanders, there's always a chance that someone will find it all too exciting and mention something to their compatriots—even just that something is afoot. Such rumblings will inevitably reach someone like me. The villains, whoever they are, knew that. Appreciated that. So they designed their plot to not just take advantage of the gullibility of certain Young Irelander sympathizers but also to have a clean break—a point where, if I or anyone else started to follow the Young Irelander trail, that trail would come to an abrupt and uninformative end."

He glanced again at Michael and Cleo. "The Young Irelander trail leads to the warehouse—then stops. The barrels are no longer there, nor is there any trace of unaccounted-for barrels ever having been there."

Cleo caught his gaze. "By that reasoning, whoever moved the barrels on, and wherever they've been secreted, will have nothing to do with the Young Irelander movement."

Drake nodded. "Precisely."

"You think the local Chartists have been drawn into assisting," Sebastian stated.

"That's what I fear." Drake grimaced. "At least I now have an introduction to the local militia leaders, and it's possible we might learn more that way, but I'm not holding my breath that we'll learn anything quickly enough."

After several seconds dwelling on that, he straightened in the chair. "But let's not get sidetracked. To summarize the present situation, we know the ten barrels of gunpowder are still within a specific area of Southwark. We've also killed one of the primary villains—either the man behind the plot if he's acting alone or, more likely, one of his lieutenants. Given the man's age—about thirty-six—then I would wager it'll be the latter."

"Aside from all else," Sebastian dryly remarked, "the former would be too easy—the plot would likely end with the man's death."

Drake inclined his head. "Fate is never that kind." He looked at Cleo. "One thing I wanted to ask. What, exactly, did he—our now-dead rider—say when he seized you?"

Cleo stared at Drake, then frowned and closed her eyes, the better to remember. She was back in the murky darkness of Black Lion Court, creeping along on the slippery cobbles... She tightened her fingers, gripping Michael's; his hand closed more firmly about hers. A moment passed, then she drew in a long, slow breath, opened her eyes, and looked at Drake. "The first thing he asked was who I was and why I was there, then immediately followed that—as if it was more important—by asking who I was working for. Then he suggested I might be working for his cousin."

"His cousin?" Drake glanced at Michael.

Also clearly thinking back, Michael nodded. "I was near enough to hear, and that's what he said."

Drake looked at Cleo. "What did you reply?"

She grimaced. "That I had no idea who his cousin was, and that's when he panicked. I'd forgotten to speak like a streetwalker. He pulled out a knife and demanded to know who had sent me and who knew about, as he termed it, *our little enterprise.*"

"*Our* little enterprise." His features hardening, Drake nodded. "So there's more than one of them involved, and this plot won't die with the rider."

After a moment of thought, Drake refocused on Cleo. "Would it be true to say that the rider found your presence relatively unsurprising and unthreatening while he thought you an average streetwalker hired by his cousin to spy on what he was doing?"

Cleo nodded. "He was more...amused to begin with. Until he heard me speak."

"Until he realized you weren't a streetwalker but a real spy—one sent by the sort of agency who might recruit women of your class..." A moment passed, then, his jaw tightening, Drake met Michael's eyes, then looked at Sebastian. "The rider knew enough to panic when he realized Cleo was a lady disguised as a streetwalker. Someone had warned him of what finding such a watcher as Cleo would mean." His tone growing colder, his accents more clipped, Drake concluded, "Whoever is pulling the strings of this plot either knows about me, about what I do, or at the very least, that an agency such as the one I oversee exists."

They all thought about that, then Sebastian said, "All those in Whitehall above a certain level know."

His lips tight, Drake nodded. "Indeed." He paused, then continued, "That would account for the...feeling I have that the mastermind behind this plot knows a very great deal about politics and government and how things are done. What is possible and what isn't. Their harnessing of the wider situation has been masterly—it's allowed them to throw up deflections and distractions. In hindsight, I think it likely they planted the whispers I heard to ensure I would go to Ireland, and more recently up north, to clarify what was going on—while the real action was occurring here."

"But if they know that much, then presumably they know about 'the sons of the nobility,'" Michael said. "That in such situations, you call on us."

"They probably do know," Drake said. "That's why the rider had been warned. But in their view, getting me out of the immediate picture reduced the risk for them. And they weren't at all concerned about me learning that the plot isn't either a Young Irelander or a Chartist plot. If anything, that's a part of their Machiavellian plan—it increases my, and Greville's, reluctance to risk issuing an effective alert." He shook his head. "The more I learn about our ultimate villain, the more I'm left with the impression that I'm playing chess with someone who knows more about the possible moves than I do."

Drake didn't bother stating that he'd never had to grapple with such a situation before.

Sebastian shrugged. "So he's someone with an intimate knowledge of Whitehall, and he's older and therefore more experienced than you." He met Drake's eyes. "Regardless, he's going to have things go wrong—and one of those things is, as we speak, on its way to some helpful morgue."

Drake held Sebastian's rather pointed, pale-green gaze, then humphed. "All right. Let's move on to what we need to know and what we can do to nullify this plot." He paused for a second, then went on, "We need to find the gunpowder, defuse it as a threat, and then identify the blackguard behind the plot. The gunpowder comes first." He looked at Michael. "Let's accept we can't go in, search, and seize it. That leaves keeping a tight cordon about that area as the only viable way to guard against the barrels being moved to the target and subsequently detonated." He held Michael's gaze. "Can you be certain the barrels are still there?"

Michael took time to assess before replying, "I believe so. They had no chance to move the barrels earlier, and we've tightened our watch. Tom reported that as of two o'clock, there'd been no sight of them. Plenty of activity—people and things going in and out, as you would expect— but not those barrels." He glanced at Cleo. "Cleo passed on a description of the brand on the barrels—the stamp of the Irish mill—so the men know what they're looking for."

"I hesitate to ask," Antonia put in, "but could the gunpowder be transferred into some other container—something our watchers won't recognize and so allow past?"

Silence held them for a moment, then Drake said, "That has to be possible. So just keeping watch isn't good enough." He looked again at Michael. "Nevertheless, can you continue your tight watch—enough to guarantee the ten barrels from the Irish mill won't slip through?"

Michael nodded decisively. "That, we can definitely do." He glanced at Sebastian. "I've already sent word to the various households—to the butlers and housekeepers currently in charge—so they're aware of our need." His lips curved. "Unsurprisingly, all I've received in response are a host of avowals of unwavering support."

Sebastian's features briefly lightened. "It's lucky that, these days, most branches and even twigs of the family keep their houses in London staffed throughout the year."

"So we have the watch covered," Drake went on. "And if the barrels are spotted leaving the area, we revert to our earlier plan—we follow rather than intercept, but as soon as the barrels reach any destination, we'll move in and replace the gunpowder, then watch for whoever comes to deal with it next. Simultaneously, we'll follow all those who've assisted in the move." He paused, then added, "Ultimately, we need to identify whoever is behind this. Until we have our mastermind in custody, we can't be sure we've fully deactivated his plot."

After a moment, he went on, "One of the few things we can feel a degree of confidence in is that the next stage of the plot won't go any more quickly than the last. It might even go more slowly, given that it seems likely he's switched from using Young Irelander sympathizers to using the local Chartists. Whoever he is, he's cautious to the bone." Drake snorted softly and looked at Sebastian. "Very like a longtime bureaucrat."

Michael glanced at Cleo, then looked at the others. "I'll continue to manage the watchers, but as Cleo and I will recognize the barrels, and given the Hendon Shipping Company's name and reputation, I suggest that she and I also see if, by asking around, we might stumble on some hint of where in the area the barrels might be hidden." He grimaced. "It's a long shot, but you never can tell."

"Also," Cleo put in, "we should learn what other types of barrels or containers are commonly taken out of that area. And a visit to the office of the Inspector General of Gunpowder might give us some idea of other ways to store and transport gunpowder."

Drake studied them. "Will you have time?"

Michael nodded. "We've postponed any official announcement until after this mission is concluded. My parents were here earlier, and over luncheon, we learned of the missions they assisted your father with—and the Hendons were often also involved. So we have precedent, so to speak. We're not anticipating any distractions from that quarter."

Drake's brows had risen. "I'd forgotten about your parents' past involvements. But that's certainly a boon if it means you can continue investigating along the lines you suggest. We need to follow every avenue we can."

He settled in the armchair. "So that covers the barrels and their possible movement. Next on our slate is the trail of dead bodies our villain leaves behind. Not his dead lieutenant—I'll come to him in a minute—but the others. Boyne, the carters, the foreman. Our villain's aim is quite clearly to ensure that he leaves no possible sources of information alive. However, if he's continued following that pattern and killed the two drivers who helped him move the barrels last night, we might just have a potential lead."

Drake glanced at Michael. "I have contacts—probably the same as yours—in the River Police. I'll ask them to advise us immediately they pull any bodies from the river—those of men who've been killed since last night. Putting names and addresses to faces might be difficult, but we might get help with that via the Chartist militias. If we can identify the drivers and where they worked, then we'll at least know where those drays came from, and someone there might know more."

He paused, then acknowledged, "That's a long shot, too, but as I said, we have to pursue every possible avenue."

He drew in a breath, ordered his thoughts, and continued, "That brings us to the Chartists. I've secured an introduction to the three local militia leaders. I gather that each controls and speaks for a separate group of militiamen. Interviewing them has to be at the top of my list—if the drivers from last night haven't yet met an untimely end, then alerting the Chartist leaders to the game they've been unwittingly drawn into might save those men's lives and get us a good deal further forward. At the very least, those men will know where the gunpowder is now." He grimaced. "That said, I'm not expecting anything to go so smoothly, and I don't hold much hope for finding those drivers alive. But if I can convince the local Chartist leaders that continuing to assist in this plot is the last thing their headquarters wants them to do…if the villain intends to call on the Chartists for any further assistance—for instance, in moving the barrels to his ultimate target—that will disrupt his next step."

Sebastian nodded. "All to the good as far as we're concerned."

The others murmured agreement.

"And that," Drake continued, "brings us to our dead gentleman. Obviously, learning his identity is a matter of urgency." Drake tipped his head toward Cleo. "Especially as we now know he was sufficiently trusted to be warned of the dangers posed by well-born spies."

"I have to wonder," Cleo said, "what sort of gentleman has a cousin who would hire a streetwalker to spy on him."

After exchanging brief glances with Sebastian and Michael, Drake said, "It's possible, even likely, that his assumption that you were his cousin's spy relates to some family disagreement and has nothing to do with the plot per se. However, the remark confirms that our gentleman has living family."

He paused, reviewing their options, then went on, "Finnegan's pursuing the man's name, and knowing his tenacity, he'll find it. Once he does, we'll need to meet again and pool our knowledge and resources to gather as much intelligence as we can about our mystery gentleman and his connections before we start actively investigating." After a second, he added, "By all accounts, this man was confident and probably ex-cavalry. That's a significant step above even Connell Boyne. I suspect our gentleman-rider will prove to be not the mastermind—that would be too easy—but a personal proxy. Someone who acted on the mastermind's orders and reported directly to him."

Drake turned toward Sebastian and Antonia.

Before he could speak, Antonia fixed him with a demanding look. "What about us? We want to help, too."

Drake took in Sebastian's steady gaze, one that hadn't flickered despite Antonia volunteering his—their—services... Clearly, Sebastian had no problem with that.

It struck Drake then; Sebastian and Antonia were operating as one. Two people, but with one aim, one goal—one shared direction. He didn't need to glance at Michael and Cleo to know he would see the same...*togetherness* between them.

But Sebastian and Antonia were officially engaged. Drake kept his gaze on them and picked his way forward with care. "I know you want to be in the field, as it were, but given that your engagement has been announced, if you turn your back on society's expectations and devote your time to this mission too openly, you'll call attention to its existence, and that won't be helpful at all."

Antonia's eyes sparked, and her chin set.

Drake held up a hand to stay her transparently imminent protest. "However, one truly valuable contribution you two can make is to keep the spotlight off the rest of us. Until now, social pressure hasn't been a problem, but with more and more of the ton returning to town for the autumn session, the invitations will start to descend even on my poor self. But you and your engagement can hold the spotlight well enough for me, Michael, and Cleo to be able to pursue our tasks unhindered. And once we have our dead gentleman's name and need to learn more about him, while being feted and fawned upon throughout the ton, you will be in the perfect position to do that. You'll have opportunities to slip in questions, and people will answer and instantly forget, too dazzled by talk of your upcoming nuptials."

Antonia looked suspicious, but it was obvious she was tempted by the prospect. Eventually, she glanced at Sebastian.

He met her gaze, smiled, and lightly squeezed her hand.

Then they looked at Drake and both nodded. "Very well. We'll act as a social shield for you three"—with a glance, Sebastian included Michael and Cleo—"and hold ourselves ready to assist on that point."

Drake held up a finger. "And possibly with one other matter."

Sebastian arched a black brow.

"It would be exceedingly helpful to know how many, for want of a better word, *order-givers* there are running this plot. I think we can agree there's an older bureaucrat-like figure ultimately pulling the strings, but how many proxies does he have in the field, doing his direct bidding? We've speculated that the rider was one. Was the man who killed Connell Boyne another? Or was he the same man?" Drake arched a brow back at Sebastian. "If we've eliminated the mastermind's only direct assistant, then we've removed an essential piece of his plan, and it will take significant time for him to recruit a new proxy. However, if our dead gentleman is one of a group, then we can assume the plot will continue, more or less as scheduled. We—Michael, Cleo, and I—can give you a sound description of our dead man. If you can compare that with men seen in the area around the time of Boyne's murder, we might learn more."

Sebastian glanced at Antonia. "We could take a day's break from the social round and go down to Kent. We didn't stay long enough after finding Boyne to inquire if any locals had seen anyone about."

"We don't need to go to Kent." Antonia met Sebastian's eyes. "We only need to go to Scotland Yard—Inspector Crawford would surely have made inquiries. He will know if any stranger seen in Kent who might have been Connell's murderer matches the description of our dead man."

"An excellent notion." Sebastian looked at the others. "So what does our dead gentleman look like?"

Between them, Drake and Michael conveyed a detailed image of the man.

Cleo added, "And he has a scar anyone who got close enough—such as an ostler or barman—would have noticed." She traced a line from the corner of her lips to the point of her jaw. "A fine slash, like a sword cut."

Sebastian nodded. "That's nicely distinctive. We'll go to Scotland Yard tomorrow and see what we can learn."

"Good." Rapidly, Drake reviewed all they'd discussed, searching for other avenues they could explore.

Michael shifted, drawing Drake's attention. "Two things we've yet to touch on—the timing and the likely target." Michael glanced around their small circle. "Those barrels are in Southwark and, so we think, not yet at their ultimate destination."

"Without knowing who's behind this, we have little hope of identifying the target prior to the barrels reaching it," Drake stated.

Michael inclined his head. "True, but I think we can all agree the target is highly likely to be over the river."

Drake nodded, as did the other three.

Frowning slightly, as if following this line of thought for the first time, Michael continued, "So either via the river or across one of the bridges, the gunpowder must be moved again—and as we all agree, it's not going to be just a short distance, this time, and so not so simply done."

Michael looked at Drake. "If *you* were this mastermind, and you only just today learned that your people have been successful in shifting the gunpowder from the warehouse—a traceable place, as we've proved—to its new and entirely secret location, all ready for the next step, which for argument's sake we'll say involves moving the cache to a basement adjacent to the Bank of England, how would you proceed—and how long would it take you to get everything ready to take that next step?"

"And," Sebastian added, "if you were running this plot, how long would you leave between achieving that final deployment to the target and detonating the gunpowder?"

Drake sat back and stared at Michael, then glanced briefly at Sebastian. Those were excellent questions via which to explore what might come next. "If it were me…"

Facing forward, Drake turned his mind to the notion. He juggled what he knew, what he could estimate and project. After several minutes' silence, he said, "Moving that much gunpowder, in whatever disguise—and there really aren't that many ways to move gunpowder across water without risking ruining it—all in complete secrecy… As to the time it would take, even I would need days, if not a week, to arrange that, even if I'd been hoping to have the pleasure and had all my plans worked out." He paused, then went on, "As we've already discussed, it's unlikely the mastermind has activated those plans yet—he would be aware that the longer his pawns know about a plot like this, the more chance of something leaking out and bringing the authorities down on their heads. No—he's careful and intends to succeed. He'll have a plan, but he'll only start contacting people and getting matters organized once he's certain all has gone as he wishes."

Some of the tension that had gripped him eased. He paused, then more lightly said, "Operating on the assumption that if *I* can't move more rapidly—and I have contacts and powers he can't possibly have to call on —then he can't manage things any faster, we have at least...four days, more likely five, before those barrels are deployed to their target.

"However, once the gunpowder is moved into position"—his tone hardened, and he felt his features do the same—"I predict we'll have very little time to stop the detonation." He met Sebastian's eyes. "If I were he...then assembling the barrels at the target is the point at which his entire plot is at maximum risk. If the gunpowder is found, the plot fails, and the target—being a place of note and therefore almost certainly under guard of some sort—is not going to be the type of place where gunpowder will remain undetected for long."

After a heartbeat, he qualified, "By long, I mean more than twelve to twenty-four hours, and much will depend on how the gunpowder is concealed or disguised. Given that it seems he'll be using pawns to move the gunpowder into position, then he'll most likely want them well away, and possibly even murdered as well, before he lights the fuse—or orders it lit. Again, given his cautious nature, that might—*might*—stretch things out for longer than twenty-four hours, but that's not something I would wish to wager on."

Sebastian drew in a breath, then let it out on a long exhalation. "So"— he looked at Michael—"we need to intercept the gunpowder before it reaches the target."

Drake also turned to Michael. "One thing to remember—the ultimate target might not be the place the gunpowder moves to next. We can't assume that, although to this point, we've been talking as if we have. If your men spot the barrels being moved, they need to follow and get word to us as soon as possible."

Somewhat grimly, Michael nodded.

Beside him, Cleo said, "Here's another question. You've stressed how careful and also how cunning our mastermind has been thus far. He's used the Young Irelanders as a façade, and now he has, you believe, drawn the local Chartists into being his pawns." She fixed her bright hazel gaze on Drake's face. "But won't he assume you'll see the pattern—that you'll get hold of the local Chartist leaders and interfere?" Her gaze steady, she tipped her head. "Surely he'll be planning on using someone else— neither the Chartists nor the Young Irelanders—for the upcoming stage?"

Drake blinked. He sat back and thought, then, slowly, he nodded.

"You're absolutely right. He's used the Chartists just enough to implicate them and force me to deal with them, to contact and question them. They might be able to lead us to where the barrels currently are." He met Michael's gaze. "But by that time, the barrels—or at least the gunpowder —will have been moved." He flashed a faint, tense smile at Cleo. "Cleo's right—he'll use some other group. But who?"

After a moment, Sebastian suggested, "Some group he trusts?"

Michael snorted. "Who would a bureaucrat trust?"

Antonia leant forward and poked Drake's arm. "If you were in his shoes, who would you use?"

Drake thought, then grimaced and met her gaze. "I would use people who are completely innocent and have no notion of what they're doing. As I said, the last move leading to the final deployment at the target site is absolutely critical. I would find some way to make the transfer of whatever container the gunpowder is in look like something normal. Something so ordinary in day-to-day life that people will do what's needed without any idea of what they're shifting into place."

"That means," Cleo said, "disguising the barrels or whatever container the gunpowder is in as something else. Something not gunpowder." She frowned. "I really don't think there are that many types of containers that are useful for moving gunpowder."

After a moment, Drake shrugged. "My suggestion is pure speculation, but that's what I would do—disguise the gunpowder as something harmless and unremarkable that would normally be found at the target site."

At that moment, they heard footsteps approaching, a swinging stride that slowed, then hesitated outside the door.

They all turned to stare at the door that, as Drake had noticed earlier, stood fractionally ajar.

Then a polite tap sounded on the panels.

Drake glanced at Sebastian, who called, "Come."

The door swung open, and Finnegan came in. He saw them, and his face lit; he turned and shut the door. He started across the room, but then glanced briefly back at the door—which, once again, had eased open. Drake assumed the latch was faulty.

Finnegan halted beside Drake's chair, his face radiating delight. "Success, my lords, my ladies." He swept them all a flourishing bow.

Drake forced his lips to remain straight. "Cut line. Out with it. What have you found?"

The look his ebullient gentleman's gentleman bent on him suggested

Drake was no fun, but when Drake coolly arched his brows, Finnegan straightened and announced, "The dead gentleman's name, my lord, is Mr. Lawton Chilburn. The bootmaker knew, of course. His boots are numbered, so it was simply a matter of checking his ledgers, and I confirmed that Mr. Chilburn had all the same characteristics as the dead man, including that rather distinctive scar across the lower part of his face."

"Excellent work. Thank you, Finnegan." The name struck not a single chord with Drake. He glanced, brows raised in invitation, at Sebastian and Antonia, then at Michael and Cleo, but they all looked as mystified as he.

Drake tipped back his head and appealed to the room at large, "Who the devil is Lawton Chilburn?"

For a second, silence reigned, then a primitive sensation—a ripple of awareness—brushed across his nape.

He tensed.

It can't be. She's nowhere near.

But then, from behind him, came the gentle tap of a lady's high heels on the parquet floor and the telltale rustle of silk and stiff petticoats, and the words "Lawton Chilburn is the youngest of Viscount Hawesley's four sons" fell like the tones of a bell on his ears, uttered in a voice he immediately recognized, no matter that he'd avoided its owner for years.

A voice that sent a chill through him—along with a thrill he didn't want to feel.

Ruthlessly clamping an unrelenting hold on every reaction and impulse he possessed, Drake ensured his impassive mask was in place, smoothly rose, and turned to face the woman—the lady, the noblewoman—who had swept into the room.

He inclined his head. "Louisa."

His gaze had locked on her pale-green silk skirts; as he straightened his head, he couldn't stop his gaze from traveling upward, over her tiny waist, smoothly up over the alluring curves of her breasts, over the glimpse of throat that showed between the peaked collars of her dress, to her pointed chin, perfect alabaster complexion, and the striking, animated features that had driven any number of his peers to drink.

Her pale-green eyes, lushly lashed with black, were similar to her grandmother's, her father's, and Sebastian's in hue, but her soul infused them with such vibrancy they literally sparkled with life—more vital and less distant than those of the others of her family blessed with eyes of that curious shade. Those entrancing eyes looked into his, and Drake felt his gut tighten.

Then, with her lips lightly curving, she transferred that disturbing regard to the others, all still seated; she swept them with her bright, imperious gaze. If she noticed that only Antonia and Cleo were smiling back—and in Cleo's case, her smile was tentative—Louisa gave no sign. Her own smile bloomed, ineffably radiant and warming. "I understand," she said, and the timbre of her voice—a husky contralto that feathered over any red-blooded male's senses—made Drake mentally curse, "that congratulations are in order."

Sebastian had managed to blank his expression, but his eyes were filled with a species of horror.

Michael, on the other hand, stared—rather more openly perturbed—at his sister. "We thought you weren't returning until tomorrow."

One finely arched black brow rose. Her own expression a serene mask, Louisa considered Michael for several seconds—long enough for him to become aware of the implications of what he'd just blurted out—then her smile deepened a fraction, growing subtly more edged. She glanced at Sebastian. "I heard of your news, and of course, I hurried home. And now I discover that we have *two* engagement balls and *two* weddings to which to look forward." She smiled entirely genuinely at Antonia and bestowed an approving nod, then included Cleo with both smile and gesture. "Excellent work, ladies."

With that, she swung to face Drake. Her gaze clashed with and effortlessly captured his. "And clearly, it's just as well that I returned without delay." With an expression that was close to a playful pout—a truly enchanting moue, an expression only she could pull off—still holding his gaze, she walked behind the sofa on which Michael and Cleo sat to claim the armchair beyond, angled to the gathering. She sank down with a susurration of silks, her gaze still holding Drake's. "I understand," she said, sitting upright with her forearms on the armrests, strikingly like a queen on her throne, "that you've all been having quite an adventure."

From the corner of his eye, Drake saw Antonia draw breath to speak. Before she could, he baldly asked, "How much did you hear?"

His question, devoid of any tone that could be considered remotely encouraging, drew Louisa's gaze, which had drifted expectantly to Antonia, back to his face.

Her expression remained serene, but there was an intensity in her eyes he found deeply unsettling. She studied him for a long moment, then calmly replied, "All of it. I was in the gallery when you arrived. I followed you and"—she waved toward the door—"listened."

That was why the door had been ajar and also explained Finnegan's curious behavior.

Drake flicked a glance at Finnegan. The Irishman had good instincts; he'd stepped back in a self-effacing way, but was watching Louisa as if she was a strange and unpredictable creature of uncertain and potentially dangerous powers.

Which was not far from the truth.

She hadn't shifted her gaze from Drake's face. Knowing that, when she wished, she had well-nigh-inexhaustible patience, he ignored her long enough to glance at her brothers. On his left, Sebastian met Drake's eyes with a look of almost panic-stricken consternation. Michael, to Drake's right, still appeared overtly horrified.

Both were as aghast as Drake at Louisa's advent, at her transparent intention to deal herself into this mission. Yet the message in her brothers' eyes was clear.

Both had too much experience of their sister's exceedingly willful ways to attempt to deny her.

Which meant that dissuading her from pushing her way into his mission fell entirely to Drake. His the battle to ensure she kept her distance, from him as well as from all possible danger.

And somehow, he had to succeed.

Because the very last person Drake needed helping him was Lady Louisa Cynster—widely known, for excellent reasons, as Lady Wild.

Dear Reader,

I had great fun crafting Michael and Cleo's romance—although they were neither the opening act nor the grand finale in the on-going drama, they still had plenty of hurdles to overcome on their way to their emotional just reward. I hope you've enjoyed this second act in the Devil's Brood Trilogy.

And now the scene is set and, indeed, the players have already taken the stage for the third and final act. Louisa and Drake's story, oh-so-aptly titled *The Greatest Challenge of Them All,* brings everything to a head, and as you might expect with those two characters, the sparks do fly. In addition, as the trilogy's storyline, of all my many works, draws on real events of those times, as I did with the previous volume, I've included an Author Note, in which I detail the historical facts that feature or have influenced what is otherwise a work of fiction. If you want to know: *How much of this is real?* that note is for you.

So we know the problem Drake, Louisa, and the others face—and the clock is inexorably ticking. Not only has the gunpowder vanished, but a murderer is removing all witnesses to its location. In the thrilling final volume, Louisa joins forces with Drake, and assisted by Sebastian, Antonia, Michael, and Cleo, they race to uncover the truth—of the location of the gunpowder, the mastermind behind the plot, and his target—in time.

Before one thousand pounds of gunpowder is detonated somewhere in London.

Stephanie.

For alerts as new books are released, plus information on upcoming books, exclusive sweepstakes and sneak peeks into upcoming novels, sign up for Stephanie's Private Email Newsletter http://www.stephanielaurens. com/newsletter-signup/

Or if you don't have time to chat and want a quick email alert, sign up and follow me at BookBub https://www.bookbub.com/authors/stephanie-laurens

The ultimate source for detailed information on all Stephanie's published books, including covers, descriptions, and excerpts, is Stephanie's Website www.stephanielaurens.com

You can also follow Stephanie via her Amazon Author Page at http://tinyurl.com/zc3e9mp

Goodreads members can follow Stephanie via her author page https://www.goodreads.com/author/show/9241.Stephanie_Laurens

You can email Stephanie at stephanie@stephanielaurens.com

Or find her on Facebook
https://www.facebook.com/AuthorStephanieLaurens/

FOR THE GRIPPING CONCLUSION OF THE DEVIL'S BROOD TRILOGY:
The thrilling third and final volume in the Devil's Brood Trilogy
THE GREATEST CHALLENGE OF THEM ALL
Cynster Next Generation Novel #6

A nobleman devoted to defending queen and country and a noblewoman wild enough to match his every step race to disrupt the plans of a malignant intelligence intent on shaking England to its very foundations.

Lord Drake Varisey, Marquess of Winchelsea, eldest son and heir of the Duke of Wolverstone, must foil a plot that threatens to shake the foundations of the realm, but the very last lady—nay, noblewoman—he needs assisting him is Lady Louisa Cynster, known throughout the ton as Lady Wild.

For the past nine years, Louisa has suspected that Drake might well be the ideal husband for her, even though he's assiduous in avoiding her. But she's now twenty-seven and enough is enough. She believes propinquity will elucidate exactly what it is that lies between them, and what better opportunity to work closely with Drake than his latest mission, with which he patently needs her help?

Unable to deny Louisa's abilities or the value of her assistance and powerless to curb her willfulness, Drake is forced to grit his teeth and acquiesce to her sticking by his side, if only to ensure her safety. But all too soon, his true feelings for her show enough for her, perspicacious as she is, to see through his denials, which she then interprets as a challenge.

Even while they gather information, tease out clues, increasingly desperately search for the missing gunpowder, and doggedly pursue the killer responsible for an ever-escalating tally of dead men, thrown together through the hours, he and she learn to trust and appreciate each other. And fed by constant exposure—and blatantly encouraged by her—their desires and hungers swell and grow…

As the barriers between them crumble, the attraction he has for so long restrained burgeons and balloons, until goaded by her near-death, it erupts, and he seizes her—only to be seized in return.

Linked irrevocably and with their wills melded and merged by passion's fire, with time running out and the evil mastermind's deadline looming, together, they focus their considerable talents and make one last push to learn the critical truths—to find the gunpowder and unmask the villain behind this far-reaching plot.

Only to discover that they have significantly less time than they'd thought, that the villain's target is even more crucially fundamental to the realm than they'd imagined, and it's going to take all that Drake is—as well as all that Louisa as Lady Wild can bring to bear—to defuse the threat, capture the villain, and make all safe and right again.

As they race to the ultimate confrontation, the future of all England rests on their shoulders.

Third volume in a trilogy. A Cynster Next Generation Novel – a classic historical romance with gothic overtones layered over an intrigue. A full-length novel of 129,000 words.

If you missed the first volume of the Devil's Brood Trilogy
THE LADY BY HIS SIDE
Cynster Next Generation Novel #4

A marquess in need of the right bride. An earl's daughter in search of a purpose. A betrayal that ends in murder and balloons into a threat to the realm.

Sebastian Cynster knows time is running out. If he doesn't choose a wife soon, his female relatives will line up to assist him. Yet the current debutantes do not appeal. Where is he to find the right lady to be his marchioness? Then Drake Varisey, eldest son of the Duke of Wolverstone, asks for Sebastian's aid.

Having assumed his father's mantle in protecting queen and country, Drake must go to Ireland in pursuit of a dangerous plot. But he's received an urgent missive from Lord Ennis, an Irish peer—Ennis has heard something Drake needs to know. Ennis insists Drake attends an upcoming house party at Ennis's Kent estate so Ennis can reveal his information face-to-face.

Sebastian has assisted Drake before and, long ago, had a liaison with Lady Ennis. Drake insists Sebastian is just the man to be Drake's surrogate at the house party—the guests will imagine all manner of possibilities and be blind to Sebastian's true purpose.

Unsurprisingly, Sebastian is reluctant, but Drake's need is real. With only more debutantes on his horizon, Sebastian allows himself to be persuaded.

His first task is to inveigle Antonia Rawlings, a lady he has known all her life, to include him as her escort to the house party. Although he's seen little of Antonia in recent years, Sebastian is confident of gaining her support.

Eldest daughter of the Earl of Chillingworth, Antonia has abandoned the search for a husband and plans to use the week of the house party to decide what to do with her life. There has to be some purpose, some role, she can claim for her own.

Consequently, on hearing Sebastian's request and an explanation of what lies behind it, she seizes on the call to action. Suppressing her senses' idiotic reaction to Sebastian's nearness, she agrees to be his partner-in-intrigue.

But while joining the house party proves easy, the gathering is thrown into chaos when Lord Ennis is murdered—just before he was to speak with Sebastian. Worse, Ennis's last words, gasped to Sebastian, are: *Gunpowder. Here.*

Gunpowder? And here, where?

With a killer continuing to stalk the halls, side by side, Sebastian and Antonia search for answers and, all the while, the childhood connection that had always existed between them strengthens and blooms...into something so much more.

First volume in a trilogy. A Cynster Next Generation Novel – a classic historical romance with gothic overtones layered over a continuing intrigue. A full-length novel of 99,000 words

ALSO AVAILABLE NOW:
A CONQUEST IMPOSSIBLE TO RESIST
Cynster Next Generation Novel #7

#1 New York Times *bestselling author Stephanie Laurens returns to the Cynsters' next generation to bring you a thrilling tale of love, intrigue, and fabulous horses.*

A notorious rakehell with a stable of rare Thoroughbreds and a lady on a quest to locate such horses must negotiate personal minefields to forge a greatly desired alliance—one someone is prepared to murder to prevent.

Prudence Cynster has turned her back on husband hunting in favor of horse hunting. As the head of the breeding program underpinning the success of the Cynster racing stables, she's on a quest to acquire the necessary horses to refresh the stable's breeding stock.

On his estranged father's death, Deaglan Fitzgerald, now Earl of Glengarah, left London and the hedonistic life of a wealthy, wellborn rake and returned to Glengarah Castle determined to rectify the harm caused by his father's neglect. Driven by guilt that he hadn't been there to protect his people during the Great Famine, Deaglan holds firm against the lure of his father's extensive collection of horses and, leaving the stable to the care of his brother, Felix, devotes himself to returning the estate to prosperity.

Deaglan had fallen out with his father and been exiled from Glengarah over his drive to have the horses pay their way. Knowing Deaglan's wishes and that restoration of the estate is almost complete, Felix writes to the premier Thoroughbred breeding program in the British Isles to test their interest in the Glengarah horses.

On receiving a letter describing exactly the type of horses she's seeking, Pru overrides her family's reluctance and sets out for Ireland's west coast to visit the now-reclusive wicked Earl of Glengarah. Yet her only interest is in his horses, which she cannot wait to see.

When Felix tells Deaglan that a P. H. Cynster is about to arrive to assess the horses with a view to a breeding arrangement, Deaglan can only be grateful. But then P. H. Cynster turns out to be a lady, one utterly unlike any other he's ever met.

Yet they are who they are, and both understand their world. They battle their instincts and attempt to keep their interactions businesslike, but the sparks are incandescent and inevitably ignite a sexual blaze that consumes them both—and opens their eyes.

But before they can find their way to their now-desired goal, first one accident, then another distracts them. Someone, it seems, doesn't want them to strike a deal. Who? Why?

They need to find out before whoever it is resorts to the ultimate sanction.

A classic historical romance with neo-Gothic overtones, set in the west of Ireland. A Cynster Next Generation novel—a full-length historical romance of 125,000 words.

If you haven't yet caught up with the earlier books in the Cynster Next Generation Novels, then BY WINTER'S LIGHT is a Christmas story that highlights the Cynster children as they stand poised on the cusp of adulthood – essentially an introductory novel to the upcoming generation. That novel is followed by the first pair of Cynster Next Generation romances, those of Lucilla and Marcus Cynster, twins and the eldest children of Lord Richard aka Scandal Cynster and Catriona, Lady of the Vale. Both the twins' stories are set in Scotland. See below for further details.

BY WINTER'S LIGHT
Cynster Next Generation Novel #1

#1 New York Times bestselling author Stephanie Laurens returns to romantic Scotland to usher in a new generation of Cynsters in an enchanting tale of mistletoe, magic, and love.

It's December 1837 and the young adults of the Cynster clan have succeeded in having the family Christmas celebration held at snow-bound Casphairn Manor, Richard and Catriona Cynster's home. Led by Sebastian, Marquess of Earith, and by Lucilla, future Lady of the Vale, and her twin brother, Marcus, the upcoming generation has their own plans for the holiday season.

Yet where Cynsters gather, love is never far behind—the festive occasion brings together Daniel Crosbie, tutor to Lucifer Cynster's sons, and Claire Meadows, widow and governess to Gabriel Cynster's daughter. Daniel and Claire have met before and the embers of an unexpected passion smolder between them, but once bitten, twice shy, Claire believes a second marriage is not in her stars. Daniel, however, is determined to press his suit. He's seen the love the Cynsters share, and Claire is the lady with whom he dreams of sharing *his* life. Assisted by a bevy of Cynsters—innate matchmakers every one—Daniel strives to persuade Claire that trusting him with her hand and her heart is her right path to happiness.

Meanwhile, out riding on Christmas Eve, the young adults of the Cynster clan respond to a plea for help. Summoned to a humble dwelling in ruggedly forested mountains, Lucilla is called on to help with the difficult birth of a child, while the others rise to the challenge of helping her. With a violent storm closing in and severely limited options, the next generation of Cynsters face their first collective test—can they save this mother and child? And themselves, too?

Back at the manor, Claire is increasingly drawn to Daniel and despite her misgivings, against the backdrop of the ongoing festivities their relationship deepens. Yet she remains torn—until catastrophe strikes, and by winter's light, she learns that love—true love—is worth any risk, any price.

A tale brimming with all the magical delights of a Scottish festive season. A Cynster Next Generation novel – a classic historical romance of 71,000 words.

THE TEMPTING OF THOMAS CARRICK
A Cynster Next Generation Novel

#1 New York Times *bestselling author Stephanie Laurens returns to Scotland with a tale of two lovers irrevocably linked by destiny and passion.*

Do you believe in fate? Do you believe in passion? What happens when fate and passion collide?

Do you believe in love? What happens when fate, passion, and love combine?
This. This...

Thomas Carrick is a gentleman driven to control all aspects of his life. As the wealthy owner of Carrick Enterprises, located in bustling Glasgow, he is one of that city's most eligible bachelors and fully intends to select an appropriate wife from the many young ladies paraded before him. He wants to take that necessary next step along his self-determined path, yet no young lady captures his eye, much less his attention...not in the way Lucilla Cynster had, and still did, even though she lives miles away.

For over two years, Thomas has avoided his clan's estate because it borders Lucilla's home, but disturbing reports from his clansmen force him to return to the countryside—only to discover that his uncle, the laird, is ailing, a clan family is desperately ill, and the clan-healer is unconscious and dying. Duty to the clan leaves Thomas no choice but to seek help from the last woman he wants to face.

Strong-willed and passionate, Lucilla has been waiting—increasingly impatiently—for Thomas to return and claim his rightful place by her side. She knows he is hers—her fated lover, husband, protector, and mate. He is the only man for her, just as she is his one true love. And, at last, he's back. Even though his returning wasn't on her account, Lucilla is willing to seize whatever chance Fate hands her.

Thomas can never forget Lucilla, much less the connection that seethes between them, but to marry her would mean embracing a life he's adamant he does not want.

Lucilla sees that Thomas has yet to accept the inevitability of their union and, despite all, he can refuse her and walk away. But how *can* he ignore a bond such as theirs—one so much stronger than reason? Despite several unnerving attacks mounted against them, despite the uncertainty racking his clan, Lucilla remains as determined as only a Cynster can be to fight for the future she knows can be theirs—and while she cannot command him, she has powerful enticements she's willing to wield in the cause of tempting Thomas Carrick.

A neo-Gothic tale of passionate romance laced with mystery, set in the uplands of southwestern Scotland. A Cynster Next Generation Novel – a classic historical romance of 122,000 words.

A MATCH FOR MARCUS CYNSTER
Cynster Next Generation Novel #3

#1 New York Times *bestselling author Stephanie Laurens returns to rugged Scotland with a dramatic tale of passionate desire and unwavering devotion.*

Duty compels her to turn her back on marriage. Fate drives him to protect her come what may. Then love takes a hand in this battle of yearning hearts, stubborn wills, and a match too powerful to deny.

Restless and impatient, Marcus Cynster waits for Fate to come calling. He knows his destiny lies in the lands surrounding his family home, but what will his future be? Equally importantly, with whom will he share it?

Of one fact he feels certain: his fated bride will not be Niniver Carrick. His elusive neighbor attracts him mightily, yet he feels compelled to protect her—even from himself. Fickle Fate, he's sure, would never be so kind as to decree that Niniver should be his. The best he can do for them both is to avoid her.

Niniver has vowed to return her clan to prosperity. The epitome of fragile femininity, her delicate and ethereal exterior cloaks a stubborn will and an unflinching devotion to the people in her care. She accepts that in order to achieve her goal, she cannot risk marrying and losing her grip on the clan's reins to an inevitably controlling husband. Unfortunately, many local men see her as their opportunity.

Soon, she's forced to seek help to get rid of her unwelcome suitors. Powerful and dangerous, Marcus Cynster is perfect for the task. Suppressing her wariness over tangling with a gentleman who so excites her passions, she appeals to him for assistance with her peculiar problem.

Although at first he resists, Marcus discovers that, contrary to his expectations, his fated role *is* to stand by Niniver's side and, ultimately, to claim her hand. Yet in order to convince her to be his bride, they must plunge headlong into a journey full of challenges, unforeseen dangers, passion, and yearning, until Niniver grasps the essential truth—that she is indeed a match for Marcus Cynster.

A neo-Gothic tale of passionate romance set in the uplands of southwestern Scotland. A Cynster Next Generation Novel – a classic historical romance of 114,000 words.

And if you want to catch up with where it all began,
return to the iconic
DEVIL's BRIDE
Volume 1 of the Cynster Novels

the book that introduced millions of historical romance readers around the globe to the powerful men of the unforgettable Cynster family – aristocrats to the bone, conquerors at heart – and the willful feisty women strong enough to be their brides.

AUTHOR'S NOTE

I incorporated several of those "too good to pass up" historical facts into this volume, and as promised, I describe them more fully below. In addition, as usual, the streets I have my characters strolling, running, or skulking down are real to the time. The map I use as reference is by Cross, dated 1850.

So, to the nuggets of history buried in this book:

1) the Worshipful Company of Carmen
- is officially the 77th Livery Company of the City of London. Yes, it still exists today. The company was granted livery status in 1848, the only such grant made in Queen Victoria's time. However, the company dates from 1517, although the controlling of carts and carriers (carrs) by the City first formally commenced in 1272. The Corporation of the City of London has exercised its rights over cartage since the corporation's inception as transport is so obviously vital to commerce.

After 1655, all licensed vehicles had to carry the City's arms on the shafts and a specific number on a brass plate—much like modern license plates. In 1835, there were 600 licensed carts. The "Hallkeeper" was/still is empowered to license and mark carrs and carts to "stand" at places known as "carrooms" and there to ply for hire in the City's streets. I suspect these were the equivalent of modern taxi-ranks, but for carts. The criteria for a cart or carr to be licensed was that the owner had to be a freeman of the City and also a member of the Fellowship of Carmen (i.e.

the Worshipful Company of Carmen). Once a year, every vehicle had to be brought to the Guildhall for examination and to be re-marked. This was necessary to enforce the rule that no cart could ply for hire within the City of London unless licensed by the Carmen. As noted in this book, this rule was not lightly or easily broken and was strongly enforced. Consequently, the carters who collected the gunpowder from Kent and drove it into London would have had to be members of the Worshipful Company of Carmen.

Plaisterers Hall, the building I have used to house the Worshipful Company of Carmen, is in fact their current address at Number 1, London Wall. As far as I can determine, Plaisterers' Hall existed in 1850, and the Worshipful Company may even then have had their offices there. However, London Wall did not exist in 1850. The location given in the book—the western end of Falcon Street where it runs into Aldersgate—is the equivalent location. The interior of Plaisterers Hall described in the book is entirely fictitious.

2) Gunpowder and the Manufacture of Fireworks

Much of the details of gunpowder itself and the difficulties of its storage and transport were given in the Author's Note of the previous volume.

Fireworks were hugely popular in England from Elizabethan times on (Elizabeth I was a fan) and in 1850 there were numerous firework manufactories dotted around London. These included Brocks Fireworks, recently moved to Sutton from Whitechapel after an accident (detailed below), Madam Coton's factory in Westminster Road, and Pains Fireworks in Brixton. Indeed, firework manufactories were located in inner London well into the 1900s—Wizard Fireworks were still in Shoreditch in 1949.

While I have hypothesized that warehouses supplying the firework manufactories existed and several were located in Morgan's Lane in Southwark, it is possible, even likely that such warehouses existed. Their location in Morgan's Lane, however, is entirely imagined.

Gunpowder was an essential ingredient for fireworks, along with saltpeter.

The explosive capacity of gunpowder is illustrated by the report of the accident (noted above) that in 1832 caused the removal of Brocks Fireworks factory from its then location at 11 Baker's Row, Whitechapel, in a residential area and nearly opposite the London Hospital. A boy ramming gunpowder into a firework tube accidentally created a spark, which ignited the firework—in a blind panic, he tossed the tube aside and fled. Fifty pounds of gunpowder plus a large amount of saltpeter exploded, blowing off the roof, setting fire to the building, and breaking every pane of glass for several blocks around. In the late 1850s, Madam Coton's factory in Westminster Road also went up rather spectacularly.

Given that our protagonists are chasing over one thousand pounds of gunpowder, it is pertinent to note the damage done by a mere fifty pounds.

3) the Chartists

Chartism was a working-class movement for political reform that was active in Britain from 1838 to 1857. The name derived from the People's Charter of 1838 and in a nutshell, the aim was to achieve adult male suffrage.

The People's Charter of 1838 laid out six simply-stated aims, the achievement of which would give working men a say in law-making— they would be able to vote, their vote would be protected by secret ballot, and by abolishing the requirement for owing property as a qualification for running for Parliament and introducing payment for MPs, working-class men would be able to stand for election. None of the demands were new, but the People's Charter became one of the major political manifestos of the century.

Given that the Chartists wanted to participate in Parliament, their strategy was to influence Parliament via demonstrating the scale of support for their cause—primarily via massive "meetings" and peaceful demonstrations. Consequently, in 1839, the 1838 Charter was presented to Parliament with a petition backed by 1.3 million (male) signatures. The MPs of the Commons voted not to hear the petition.

In 1842, a second petition was presented to Parliament with 3.5 million signatures. Again, it was rejected.

On April 10, 1848, in the spring during which political uprisings occurred throughout Europe, the Chartists held a massive meeting on Kennington Common. They planned to march on Parliament to present the latest petition, this time signed by 6 million men. The authorities had recruited 100,000 special constables to bolster the police force, and the crowd was not permitted to cross the Thames. Subsequently, the petition was delivered by a handful of leaders, and Parliament once again rejected it.

After the "defeat" of 1839 and again in 1842, uprisings of various sorts were planned and some occurred, but were ineffective and were severely repressed.

The Chartist leadership was diverse, but over time, Feargus O'Connor, owner and publisher of the Leeds' Northern Star newspaper, became the ultimate leader. He was devoted to achieving reform through peaceful parliamentary means, and was eventually elected to Parliament in 1847.

The "defeat" of 1848 lead to a significant rise in Chartist plots and insurrection, led by so-called "physical force" Chartists, but none of these plots or uprisings were supported by the established Chartist leadership and were, once again, suppressed by the authorities.

Gradually, Chartism as a movement faded into obscurity. However, while the movement did not directly achieve any reform, all of its six stated aims eventually became law. Many ex-Chartists swelled the ranks of the Reform League which campaigned for manhood suffrage and partially succeeded with the passage of the Reform Act of 1867, which granted the vote to urban working men.

While the hotbeds of Chartism lay in Wales and the north of England, from 1836, London was established as the home of Chartists in the southeast of the country. More on the London Chartists in the next volume.

The third volume of this trilogy incorporates further historical facts. For your interest, I will describe those in a similar note at the back of that volume.

Stephanie.

ABOUT THE AUTHOR

#1 *New York Times* bestselling author Stephanie Laurens began writing romances as an escape from the dry world of professional science. Her hobby quickly became a career when her first novel was accepted for publication, and with entirely becoming alacrity, she gave up writing about facts in favor of writing fiction.

All Laurens's works to date are historical romances, ranging from medieval times to the mid-1800s, and her settings range from Scotland to India. The majority of her works are set in the period of the British Regency. Laurens has published more than 75 works of historical romance, including 40 *New York Times* bestsellers. Laurens has sold more than 20 million print, audio, and e-books globally. All her works are continuously available in print and e-book formats in English worldwide, and have been translated into many other languages. An international bestseller, among other accolades, Laurens has received the Romance Writers of America® prestigious RITA® Award for Best Romance Novella 2008 for *The Fall of Rogue Gerrard*.

Laurens's continuing novels featuring the Cynster family are widely regarded as classics of the historical romance genre. Other series include the *Bastion Club Novels*, the *Black Cobra Quartet*, and the *Casebook of Barnaby Adair Novels*. All her previous works remain available in print and all e-book formats.

For information on all published novels and on upcoming releases and updates on novels yet to come, visit Stephanie's website: www. stephanielaurens.com

To sign up for Stephanie's Email Newsletter (a private list) for heads-up alerts as new books are released, exclusive sneak peeks into upcoming books, and exclusive sweepstakes contests, follow the prompts at Stephanie's Email Newsletter Sign-up Page

To follow Stephanie on BookBub, head here https://www.bookbub.com/authors/stephanie-laurens

Stephanie lives with her husband and a goofy black labradoodle in the hills outside Melbourne, Australia. When she isn't writing, she's reading, and if she isn't reading, she'll be tending her garden.

www.stephanielaurens.com
stephanie@stephanielaurens.com

9 781925 559392